William Robinson Clark

Savonarola

His life and times

William Robinson Clark

Savonarola
His life and times

ISBN/EAN: 9783337314712

Printed in Europe, USA, Canada, Australia, Japan

Cover: Foto ©Raphael Reischuk / pixelio.de

More available books at **www.hansebooks.com**

His Life and Times

BY

WILLIAM CLARK, M.A., LL.D.

PROFESSOR OF PHILOSOPHY IN TRINITY COLLEGE, TORONTO

CHICAGO ·
A. C. McCLURG AND COMPANY
1890

PREFACE.

THE life and character of Savonarola have been rightly supposed to present great difficulties to the historian. From the day of his death — nay, more, from the day of his power in Florence — up to our own times, opinions the most diverse have been entertained respecting his character, his motives, his conduct. While his enemies have denounced him as a rebel against the sovereign Pontiff — in later times they have hardly dared to call him a heretic.—and as a disturber of the commonwealth, his followers and admirers have regarded him as a saint and a hero, and have venerated his memory as that of a martyr.

The supporters of despotism, ecclesiastical and civil, have cherished a feeling of bitter enmity against the man who had such an ardent love of liberty ; and they have been joined by the prophets of scepticism, who have had nothing but contempt and hatred for one who was so powerful a witness for religion and for God.

According to the sceptic Bayle, he was a ridiculous and base impostor, who richly deserved the fate that befell him. According to Roscoe, who found it difficult to believe anything good of one who was so consistent and steadfast an opponent of his idolized Medici, he was an arrogant and ambitious priest, half impostor and half fanatic. The errors of Roscoe were partly traditional, partly depended upon his defective point of view, and partly arose from his being unacquainted with many of the original documents which throw light upon the age of which he wrote.

It was only quite lately that an attempt was made to re-write the history of Savonarola and his times on the basis of contemporary documents and the testimony of contemporary writers. Rudelbach was the first who seriously undertook this work, and he accomplished his task with German industry and thoroughness. Although he has considerably detracted from the value of his book by his persistent attempt to prove that Savonarola was a Protestant, all subsequent writers are greatly indebted to his researches.

Rudelbach's work was published in 1835, and was succeeded in 1836 by that of his countryman, Meier, who also brought to light documents and facts which had been previously unknown. This writer also marred his work by endeavoring to prove that Savonarola held the doctrines of Luther. In spite of this, I have been greatly indebted to him and his predecessor.

The next important life of Savonarola was written by M. Perrens, an eminent authority on Florentine history, and published in 1853. This writer had the advantage of using the materials collected by the Padre Marchese, who had taken a deep interest in the life of Savonarola, and belonged to his own order.[1] It cannot be denied that Perrens made diligent use of these materials and of other documents which he found at Florence. He made himself thoroughly acquainted with his subject, and he produced a well-written and readable book; still, there is a want of consistency in his views of Savonarola's character and history which renders his work in many respects unsatisfactory.[2]

---

[1] He edited some of the unpublished letters of Savonarola, and published a history of the convent of St. Mark's, and other. works bearing on the same subject.

[2] It is the more necessary to note this, since Dean Milman's article in the Quarterly Review, subsequently republished among his miscellaneous works, has given currency, among readers of English, to the view of M. Perrens.

The life of Perrens was, however, the best that had been written until Professor Villari published his "History of Girolamo Savonarola and his Times."[1] Whether we consider the fulness of his researches, or the true historical spirit in which Villari composed his book, it must be allowed that he has done the work almost as well as it can be done. As a book for Italians and for those who take an interest in the philosophical doctrines of Savonarola, it can hardly ever be excelled, and can never be entirely set aside.

To Signor Villari I owe much more than to any other writer, and I have hardly ever ventured to differ from him without much consideration. It will be evident, however, to careful readers that I have followed him in no servile spirit. I have done my best to understand the history and character of the man whom I have undertaken to describe, and I have endeavored to tell the story simply and plainly, as I have myself been able to understand it.

Since the fruits of my study of the life of Savonarola were first published, several contributions to the subject of considerable importance have appeared. First and chief of these is an essay on Savonarola in a volume of historico-biographical studies by the great German historian Ranke (Leipzig, 1877). Next comes a very interesting study by Père Bayonne (Paris, 1879), a member of the same order and an enthusiastic admirer of Savonarola. Finally, Professor Villari has put forth a carefully revised and almost rewritten edition of his great Life (Florence, 1888), in which he has made a few corrections and alterations, some of them based upon documents previously unknown.

I have been careful to consult all those modern writers from whom I expected to obtain help for my work, and I have made ample acknowledgment of my obligations

---

[1] La Storia di Girolamo Savonarola e de' suoi tempi, narrata da Pasquale Villari, con l' aiuto di nuovi documenti. Firenze: Le Monnier, vol. i. 1859; vol. ii. 1861.

wherever I was conscious of them. Sometimes I have thought it better to quote their very words. But it must not be supposed that I have obtained my information generally at second hand. I have studied all the principal original sources, and have commonly told the story in their language. For the sake of any who may care to follow me in these studies, I may mention the Lives of Giovan Francesco Pico della Mirandola and Burlamacchi, the work of Barsanti, and the " Cedrus Libani " of Frà Benedetto, published in the splendid Italian "Archivio Storico." I should add that I have been much indebted to the various works of Padre Marchese, published in the same collection.

Of the works of Savonarola I have carefully studied the " Compendium Revelationum," the "Trionfo della Croce," and many of his sermons and smaller works, as well as his poems. I have also used the works of Machiavelli, Guicciardini, and Sismondi ; and among later works, Capponi's " Storia della Repubblica di Firenze " and Von Reumont's " Lorenzo de' Medici."

WILLIAM CLARK.

Trinity College, Toronto.
Midsummer, 1890.

CONTENTS.

SAVONAROLA.

CHAPTER I.

ITALY IN THE FIFTEENTH CENTURY.

IN order to understand the character and work of a
man who belonged so entirely to his own age as Savonarola, it will be necessary to attempt some estimate,
however slight and imperfect, of the times in which he
lived. We must try to understand something of the
state of the Roman Empire, of which Italy was, in theory at least, the centre ; of the condition of the Papacy,
the great fountain of authority in the Western Church ;
of the religious orders ; of the intellectual and moral
condition of the people at large.

Although it would be quite impossible to understand
the course of Florentine history, with its fierce struggles
between Guelfs and Ghibellines, apart from the history
of the Empire, these struggles had long ceased before
the age of Savonarola. They had, indeed, left behind
them political parties which had sprung out of them,
and party feelings whose roots were buried deep in those
ancient animosities ; but as a practical question, the
state of the Empire hardly concerns the student of
Italian ecclesiastical history in the fifteenth century.
The Empire was at its lowest point, and the Papacy at

its highest.   Frederick III. was Emperor and Nicholas V. was Pope when Savonarola was born.   "In Frederick the Third's reign," says Dr. Bryce,[1] "the Empire sank to its lowest point.   It had shot forth a fitful gleam under Sigismund, who, in convoking and presiding over the Council of Constance, had revived one of the highest functions of his predecessors. . . . Never afterwards was he [the Emperor], in the eyes of Europe, anything more than a German monarch."   It was just the reverse with the Papacy.   "The Pontificate of Nicholas V.," says Dean Milman,[2] "is the culminating point of Latin Christianity."

Slowly, gradually, surely, the change had taken place. The time had long gone by when men had dreamed of a state of things in which the world should be governed by two masters acting in harmony, the Emperor and the Pope.   The theory of Dante, born a Guelf, but forced by the violence of the papal party into the Ghibelline ranks, was a beautiful one, but it could not be worked. Even when the faith of the Church was the religion of the Empire, it became a hopeless task to reconcile the claims of the master of the world with those of the Vicar of Christ.   That the Pope should hold his secular possessions of the Emperor as his suzerain ; that the Emperor should receive his authority from the Head of the Church, — through His Vicar, by whom he was anointed and crowned, — all this might seem reasonable, natural,

---

[1] The Holy Roman Empire, ch. xvii.   This work can hardly be too highly recommended to the student of mediæval history.   A knowledge of its subject is of the greatest necessity for such ; and it is difficult to mention a work from which it could more easily and effectually be obtained.

[2] Latin Christianity, bk. xiii. ch. xvii.

simple in theory; but innumerable complications arose in working it out. The difficulty of serving two masters continually presented itself; and men drifted into the party of the Guelfs or into that of the Ghibellines, not only from the intelligible reason that they sided with the papal party on the one hand, or with the Imperialists on the other, but from multitudes of other reasons, arising out of local position and family or national history. To us, for instance, it seems strange to find the most strenuous supporters of the Papacy among the strongest republicans; but our surprise vanishes when we remember that the aristocratic party was headed by those great nobles who derived their chief authority from the Emperor, and were devoted to the support of his claims.

It would be out of place to sketch here, even in barest outline, the rise of the papal power, and therefore we must be contented merely to indicate those points which will render our narrative intelligible. The power of the Roman Bishop had grown up by slow degrees, and had derived its strength from a variety of elements. It would be a mistake to fasten upon any one cause as sufficient to account for the almost absolute dominion which the Bishop of Rome came to exercise over the Western Church.

It was not only his position in the metropolis of the world-empire,— although this went for much,— it was not simply the early fable that the Pope was the successor of Saint Peter, that gave him his authority. This was an effect quite as much as a cause of his predominance. The New Testament knows nothing of Saint Peter as the founder of the Church of Rome. When he is mentioned in this connection by Irenæus, it is only as associated on equal terms with Saint Paul.

But there were other causes at work. The piety, orthodoxy, learning, and ability of a series of Pontiffs who
adorned that chair in the earliest days contributed to
strengthen the influence and confirm the power which
seemed naturally to belong to the Bishop of the Mother
City, and to engender the idea that this was the Mother
Church.[1] Perhaps it must be added that a strong cen-
tral ecclesiastical power was almost a necessity in the
ages through which the Church had to pass from Constantine to Charles the Great, and from his days to
those of another Charles, who witnessed the beginning
of the great and widespread revolt against the papal
power. We have said nothing of the false decretals.
Although they did undoubtedly lend support to the
papal theory in its days of advance and development,
it must yet be confessed that the main points of that
theory were set forth and conceded before those famous
documents were promulgated.[2]

Whether a sagacious anticipation of the dangers in-
herent in the secular character which began to be asso-

[1] Dr. Freeman remarks: "From the time of Constantine on-
wards, the divisions of the Empire and the constant absence of
the Emperors from Rome had greatly increased the power of the
Popes. They had not, like the Patriarchs of Constantinople, a
superior always at hand. Charles the Great had fully asserted
the imperial power over the Church; but after his Empire
broke up, the power of the Popes grew again. It was checked
only by their own wickedness and their divisions among themselves, which kings like Otto the Great and Henry the Third
had to step in and put an end to" (General Sketch of Euro-
pean History, ix. 2).

[2] The first steps in the progress of papal power are strikingly
illustrated in Dr. Lightfoot's appendix to his edition of Saint
Clement's Epistles, pp. 252 ff. On the general subject, cf. Papal
Claims (London and New York).

ciated with the spiritual power of the Papacy would have led to their being averted, we cannot tell. Humanly speaking, it is difficult to imagine, as we trace the course of history, that the Popedom could have been very different from what it was. Be this as it may, it seems inevitable that it should have become a secular power, and equally so that its spiritual character, the world being what it is, should have suffered from the connection.

The deterioration is, in fact, undeniable. As we follow the solemn and impressive history from Pontiff to Pontiff, from age to age, we become aware that the voice of the Vicar of Christ no longer speaks in the pure tones of a Leo or a Gregory; the world also has its prophet on the throne of Peter, and the spirit of the world is blended, in a combination sometimes blasphemous, sometimes touching upon the ludicrous, with the higher spirit of the kingdom. The first Bishop of Christendom is serving two masters.

The moral deterioration of the Roman See is a simple fact of history. It was not rapid, and there were breaks and suspensions and recoils in its course; but it was, on the whole, gradual and certain. We mark it, perhaps, most in the period which elapsed between the beginning of the fourteenth century and the era of the Reformation. The evil, however, was at work long before this time. In the struggles between the great Popes, like Gregory VII. (Hildebrand), and the great Emperors, like Henry IV., there was of necessity a secularizing of the spirit of the ecclesiastical power, far more than a spiritualizing of the secular; and the Popes were quite as much the victims as they were the causes of the circumstances in which they found themselves.

John of Salisbury, almost exactly a century later than Gregory VII.,—he died in 1180,—tells us that when asked by his friend Hadrian IV. what people said of him and of the Roman Church, he replied:—

" Many people say that the Roman Church, which is the mother of all other Churches, shows herself to other Churches, not as a mother, but as a stepmother. 'Scribes and Pharisees sit upon her seat, who bind heavy burdens, and grievous to be borne, and lay them on men's shoulders; but they themselves will not move them with one of their fingers.' They lord it over God's heritage, and do not walk in the way of life, as ensamples to the flock. They heap up precious things, and load their tables with gold and silver. . . . With them godliness is practised for the sake of gain, not for the dissemination of the truth. . . . To many even the Roman Bishop has become unbearable; and people complain that while the churches which were built by the devotion of our fathers are falling to ruin, and while the altars are deserted, he is going about in purple and gold. The palaces of the priests are resplendent, while the Church of Christ is left polluted and uncared for. . . . In my judgment," he added, " so long as they go this way, the scourge of the Lord will never depart from them."

This was towards the end of the twelfth century; but about a century later began a period which tended still further to destroy the better features of the papal power. This was the famous Babylonish Captivity,—the residence of the Popes for a period of seventy years (1305–1376) at Avignon in France. One of its evil results was seen in the schism which immediately followed, and lasted for about half the time of the Captivity, — until the Council of Constance, when Martin V. was raised to the papal throne in 1417, and was finally accepted by the whole Western Church.

When Milman speaks of the Pontificate of Nicholas V. as "the culminating point of Latin Christianity," he does not ignore the facts and circumstances which had long been at work to undermine the monarchy of Hildebrand. "The papal power," he says, "had long reached its zenith. From Innocent III. (1198-1216) to Boniface VIII. (1294-1303) it had begun its decline." That is to say, from near the time of John of Salisbury to the beginning of the period of the papal residence at Avignon, the power of the Pope relatively to that of the secular rulers began to decline; and the Captivity and the schism almost annihilated any real authority that still remained in his hands. But the Pope as the representative of the Church — perhaps, rather, the Church presided over by the Pope — was supreme in the middle of the fifteenth century. It had burned Huss and Jerome of Prague, and it seemed at peace and irresistible. This was the appearance of things as it would strike the eye of a statesman. But there were unseen forces at work which we, at least, cannot overlook. An age which endured a Papacy in virtual subjection to the French Crown for the best part of a century, another which could tolerate the worse scandal of rival Popes for more than a whole generation, must have fallen from the faith, as well as the order, of earlier times.

"The transfer of the papal throne from Rome to Avignon for a space of seventy years, during the early part of the fourteenth century, entailed enormous evils on Europe, and on the estates of the Church in particular. It was a deliberate renunciation by the Popes of their most sacred duties as Bishops of Rome and as temporal sovereigns. While

they passed their days in epicurean ease and luxury on the
banks of the Rhone, the patrimony of the Church was trodden down by lawless barons and contending factions, and,
as was natural in such a state of things, the people, both
clerical and lay, equally despised the laws of God and of
man. Venality, impurity, and licentiousness pervaded the
papal court, and had reached such a pitch at the time that
Petrarch was a resident at or near Avignon that he points
to the Romish court there, in his epistles *sine titulo* and in
three of his sonnets, as the Western Babylon, a sink of
iniquity, a very hell upon earth." [1]

It would be absurd to charge the Popes with the
whole guilt of the corruption of the fifteenth century.
If they were in part the causes, they were also in part
only the indications, of a state of things against which
some of them struggled hard, but which for the most
part, they were powerless to amend. It is by no means
true that the Popes of this time were all bad men ; but
unfortunately some of the best seemed the least fitted
for the evil times on which they had fallen. Nicholas V., [2]

---

[1] Harford's Life of Michael Angelo, vol. i. ch. viii. pt. i.,
where the references will be found.

[2] In Nicholas V., in three short years, the Pope had become
again a great Italian potentate. . . . Nicholas V. laid the foundation of his power not so much in the strength of the Roman See
as a temporal sovereignty as in the admiration and gratitude of
Italy, which was rapidly reported over the whole of Christendom.
. . . The famous architect Leo Alberti describes the unexampled
prosperity under Nicholas, for which the conspirators would have
made that cruel return. " The whole of Latium was at peace. . . .
The domain of the Church was in a high state of cultivation ; the
city had become a city of gold through the jubilee; the dignity of
the citizens was respected; all reasonable petitions were granted
at once by the Pontiff."— MILMAN : *Latin Christianity* (2d ed.),
vi. 169.

one of the best of Popes, had his soul saddened, his heart almost broken, by rebellion breaking out among his ungrateful Roman subjects.

To him succeeded Pius II. (1458–1464), the famous Æneas Sylvius, who, although he was not a man of the same depth and spirituality as his predecessor, would yet, by the elevation of his mind, the purity of his character, and the splendor of his abilities, have shed lustre upon any throne. If it was the age of silver succeeding the age of gold, it was succeeded by one far baser than itself. Paul II. (1464–1471), the successor of Pius, was the sister's son of Eugenius IV., who reigned during the sixteen troubled years which intervened between Martin V. and Nicholas V. If his character as Pope had resembled that of his earlier years, he might have left behind him the reputation of his uncle; but the arrogance of his pretensions, his love of display, his unscrupulousness in accumulating money, and his disregard for his word, or even his oath, have deeply stained his name. "You venture to appeal to judges," he cried, with a glare [1] at Platina. "As if you did not know that all laws are lodged in our breast! The sentence is given. I am Pope, and I have power to rescind or to approve, at my pleasure, the acts of all other men."

It has been truly said that, at this time, every other precious thing was as cheap at Rome as the Pope's oath. But the course was still downwards: Paul II. was succeeded by Sixtus IV. (1471–1484). In his reign simony was open and undisguised; no benefice was given away without being paid for. The unscrupulousness of his conduct towards his opponents we shall have

[1] Torvis Oculis. Cf. Bower, Popes, A. D. 1465.

to notice when we come to speak of his quarrel with the
Medici. Murder he held in certain cases to be justifi-
able ; and his general character may be judged from the
generally believed report that his death was brought on
by chagrin at a peace being concluded, without his
sanction, between the Venetians and certain allied powers who were at war with them. Of darker charges
against him, made and believed, we say nothing. The
chief excuse alleged for his crimes consists in the plea
that they all proceeded from an immoderate affection
for his relations, and his desire to promote and enrich
them.

Innocent VIII. (1484–1493), if not as bad a man, was
possibly a worse Pope than Sixtus had been. When the
latter died, a contemporary wrote : " On this most happy
day God Almighty showed His power upon earth, and
delivered His people out of the hand of this most im-
pious and iniquitous sovereign, in whom dwelt no fear
of God, no love for the flock of Christ, but shameful
lust, avarice, and vain-glory." But it was worse in the
days of his successor. Murders were frequent, and were
seldom punished when their authors were protected by
the princes of the Church. A man who had murdered
his own two daughters was set at liberty on the morning
of the day appointed for his execution, because he had
paid eight hundred ducats. And the papal Vice-Cham-
berlain, when asked why such criminals escaped, gave
with bitter irony the reply : " God willeth not the death
of a sinner, but that he shall pay and live ; and so we
think in Bologna."[1] One incident of this Pope's reign
may suffice to show its character. We suppress the

[1] No mere story. Steph. Infessura declares that he was present when it was said (Diar., p. 1988, in Rudelbach).

most offensive portion of the Pope's words in reference to it.

The Pope's vicar for the city of Rome on one occasion issued an edict forbidding concubinage, and threatening the laity who were guilty of it with excommunication, and the clergy with suspension and loss of their benefices. Innocent had the vicar summoned before him, and gave orders that the edict should be withdrawn, as concubinage, or something worse, was universal. It should be added, however, that he did, although apparently with reluctance, consent to the renewal of a constitution of Pius II. forbidding priests to keep taverns, play-houses, and houses of ill-fame, or to act as the secret agents of prostitutes. This Pope, let it be remembered, was the friend of Lorenzo de' Medici; and one of his natural sons married Lorenzo's daughter Maddalena. It was he who, on account of this family connection, conferred the cardinal's hat on Giovanni, the brother of Maddalena, afterwards Leo X., when he was only thirteen years of age.

This brings us to the reign of Alexander VI. (1493–1503). It was under this Pope — one of the worst, perhaps the very worst, that ever brought dishonor upon the loftiest seat in Christendom — that Savonarola was put to death.

The hasty sketch which has been given of the occupants of the Roman See during these years — nearly half a century — will prepare our readers to understand something of the times to which our narrative belongs. We turn from the Popes to the monks, — in other words, to the special representatives of the inward and religious life of the Church.

There was a time when, however it might be in the

world, there was purity and devotion in the cloister. Without arguing the question whether those who fled from the world to the convent did not carry the world with them into their retreat, — or the other question, whether the monastic life was more a means of deepening or of narrowing the spiritual life of men, — there can be no question that we are indebted to the religious orders for splendid examples of learning, of piety, of intellectual power and influence.

But it is equally undeniable that, like other human institutions, these were liable to corruption and decay. We see recurring evidences of their degeneracy in the rise of reformed communities, — like that of Clairvaux breaking off from Clugny, for example. The most remarkable attempt to deliver monasticism from its tendency to luxury and self-indulgence, from its forgetfulness of the vow of poverty, was the almost contemporaneous rise of the two great mendicant orders of the Dominicans, or Preaching Brothers, and the Franciscans, or Lesser Brothers. Of the vast achievements of these two great orders there could be no question, even if we had only the name of Aquinas as a son of the former, and that of Bonaventura as belonging to the latter. Yet these also fell into such decay that their reformation seemed almost hopeless; as we shall have occasion to remark in the course of this history.

On this subject one witness may be adduced, and one shall suffice, — Nicolas de Clémangis.[1] He was born in the latter half of the fourteenth century, and survived the period of the Council of Basel, dying about 1434. He was rector of the University of France, and together

[1] Cf. Wetzer and Welte, Kirchenlexicon, *s. v.*, and Rudelbach.

with his master, Pierre d'Ailly, and Gerson, formed the
triumvirate of Catholic reformers who were the glory of
France at the beginning of the fifteenth century. The
sad condition of the Church was the subject of various
appeals which he addressed to the king of France,
Charles VII., and to the Anti-pope, Clement VII.; but
his principal work was his treatise on the corrupt condition or ruin of the Church.[1] In this treatise he has the
following remarks : —

"As for the monks, what can we say in commendation of
those who, according to their vows, ought to be the most
perfect of all the sons of the Church, since they are removed from anxiety about the things of the world, and are
thus able to devote themselves to the contemplation of
heavenly things, but who are plainly the reverse of all
this? For they are, in fact, the most covetous and avaricious of all, and are mere slaves of the world, instead of
fleeing from it. Nothing is so hateful to them as their
cell and their convent, reading and praying, their rule and
religion. Monks they are externally in their dress, but in
their life and works they are as far as possible removed
from perfection. And this is the righteous punishment
which they suffer, that they do not find what they seek ; for
the revenues of the convents dwindle away more and more
from their insatiable pursuit of earthly goods ; so that
where formerly a hundred could live conveniently, now
hardly ten can exist with the greatest care ; and they
are scarce able to keep their buildings in a habitable
condition.

"And what shall I say of the mendicant friars, who by
their vow are devoted to the most absolute poverty, and
glory in being the true disciples and followers of Christ,
and boast that they alone can give to the people the true
food of the soul, and show them the way of eternal life;

---

[1] De Corrupto Ecclesiæ Statu, s. de Ruina Ecclesiæ.

that they alone fulfil the obligations of the true servants of God, and by their zeal make amends for the neglect, ignorance, and omissions of others who are lukewarm and asleep? In truth, if they had attained to such a degree of perfection, they certainly would not thus exalt themselves, and despise all others in comparison with themselves. For it is the true perfection of the righteous that they never regard themselves as perfect, but ever increase in humility as they grow in grace. By the contrary course the good which they really have is corrupted and destroyed. Just as the synagogue had its Pharisees, against whom Christ spoke most strongly in the Gospel, so are these new apostles to be regarded as the Pharisees of the Church, to whom is applicable all that Christ said of the Pharisees, or even much worse. For they are like ravening wolves in sheep's clothing, who have the outward appearance of holiness, but inwardly are defiled with all lusts ; who, like the priests of Bel, consume that which is offered to God in their secret chambers, revelling with their wives and children, — preaching, indeed, what people ought to do, but not doing it themselves, and thus through their own preaching becoming reprobate ; clothing themselves like an angel of light, and in that garb serving not Satan, indeed, and yet not Christ either, but their own bellies ; alluring the hearts of the innocent by their seductive words.

"And what shall we say of the nuns, if we would avoid the appearance of describing, not virgins consecrated to God, but brothels and deeds of shame? In truth, the nuns' convents are in these days nothing else than public houses of unchastity, places for receiving immoral and licentious young men, so that to let a maiden enter a convent is very much the same as offering her for open prostitution."

There is no reason for doubting the general truth of this testimony, and the condition of the Papacy at the time sufficiently prepares us to believe it. But if these

were the shepherds, what must have been the character
of the flock? Doubtless God had, then as always, many
secret ones who served Him faithfully and devoutly, and
of these it was the delight of Savonarola to speak;
but as regards the Church at large, the times were
evil, and nothing but revolution or root-and-branch
reformation could save the Christian communion from
dissolution.

The moral tone of Christendom at least had never
been lower. The most brutal selfishness stalked shame-
lessly abroad. Despotism, oppression, cruelty, were
practised all but universally by the rulers of the people.
Murder had become a trade, and poisoning an art; and
both became part of the policy of princes. " In Italy,"
said Pontanus, " there is nothing cheaper than human
life." The Church was worst of all. " Through the example of the papal court," said Machiavelli, " Italy has lost
all piety and religion. We have to thank the Church
and the priests for our abandoned wickedness."[1]

In considering the work of Savonarola, and the various reforming tendencies which were in operation in his
times, there is another class of influences which must
not be overlooked. Leaving out of consideration for
the moment the spirit of mysticism, which had awakened in Germany and was extending itself widely and
fostering a more inward and spiritual life, there was the
spread of learning through the universities, the invention
of printing, and that great classical movement which is
known as the Renaissance.

The organization of the higher instruction of the nations in universities was preparing also for the great
revival of learning which was to work a revolution, not

---

[1] Discorsi, i. 12.

only in the opinions of men, but in their very modes of thought, of reasoning, and of investigation. Paris and Oxford arose in the thirteenth century, Köln and Prague in the fourteenth ; and these not only produced controversialists who called in question the absolute authority claimed for himself by the Roman Bishop, but earnest reformers who had no thought of creating a schism in the Church, but urgently demanded her purification. If Paris had the great names which have just been mentioned, England is not likely to forget that Oxford had her Wickliffe, or even that Prague had her Huss.

With respect to the great literary movement known as the Renaissance, so full of light and of darkness, of liberty and of bondage, the subject is not merely of great extent, but involves so many points of controversy that we must keep simply on its outskirts ; yet certain facts may be noted with regard to which there is at least a substantial agreement.

The Renaissance, so often connected with the capture of Constantinople by the Turks in 1453, was not simply the result of an event which led to the emigration of a large number of Greeks to Italy. No doubt it received its most powerful and most visible impulse from this occurrence ; but it was in full progress before. The literary movement in question "is anterior by more than a century to the great event which is assigned as its date. It is impossible to deny that there was a strong taste for antiquity during the period of the sojourn of the Popes at Avignon. Cola di Rienzi was a distinguished humanist before becoming a celebrated revolutionary."[1] It would be easy to add other names in whom the same tendency is conspicuous.

[1] Christophe, La Papauté pendant le quinzième Siècle, i. 431.

In regard to the inward character of the movement, it was essentially humanistic or naturalistic, and in so far it was a revolt, not only against Catholicism, but against Christianity. It was virtually a return to Greek Paganism. It knew nothing of grace; it was the mere worship of nature. A Protestant, looking back upon those days from his own present point of view, is apt to imagine that it was essentially a protest against the corruptions and tyranny of the times, especially as that tyranny was embodied in the Roman See. No doubt it was, in a measure, such a protest; but for the most part accidentally. We may even say that it was become a necessity for the age in which it arose, and at least a means in the hand of Divine Providence for bringing about certain sorely needed changes in the Church and the world. All this may fairly be allowed.

To attribute such high principles and purposes to the movement itself, however, would be palpably absurd. It had no genuine sympathy — to take one example — with rational liberty as being the right of all men, and a benefit to humanity at large. No doubt it despised monkery, asceticism, and restrictions of all kinds. But the liberty which it preached was the liberty of education, philosophy, refinement, culture. No Horace could have more hated and despised the profane mob. The Renaissance would never have emancipated the serf, or struck the fetters from the hands and feet of the slave.

In short, it was heathen, and not Christian, and so it had no conception of the lofty charity of the Gospel, even as it was destitute of its spiritual power. This judgment is not a mere theoretical opinion deduced from the nature of the case, it is amply confirmed by the facts of history. The Renaissance had no more sympathy with the self-denial of Christ than it had with the absurdities of mediæval self-torture. It had no more sympathy with downtrodden humanity than it had with ecclesiastical despotism.

To a certain extent it was a power working in favor of reform. Perhaps its best fruits may be seen in men like Erasmus. But it had no real depth of earnestness. When the necessity for sacrifice arose, then came the evidence that it was not of Christ. It could criticise, gibe, sneer, even denounce; but it could not suffer. At bottom it was much more in sympathy with a cultivated tyrant than with his uncultivated victims.

"That spirit," says Dr. Bryce,[1] "whether we call it analytical, or sceptical, or earthly, or simply secular, for it is more or less all of these, — the spirit which was the exact antithesis of mediæval mysticism, — had swept in and carried men away with all the force of a pent-up torrent. People were content to gratify their tastes and their senses, caring little for worship and still less for doctrine; their hopes and ideas were no longer such as had made their forefathers crusaders or ascetics; their imagination was possessed by associations far different from those which had inspired Dante; they did not revolt against the Church, but they had no enthusiasm for her, and they had enthusiasm for whatever was fresh and graceful and intelligible."

It might seem strange, but to a deeper view of human nature it will seem not unreasonable, that along with the sceptical indifference to Divine revelation and Christian truth begotten by this movement there came a growing belief in astrology and cognate superstitions.

---

[1] Holy Roman Empire, ch. xvii.

Popes who did not believe in God believed in the influences of the stars and in the power of magic ; just as unbelievers in our own day have attained to a faith in table-turning and " spiritualism." Even at the universities they taught astrology as a science. Paul II. declared that the astrologers had predicted that he should become first cardinal, and then Pope ; and the same destiny was assigned to Giovanni de' Medici, afterwards Leo X., by Marsilio Ficino, who cast his horoscope at his birth. Later on, it is asserted, Paul III. never held a consistory without first ascertaining from the astrologers what hour would be favorable for the purpose.

The characteristics of this movement, as here indicated, will receive illustration from the history of Savonarola. The Renaissance at first helped him. It was high-toned, liberal, educated, and therefore it would give a hearing to this new prodigy. Nay, it took in hand to patronize him. Savonarola knew, by a spiritual instinct, how alien its spirit was from his, and kept aloof. Some of its better representatives, like the elder Pico della Mirandola and Angelo Poliziano, came under his influence and died his disciples ; the movement itself was apart from his work, was ultimately opposed to it, and became his persecutor.[1]

[1] On the general subject of this chapter, besides Gibbon, Milman, and other standard authorities, cf. Gebhart's Essais : De l'Italie (Paris : Hachette) ; Historisches Taschenbuch for 1875.

CHAPTER II.

SAVONAROLA'S BIRTH AND EARLY YEARS.

GIROLAMO SAVONAROLA was born at Ferrara on St. Matthew's day, Sept. 21, 1452. His grandfather, a native of Padua and the member of a noble family belonging to that city,[1] had been invited to Ferrara by Niccolò d' Este.[2] The house of Este, hardly less distinguished than that of the Medici for its patronage of literature, art, and science, gloried in attracting to the city which it ruled, the most distinguished men of the day. Michele Savonarola, equally renowned as a man of letters and a physician, removed to Ferrara in the beginning of the fifteenth century, and had two sons, Giovanni and Niccolò.

Of this Niccolò, his second son, we have very little information ; even his profession, if he had one, is unknown. What is certain is, that he married a daughter of the illustrious house of Bonaccorsi [3] of Mantua, Elena

[1] The Porta Savonarola at Padua recalls to mind the neighboring residence of that noble family ; and in the Prato della Valle stands a statue of Antonio Savonarola, who manfully defended his native city in the middle of the thirteenth century. — VON REUMONT : *Lorenzo de' Medici*, bk. vi. c. 6 (Mr. Harrison's translation).

[2] This Este is known as Niccolò III., Marquis of Ferrara.

[3] Thus Pico, and Villari in his first edition. In his second (i. 2), he spells the name Bonacossi.

by name, and that they had two daughters and five sons, of whom our Girolamo was the third.[1] Born, as we have said, September 21, he was baptized on October 4, the feast of St. Francis, in the church of Santa Maria del Vaio, and received the baptismal names of Girolamo Maria Francesco Matteo.[2]

If we know nothing of Savonarola's father, we are told enough of his mother to prove that there was in his case no exception to the theory that great men have usually had remarkable mothers. She was a woman of a powerful understanding, and of a masculine force of character; and we have a touching proof of the affection with which her greatest son continued through life to regard her in the fact that, whilst his first letter after entering the Dominican order was written to his father, it was to his mother that he addressed himself in the days of sorrow and trial which were so frequent in his later life.

As a child it would appear that Savonarola was distinguished by the seriousness, it might be said almost the sorrowfulness, which was his lasting characteristic, as

[1] Burlamacchi gives us the following information respecting them. The sons were: 1. Ognibene, who became a soldier; 2. Bartolommeo, whose profession is unknown; 3. Girolamo; 4. Marco, first a secular priest, afterwards a Dominican monk under his brother, taking the name of Fra Maurelio or Marco Aurelio; 5. Alberto, a skilful physician and kind to the poor, in both respects emulating the fame of his grandfather. The daughters were Beatrice, who remained unmarried, and Clara, who, losing her husband while young, lived a widow with her mother and her brother Alberto. Burlamacchi, *Vita di Savonarola*, p. 3 (Lucca, 1764).

[2] The names are given by his father in a note appended to a copy of his son's work, *Sul Dispregio del Mondo*; also by Burlamacchi.

well as the character of the higher mind of the whole age to which he belonged.   In person, as we may judge from the agreement of several existing portraits, he was by no means attractive; and the fascination which he exercised over those who came in contact with him proceeded from tone, spirit, and character, and not from any physical endowments.   Of his personal appearance we are enabled to judge, not only from the portraits,[1] but also from the careful descriptions of his three contemporary biographers.[2]

In stature he was rather below the middle size, but erect and easy in carriage.   His complexion was fair, and somewhat ruddy.   His forehead was massive and broad,[3] and deeply furrowed with wrinkles; his eyes dark blue, bright, and penetrating, with long, reddish eyelashes, and surmounted by thick eyebrows.   His nose was prominent and hooked, and he had a large mouth with full under-lip, which is said to have communicated a most pleasing expression to his whole countenance.   His limbs were well proportioned, inclining neither to leanness nor corpulency, but of a fine

[1] Besides an intaglio and some portraits of uncertain origin, there are three of great value: the first a fresco in Savonarola's cell at St. Mark's, from the pencil of Frà Bartolommeo, one of his own *frati*.   The second, by the same painter, is in the Academy of Fine Arts at Florence, and represents Savonarola as Peter Martyr.   A third portrait, of considerable merit, is preserved in the Rubieri family, and is also attributed to Frà Bartolommeo.

[2] Pico della Mirandola, c. i.; Burlamacchi; and Frà Benedetto, Cedrus Libani, c. 5.

[3] Burlamacchi speaks of it as " eminente e elevata," and Pico as "sublimis;" but, judging from all the portraits, this must describe the effect produced by its massiveness, and not by its height.

and delicate organization. His hands were very thin, — so thin that when he was preaching they seemed transparent, and his fingers were unusually long and tapering. Naturally he was of the sanguino-bilious temperament;[1] but his face was wonderfully calm, and of such sweetness of expression that "it seemed to have descended from heaven." In conversation and deportment he was of unequalled gentleness, "affable, sweet, and without any asperity." Such was the man as he appeared to his most intimate friends in the maturity of his life, activity, and power. We can imagine what the boy was like in those early days at Ferrara, before that massive brow was furrowed, when the sorrows of the future were only dimly foreshadowed in the calm and serious life of the brooding, meditative, retiring boy.

Whether because his eldest brother Ognibene was early marked out for the army, and his second brother Bartolommeo was destined to succeed to his father's possessions, or because of his own conspicuous native powers, he was intended by his parents and by his illustrious grandfather for the medical profession, — the chief source of their glory as a family. It was perhaps for this reason that the aged Michele Savonarola interested himself so deeply in this grandchild that for several years he superintended his education, and taught him with the greatest energy and patience, and with more than fatherly affection. The instructor did not want an apt and willing pupil; he found in his grandson a mind thirsting for knowledge, of more than ordinary clearness and acuteness, and endowed with a

1 "Sanguigno-bilioso," says Villari, — corresponding to what we should call choleric and melancholic.

"marvellous love of truth," and a "judgment which seemed carried towards truth by its own nature."[1]

When Savonarola was but ten years of age, in 1462, his grandfather died, and he was sent to one of the public schools of his native town, while his father privately instructed him in logic and philosophy. His progress at school was most decided. The devotion with which he addicted himself to his studies was not more remarkable than the quickness which he displayed ; and he particularly distinguished himself by the "skill and acuteness" which he showed in debate, so that even in those early days his companions began to predict his future greatness. It was indeed "difficult to decide whether he most excelled in learning or in the gravity of his manners ; " but the gentleness of his disposition seems to have secured for him the esteem even of those whom he excelled.

In those days, as in after life, he loved retirement and shunned publicity. When playing with the other boys, he would run away and employ himself in erecting little altars ; but this kind of tendency is so common among boys in every country that it would be unsafe to infer that he was already thinking of devoting himself to the monastic, or even to the clerical life. There is no doubt that in later years he often spoke of the "religious life" as that which is supremely happy, and that he strove to lead men and women to enter this state ; but it was long before the thought of it was deliberately adopted by himself. When at last he took refuge in the convent, his parents were evidently unprepared for

---

[1] Sentences or phrases thus marked will be understood to be derived from one or other of the original authorities, unless when it is otherwise specified.

such a step, and in one of his sermons he tells us that he had declared a thousand times, while still living in the world, that he "would never become a monk." [1]

The determination to enter the religious life was brought about by a variety of causes, and not by any single incident or series of events. As a child he was of a serious and devout disposition; his studies inclined him in the same direction. A personal disappointment doubtless disposed him to take the darkest views of the evil age in which his lot was cast, and he refers to a sermon which he heard when about two and twenty as a kind of turning-point in his spiritual history.

At the time that Savonarola was being educated for the medical profession, the sciences were so little distinguished that the scholastic philosophy was an essential part of his professional studies. In this way he became acquainted with the writings of Saint Thomas Aquinas and with the Arabic commentaries on Aristotle. The hold which these studies gained on his mind, and the attachment to the great schoolman which grew up within him, fostered his native tendencies, and gave that direction to his intellectual and religious convictions and purposes by which he was influenced through life. Indeed, so absorbed did he become in philosophy and theology — spending whole days over them — that he could hardly spare any thoughts for the special department of medicine.

The study of Plato belongs to a later period. It was, indeed, impossible for a thoughtful Italian to remain ignorant of the Platonic philosophy in the days of Politian and Pico della Mirandola. It was impossible for Savonarola to escape entirely the influence of the Renais-

---

[1] Prediche sopra Amos e Zacharia, Venet., 1528, fol. 251.

sance; and he tells us that he studied the Dialogues with care and wrote many notes on them, and that he was in some danger of being misled by their fascinations. He speaks in one of his sermons of the fashion for Platonism having become so strong that one heard of nothing from public teachers "but Plato, that divine man." "I was in that error myself," he says, "and studied much those dialogues of Plato; but when God gave me light I destroyed all that I had written on that subject."

There was much in the circumstances of his times to deepen the natural seriousness of Savonarola. The state of Ferrara must have given rise to grave reflections in one who was little apt to be dazzled by the splendor of pomp and show. Few could have been more welcome in the halls of the Este than the members of the house of Savonarola; but we are told that never but once could Girolamo be induced to appear at court.

Niccolò III., who had invited Michele Savonarola to Ferrara, had died before the subject of this memoir was born, and was succeeded by his two natural sons, Lionello and Borso, whom he had caused to be legitimized in his lifetime, in consequence of the youth of his legitimate son Ercole. Lionello succeeded his father in 1441, and died in 1450. He ruled with such success in troubled times that his country was called the "land of peace." Borso was a man of a different stamp.[1] He was the "Magnificent" of Ferrara, as Lorenzo de' Medici was of Florence; and was so renowned for the splendor of his court, and for his abilities and influence, that in distant lands he was spoken of as the king of Italy.

It was while Borso was Marquis of Ferrara, and in

---

[1] Cf. Signor Villari's remarks, lib. i. cap. i. p. 7.

the very year of Savonarola's birth (1452), that Frederick III. passed through Ferrara, on his way to Rome to
receive the imperial crown at the hands of the reigning
Pope, Nicholas V. He was received with great state
by the Marquis and court of Ferrara; but as he had
decided, on his return from Rome, to raise Borso to
the ducal dignity, preparations were made on the most
splendid scale for the celebration of the event.

But these festivities were entirely thrown into the
shade by the reception accorded to Pius II., in 1458,
on his way to the Council of Mantua, at which he was
hoping to stir up Western Christendom to undertake a
crusade for the recovery of Constantinople. We need
not dwell upon the hopeful beginning or the ridiculous
failure of this enterprise; and we have no means of
knowing how the youthful mind of Savonarola was impressed either by the splendid pomps of his native city
or by the hopes excited on behalf of the suffering Eastern Christians. He was only six years of age when the
Pope passed through Ferrara, on his way to the council.
He must have been a witness of these festivals; and he
probably knew something of the miseries and the hopes
of the Greeks. All that we know is that he was not
attracted to the ruling family. When Borso died, and
his half-brother, the legitimate son of Niccolò III., came
to the throne as Ercole I., in 1471, Savonarola was
nineteen.

The glory of the Este had not dazzled him. His true
eye saw the hollowness of courtly splendor. His deep
religious nature was shocked by the worldliness and
worthlessness of the lives of the great. His instinctive
and unquenchable love of liberty could never delight
in the degradation and misery of his fellow-men, which

always result from even the most graceful despotism. The chains might be gilded, or even golden; but in his eyes they were none the less fetters upon the bodies and souls of men.

Of his early thoughts we know nothing. Of the progress of his education we have hardly any information from his biographers, only such scanty facts as we have noted, besides occasional allusions in his sermons. But we are now coming to the period in which we have his own record of the thoughts and emotions that were passing in his mind. He had been a solitary, brooding boy, "living little in the society of his fellows, much in his own," caring only for learning and knowledge, and for these only as the way to truth. Much he thought and meditated on the life of man and the end for which he was created; but as the light within grew brighter, he became more and more conscious of the darkness without. *Hora novissima; tempora pessima:* "The world is very evil; the times are waxing late,"—this was the burden of his thought. The words which the spirit of Polydorus uttered with groans in the ears of Æneas, as he told his father afterwards, he recited many times in a day with tears: *Heu! fuge crudeles terras, fuge litus avarum!*—"Ah! flee from this cruel land, flee from this covetous shore."[1]

Of the letter in which he makes this declaration we shall have to speak presently. It contains his reasons for abandoning the world. The desire arose, he says, from his beholding "the great misery of the world, the iniquities of men, the rapes, the adulteries, the robberies, the pride, the idolatry, the cruel blasphemy, which have come to such a height in the world that there is no

---

[1] Æneid, III. 44.

longer any one found who does good. I could not bear," he goes on, " the great wickedness of the blinded peoples of Italy; and so much the more that I saw virtue everywhere disdained, and vice held in honor. This was the greatest suffering that I could have had to endure in this world; on which account I prayed every day to the Lord Jesus Christ that He would deign to raise me up out of this mire. And I made continually short prayers to God with the most earnest devotion, saying, ' Show Thou me the way that I should walk in, for I lift up my soul unto Thee,' — *Notam fac mihi viam in qua ambulem, quia ad Te levavi animam meam.*" [1]

It is clear that these were not mere afterthoughts which suggested themselves as a justification of the course he had taken; for the same feelings are expressed in a poem which he composed three years before, when he was only twenty, in 1472, " On the Ruin of the World." [2]

If he did not believe, he says, in the infinite providence of God, what he saw in the world would make him agree with those who deny Him or say that He sleeps; for everywhere virtue is perished and every decent custom, and there is no true light in the world, nor even shame for vices. Rapine and murder are so common that he is happy who practises such sins.

At one moment in his life at Ferrara it seemed as though the world might begin to have a new interest for him; but this new hope had scarcely arisen upon him when it set, leaving him involved in a thicker darkness. It is curious that his biographers, with one exception, seem to have known nothing of Savonarola's

[1] Psalm cxliii. 8.

[2] De Ruina Mundi, in Poesie (Firenze), 1847, pp. 3–6.

disappointment in love ; and it was only quite recently that this incident in the history of his early manhood was brought to light. It is, however, recorded by his own disciple, Frà Benedetto,[1] and there is no reason to doubt the truth of the story.

It would be inconsistent with all the testimonies respecting his early character to suppose that it was this event which gave all its sadness to his life. But it can hardly be doubted that it added greatly to his previous despondency. The incident is not only interesting in itself, but throws some light upon his natural disposition.

A citizen of Florence, of the noble family of the Strozzi, banished from his native city, had come to Ferrara, bringing with him a natural daughter. Living in the house next to Savonarola's, she attracted the attention and gained the affections of Girolamo, who one day availed himself of the opportunity offered of speaking to her on the subject of his affection. The answer which he received was haughty and insolent: " Do you imagine that the blood and the great house of the Strozzi could form an alliance with that of Savonarola ? " It was an unfortunate reply. The girl remembered only one half of her parentage ; and the mortified lover, provoked by her foolish pride, fiercely reminded her of the stain on her birth. We may be sure that he repented of his anger when the flushing face revealed the feelings which she could find no words to express. We may be quite sure that the bitter taunt which he had cast at her often came back with pain to the memory of the chastened Frà Girolamo in after years.

[1] Vulnera Diligentis, lib. i. c. g. It was first discovered by Meier (cf. Meier's Leben, c. i. s. 15).

The feelings of weariness and revulsion which the condition of the Church and the world had aroused within him went on deepening, until at last he resolved to leave his home and enter a monastery. By day and by night his thoughts were of God and eternity, and he was meditating continually on the possibility of living a better and a higher life. When he was twenty-two years of age, we are told, he spent a whole night in considering what course he ought to take. In order to assist his meditations he had sprinkled his body with the coldest water; and he ended by dedicating himself entirely to the service of Jesus Christ.[1] It was about this time that he was deeply moved by the preaching of an Augustinian monk at Faenza, which seems finally to have decided his taking the step he had been already meditating. Long afterwards he refers to the impression then made upon him as deep and powerful. "Once," he says, "while I was still in the world, I went .for amusement to Faenza, and entering by chance the church of St. Augustine, I heard a word from an Augustinian preacher, which I will not tell you now, but which to this hour I have in my heart; and I went and became a friar before a year had passed." Frà Benedetto says that Savonarola would never repeat that word; and that, strangely, the monk from whom he heard it was known as a man of irregular life; from which Savonarola took occasion to observe that we might learn to do well from the Divine Word, whoever preached it.

When he had once resolved to become a monk, he had little difficulty in deciding for the Dominican order,

---

[1] An incident mentioned, and his age at the time, both by Pico and Burlamacchi.

[2] Prediche sopra Ezechiel, Ven., 1541, fol. 172.

to which he was probably attracted by many considerations, but chiefly by his devotion to Saint Thomas, the
great glory of the order. We can imagine the emotions
with which he passed through Bologna (probably the
route he took), on his way back from Faenza to Ferrara,
with these new resolves working in his mind.

The resolution he had formed at once lifted a burden
from his heart, for he felt he had now broken with the
ungodly world ; but this joy was darkened by the thought
of the pain he was about to inflict upon his parents, to
whom he did not dare to disclose his purpose. It
seemed to him that his mother was watching him with
a new and painful interest, as though she were striving
to read his very heart. For a whole year this struggle
went on.   In the letter to his father from which we have
already quoted he says, " If I had shown you my purpose, I believe verily my heart would have broken before
I could have parted from you, and I should have abandoned the intention I had formed."

It was hard to leave them, in any case. The night
before he set forth on his new life, he took his lute in
his hand and played on it a strain so sorrowful that his
mother seemed to divine what was passing in his heart,
and turning to him with saddened looks exclaimed, " My
son, this is a sign of parting."   By a great effort he kept
his eyes on the ground, and continued with a trembling
hand to touch the lute, without venturing to answer.

On the 24th of April the whole city of Ferrara was
celebrating the festival of St. George ; and it was this
day, when the thoughts of the populace and of his own
family were entirely occupied with the festivities, that
Girolamo had chosen as a time when he could escape
without being observed.   He took his way to Bologna

and prayed for admission to the Dominican convent of that city, where the great founder of the order lies enshrined. He made but one special request, that he might be appointed to perform the most menial duties of the fraternity.

To a mind like that of Savonarola, the convent might have possessed many attractions. His tendencies were towards solitude rather than intercourse with his fellowmen; and here he might gratify his tastes. His love for Saint Thomas and for theological study might have led him to desire a manner of life in which such studies might reasonably have formed his principal occupation. How little such considerations weighed with him, we may judge not only from his declaration to his father that he had come to the resolution of leaving the world, because he could no longer endure the corruption of the age, but also from the purpose which he formed respecting his employments when he entered the convent.

Savonarola was not unaware of the dangers and temptations of the monastic life. He was, indeed, so fearful of putting on the habit of the religious in a worldly spirit that, as he afterwards informed his friend and biographer, Pico della Mirandola, he had resolved not to take holy orders, nor even to addict himself to his favorite philosophical studies. It was his fixed intention to ask to be employed in manual labor, to work in the garden, to make clothes for the brethren, and the like. This resolution, says Pico, he providentially forgot, God intending him for a teacher of others. It is equally probable that in the same spirit of humility which prompted the resolve, he abandoned it in obedience to those under whom he was placed, and who discerned in him a fitness for higher work.

Although he had shrunk from divulging to his parents

his intention of taking the religious habit, yet he would not, for a moment longer than he thought necessary, leave them in ignorance or anxiety as to the step he had taken. Among his books in his desk he left a paper, of which a copy has recently been found, on "Contempt of the World;" and on the following day he wrote a letter to his father, explaining the reasons which had moved him to leave his home.

The treatise simply sets forth the thoughts which had been growing so strong within him of the evils of the world. The copy recently discovered bears upon it the following touching words, in Italian, from his father's hand : —

"I remember how, on the 24th of April, which was St. George's Day in 1475, Geronimo my son, student in arts, departed from his home and went to Bologna, and entered among the brothers of St. Dominic in order to become a brother; and left me, me Niccolò della Savonarola, his father, the underwritten consolations and exhortations for my satisfaction."

The letter from which we have already quoted was marked by the most tender affection as well as by the greatest earnestness. He tells his father, "I wish you, as a true man and one who despises fleeting things, to be influenced by truth, and not by passion, like women, and to judge, under the dominion of reason, whether I am right in fleeing from the world." And then he speaks of the evils of the age in words already quoted.

"And so, dear father," he goes on, "instead of weeping, you have rather to thank the Lord Jesus, who has given you a son, and then has preserved him to you for twenty-two years ; and not only this, but besides has designed to make him His knight militant (*militante cavaliere*). Ah! do you not regard it as a great grace to have a son a knight of Jesus Christ? But, to speak shortly, either it is true that you love me, or it is not true. I know well that you will not say you do not love me. If then you love me, since I have two parts, that is, the soul and the body, do you love most the soul, or the body? You cannot say the body, because you would not love me if you loved the baser part of me. If then you love the soul best, why should you not seek the good of the soul? Therefore you ought to rejoice, and to regard this as a triumph. . . . Do you believe that it is not a great grief for me to be separated from you? Believe me, that never since I was born have I had a greater grief nor a greater affliction of mind, seeing myself abandon my own blood, and go among people unknown, in order to make a sacrifice to Jesus Christ of my body, and to sell my will into the hands of those whom I never knew. But yet, considering that God calls me, and that He does not disdain of us worms to make Himself servants, I could not be so bold as not to incline to His most sweet voice, which says, 'Come unto Me, all ye that labor and are heavy laden, and I will give you rest. Take My yoke upon you.' . . . I pray you then, my dear father, put a stop to your lamentations, and do not give me more sadness and grief than I now endure, — not for grief of that which I have done, which I certainly do not wish to recall, even if I thought I could become greater than Cæsar, but because I am still made of flesh, as you are, and the senses fight against the reason. . . . It only remains for me to pray you, like a man, to comfort my mother, whom I pray, together with you, to give me your benediction: and I will always pray fervently for your souls. *Ex Bononia, die* xxv. *Aprilis* (Bologna, April 25), 1475. . . . *Hieronymus Savonarola, filius vester.* To the noble and excellent man Nicolas Savonarola, the best of parents (*parenti optimo*)."[1]

[1] This letter has been often published, but an accurate copy was for the first time printed from the autograph by the Count Carlo Capponi. Villari reproduces this text, and from his work our translation is made.

What effect this letter may have produced we cannot tell, but there is a second letter extant, without date, in which he complains of their excessive grief.

"Why do ye weep, blind ones?" he begins. "Why do ye complain so much? If our temporal prince had called me now to gird a sword on my side in the midst of the people, and to make me one of his knights, what joy you would have experienced! And if I had then repudiated such an honor, would you not have thought me a fool? . . . And now the Prince of princes, He who is of infinite power, calls me with a loud voice, even prays me (O great love !) with a thousand tears, to gird a sword on my side, of the finest gold and precious stones, and wishes to place me among the number of His knights militant. And now, because I have not refused so great honor, although I am unworthy (and who would refuse it ?), — because I, giving thanks to so great a Lord, since He thus wills, have accepted it, — you all afflict me, when you ought to rejoice and give thanks ; and the more you do so, the more you show that you love me."

CHAPTER III.

MONASTIC LIFE AT BOLOGNA.

WHEN Savonarola arrived in Bologna, the city, after many variations of fortune, had become, in name at least, the second capital of the Papal States, although the family of Bentivoglio, by whom it was governed, held the papal supremacy very lightly. But the young novice had at this time no thoughts for questions which he afterwards felt to be of vital importance to the well-being of Italy. We may even doubt whether that splendid shrine in the convent church, one of the greatest works of Nicolà da Pisa, upon which so many pilgrims have gazed with admiration, interested him otherwise than as the resting-place of the great founder of his order.

During his novitiate, and indeed during his whole life at Bologna, he abstained, as far as possible, from all social intercourse with his fellow-men. Every hour that he could gain for the purpose he spent in silent meditation and prayer. His companions compared his manner and conduct to those of the ancient ascetics and hermits of Egypt, as they saw him moving about like a ghost, worn to a shadow by fasts and vigils.

In every respect he kept his vow of poverty to the letter, or rather in excess. He ate only enough to sustain life. His garments were the roughest and the coarsest that he could procure, but always scrupulously clean. His shoes were long and turned up at the points, for, he said, "they would be full of precious stones in Paradise." His bed consisted of pieces of wood and sticks laid across so as to form a kind of lattice-work, on which were placed a sack of straw and a woollen sheet, with a coarse frock thrown over them.

As regards his vow of purity, his biographers speak of his eminence in this respect as being represented in his writings, and as the reason for his being favored with visions of the world of spirits. Nor was his obedience less remarkable ; for while he was in most perfect subjection to his superiors, he was humble and gentle to equals and inferiors, and although he spoke very little, he was always kind and affable in manner. It was perhaps the happiest and most tranquil period in all his life. Speaking of it afterwards,[1] he says : "It was said to me, Go forth from your home and your country, and leave all. And I was guided to the harbor of the sea, that is, to religion, which is the true and safe harbor to him who seeks for salvation. And I came to this port when I was twenty-three years old. And two things above all others I loved, which drew me to this harbor, — liberty and peace."

With all his gentleness and humility, he did not lack those powers of sarcasm which were afterwards displayed in his preaching. There is a story told of two monks of Vallombrosa who came to visit him, who were themselves so struck by the contrast between his coarse garments and their own more luxurious attire that they thought it necessary to give some explanation of their usages. Their frocks, they said, were made of fine

[1] Prediche sopra alquanti Salmi ed Aggeo, Ven., 1544, fol. 141.

cloth because it wore so much longer. " Ah," replied the Frate, dryly, " what a pity it is that Saint Benedict and Saint Giovanni Gualberto did not know that ; for then they might have worn the same ! " [1]

During the seven years that he remained in the convent at Bologna he was unremitting in his studies. His old favorite, Saint Thomas, he never abandoned, and he greatly delighted in works of devotion like those of Augustine and Cassian ; but there grew in him an ever-increasing tendency to turn from other books and give himself more and more to the study of the Holy Scriptures. He is said [2] to have committed the whole of the Canonical Books to memory, — a practice which bore abundant fruits in his after labors ; and it was here that he formed the habit, never afterwards abandoned, of making notes on the margins of his Bible, his Breviary, and other books. Several of these are still in existence, and one of the most interesting objects now shown in the convent of St. Mark at Florence is one of his Bibles, kept in his cell, the margins of which are covered with notes in his beautiful but minute handwriting. It is an instance of the affectionate interest which his early biographers took in the smallest particulars of his life and habits, and also of the uncertain inferences they drew from them, that Burlamacchi mentions that this habit of annotating his Bible and Breviary with all that was necessary for preaching and hearing confessions enabled him to travel without a valise (*la valigia*) !

It was not long before his superiors determined to make use of his gifts for the benefit of the community ;

---

[1] Burlamacchi gives the story here ; it is quite as likely, however, to have belonged to the period of his reforms at Florence.

[2] Burlamacchi.

and therefore they set him to instruct the novices of the convent. It was with no small reluctance that he complied with this command, foreseeing, as he did, that it would involve the sacrifice of many hours of solitude, of meditation and prayer; but he obeyed, and in this, as in every other occupation, he gained the esteem and admiration of his brethren.

The " peace and liberty " which he had sought and found might now have secured to him a calm and tranquil life, if he could have forgotten the evils of the world, if he had not found these evils asserting their dominion within the walls of the convent. Already, we are told, he was struck with the contrast between the monks of his own day and those of earlier and better days, when he saw multitudes around him heedless of the Word of God and the life of grace, and " intent only upon enriching the churches and building the most beautiful convents, and many others occupying themselves in numberless vanities."

It might seem to be a proud boast which he uttered in later days, that he was entirely devoted to the pursuit of truth; but those who follow him from the time of his entering the Dominican order throughout his life, and thoughtfully ponder his words and his deeds, his utterances in public and in private, and his conduct as a priest and a patriot, will hardly refuse to allow the truth of his claim.

" I have always," he says, " striven after truth with all my might, and sought unceasingly to win all men to it, as I have declared a constant war against falsehood, which I have always hated. The more trouble I bestow upon it, the greater becomes my longing, so that for it I could abandon life itself. When I was but a boy, I had such thoughts; and from that time the desire and longing after this good has gone on increasing to the present day."[1]   "Truth," he says in another place, "should be loved for its own sake, and brings great joy to those who find it.   It enlightens the spirit with a divine splendor, and leads the soul to communion with God, who is Truth itself."[2]

To such a man the condition of men and things around him was intolerable.   His first poem has shown us what he thought of the world before he left it.   He had not been long in the convent before he wrote a second on the ruin of the Church ("De ruina Ecclesiæ")· It is said to have been composed in the year 1475, the first of his monastic life.   "Where," he asks, addressing the Church as a "chaste virgin," to whom he, although unworthy, belongs, being one of the members of her eternal Spouse, — "where is the light of the early days? Where are the gems and the fine diamonds?   Where are the burning lamps and the beautiful sapphires?" — meaning the saints and martyrs, the love and devotion of the early Church.   "Where are the white stoles and the sweet chants?"   The virgin takes him by the hand and leads him to a cave, and tells him that, when she saw proud ambition enter Rome, she departed, and dwelt where she could lead her life in lamentation.   Then she shows him her wounded body and her dishevelled hair; and when he asks who it is that has thus dethroned her and broken her peace, she answers: "A false, proud harlot, Babylon."   "And I: 'In God's name, lady tell me, can these great wings be broken?'   And she:

---

[1] Dialogo della verità profetica, fol. 72.
[2] Prediche sopra diversi Salmi, etc., fol. 42. (Qu. by Meier, p. 21.)

'Mortal tongue must not speak it; nor is it allowed to take up arms.   Weep and be silent, for this is best.'"[1]

When we remember that Sixtus IV. was Pope during the whole of the seven years that Savonarola spent at Bologna, we shall understand what hope of reformation he could have drawn from the character of the Head of the Church.   But the secular rulers of Italy were no better — how could they have been better? — than its spiritual chief.   Liberty had perished in all the ancient republics, Venice alone, perhaps, excepted.   Bologna was ruled by a Bentivoglio.   Milan was under the weak but tyrannical Galeazzo Sforza.   Florence, after being ruled by the wise and able Cosimo de' Medici, who never discarded the forms of liberty even when the reality was gone, had been succeeded (1464) by his weak and incapable son, Piero,[2] who, happily for the prospects of his family, died in 1469, and was succeeded by Lorenzo.

It is not merely in order to illustrate the condition of the world at this time, but also on account of its direct bearing upon the history of Savonarola, that we pause for a moment to relate the history of a tragedy, neglected by no historian of this period, which took place at Florence in 1478, three years after Savonarola entered the convent at Bologna, four years before he left it and came to Florence.   Whether we consider the character and position of the family assailed, the nature and ramifications of the conspiracy formed against them, the designs of

---

[1] The poem is given, with copious notes, in the Poesie, edited by Audin de Rians (Firenze, 1847).

[2] Von Reumont shows, however, that this Piero was a man possessed of many admirable qualities, — very different from his grandson who bore the same name.

the conspirators, or the actual results of the attempt, the conspiracy of the Pazzi will appear to be one of the most remarkable events of the period to which it belongs.

The name of the Medici will hold a prominent place in these pages. They were the most powerful family in Florence, and in some respects they had merited the influence to which they had attained. The Pazzi were among the oldest families and the greatest of the same State. They were connected with the Medici by marriage; but for some reasons, real or imagined,[1] they bore a grudge against them, and they envied them the power which they possessed in Florence. But the Pazzi were not alone in the conspiracy. It has even been doubted whether they were its prime movers. That place has, by some historians, been assigned to the Holy Father himself; and if Sixtus IV. was not the instigator of the attempt,[2] there is no doubt that he gave it the most energetic support, and his nephew, the Count Girolamo Riario, took an active part in the whole scheme. Their design was to murder Lorenzo de' Medici and his brother Giuliano, and thus to crush the power which was inconvenient to the Pope and hateful to the Pazzi. Determined to stop at no obstacles, when they found it almost impossible to slay the two brothers at once, they determined at last to assassinate them at the time of High Mass, on the occasion of a great solemnity in the cathedral of Florence.

A soldier of some reputation, by name Montesecco, had been employed to perpetrate the crime; but the

---

[1] They were not merely imaginary. Cf. Von Reumont, Lorenzo de' Medici, bk. ii. c. i.

[2] The Pope professed, at least, to discountenance the murder.

man who was ready to commit murder was not prepared to incur the guilt of sacrilege. They had to find
other tools, and they found them in two priests. This
can hardly seem wonderful, when the conspirators were
supported by the Pope, and had for their most active
leader Francesco Salviati, Archbishop of Pisa. This
man had been appointed by the Pope in opposition to
the wishes of the Medici, and he was now in Florence,
taking counsel with the other conspirators, waiting to
reap his revenge. The murder accomplished, they were
going to raise the populace, under the pretence of restoring their lost liberty, and then to take possession of
the property of the murdered men.

The signal for the striking of the blow was the bell
which announced the elevation of the host; and Giuliano de' Medici[1] fell dead under the knife of one of the
assassins. Lorenzo was only wounded, and was able to
defend himself until, with the assistance of his friends, he
escaped into the sacristy of the church. Still, the conspirators hoped their work was not in vain; they might
raise the populace, and finish it by open violence. The
populace rose in defence of the Medici. In a few hours
the Archbishop of Pisa was swinging, in his episcopal
robes, from a window of the Palazzo Vecchio, and one
of the Pazzi was hanged beside him. The conspiracy
had failed, and many of the conspirators were hunted
down and slain.

The wrath of the Pope knew no bounds, and broke
forth in threats and anathemas, — not against the sac-
rilegious desecrators of temples, the conspirators, the
assassins, but against Florence and the Medici. It is

[1] Of this Giuliano, Pope Clement VII. was the illegitimate
son.

worth while to glance at the document in which he set forth the wrongs he had suffered from the Florentines, and the punishment he found it necessary to inflict upon them. "According to the example of the Saviour," said his Holiness, "he had long suffered in peace the insults and the injuries of his enemies, and he should still have continued to exercise his forbearance, had not Lorenzo de' Medici, with the magistrates of Florence and their abettors, discarding the fear of God, inflamed with fury, and instigated by diabolical suggestions, laid violent hands on ecclesiastical persons, hung up the archbishop, imprisoned the cardinal [his nephew], and by various means destroyed and slaughtered their followers [the accomplices of the assassins]." He then proceeded to excommunicate Lorenzo and the magistrates of the republic, and their "immediate successors, declaring them incapable of receiving or transmitting property by inheritance or will, and prohibiting their descendants from enjoying any ecclesiastical employment. By the same instrument he suspended the bishops and clergy of the Florentine territories from the exercise of their spiritual functions."[1]

These things were not done in a corner, the sound of them went throughout all the world. We may judge whether the Dominican friar at Bologna who, three years before, had in his *Canzona* spoken of Rome as Babylon, "a false, proud harlot," could now shake off the horror with which he regarded the state of the visible Church in its root and in its branches. The Pope, be it remembered, was that Sixtus IV. who occupied the "chair of Peter" during the whole of the seven years in

____

[1] Roscoe, Life of Lorenzo de' Medici, c. iv. Cf. also Capponi, Repubblica di Firenze, lib. v. c. 5.

which Savonarola was watching and praying, and study-
ing and teaching, and grieving over the ruin of the
Church at Bologna. Amid such circumstances were his
thoughts and purposes for the future being shaped.
Under such influences was he trying to learn what work
his Master had set him to do in the world.

Savonarola's success as a teacher was so great that his
superiors appointed him to preach ; nor was he slow in
yielding obedience to the command. The fire was
kindling within him, and he was preparing, unconsciously, perhaps, to speak with his tongue words that
would be felt and remembered. This result was not,
however, achieved at once. It is with some astonishment that we learn how little his first sermons seem to
have gained the attention of his hearers. The reasons
were manifold, and they are to be sought partly in the
corrupt taste of the age, and partly in the peculiar genius
and mission of the preacher.

It had been the fashion with the popular preachers of
those days to indulge in the most fanciful conceits and
tricks of rhetoric, for the purpose of attracting and amus-
ing their hearers. A sermon was, in their eyes, either a
light recreation or a means of exercising their own dialectical subtlety. To the deep moral earnestness of
Savonarola all this was horrible and revolting ; and it is
possible that in shrinking from the use of artifice in the
pulpit, he may have shown a disregard of those rules of
spoken composition which few can afford to neglect.
None of the early sermons have been preserved, so that
we have no means of judging of them. It is very probable, however, that the Frate had not yet found his own
proper manner of address ; that the emotions which
were struggling within him had hardly shaped themselves

into definite thoughts, so as to be ready for articulate and coherent utterance. Indeed, the testimony on the subject is not quite consistent. We learn, for example, that he was ordered by his superiors to go and preach at Ferrara; and while we are told that his fellow-citizens heard his preaching with great favor, he himself complains, in a letter written to his mother from Pavia, eight years after, that in him was fulfilled the saying : *Nemo propheta in patria sua,* — " No prophet is accepted in his own country." [1] On the occasion of this visit to his native town he avoided meeting any of his old acquaintances, and he saw very little even of his parents, for fear of awakening sentiments which he wished to remain forever dead.

Although his public teaching seems to have been unsuccessful, this was not the case either with his private instructions or his personal admonitions. A story is told by his biographers of the remarkable effect produced on a number of hardened and reckless men by his remonstrances. On a certain occasion he journeyed from Ferrara to Mantua in a boat alone with eighteen soldiers, who were playing and using obscene language, when he asked leave to speak a few words to them. Pico says that he spoke to them for the space of half an hour most earnestly on the sinfulness of their life ; and both he and Burlamacchi relate that, before he had ended his address, eleven of them fell prostrate at his feet, confessing their great and innumerable sins, and asking pardon with tears for the offences of which they had been guilty against the Frate and against God.

But a series of events were about to occur which

---

[1] St. Luke iv. 24.

were destined to alter the whole course of his life. In the same year in which he had been sent to preach in his native town (1482), a war broke out between Venice and Ferrara, which was at first carried on between these two States, but soon divided all Italy into two hostile factions. Florence alone remained undisturbed by the tumult which arose, while Ferrara was its very centre. It was in many respects a strange and curious struggle. Pope Sixtus, it is said, had stirred up the Venetians at the beginning of the war, and there is no doubt that he was on their side; but he shortly afterwards came to see that his interests would be more advanced by espousing the cause of their enemies. He thereupon turned round, excommunicated the Venetians, and did his utmost to inflame and keep alive the strife he had kindled. With such an ally on either side, it is not wonderful that the contending powers became anxious to conclude a peace; and this they accomplished in two years from the beginning of the war, 1484. This was the peace which proved the death of the Holy Father. "You announce to me," he said, "a peace of shame and disgrace." His grief and rage brought on an attack which carried him off on the following day.

Savonarola was at Ferrara, in the convent of Santa Maria degli Angeli, when the war broke out; and the Venetians having threatened to storm the city and massacre the inhabitants, a number of the brethren were sent away and distributed among different cities of Italy. Savonarola was among those who were sent to the convent of St. Mark at Florence.

It was apparently with reluctance that he had gone to Ferrara, and in a letter afterwards written to his mother, he points out that it was better he should not remain there.

"It is very seldom," he says, "that a monk can do his best work in his native country. People have less confidence in the counsels of a fellow-citizen than in those of a stranger. ' No prophet is accepted in his own country,' said our Saviour; and He was not accounted one by His own countrymen. If I wanted. to do in Ferrara what I do in other cities, they would say, as they said of Christ : ' Is not this the Carpenter, the son of a carpenter and of Mary ?' — so of me : ' Is not this Master Girolamo, who committed such and such sins, and who was no better than we were ? We know him well.' And they would give no heed to my word. . . . Out of my own country," he adds, — it is a son writing in all simplicity to a mother — "it is not so. On the contrary, when I want to leave, men and women weep."

It was not destined that the brother should remain at Ferrara ; and this change in his circumstances was of the greatest import as a turning-point, perhaps the most important, in his life. He was bidding a last farewell to Ferrara and to those whom he loved so tenderly, and whom he was never again to see on earth. But what was the past which he was leaving, compared with the future upon which he was now entering? He might continue to be spoken of as Girolamo of Ferrara, but henceforth it is as a brother of St. Mark's and a citizen of Florence that he belongs to the world and to history.

How much depends upon what men call accidents ! Who can tell what the fortune of Savonarola would have been if he had been sent to some other town of Italy, undisturbed by the storms which raged in his new home ?

There was not a second Florence; and at a distance from this great city he might have been a great teacher, preacher, reformer,— he could hardly have been insignificant anywhere,— but his place in history would have been altogether different; and so, indeed, would the history of Italy itself have been, for we may say, without hesitation, there was no other man of that age who could have filled his place. If there was no second Florence, there was no second Savonarola.

CHAPTER IV.

THE BROTHER OF ST. MARK'S.

THE convent of St. Mark in Florence was originally built by a company of Sylvestrine monks from Vallombrosa at the close of the thirteenth century, about the same time that the Palazzo Vecchio was built for the Signoria. The order of the Sylvestrines had its beginning some sixty years before, and came to have as many as twenty-five convents and three hundred brethren; but it is now almost extinct, many of its members having been absorbed into other societies. For a whole century these monks lived in their convent, honored by the citizens of Florence for their virtues and their work. But the great plague of Florence, which broke out in 1400, and which has been so powerfully described by Boccaccio in the introduction to the Decameron, seems to have produced the same twofold effects which resulted from the plague at Athens, described by the still more powerful pen of Thucydides. While some had their devotion deepened and strengthened, others became reckless, or fell into thoughtless and irreligious courses.

With the Sylvestrines of St. Mark's the effect of the plague was to relax their discipline and to engender all those evils which flow from a neglect of rule. This degeneracy seems to have gone on for a whole genera-

tion.   About the time of the plague there was a society
of Dominicans which, after several vicissitudes of fortune
and of character, had been settled at the small convent
of San Georgio, on the south side of the Arno, in the
San Miniato district, behind the Boboli Gardens.[1]   This
Dominican society had undergone more than one removal, but had been so improved by the discipline that
it was determined by the Pope and the Signoria that
they should take possession of the larger convent of
St. Mark, and transfer their own to the Sylvestrines.

When these reformed Dominicans of the Lombard
congregation [2] took possession of San Marco it was in a
state of the utmost dilapidation.   The dormitory had
recently been destroyed by a fire, so that the monks
were forced to seek for shelter in wooden huts.   Cosimo
de' Medici, the great founder of Medicean influence in
Florence, undertook the restoration of the buildings.
He promised the monks ten thousand scudi for the
purpose, but he is said to have spent as much as thirty-
six thousand.   The work extended over nearly seven
years (1436–1443), and was carried on under the direction of Michelozzo Michelozzi, an architect of some
celebrity.   It should be stated, however, that the buildings have since his time been greatly altered.   The
church, for example, which dates back as far as 1290,
had its façade reconstructed by Pronti in 1777.   It
should be added that Cosimo — *Pater Patriæ*, as he
was called, and not altogether without reason — did

---

[1] The gardens were, of course, still in the future.   In fact,
the Pitti Palace is said to have been undertaken in the very
year of the exchange mentioned in the text, and the building to
have been commenced five or six years later.

[2] It is of some importance to note their description.

not rest contented with having merely reconstructed the buildings of the convent. He resolved upon a more difficult enterprise, — to bestow upon the monks the gift of a valuable library. Luckily for his purpose, there had just died Niccolo Niccoli, the most celebrated collector of books and manuscripts, and one of the most learned men of that age. His collection, which was of great value, he left to the public, but burdened by very heavy debts. Cosimo paid off the debts, and after retaining some valuable manuscripts as his own, he presented the remainder to the convent of St. Mark. It was the first public library in Italy, and was not merely highly prized by the brethren, but was the means of stimulating the literary industry of the society.[1]

But the rebuilding of the monastery was only a preparation for those nobler works of art which are some of the most striking illustrations of the heavenly spirit of a brother of the newly settled society, Frà Angelico, or as he was then called, Frà Giovanni da Fiesole. It was a wonderful era in Florentine art. Exactly a century before, Giotto had been raising his matchless Campanile by the side of the ancient Baptistery of St. John. While Frà Giovanni was covering the walls of San Marco with the fruits of his devotion, Brunelleschi was planning and carrying out the execution of that glorious dome, the admiration and perhaps the inspiration of Michael Angelo,[1] which was to soar aloft and dominate the whole city, rising a hundred feet higher even than Giotto's tower. Of these charming frescos we can say but

[1] Michael Angelo's reply is well known, when he was told that he was about to erect for St. Peter's at Rome a finer dome than Brunelleschi's. " Più grande," he said, " ma non più bello."

little here.   No one who has seen them in their marvellous freshness on the walls of St. Mark's is likely to forget them.   Untravelled Englishmen may study them in the admirable copies of the Arundel Society; and we may well believe that they often kindled the pious imagination and soothed the troubled heart of the new friar.

Frà Angelico's is not the only great name connected with San Marco.   There was another, which in those days, at least, was held in still greater esteem, that of Antonino, "one of those characters which do real honor to the human race."[1]   He was the creator of many beneficent institutions in Florence; and he renovated and reorganized many others.   It was he who converted the society of the Bigallo, founded by Saint Peter Martyr for the extermination of heretics, into a charitable institution. Instead of carrying on the bloody work of the Inquisition, the brethren now devoted themselves to the care of orphan children.   He was also the founder of the "Good Men of Saint Martin" (*Buon' Uomini di San Martino*), who collected alms for the relief of the deserving and shamefaced poor (*poveri vergognosi*) at their own houses.   His self-denial was equal to his warm love for God and man and his active charity on behalf of the suffering and needy.   He died in 1459, lamented as a public loss by all Florence; and Savonarola found his name revered, and his life held up as the highest example for the imitation of the brotherhood, when he arrived in Florence in 1482.

When Savonarola came to Florence he often heard the brethren of San Marco extolling the piety of Sant' Antonino; but it was not long before he discovered that

[1] Villari.

their admiration did not involve the purpose of imitation. His was more a name to boast of than an ideal
to reach after. In this convent, too, all was worldliness
and irreligion. The immorality of the people had assumed a more refined form under the influence of the
prophets of the Renaissance. In this mediæval Athens
there was little that seemed coarse and outwardly repul-
sive; but its polished cynicism, its refined sensuality, its
utter heartlessness and unbelief were, if possible, more
disgusting to the serious, earnest spirit of Savonarola than
evil more coarse and less disguised would have been.
The "religious" were hardly different from the men of
the world. Religion was the thing they cared for least;
even theology had little interest for them. We can imagine with what bitter grief and disappointment Savonarola beheld the eager interest manifested in Plato and
Aristotle, and the utter neglect of Saint Thomas and even
of Saint Paul.

It must be remembered that Frà Girolamo had no
personal reason for mortification. His reputation had
gone before him, and he had hardly entered the new
brotherhood when the prior, Vincenzo Badella, appointed
him to the same post which he had held at Bologna,
that of *Lettore*, or instructor of the novices; and he dis-
charged the duties of his office with great success for
the four years of his first residence at Florence (1482–
1486). It was probably for this reason that he was appointed in the year 1483 to preach the Lent sermons at
St. Lorenzo; but here, as in his former attempts, he met
with no success. It is said that only five and twenty
persons could be induced to listen to his sermons; and
this at a time when the church of Santo Spirito was
crowded by multitudes who listened eagerly to a rival

preacher, a favorite of the Medici, named Mariano da
Gennazzano.

The reasons for Savonarola's failure are to be found
both in his subjects and in his manner. The topics on
which alone he cared to preach were connected with
those subjects in which his hearers took no interest.
The Frate was in deadly earnest, whilst the Florentines
had lost all depth and seriousness of thought. He had
started on a crusade against sin and unbelief in all their
forms, burning with an unquenchable love of God and
an irrepressible zeal for the salvation of souls. To them,
for the time at least, sin and holiness, condemnation and
salvation, were become almost unintelligible expressions.

It would hardly be possible to give a more clear and
intelligible idea of the contrast than that which is set
forth by contemporaries respecting the preaching of
Savonarola on the one hand, and this Mariano da Gennazzano on the other.[1]

Benivieni, in a letter written long afterwards to Pope
Clement VII., the natural son of the murdered Giuliano
de' Medici, in defence of Savonarola's teaching, relates
that on one occasion he said to the Frate, " Father, it
cannot be denied that your doctrine is true, useful, and
necessary ; but your manner of expression is wanting in
grace, especially as this admirable Frà Mariano is here
every day." Savonarola replied, " This elegance of language must be allowed to give way before the simplicity
of preaching sound doctrine." There is no doubt that
Savonarola's preaching was at that time defective in various respects. His voice is said to have been weak,
his intonation bad, his action awkward, his pronuncia-
tion wanting in refinement, his style heavy. Oppressed

____

[1] For this I am indebted to Villari.

by the weight of his matter, he probably neglected the order and method without which it is almost impossible to convey effectively and impressively one's thoughts in public speaking. But there were other reasons to be found in the utter corruption of the public taste, in the false notions almost universally prevailing on the mission and work of the Christian preacher.

A better proof of this statement could hardly be adduced than that which is found in the judgment pronounced on the preaching of Frà Mariano by a critic no less competent than Politian. His commendations of this preacher, as Villari remarks, form the best illustration of his own defects and those of the admiring audience in general. " I went," he says, " rather prejudiced against him, for the loud applause had made me distrustful. I had hardly, however, entered the church, when the dress, the countenance, the figure, changed my mind, and I instantly desired and expected something great. I confess that sometimes in the pulpit he seemed to grow to a superhuman stature. He began to speak. I am all ears [mark] at his melodious voice, his well-chosen words, his sonorous sentences. Then I remark the divisions, I observe the periods, I am dominated by the harmonious cadence," and so forth. This was the judgment of a man of great learning and of the most refined taste. What, then, must have been the opinion and sentiments of the masses? It can hardly be surprising that the rough prophetic utterances of Frà Girolamo failed at first to gain the ears [1] which sought

---

[1] Burlamacchi says that his failure seemed then so complete that he thought of giving up preaching, and keeping to the exposition of Scripture; that he was advised to do this, and actually announced publicly his intention of doing so.

for gratification in elegant language, apt quotation, classical allusions, graceful gestures, — in oratory which was intended merely to charm, sometimes to amuse, but which was never animated by any more lofty purpose.

Brooding on the evils of the age, striving with all his might to deliver his testimony for God and for righteousness, preparing himself by long vigils, fasts, prayers, Savonarola found that his was indeed a voice "crying in the wilderness;" and he must often have asked whether some clearer and higher guidance might not be vouchsafed from on high to one who so truly desired and labored to win back this people to Christ. In two things he never wavered, — in his faith in God, and in his consciousness of a divine mission. He knew the righteousness of God and the love of God. He was sure that such a Being could not look with complacency upon the corruptions of Florence, of Italy, of the world and the Church. It must be His will not to destroy these erring children, but to bring them back to Himself, — to bring them back by loving and gentle ways, if that could be done; if otherwise, by chastisements and sufferings. And what was his own part in this work, and how could he accomplish it? If he alone were left of the prophets of the Lord, he must not shrink from his mission.

Then he turned to the Bible, which was now, more and more, his constant, almost his exclusive companion, and he found in the condition of Israel of old a picture of that which was passing around him in the Christian Church, and in the voices of the prophets those very warnings which were forming themselves within his own heart and striving for utterance on his tongue. If God spoke to His servants then, why should He not speak now? The need could never have been greater, more urgent; the perplexities of the age could never have been more involved. What could man do in such a case? Must not God speak?

At last the vision came. One day the heavens seemed to open before him, and there appeared a representation of the future calamities of the Church. At the same time a voice was heard commanding him to go and proclaim these things to the people. At last he had obtained the guidance for which he had been waiting, the command which he had no right and no power to disobey. He had seen a vision which told him that the Church was to be chastised and reformed, and he was ready to go forth, like the Baptist of old, and cry, " Repent, for the kingdom of heaven is at hand ! " "Now also"—the words seem to express exactly what was passing in his mind, what he believed he was receiving from God—" the axe is laid unto the root of the trees : therefore every tree which bringeth not forth good fruit is hewn down, and cast into the fire."

This was in the year 1484. It must almost have seemed as though Divine Providence were preparing for a change in the state of the Church ; for in this very year Sixtus IV. died. Surely there must be a change for the better. We have already heard what the change was. Sixtus was succeeded by Innocent VIII. The hopes that were excited by the death of his predecessor were now abandoned. The Papacy, at least, would give no help in the reformation of the Church.

Whether because of his failure in Florence, or for some other reason, Savonarola was sent on the two following Lents (1484 and 1485) to preach at San Geminiano, a small town in the mountains of Siena.

In those days a place of greater importance than at present, San Geminiano was found to contain a population more open to impressions such as Savonarola wished to produce. It may have been for this reason in part, but doubtless also, and far more, in consequence of the new convictions which had been wrought within him, that he now began to announce, as with prophetic voice, the three points which were henceforth to be the great subject of his preaching. That he did already believe them to be the subject of revelation to his own spirit, there can be no doubt; although for the present he was contented to declare them as deductions from the Bible, regarding his hearers as not yet ready to receive them as the echoes of the voice of God. The three statements which he now for the first time clearly set forth were the following: —

1. That the Church will be scourged,
2. And then renovated;
3. And this will be soon.[1]

It appears that he obtained a hearing from these mountaineers which had not hitherto been accorded to him; and when he returned to Florence, it was with the conviction deepened that he was now walking in the path marked out for him by the providence and grace of God.

But his first period of residence at Florence was drawing to a close, and he was now to leave it for four years. These four years form a very obscure part of his history; but we can trace his life and his work at various points during that period of time. Of his thoughts at this time we know little; only we are sure that a great part of his solitary hours was spent in

---

[1] La Chiesa sarà flagellata, e poi rinnovata; e ciò sarà presto.

meditating upon the evils of the age and upon the work which it was given him to perform; and we know that this consciousness of his work was ever and anon breaking out in his public utterances.

It is at Brescia that we first meet with him (1486), and now expounding the Apocalypse. From this time we must date his plain and open announcement of the evils coming upon Italy, and the powerful effects of his words. Visions now seem to multiply, and he is no longer, in his own consciousness at least, a mere expositor of the written word; he is, in some sense, a prophet sent by God, proclaiming his warnings and counsels with the tone of one who can say, " Thus saith the Lord."

It may be expected that something should be said on the nature of these visions and revelations; but history refuses to give a decisive explanation of questions like these. Who can tell when a gracious illumination passes into a supernatural guidance? Who can tell when the perception of the thoughts and destinies of men arises from a devout meditation on Holy Scripture and an earnest contemplation of the ways and works of men and of nations, and when it is given by direct revelation from God? How uncertain the Frate himself felt about this line of division we shall have occasion to see hereafter. It may here be said, once for all, that we make no pretension to solve these mysteries. Of one thing only we are sure, that Savonarola was profoundly convinced of the reality of his visions, that he believed he was speaking in the name of the Lord, that he was prepared to suffer even death itself in vindication of his testimony, and that, before long, he saw clearly enough that this was the probable end of the work to which he felt himself called.

At Brescia, as we have said, he began to expound the Apocalypse, and this with special reference to Brescia itself. One of the four and twenty elders mentioned in that book, he declared,[1] had come to him, and had foretold the terrible calamities that were in store for this city. It was to become a prey to its enemies; wives were to be snatched away from their husbands, and virgins were to be violated; children would be slain before the eyes of their mothers, and the streets would flow with blood. His words were not forgotten; and when, six and twenty years afterwards, the city was sacked by the soldiers of Gaston de Foix, and six thousand of its inhabitants perished, it was believed by many that the prophecy of Frà Girolamo was being fulfilled.

From this time he seemed to be assured, not only of his mission, but of the divine communications which he received respecting the future of the Church. He told his friend and biographer, the younger Pico della Mirandola, that on one occasion, while meditating on the text, *Bonus es Tu, et in bonitate Tua doce me justificationes Tuas,*—" Blessed art Thou, O Lord: teach me Thy statutes,"[2] he felt his mind illuminated, and all doubts left him, and he felt more certainty of the things that were shown to him than a philosopher did of first principles.[3]

---

[1] Burlamacchi states that this was related to the brethren of St. Mark's in 1520 by the Prior of Brescia, who had heard the sermon in which Savonarola announced these future calamities.

[2] Ps. cxix. 12.

[3] Burlamacchi, p. 22.

It was not Savonarola alone who received these convictions during his residence at Brescia. Razzi relates that a lady wrote to the Frate, announcing that she had received a revelation of his future history; but he, regarding her communication as a device of the devil, threw the letter into the fire. It is further related by his biographers[1] that, on Christmas Eve in this year, he remained immovable for five hours, in an ecstasy, and that his face shone so as to illuminate the whole church; and this, it is said, occurred several times.

Shortly afterwards we find him at Reggio, still absorbed in those great thoughts of the reformation and renovation of the Church and the world. A chapter of Dominicans was assembled for the consideration of questions of theology and of discipline. While points of casuistry were being discussed, Savonarola sat silent and, as it seemed, wrapped in his own meditations, his monk's cowl drawn over his wrinkled forehead. In mere theoretical disputations which tended to foster curiosity and dialectical subtlety, he took no interest. When, however, they turned to the question of manners and discipline, then the prophet of Brescia arose, and in the midst of the assembled clergy and laity who had come to take part in the deliberations of the meeting, he spoke those words which had already moved the hearts of men when uttered from the pulpit. It was like a thunderbolt falling in the midst of them, and they sat as though transfixed with astonishment. He spoke of the evils of the Church, but still more earnestly of the fearful corruption of the clergy as the fountain from which those evils flowed. Clergy and laity were

---

[1] On the testimony of a brother, called by some Sebastiano, by others Angelo.

alike impressed by his words. The fame of his power spread throughout Northern Italy, and many princes and others, who had begun to see the necessity for reform, entered into correspondence with the man who had given such distinct and powerful utterance to their own reflections.

Among the laymen who were present at the conference was one who bore a distinguished name, whose friendship was once and forever secured for the Frate by the impressions which he then received from his words. This was the elder Pico della Mirandola, the intimate friend of Lorenzo de' Medici, then only twenty-three years of age. Savonarola, it will be remembered, was thirty-four, and Lorenzo four years older, — thirty-eight. This Giovanni Pico della Mirandola was the uncle of that Giovanni Francesco Pico della Mirandola who was afterwards the friend and subsequently the biographer of Savonarola.

It was indeed a remarkable conquest in many ways. It was, so to speak, the first point at which the Frate had touched the men of the new learning. It was a victory where one could be least expected. Pico was one of the most refined and cultivated men of his age, one of those who took the greatest delight in the intellectual subtleties which Savonarola had already learnt to despise. He did not despise them because he had a mind incapable of discerning them. Perhaps it was the sense of their attraction for him, together with his conviction of their utter worthlessness, that made him turn from them almost with indignation. What things had been gain to him, these he now " counted loss for Christ."

It was perhaps the sense of these twofold elements

in his spirit that was the secret of the fascination he immediately exercised over Pico. This illustrious man, even in his youth — and he did not live to be an old man — was reckoned the marvel of his age. His knowledge of Latin was not perhaps wonderful: it was the literary language of his time and of his country. Greek, too, had begun to be extensively and profoundly studied. It is said that he knew both languages as well as his own. But he had also studied Oriental languages with success, — a much more rare accomplishment; and he was an expert logician and a well-read philosopher. It is likely enough that the charge of shallowness which was brought against him was well founded. Few men can play the part of an Admirable Crichton without some compensating disadvantages. Still, he was a man of prodigious attainments, of an unresting activity, with a memory the most retentive; adding to all a simplicity and unworldliness which were rare among scholars, and a grace and vivacity which attracted and fascinated every one who came within the sphere of his influence.

This was the man, distinguished beyond all who were present at this conference, into whose heart the words of Savonarola now fell with an irresistible power. From that moment Pico "felt," says Burlamacchi, " as if he could not live without him; " and it appears he lost no time in giving effect to his new sentiments, for he shortly after sought to induce Lorenzo de' Medici to have the Frate recalled to Florence and San Marco. This request of Pico, the same writer tells us, Lorenzo immediately complied with, because " he was much loved by him." The feelings now engendered in the heart of Pico towards his new friend were never extinguished. It was only his premature death, as we shall see in the sequel of our narrative, that prevented his entering the Dominican convent; and it was his last request that he might be buried within its walls, in the habit of the order.

Savonarola did not return to Florence for three years after this meeting. He had still work to do in Lombardy. His course we are able to trace only somewhat indistinctly. In July, 1489, we find him in his first convent at Bologna, where they wish him to undertake his old office of *Lettore*. On Christmas Day, in the same year, he is again at Brescia. In the following January he is at Pavia; and he preached the Lent sermons at Genoa shortly afterwards. These bare facts have been recently made out, but nothing more is known of his work or its effect. As we were told that when he left Ferrara for Florence, eight years before, he then bid a last farewell to his home, we may infer that he did not renew his intercourse with his family during these journeys. It was not that he forgot his parents or was destitute of natural affection. Before he left Pavia, on the 25th of January, 1490, he wrote a long and affectionate letter to his mother, regretting that his religious profession prevented his helping them in future otherwise than by his prayers. Although he could no longer see them face to face, he told them that he sympathized with them in all their joys and sorrows; but he had forever renounced the world, and given himself to labor in the vineyard of the Lord, for the salvation of his own soul and the souls of others. If God had given him this power, it must be his duty to use it; and since he was chosen to this holy office, his mother must be contented to see him exercise it away from his native place, because he would have more fruit elsewhere than at

Ferrara. And then he uses the language already quoted. " Be assured," he concludes, " that my heart is still more firm in its purpose to give up all for the love of God and the salvation of my neighbors; and since I could not do this in my own native place, I must do it elsewhere." He had " forsaken all " and taken up his cross, and he would not lay it down for a moment.

Although it is distinctly stated by his biographers that Lorenzo de' Medici did, in accordance with the request of Pico, at once invite Savonarola to return to Florence, some doubts have been suggested on the subject by M. Perrens, on the ground that he did not receive a call from the Prior of San Marco until July, 1489, and did not actually return to Florence until August, 1490. Such a theory, entirely unsupported by testimony, would need stronger arguments to render it credible. It is possible that the invitation of Lorenzo, who on account of his father's and his own munificence to the convent regarded himself as almost its proprietor, or at least its patron, may have seemed to Savonarola no sufficient reason for a monk's adopting a particular society as his own. Even if at that time the prior joined in the invitation, Savonarola may have formed engagements which required his continued residence in Lombardy. Whatever the reason may have been, we find he did not return to Florence until a whole year after the prior had invited him to do so.

But Perrens adds a suggestion still more improbable. Lorenzo, he thinks, had refused to comply with Pico's request because he did not wish to have the Frate in Florence again; and Savonarola resented his backwardness. This, he imagines, was the beginning of his antipathy to the Magnificent ! Such a theory is quite inconsistent with the whole facts of the case, and it is inconsistent with the view which the French biographer himself gives of the character and conduct of Savonarola. Lorenzo never showed the slightest disposition to keep Savonarola at a distance. The Frate, in shunning all intercourse with the Medici, was only acting as the boy had done at Ferrara. The disciple of Him who was " not of the world," and who told His disciples that they were not of the world, stood in need of no personal affront to make him careful to avoid the appearance of the slightest compliance with the most refined and inveterate worldliness which perhaps Christendom had ever seen.

It is related that he accomplished the journey from Genoa to Florence on foot, but that his strength was unequal to the journey, and failed him near Bologna. From that point, it is told, he received supernatural assistance, which was continued to him until he came to the gate of San Gallo. Be this as it may, he reached Florence in the year 1490, and from this point we are able to trace his history continuously and without interruption to its close. We must now make a brief pause, and try to understand his position and circumstances in this new and most important stage of his career.

CHAPTER V.

FLORENCE AND THE MEDICI.

THERE are names which carry with them something of a charm. We have but to say " Athens ! " and all the great deeds of antiquity break upon our hearts like a sudden gleam of sunshine ; " Florence ! " and the magnificence and passionate agitation of Italy's prime sends forth its fragrance towards us like blossom-laden boughs, from whose dusky shadows we catch whispers of the beautiful tongue.

Athens was the first city of Greece, — rich, powerful, with a policy which extended almost over the entire world of that age. Florence, however, in her fairest days, was never the first city of Italy, and in no respect possessed extraordinary advantages. She does not lie on the sea, and the Arno has never been navigable. The situation of Naples is more beautiful, that of Genoa more royal, Rome is richer in treasures of art, Venice possessed a greater political power ; and yet, notwith-standing, all that happened in Italy between 1250 and 1530 is colorless when placed side by side with the history of this one city.' Her internal life surpasses in splendor the efforts of the others at home and abroad. The events through the intricacies of which she worked her way with vigorous determination, and the men whom she produced, raise her fame above that of the whole of Italy, and place Florence as a younger sister by the side of Athens.[1]

The origin of Florence is lost in obscurity, and its early history is mingled with fable.[2] Machiavelli, following Dante and Villani, tells us that the city of Fiesole, being situated on the summit of the mountain, the inhabitants, in order to make its markets more convenient, had removed them to the spot between the roots of the mountain and the river Arno. By degrees this settlement, which is said to have originally borne the name of Villa Arnina or Camarzo, was greatly augmented, — among others by the soldiers of Sulla, and afterwards by those of Cæsar, who were stationed there.

The origin of its name, Florentia, — afterwards and still called Firenze — has been disputed; some thinking that it was originally Fluentia, others that it was derived from the fact that the valley in which the city stands is richly covered with flowers. It would appear at least that the Florentines themselves inclined to this opinion, since they gave their cathedral church the name of Santa Maria del Fiore. The lily, too, is painted on the shield of the republic and on the banner of Santa Reparata, the patron saint of Florence, who gave its name to the church which formerly stood on the site of the cathedral.

Cicero and Sallust both speak of the wealth of the Florentines; and Tacitus relates that in the reign of

---

[1] These paragraphs are condensed from chap. i. of Grimm's Life of Michael Angelo.

[2] On the general subject of this chapter see Machiavelli, Istorie Fiorentine; Sismondi, Républiques Italiennes; and G. Capponi, Storia della Repubblica di Firenze. A very full account is given in the Misses Horner's Walks in Florence.

the Emperor Tiberius (A. D. 17) a Florentine embassy came to Rome to petition the Senate that the waters of the Chiana — Tacitus calls it Clanis — should not be allowed to flow into the Arno, which, they said, would bring destruction upon them.

When the Empire fell, Tuscany, like the other provinces of Italy, became subject to the Goths. It is said that a horde of these barbarians attacked the city, A. D. 405, under a leader called Radagasius, but were defeated by the Roman general, Stilicho. This battle was fought on the 8th of October, the feast of Santa Reparata, — a young Cappadocian martyr who was put to death at the age of twelve. It was reported that she appeared in the thick of the battle, bearing a red banner in her hand, on which was emblazoned the lily, — the emblem of the Blessed Virgin. Hence the Florentine devotion to this saint, whose festival they continued to celebrate in memory of that day; hence the adoption of her banner as the shield of the republic, and the dedication to her memory of that which was formerly their principal church. The story of the destruction of the city by Totila, and its subsequent reconstruction by Charles the Great, is a fable.

Florence had bishops in the fourth century; and towards the end of this period the most distinguished among them was Zenobis, or Zanobius, in whose time Saint Ambrose, who was a friend of his, is said to have come to Florence and consecrated the church of San Lorenzo.[1] It was believed that the appearance of Santa Reparata was an answer to the prayers of Zanobius, who was then bishop. Slowly the city went on increasing,

---

[1] This is what Capponi says. Miss Horner says he consecrated Zanobius bishop in the church of San Lorenzo.

stretching out towards Fiesole, until about the year 1000 the inhabitants of the two cities had become one people, when they decided to unite their armorial bearings, making them red and white : the red with a white lily being the ancient arms of Florence, and the white with an azure moon the arms of Fiesole. There is no truth in the story that Fiesole became subject to Florence by conquest.

In the wars between the Empire and the Papacy Florence was deeply implicated, and was driven by her undying love of liberty to devote herself ardently to the side of the Pope. Such a statement may seem extraordinary and unintelligible to ourselves in these days, but it is notwithstanding susceptible of easy explanation. In the conflict with the Emperors, the Popes when driven from Rome not infrequently came to reside at Florence, and Victor II. died there in 1057; but the reason for the espousal of the papal cause by the Florentines lies deeper. It is easy to understand the point of view of either party in this long-standing quarrel. From the German, or imperial, side, nothing could be more natural than the Ghibelline view of the matter. From the Italian, or papal, side, the Guelf policy was equally defensible. The Florentine leaning in this dispute, however, did not arise from any high notions of the papal prerogatives, but from the conviction that only in proportion as the Empire, and with it the power of the nobles, was held in check, could the liberties of the republic be established and secured. In illustration of this view of the subject, it may be noticed that during the ascendency of the aristocracy Florence was generally Ghibelline.

Florence, like Athens, seems to have had, through-

out all the days of its greatness, at least, an unquenchable passion for liberty ; and it owed all its greatness to
its freedom.   It is true that Florence, like other republics, was fickle, capricious, wayward, ungrateful ; but the
free constitution of the city, in spite of all the abuses connected with its exercise and its history, gave scope to
industry and rendered possible the development of the
resources of the city.   A man had power not alone or
chiefly because he bore an honored name, but because
he actually possessed in himself that vital force which the
public conscience and the public will were constrained
to acknowledge.   A man was raised to authority because
he was worthy of authority.   It is true that jealousy
and envy might remove him from his place and drive
him from the State ; but the commonwealth had profited
by his services even when it had proved itself in a measure unworthy of them.   The Florentines knew that the
aristocratic party were hostile to their liberties and that
the oligarchy was sustained by the Emperor·as suzerain ;
and therefore they were Guelfs.   In the same way Pisa,
subject to Florence, ever resenting the yoke which it
was unable to shake off, took sides with its adversaries
and became Ghibelline.   It ought to be mentioned, as an
important event in the history of the conflict, that Ma-
tilda, Countess of Tuscany, who held Florence and the
other cities of that province under the Emperor, warmly
espoused the cause of the Pope, and placed her wealth
and her possessions at his service.   In the great struggle
between Gregory VII. (Hildebrand) and the Emperor,
Florence voluntarily took the same side.   At her death
the countess left to the Roman See the whole of her
vast territories, which enormously increased the power
of the Pope, but naturally embittered the strife between

him and the Emperor, who regarded these possessions as legitimately falling by reversion to himself.

From ancient times the Italian cities had ordinarily been governed by two consuls, in imitation of their mistress, Rome; and about the time of its union with Fiesole, Florence had associated with these one hundred senators, chosen from the best men of the State. The consuls afterwards varied in number, sometimes being as many as twelve; but they were always chosen from the nobility. By degrees — we cannot be quite sure of the time; it was probably about the beginning of the thirteenth century — these consuls came to be called Consuls of the *Arti*, or trades; and here we have the germ of that institution which endured, under various names, as long as the liberties of Florence endured. Sometimes they were called Priors (*Priori*), sometimes *Buon' uomini* (Good men), sometimes *Anziani*, or Ancients, sometimes they numbered four or six, sometimes ten, twelve, or twenty-four; but the general character of the office was maintained throughout.

Amid all the changes in the form of the government the Emperor was always, in theory, at least, regarded as supreme, however little of actual power might be conceded to him. But when, by means of the Lombard league, the cities of Italy obtained at the peace of Constance a local government, there was appointed an officer of a very mixed character as regarded both his position and his functions. He was named the Podestà, or Potestà, and was, during his term of office, at once the head of the State and the representative of the Emperor. His powers were both judicial and administrative: he had the power of the sword, and he was known as the lord of the place. The Emperor originally intended that this official should be appointed and invested by himself; but this prerogative was rarely exercised, and eventually fell into disuse, so that the Podestà was elected by the citizens. The election was only for a year or six months, to prevent the abuse of powers so great as those with which he was entrusted. He was required to be of a noble family; and to prevent his giving partial judgments, he was never chosen from among the citizens, but from another city or country. Originally, in Florence, he had his residence at the arch-bishop's palace; afterwards in the palace which bore his name, — the Palazzo del Podestà, now known as the Bargello; finally in the Palazzo della Signoria, or Palazzo Vecchio. He was supreme over all the other magis-trates, and all public acts were performed in his name and under his authority. His dress was, like his office, peculiar and distinctive. He wore a long robe, white, yellow, or formed of cloth of gold; on his head he wore a red cap.

In 1248, through the influence of Frederick, Prince of Antioch, the natural son of the Emperor Frederick II., the Guelfs were cast out of Florence, and the Ghibel-lines were for a time supreme; but their triumph was of short duration. In 1250 the citizens met together; and forming themselves into a number of groups, — reported diversely as thirty-six and fifty, — they chose as many leaders and captains of a kind of local militia, who were also a council of government. In place of the Podestà, they elected a Captain of the People, with very much the same qualifications and powers; but they soon afterwards restored the Podestà, assigning to him and the Captain independent tribunals, so that the one might be a check upon the other. They then divided the city into six wards, each ward, *sesto* or *sestiere* (sixth), as it was called, having over it two *anziani* (ancients or seniors),—twelve in all. These twelve seniors, who were elected for the space of two months only, were required to live, to eat, and to sleep in the public palace, and could only go out together. The collective body was called the Signoria.

We see the government of the republic here assuming the shape which, in its general outlines, it retained up to the sixteenth century. Capponi divides the history of Florence into four periods: 1. The heroic stage, from 1183 to 1321; 2. The levelling stage, from 1321 to 1382; 3. The reactionary, or aristocratic, stage, from 1382 to 1434; 4. The Medicean, or servile, stage. But each of these was characterized by many changes. Hardly had the measures just described been adopted, when the Guelfs were recalled and the Ghibellines expelled. In 1267 (two years, let us remark, after the birth of Dante) the names of the twelve magistrates were called, as we have said, *Buon' uomini.* In 1282 they are six in number, and are called *Priori delle arti;* and now they are not the elect of wards, but the representatives of guilds, these *arti*, or corporations of trades, being first three and then six. The six priors, afterwards eight, are known as the College of Priors; and over them, ten years later, is placed a *Gonfaloniere* (standard-bearer) of justice, elected, like the priors, for two months only. For our present purpose it may be sufficient to add that various councils were afterwards formed, to whom all laws proposed by the Signoria had to be referred before they were finally promulgated; besides two smaller bodies known as the "Ten of War," whose name indicates their office, and the Magistracy of Eight

(*Otto di Guardia*), who had to try criminal cases, and were appointed for a period of four months.[1]

It may be sufficient further to note here that the tendency of Florence was, for many generations, more and more to democracy. To such an extent was this tendency carried that nobility, instead of being a qualification, as in former days, became an absolute bar to office in the government of the republic; in consequence of which a member of a noble family had to lay aside his privileges of nobility before he became qualified for election. There were, of course, fluctuations in the carrying out of these tendencies. When the citizens grew weary of popular turbulence they would throw themselves into the arms of a despot, as in the case of the Duke of Athens; but their native love of freedom made them speedily throw off the yoke, and there arose among them a new nobility, which was likely to prove no less dangerous than the old, — a nobility which was derived from the trades or professions of Florence, and which drew its authority, not from ancient titles, but from intelligence, from wealth, and from the influence by which they are accompanied. One of these was the family of the Medici.

There had been various names of distinction in this family; but the true founder of its greatness was Giovanni de' Medici, the father of Cosimo, called *Pater Patriæ*, and the great-grandfather of Lorenzo, surnamed "the Magnificent." By industry and intelligent enterprise Giovanni acquired enormous wealth; and this, together with his liberality and affability, made him one

---

[1] A detailed account of the changes in the government of Florence will be found in Capponi, under the various dates; a good compressed account in Von Reumont, Lorenzo, bk. i. ch. 6.

of the most influential men in the city. He left two sons. From the younger descended that line of Medicean Grand Dukes under whom Florence fell so low as to forget all her former glory. It is with the elder, Cosimo, and his descendants that we have now to do.

Cosimo, born in 1389, was thirty-nine years of age at the death of his father in 1429. Before this time, however, he had attained to great influence and authority. He accompanied John XXIII. to the Council of Constance; and when that Pope was deposed by the council, and Martin V. elected, Cosimo redeemed him from the Duke of Bavaria, by whom he had been detained a prisoner, and gave him a shelter in Florence during the remainder of his life. It is perhaps impossible for us, who remember the evils that the Medici have inflicted on Florence, to regard with complacency their rise to power in the State. Yet it would be difficult to enumerate the attributes of a good citizen without including some of the conspicuous excellences of Cosimo de' Medici. There is at least a measure of truth in Voltaire's remark, that " no family ever obtained its power by so just a title."

By degrees Cosimo attained to so great authority in the republic that he was practically absolute. The executive power was at this time exercised by eight priors, and a *Gonfaloniere* elected every two months; the judicial power was in the hands of officers, aliens to the State, bearing the names of Podestà and Captain of the People, chosen once a year; and while Cosimo had sufficient influence to procure the election of magistrates who were willing to give effect to his wishes, he was at the same time careful to preserve the forms to which the citizens had been accustomed. While, therefore, the liberties of the people were being gradually but steadily undermined, this was carried on without any suspicion being excited that they were parting with their birthright. It was by a kind of true instinct that they entitled Cosimo the father of his country; but they did not reflect that " paternal government," which in the family is the only allowable method, has a tendency to weaken and enslave a nation.

Whether animated by sentiments of patriotism or by feelings of personal jealousy and enmity, there was a party in the city which could not regard the influence of the Medici with indifference or equanimity; and a Signoria, or body of magistrates (comprehending the priors and the *Gonfaloniere*), was elected in opposition to them (1433). Rinaldo degli Albizzi, the leader of this opposition, obtained from the new magistracy a decree sentencing the Medici and their adherents to banishment. Cosimo was exiled to Padua for ten years. It was feared, however, that his enemies, who had put him in prison, might make an attempt on his life; and Cosimo provided for his safety by bribing his keepers, and so secured his escape. During his exile, it may be mentioned, he made the acquaintance of that Michelozzo Michelozzi whom he was afterwards to employ in the reconstruction of St. Mark's.

Everywhere he was received and entertained as if he had been a prince on his travels, rather than a citizen banished from his home. Partly through his own patient fortitude, partly through the indecent violence of his enemies, a reaction soon took place in Florence; and before a year had elapsed from the time of his departure, a magistracy friendly to the Medici was appointed, and Cosimo and his brother were recalled, and their opponents driven into exile.

When Cosimo returned to Florence, although he did not spare his foes, he showed no resentment towards the citizens, but proceeded to multiply his benefactions to every useful object. Among these he gave a prominent place to the advancement of learning. It has been said that Cosimo was merciful to his enemies. The truth, however, is that he took care to preserve the forms of law while driving numbers of them into banishment.[1] We have referred to his munificence in being the second founder of San Marco and in having provided it with a library; but he may indirectly have forwarded a still greater work than this. The man whom he selected to assist in the arrangement of the library left by Niccolo Niccoli, and presented by Cosimo to the Dominicans of San Marco, was Tomaso Calandrino, the son of a poor physician of Sarzana. Within a few years this Thomas of Sarzana, as Pope Nicholas V., was to begin the formation of the great library of the Vatican.

While Cosimo was thus wisely and liberally, out of his princely fortune, promoting special works of utility, he was not only interesting himself in the government of the State, but he was effectually promoting the spread of learning, and especially the study of the Greek language, which, after being revived in the days of Petrarch and Boccaccio, had begun to languish. Among those whose studies he encouraged and assisted was Marsilio

---

[1] When remonstrated with on account of the numbers banished, and told that the city would be wasted (*guasta*), he replied: *Meglio guasta che perduta,* — "Better wasted than lost." Under his bland courtesy there was fixed and ruthless determination.

Ficino, the son of his favorite physician, whom he appointed over the academy which he established at Florence for the study of the Platonic philosophy. It was under his patronage that Ficino commenced the translations of Plato which he was enabled afterwards to publish by the liberality of Lorenzo.

Cosimo died at the age of seventy-five, in 1465. He was full of honors as of years; but his last days were not unclouded with anxieties. His younger son, Giovanni, of whom he had entertained the highest expectations, died before him; and Piero, who had married a daughter of the house of Tornabuoni, had not inherited the genius of his family. Piero's eldest son, Lorenzo, was only sixteen at the time of his grandfather's death; and although he had given promise of remarkable powers, his youth rendered any calculations respecting the future very uncertain. Indeed, Cosimo never seems to have felt very confident with regard to the fortunes of his family. When he was adorning Florence by building palaces, churches, monasteries, he used to say: "I know the humors of this city," — he had had some experience of them in this very way, — "fifty years will not pass before we are driven out of it; but the buildings will remain." "Words as wise as they were magnanimous," says Capponi,[1] "and a good foundation for the greatness of his house."

Piero lived only five years after the death of his father; and it was well, perhaps, for his house that it had not longer to suffer from his weakness and incapacity.[2] Well, also, it was for Lorenzo that his mother

[1] Lib. v. c. 3.

[2] Von Reumont has, however, shown that Piero was not so

was Lucrezia Tornabuoni, — one who was able to form his young mind, and to impress upon it a stamp which it never lost. Next to her influence was that of his tutor, his father's friend and *protégé*, Marsilio Ficino. Of this man it is necessary to say something, not only because of his part in forming the opinions and character of Lorenzo, but also on account of his place in the great intellectual movement of those times.

The great Schoolmen of the Middle Ages had been almost entirely under the influence of Aristotle; but the revived study of Plato in the East was speedily transferred to the West, and was the signal for fierce controversies between the adherents of the two schools. Men like the elder Pico might attempt a reconciliation between them; but history will have taught us the fruitlessness of such attempts, and will enable us to understand that the champions of orthodoxy, with Saint Thomas at their head, were generally Aristotelians, while the followers of Plato were frequently tainted with latitudinarianism, or even heresy. It was the intention and chief endeavor of Ficino, not merely to teach the Platonic philosophy, but to show its accordance with Christianity. His thoughts on the subject will be better conveyed by a slight description of a short treatise which he wrote, " On the Christian Religion." [1]

He sets forth with the intention of proving the Divine mission of Christ and the truth of His doctrine; and by way of introducing this theme he remarks that the coming of Christ had been many times prophesied by

contemptible as he has been represented. He was an affectionate parent and friend, and a gentle and merciful ruler (Life of Lorenzo, bk. ii. ch 4).

[1] Della religione Cristiana (Fiorenza, 1568); cf. Villari, i. 4.

the Sibyls: the famous verses of Virgil are known to all. Plato, when he was asked how long the precepts of his philosophy would endure, had replied, " Only until He shall come who shall open the fountain of all truth;" and Porphyry had said that the gods pronounced Christ supremely pious and religious, and declared that He was immortal, testifying very benignantly of Him (*molto benignamente testificando di lui*). It would not, perhaps, be quite fair to judge of the author's own most inward sentiments from arguments such as these, as it may be answered that he was here only addressing himself to Platonists, and commending to their acceptance the religion of Christ; but it is, in fact, much nearer the truth to say that he cared more for Platonism than for Christianity, and sought to find disciples for his master by conciliating those who from the side of the Church looked upon his system with suspicion. We can understand, when we reflect on tendencies like these, how Savonarola revolted from this Platonism, and turned with ever-deepening affection and reverence to his Bible. He saw clearly that the aim of the great promoters of the new learning in Florence was not to strengthen, or even to broaden, the Christian doctrine and system, but to undermine it. They Platonized the Gospel, and they professed to Christianize Platonism; but the result was simply a refined heathenism adorned with Christian phrases and sent forth with a Christian sanction.

Among the hearers of Ficino were Angelo Poliziano and the elder Pico, as well as Lorenzo. The friendship between Ficino and Cosimo was of the most intimate character. "Come to me as quickly as possible," writes the latter from his villa at Careggi, " and bring with you our Plato's treatise on the *Summum Bonum*, which you have now translated, I believe, according to your promise, from Greek into Latin." "Nobody," says Ficino, " was ever dearer to me than the great Cosimo ;" and writing to Lorenzo, after his father's death, he says: " When we had thus read together, as you well know, for you were present, Plato's treatise on the *Summum Bonum*, Cosimo died soon after, as if to enter on the abundant possession of that good of which he had tasted in discussion." [1] It is the same spirit of paganism which pervades all his thoughts and his life. He had a bust of Plato in his chamber, and a lamp continually burning before it. He considered that the character of Socrates was a foreshadowing of that of Christ, and wished that the Platonic philosophy were taught in churches. This is the man and these are the principles under the influence of which Lorenzo grew up to manhood.

The work of suppressing and exterminating the enemies of his house had been so thoroughly carried out by Cosimo that, in spite of the feeble government of Piero, and the youth of his two sons, — Lorenzo was only one and twenty, and Giuliano only sixteen, at the time of their father's death, — they succeeded at once to the authority of their family in the government of Florence and the administration of its affairs. It is to Lorenzo that we are now to look as the guiding spirit in the republic ; and we cannot understand the attitude assumed towards him by Savonarola, unless we first obtain a fairly clear notion of his character and designs. Few can be unaware that opinions on this subject the most diverse have been and perhaps still are entertained by different writers on this period of history. According to

[1] Cf. Harford's Life of Michael Angelo, ch. iv.

Roscoe and writers of his school, Lorenzo, if not fault-less, was at least a great, an enlightened, and a benignant ruler, the patron of literature and art, and the benefactor of the republic. Such a man could be opposed only by the factious, the turbulent, or the selfish. According to others, he was a crafty tyrant, seeking by every means, however unscrupulous, to gain power and popularity; preserving the appearance of liberty to Florence only that he might the more effectually enslave it; pampering every evil appetite of its citizens, that he might secure their support and destroy their power of resistance. Either side must have something to say for itself; and if the worshippers of Lorenzo are absurd and irrational in their idolatry, it is possible that his enemies do not take sufficient account of the corruption of the age in which he lived. It may be granted on behalf of the former that Lorenzo did much for Florence and its people; but it is equally certain that he made no stand against the evils which were slowly bringing the city to ruin, that he probably cared little for the deterioration which was going on around him, and that he used it for his own purposes. The more convincing are the proofs of his abilities and accomplishments, the more heavy must be his condemnation for having failed to use them for the true well-being of Florence.

There can be no doubt that Lorenzo the Magnificent was a man of varied accomplishments and of considerable attractiveness of manner. In stature he was above the middle size, and he was strongly built and robust. He had a dark complexion, weak sight, a harsh and nasal voice, a large mouth, and a nose which, like that of his great contemporary, Michael Angelo, had suffered an injury which disfigured it. For this reason, perhaps, he had lost all sense of smell. But his eye was bright and penetrating, his forehead lofty, and his manners peculiarly cultivated and graceful. In conversation he showed himself well-informed, ingenious, and vivacious; and he exercised a remarkable fascination over all who were admitted to intimacy with him. The effects of his eloquence on public auditories were on several occasions very considerable. In morals he was the reflection of his own age; to the pleasures which he encouraged among the Florentines he was, in no moderate degree, himself addicted.

There was, indeed, in the social life of Florence at this time a very remarkable combination of characteristics. If literature had degenerated, the age could still produce writers like Machiavelli and Guicciardini; but painting had entered upon a new, and its greatest era, and architecture was asserting a place beside the sister art. With all this, morality had sunk to its lowest ebb. It had become a subject for animated discussion and controversy, but it had ceased to be regarded as having a right to regulate men's lives. It was not that the principles of the Christian faith or its rules of life were contradicted or denied, they were simply ignored or refined away. If men did not deny the religion of the gospel, or express their doubts of its reality, it was because they were too indifferent as to the truth or falsehood of its claims.

Lorenzo de' Medici was essentially a man of his age. In himself, in his own character and life, he represented its contradictions, and he did his best to foster the worst side of the popular taste. His gracious manners did not proceed from a generous spirit, they were the result of training. He had inherited from his grandfather the politic sense which enabled him to discern what was most captivating to the mob; and even his encouragement of learning did not proceed entirely from enthusiasm for the spread of knowledge and truth, but was rather a means of amusement or a measure of policy. The strange contrasts in Lorenzo's life are hardly intelligible to ourselves. He was equally at home in the Platonic assembly, disputing on the nature of virtue; in the society of artists, discussing the theory of beauty and its exemplification in the creations of the Italian painters and sculptors; in the gardens of San Marco, contemplating with satisfaction his own work in advancing at once the fine arts and the interests of religion; and in the Carnival, joining in the wildest orgies of its votaries.

If testimony seem insufficient to verify the last statement, there is additional confirmation in his encouragement of this festival, and in his actually having written songs to be used in its celebration. Of these celebrated Songs for the Carnival (*Canti Carnascialeschi*), which were an invention of his own, and which were sung by the young nobles in their masquerades throughout the city, we need only say that they are so coarse and obscene that they could not now be read in any society without being regarded as an offence against ordinary decency. It is difficult to say whether he did more mischief by the destruction of liberty or by the encouragement of immorality.

" It is impossible," says Sismondi, " to place him in the rank of the greatest men of whom Italy boasts. Such honor is reserved for those who, superior to personal interests, secure by the labor of their life the peace, the glory, or the liberty of their country. Lorenzo, on the contrary, habitually pursued a selfish policy ; he sustained by bloody executions a usurped power : he every day added to the weight of a yoke detested by a free city ; he deprived the legitimate magistrates of the authority assigned to them by the constitution ; and he excluded his fellow-citizens from that political career in which, before his time, they had developed so much talent. We shall see," he adds, "in the sequel of this history the fatal consequences of his ambition and of the overthrow of the national institutions "[1]

In this extract there is an allusion to the sacrifice of human life on the part of Lorenzo ; and there is one instance of this kind of cruelty which must not be left unnoticed, on account of its connection with our story. We refer to the sack of Volterra. This was one of the subject-towns of Florence, which, in the year 1466, revolted, in consequence of the rapacity of Lorenzo himself.[2] Many of the Florentines were inclined to try gentle measures, and would have extended pardon to the offenders ; but Lorenzo, then only eighteen years of age, in a spirit which reminds us of his grandfather's " better that the city should be wasted than lost," pronounced in favor of recovering and holding it by the sword. This decision, sufficiently criminal in itself, led to others even more so. The Venetians having secretly favored the rebellion of Volterra, the work of subjugation became more difficult, and this again involved a considerable outlay of money. In order to meet the expense incurred, a sum of 100,000 florins was withdrawn from the Monte delle Doti[3] (Dowry Bank), — a

---

· [1] Repub. Ital., xi. 369.   [2] Cf. Capponi, lib. v. c. 5.

[3] Called also Monte delle Fanciulle. *Monte* was the word used in Florence for a bank.

fund instituted for providing portions for orphan girls at their marriage, — in consequence of which numbers of girls, thus deprived of their dower, abandoned themselves to an evil life. Yet Lorenzo took credit for this act, as having saved the expedition.[1] During the siege of Volterra it was promised to the inhabitants that their lives and property should be respected on condition of their surrendering. In spite of this assurance, when the Florentine army entered the gates the city was sacked, the churches plundered, the men taken prisoners, and the women ravished. There is reason to believe that these atrocities were perpetrated with the sanction of Lorenzo.

The conspiracy of the Pazzi, already mentioned, will show that the tyranny of the Medici was not acquiesced in by all; but that conspiracy was originated far more by personal envy and hatred than by motives of patriotism, and it was carried out in a manner the least likely to engage the sympathies of those who most deeply resented the tyranny under which the liberties of Florence were being destroyed. Its effect was, consequently, and quite naturally, to confirm and strengthen the power of Lorenzo, who was regarded by his sycophants as a martyr, and who availed himself of the opportunity of putting down all opposition by procuring the death and banishment of his enemies. Four years after this conspiracy Savonarola came to Florence. We have remarked on the state of the republic and of the Church which he found there; and we can understand with what feelings he regarded the family, and its living and ruling representative, through whose influence all that he most venerated was set at nought, all that he most de-

[1] See his letter in Capponi.

tested was propagated and supported.   It is important to bear these facts and considerations in mind while we follow the history of the man who began to feel that one great part of his mission in Florence must be to show a strong, continuous, and unyielding opposition to the policy of its virtual ruler, Lorenzo the Magnificent.

CHAPTER VI.

THE PRIOR OF ST. MARK'S AND LORENZO THE MAGNIFICENT.

WHEN Savonarola returned to Florence in 1490,[1] he was not unmindful of his failure as a preacher during his previous residence in the city, four years before ; and he had no desire again to encounter the cold in-difference of his fellow-townsmen. He was accordingly reinstated in his office of *Lettore,* and resumed his work of instructing the novices of the convent. But the fame of his work in Lombardy had gone before him to Florence, and the admiration and affection conceived for him by Pico della Mirandola speedily became known.

In order to meet the wishes of those who desired to have the advantage of his instructions, he was forced to remove his lectures to the convent garden, where they were delivered under a rose-tree which grew near the door of a chapel. Although this garden is now separated from the convent by a narrow street, the rose-tree has been renewed from generation to genera-tion by those who have venerated the memory of the teacher. This proved only a temporary arrangement. His expositions of the Apocalypse attracted so many

---

[1] Rudelbach, Meier, and others give the date as 1489, follow-ing the custom of the time, which made the year begin on the 28th of March. As a rule, the dates are given here as though the year began January 1.

hearers that it was found necessary to remove into the convent church.   Permission was granted by Domenico da Finario, the prior of the convent.   After some reflection, Savonarola announced one Saturday to his hearers that to-morrow he should begin to preach ; and it is said that he added, he should continue to preach for eight years, — which actually happened.

The change was greater than might appear.   As a teacher or lecturer, Savonarola addressed himself to the understanding of his hearers, and instructed them in the meaning of the subject or book which was his theme. As a preacher he spoke, as the ambassador of Christ and the servant of God, to the heart and conscience of men.   In the pulpit he was not merely the teacher, he was the prophet.   His first sermon was preached on the 1st of August, — soon, therefore, after his return to Florence, — and his success was assured from the beginning.   The church was so crowded that the brothers had to stand on the walls of the choir ; and the effect of the sermon was prodigious.   Savonarola, referring to it afterwards, said it was a terrible sermon (*una predica terribile*) ; and from the account which he has left, we may learn that he had now, once and forever, taken up that great theme which was to be the uninterrupted subject of his teaching and warnings so long as he was permitted to preach.

"On the 1st of August of this year," he says,[1] "on a Sunday, I began to explain publicly the Apocalypse in our church of St. Mark.   During the whole course of that year I continued to set forth to the Florentines these three propositions: 1. The Church of God must be renovated, and that in our time.   2. Italy is to be scourged before

---

[1] Compendio di Revelatione.

this renovation. 3. All these things will happen very soon. I endeavored to demonstrate these three points to my hearers, and to persuade them by probable arguments, by allegories taken from Holy Scripture, and by other similitudes or parables drawn from what was taking place in the Church. I insisted upon reasons of this kind, and I kept back the knowledge which God gave me of these things by other means, because men's minds did not seem to me at that time in a condition to understand those mysteries."

The same account is given by Burlamacchi, who says that he began by proving his three propositions from reason and Scripture, not considering the people prepared to believe in the visions by means of which he had obtained this knowledge; and afterwards, when he saw in his hearers a better disposition, he began to make known to them the revelations which he had received, but by way of parables and figuratively.

The impression which his preaching made upon·all classes was deep and powerful. Naturally enough, it was also diverse. Such ideas could not be promulgated without exciting opposition as well as attracting attention and interest. So it has been with all great teachers. Of the greatest of all teachers we read that "some said, He is a good man: others said, Nay; but He deceiveth the people;"[1] and the biographer of Savonarola tells us that when he began his sermons at St. Mark's, some said he was "a simple and good man," while others said he was "learned, but most cunning." Friends and foes, men of the world and philosophers, as well as earnest and simple-minded Christians, continued to crowd around the pulpit of St. Mark's, until it became

[1] St. John vii. 12.

evident that a larger arena must be found for his work and influence.

Accordingly, when the Lent of the following year (1491) arrived, he was called to preach in the cathedral, and became at once the accepted teacher, the acknowledged spiritual power of Florence, — a position which he retained, amid all the many wondrous vicissitudes of fortune and condition through which the great city was destined to pass during the next seven years. There is no reason to believe that Savonarola ever wavered in his convictions with regard to the main propositions which he had set himself to proclaim and enforce; but it appears clearly that he was not at this moment prepared, at all hazards, to force them upon an unwilling audience.[1] Finding that in certain quarters a very determined opposition was arising to the subjects of his preaching, he "became at times pusillanimous, and made up his mind no longer to preach on these points," but to restrict himself to the general doctrines of morality and religion.[2]

This course soon proved unpalatable and impossible. Everything which drew him away from these studies proved uninteresting and wearisome, and filled him with " disgust; " so that he began to " hate himself." How could he preach with full conviction and power when he was not speaking of the things of which his heart was full? Thus to preach would have been to abandon his

[1] This we learn from Burlamacchi and from his own Compendio di Revelatione.

[2] According to Villari, this change in his method was brought about, in part, by remonstrances from Lorenzo de' Medici and others. As this eminent writer has cited no authorities for changing the ordinarily received order of these events, I have preferred to follow that given by Burlamacchi.

mission, to give up the special work which he felt called upon to perform. He seems to have done his very best to tread in the paths of ordinary preachers ; but he failed in this attempt. He had resolved on one occasion that he would not preach on the subject of the future history of the Church and of Italy ; but on the Saturday preceding he found he could think of nothing else. "God is my witness," he says, "that during the whole of Saturday and through the whole night until the morning I lay awake, and every other way, every doctrine except that, was taken from me. At daybreak, wearied and depressed by this long vigil, I heard, whilst I was praying, a voice which said to me : 'Fool, dost thou not see that God wills thee to follow the same way?' And so that day I delivered a tremendous sermon."[1] It was, says his biographer, "a wonderful and stupendous sermon."

From this time he seems to have struggled no more against his convictions, — against those voices which were speaking in his heart, and which dominated all his thought and his action. It was no longer the teacher expounding the text of Scripture, and enforcing its precepts by the arguments of reason and the testimonies of experience and history, it was the seer standing face to face with the invisible world, looking away into the future, near or distant, and telling with passionate conviction all that he saw and heard in that sphere from which ordinary men were shut out. Nor did he confine himself to such general statements as were contained in his three famous propositions ; he ventured to predict particular events. It was, apparently, at this time that he announced the near death of Pope Innocent, the coming

[1] Compendiùm Revelationum.

descent of the French upon Italy, and the calamities which were about to befall the house of the Medici and Lorenzo himself.

In July of 1491 the Prior of St. Mark's died, and Savonarola was elected to fill his place. It had become a custom in the convent for the new prior to go and do homage to the head of the house to which it was so deeply indebted; but Savonarola saw in this a dangerous concession, which was at variance with his sense of independence as a priest. "I acknowledge my election," he said, "as the act of God, and to Him I will pay my homage." The remonstrances of the monks were of no avail. They were met by the simple question: "Is it God or Lorenzo who has made me prior?" When "The Magnificent" heard of this refusal, he was greatly excited. "You see," he exclaimed, "a foreigner is come into my own house, and will not even condescend to visit me." [1]

However deeply Lorenzo may have resented this want of courtesy or deference on the part of the new prior, he was too skilled in the arts of government to manifest his resentment; and he set himself to conciliate the man whom he was unable to command. Accordingly, he was often to be seen at Mass in the convent church, and he further attempted to throw himself in the way of the Frate by coming and walking in the convent garden. On one occasion this happened while Savonarola was engaged in his studies; and one of the brethren thought right to run and tell the prior that their benefactor was walking in the garden and probably expected to see him. "Has he asked for me?" inquired the

---

[1] The theory of Perrens on the original cause of Savonarola's antipathy to Lorenzo has been examined in chapter iv.

prior. "No, but—" "Very well, then; let him continue his walk as long as he pleases," was the reply. In the eyes of a man who so loved liberty, and saw in it the only hope and possibility of raising Florence out of its wretched ungodliness, frivolity, and wickedness, the man who was enslaving it could be no object of admiration or complacency. To go out of his way to recognize Lorenzo further than strict duty demanded would be, in his judgment, to make himself the accomplice of one whom he regarded as encouraging all the worst evils by which the city was afflicted.

Lorenzo was not to be discouraged. There might be other ways of conciliating a man who was becoming a power too formidable to be ignored. He continued to send gifts to the convent, which were accepted and made over to the general funds of the society, without, however, producing any alteration in the manners or attitude of the prior. He was not ungrateful for them, but he estimated them at their true value. "The good dog," he said one day in his pulpit, "always barks in order to protect his master's house; and if a thief comes and throws him a bone or anything else to put him off his guard, the good dog takes it, but at the same time he also barks, and bites the thief."

Perhaps, thought Lorenzo, he dislikes the connection between the giver and the gifts being made so evident; and he caused a considerable amount of gold to be deposited in the alms-box of St. Mark's Church. Savonarola knew too well where it came from; and separating the smaller pieces of money placed in the chest, which, according to custom, he reserved for the needs of the convent, he sent the gold to the good men (*buon' uomini*) of St. Martin, to be distributed among the poor of the city. And so, says Burlamacchi, Lorenzo came to see " that this was not the soil to plant vines in."

It would appear, moreover, that Savonarola, so far from being conciliated by this conduct, did not cease to denounce the evil that was being wrought in Florence by the arts of the Medici. In spite of every advance made by Lorenzo, he went on reproving the vices of the age, and threatening the great tribulations which he saw coming upon the earth. Whether he made direct allusion to the influence of the man in authority or not, his meaning was not obscure ; and Pico tells us that Lorenzo, hearing that Savonarola had inveighed against his tyrannical customs and ways (*tyrannicos usus*), attempted to conciliate him, while a number of citizens, " stirred up," says Burlamacchi, " by lukewarm religious, went and urged him not to go on preaching in that manner." At last Lorenzo sent to him five citizens of great authority to entreat him, as though they came of their own accord, that " for the sake of the common good and peace of the city, and also for the good of the convent, he would adopt another style of preaching, and one more general, and that he would not predict the future or refer to particular things beyond what was necessary." The names of the five are given by Burlamacchi, and it is possible that they were chosen by Lorenzo because they were known to be friendly to the Frate. If this were so, it would be another proof of his desire to win him by conciliatory measures. Be this as it may, all the five were afterwards found among his followers. One name we may mention, as we shall hear again of him who bore it, and under circumstances of deep and painful interest, the name of Francesco

Valori. When they came into the presence of Savonarola they all but lost courage to speak, and made their appeal in a very feeble and half-hearted manner. They were received with great kindness by the Frate. He told them that he knew they were not speaking their own mind, but that of Lorenzo ; and he gently rebuked them for thus allowing themselves to be the instruments of another. He bade them go and admonish Lorenzo to repent of his errors, as a calamity sent by God was now impending over him and his house.

Again, it is said, three other men came to him on the same errand ;[1] and he gave them these words for answer : "Tell Lorenzo from me that he is a Florentine and the first man in the city, and I am a foreigner, a poor, mean friar. Nevertheless, tell him that it is he who is to depart, and I who am to remain ; he will go, but I shall stay." Not knowing what to reply, they departed, and delivered their message. Lorenzo, it is said, remembered the warning in the solemn hour which was then drawing near.

Resolving not to be baffled, the Magnificent attempted other means of dealing with the unapproachable friar. If he could not win him to his side, he might, perhaps, destroy his popularity and influence among the people. For this purpose he stirred up his old rival, the Augustinian Frà Gennazzano, to resume his preaching. We remember the enormous popularity achieved by this preacher at the time that Savonarola was attempting to gain the ear of his five and twenty listeners in the church of San Lorenzo. He must have been, in some sense, a man of eminence, although, as Burlamacchi says, he was " more endowed with eloquence than with holy doctrine." Up

---

[1] Pico says he had heard that these came of their own accord.

to this time he had professed to rejoice in the success of Savonarola; but no sooner had he received from Lorenzo the hint to attack him, than he prepared to do so with all vehemence. On Ascension Day, 1492,[1] he preached in the church of San Gallo, after vespers, and taking for his text the words of our Lord, "It is not for you to know the times or the seasons" (*Non est vestrum nosse tempora vel momenta*), he made a most violent attack upon Savonarola, — denouncing him as a false prophet, as a sower of sedition and disorder, and, in short, proceeded to such lengths as to disgust his audience, so that in that one day he almost entirely lost the reputation which he had previously acquired, and many of his own friends fell away from him. Next Sunday Savonarola preached from the same text, showing that it was quite compatible with all that he had taught; so that the attempt of Lorenzo utterly failed, and left Savonarola more than ever master of the situation.

Although Gennazzano discontinued his preaching, to which those who had now been arrested by the enthusiasm of his rival were little likely to give heed, he professed the greatest regard for Savonarola, invited him to his convent, asked him to sing Mass, and joined with him in the celebration, and exchanged all kinds of courtesies with him. This was, however, only a dissembling of his real feelings. It was not easy for a man, especi-

---

[1] The date given; at present I am unable to see how this can be consistent with the time of the death of Lorenzo. If we could place this incident in 1491, before the appointment of Savonarola as Prior of St Mark's, all would be simple. Signor Villari avoids the difficulty by omitting mention of the year to which this Ascension Day belongs.

ally for a man of his character, who had been regarded as the greatest preacher of his time, to see the relative positions of himself and another so suddenly and utterly changed. It was not easy to forget the admiring crowds that had hung upon his lips in the Santo Spirito nine years before, while the immature utterances of the Frate of San Marco were resounding within the almost empty walls of San Lorenzo, and to see with patience that now, whilst he was neglected, all men had gone after that other. Hatred and the desire for revenge took possession of him. Shortly afterwards, going to Rome, he not only denounced his rival in private to the Pope, but publicly, in a sermon, declared him to be in league with the author of evil; or, as Burlamacchi puts it, he exclaimed: "'Burn, Holy Father, burn, I say, this instrument of the devil, this scandal of the whole Church,' speaking openly of the Father Frà Girolamo." When the Frate heard of it, he only expressed the hope that God would forgive him.

It is creditable to Lorenzo that he should now have abstained from any further attempts to interfere with Savonarola. Such a course may have been dictated by that regard to policy which distinguished the more able members of his family; and it is most likely that he had other thoughts, suggested by the malady which, now increasing in strength, was before long to carry him off. But there can be no doubt that he had conceived a genuine admiration for this bold friar who would not be deterred by threats or blandishments from speaking the words which he believed that God had put in his mouth, and who commended his message by the splendor of his genius and the unfeigned sanctity of his life. It is at least certain that when Lorenzo felt the approach of the last enemy, he experienced an earnest desire to see the man whom, in his lifetime, he had vainly striven to conciliate. As his sickness increased he had retired to the villa at Careggi built by Cosimo; and it became evident, early in April, that he had not long to live. For a time he was able to enjoy the society of his friends and to receive the visits of some of the more distinguished citizens of Florence. The better side of his character came out, as he was withdrawn from the temptations of the great city, and lost the power of gratifying his baser passions. Those who read only the hymns in which the undoubtedly religious character of his mind is expressed, would find it impossible to believe that he could be the writer of those Carnival Songs of which we have already heard. Politian, who was constantly with him in these last days of his life, relates that he called his son Piero to him, and gave him solemn counsels as to his conduct as a citizen and as a possible ruler of Florence in the future. "Remember," he said, — how little the warning was heeded, we shall shortly be forced to tell, — "remember in every position to pursue that course of conduct which strict integrity prescribes, and to consult the interests of the whole community, rather than the gratification of a part."

As the end drew near he expressed a wish to see Savonarola, "because," he said, "I have never yet found a religious like him."[1] "Tell him," said Savonarola, when he received the request, "that I am not what he wants, because we shall not be in accord; and therefore it is not expedient that I come." "Go back to the prior," said the Magnificent, "and tell him that

1 Burlamacchi, p. 37.

at all events he must come; for I want to be in accord with him and do all that he shall tell me." It is generally known that there are two accounts of this interview, — that of Politian, who was present at the time, and that given by the younger Pico and Burlamacchi. Roscoe, unable to see any good in the priest who would not be the mere tool of the destroyers of Florentine liberty, and hardly any evil in Lorenzo the Magnificent, treats the latter account as improbable and untrue; although if he had considered the matter more maturely, he would have found the story told by the friends and biographers of Savonarola much more illustrative of the haughtiness which he ascribes to him than the narrative of Politian, which he adopts. It may be possible to show that the contradiction between the two accounts is not so great as would at first sight appear.

Here is Roscoe's version of the interview : —

" This interview [between Lorenzo and the elder Pico] was scarcely terminated when a visitor of a very different character arrived. This was the haughty and enthusiastic Savonarola, who probably thought that in the last moments of agitation and of suffering he might be enabled to collect materials for his factious purposes. With apparent charity and kindness, the priest exhorted Lorenzo to remain firm in the Catholic faith; to which Lorenzo professed his strict adherence. He then required an avowal of his intention, in case of recovery, to live a virtuous and well-regulated life; to this Lorenzo also signified his sincere assent. Lastly, he reminded him that, if needful, he ought to bear his death with fortitude. 'With cheerfulness,' replied Lorenzo, ' if such be the will of God.' On his quitting the room, Lorenzo called him back, and as an unequivocal mark that he harbored no resentment against him for the injuries which he had received, requested the priest would bestow upon him his benediction ; with which he instantly complied, Lorenzo making the usual responses with a firm and collected voice."

The animus of this statement is evident;[1] but it is with the facts alone that we have now to deal. Roscoe refers in a note to a different account of the interview given by Pico, which is " deserving of notice," he says, " only by the necessity of its refutation." The account of which he speaks is given by Burlamacchi as well as by Pico,[2] with different degrees of detail. We shall reproduce it here, and consider briefly its internal prob- ability and its consistency with the story given by Poli- tian. According to the friends and contemporaries of Savonarola, it was at Lorenzo's earnest request that he came to see him.[3] During the interview Lorenzo

---

[1] Compare Roscoe's report with Politian's own language : " Scarcely had Pico left, when Hieronymus of Ferrara entered the chamber, — a man distinguished for his learning and holiness, an eminent preacher of heavenly doctrine (*insignis et doctrina et sanctimonia vir, cœlestisque doctrinæ prædicator egregius*)." And Roscoe professes to reproduce the testimony of Politian !

[2] Also by Barsanti, Razzi, and other authorities of no less credibility.

[3] Burlamacchi here adds that Lorenzo said he had three sins to confess, for which he asked absolution, — the sack of Volterra, the money taken from the Monte delle Fanciulle, and the blood shed in punishing those who were implicated in the Pazzi con- spiracy. It has naturally been objected that this could not have been known without a violation of the secrecy of the Confes- sional. But it must be noted that Pico's narrative makes no mention of this incident, so that we may safely regard it as fabulous. I cannot understand how Professor Villari has al- lowed it to remain in his text, notwithstanding his separate note on the subject (vol. i. p. 182). The remarks of Ranke (*Historische biographische Studien*, s. 350) seem quite conclusive.

became greatly agitated, and Savonarola, to calm him, kept on repeating: "God is good, God is merciful. But," he went on, "you must do three things." "What are they, father?" asked Lorenzo. The countenance of Savonarola became grave as, extending the fingers of his right hand, he replied: "First, you must have a great and living faith in the mercy of God." "In that I have the greatest faith." "Secondly, you must restore all that you have wrongly taken away, or instruct your sons to make restitution for you." For a moment this demand seemed greatly to distress Lorenzo; but at last, making an effort, he signified his assent by the inclination of his head. The third requirement was yet to be made. Savonarola became still more solemn in manner, and seemed to increase in stature, as with terrible earnestness he continued: "Lastly, you must restore liberty to your native country as it was in the early days of the republic of Florence." It was touching the root of the man's family pride and ambition. Summoning his remaining strength, he angrily turned his back upon the friar, and refused to utter another word. Savonarola departed without pronouncing absolution, and Lorenzo died soon afterwards, on the same day, April 8, 1492.

By those who deny the accuracy, even the general credibility, of this account, it is assumed that Politian was present during the whole of the interview, and

Whether we consider the internal probability or the external evidence, the whole story becomes clearer and more consistent by the rejection of this incident. Lorenzo's refusal to comply with Savonarola's preliminary requirements prevented any formal confession from being made, so that no absolution could be given.

heard all that passed between the confessor and his penitent. Neither assumption can be sustained. Politian himself, in his letter which describes the last day of Lorenzo's life, states that he several times went into an adjoining chamber; and Razzi asserts expressly that, during the interview, "the others left the room." Besides, is it probable that even the dearest friends of the dying man would be permitted to hear, or would desire to · hear, the last words which he spoke in confession to a priest? There is indeed a certain agreement between the two narratives, and Politian's report may refer to the first words which passed between the two men. It is customary, at the beginning of a confession, to ask and obtain the priest's blessing; and so much may have been seen before the others quitted the chamber. And this is all that Politian says. Of the withholding of the absolution he may have seen and known nothing. If he knew of it, as the devoted friend of Lorenzo he would have been little likely to record it.

M. Perrens, indeed, goes so far as to deny the internal probability of the story of the biographers. He says that the demand for the restoration of the liberties of Florence is a mere anticipation of the course of conduct which was afterwards pursued by Savonarola in the revolutionary times which were soon to follow. This objection may safely be left to the judgment of those who are acquainted with the whole history of the period. In the very height of the revolution, Savonarola never professed to be in theory a republican; he preferred the monarchical form of government where it was possible. Moreover, before the death of Lorenzo, it is agreed by all, he denounced his influence as destructive alike of the liberties of the State and of public morality. Even in the minutest details, the account of Savonarola's friends is the more probable. Was it likely that he who had refused to have intercourse with "The Magnificent" when he was lord of Florence, would have almost forced himself upon him when he was at the point of death?

The death of Lorenzo de' Medici was an event fruitful in consequences to his own family, to Savonarola, and to the State of Florence. Had he lived to the natural life of man, — he was only forty-four years of age when he died, — how different might have been the future history of the republic and of Italy !

In the same year (1492), July 25, Pope Innocent VIII. died, and was succeeded by Alexander VI. Events are thickening, and we can with difficulty realize the fact that the wonderful changes which have now to be related should have taken place within a period of time so limited.

CHAPTER VII.

THE PREACHER AND PIERO DE' MEDICI.

THE reputation of Savonarola was never at a higher pitch than in the first days of the administration of Piero de' Medici. All the attempts of Lorenzo had failed to silence, to intimidate, or to conciliate the man who felt that he was sent by God, and did not owe his position, as priest or as prior, to human authority. He had even made a conquest of the potentate who had thought to be his master as he was the master of Florence. The dying Lorenzo had sought counsel in his last moments of the Prior of St. Mark's, the terrible preacher of Santa Maria del Fiore. If he could. thus influence the greatest among them, whose word had been as law to the whole people, how could he be any longer resisted?

But these were only the effects of the real and mighty inward power which dwelt in the heart of the man himself, and which made itself felt in his every word and deed and gesture. The saintliness of his life was known to all by the testimony of his brethren and by many infallible proofs. The clearness of his spiritual perceptions gave to his utterances a distinctness and a certainty which could not be mistaken, and which produced instant conviction. The singleness of his aims, the high unworldliness of his designs, the strength of his will, the capaciousness of his intellect, all combined to make him wellnigh irresistible. He was universally recognized at this time as the great spiritual power in Florence, even as some years after he became, in fact and almost in name, the ruler of the republic.

Savonarola's biographers seem to feel, rather than to say, that here was a new starting-point in his marvellous career; for his history is the history of Florence. They pause at this crisis to speak of the man himself, — of his power as a preacher, of his character, deportment, life. "This great father," says Burlamacchi, "was endowed with infinite and most rare virtues. He was benignant and pleasant with all, humble and gentle with every one of the novices, and universally affable in conversation. The familiarity of his manner produced joy and gladness in others; and those who once came to know him had the greatest desire and avidity for his company; and when he spoke of spiritual things, no one was able to withdraw from his presence." To this he added a marvellous power of divining what was passing in the minds of others, as well as of influencing their opinions and judgments. On a certain occasion he discerned in one of the novices a desire to abandon the religious life. A glance from the prior told the halting youth that his thoughts were being interpreted, and decided him to abide in his vocation.

The testimony of Pico is entirely to the same effect. He was ever accessible, even to his enemies, and he was of wonderful placability. Pico says it was "native;" but we may be permitted to doubt this, and to ascribe his meekness and gentleness to a Source higher than nature. He was never known to utter a harsh or rough rebuke, or to raise his voice in anger, or to show a trace of passion on his countenance, however much he might be provoked. He was fervent in the denunciation and eradication of vices; but in his public admonitions it was by gentleness of speech, by simplicity of language, rather than by vehemence or exaggeration of expression, that he sought to carry conviction to his hearers.

His manner of life was in keeping with the unworldliness of his mind. He partook of the commonest food, and ate the coarsest bread that he could obtain. If a finer quality were placed before him, he would change it, and give it to some old and feeble person. He was most sparing in food and drink; and from this rule he never departed, except when he was showing hospitality, — a duty which he never neglected, although he had almost lost all taste for it himself. His dress was as plain as his diet; but although coarse, it was always scrupulously clean. He was fond of repeating the words of Saint Bernard: "That he liked poverty, but not dirt."[1]

For nothing was he more remarkable than for his deep, earnest, and constant habits of devotion. He was indeed one of those who "pray without ceasing." If he lay awake at night, he spent every moment in prayer and holy meditation. Some of the stories related of him, in connection with this habit, border upon the miraculous. /On a certain Christmas Eve, we are told, when lauds were being sung in the church, his body remained perfectly motionless for five hours; and " so entirely were his thoughts and affections absorbed in God by the presence of the Holy Spirit that his face emitted a strong light. When the divine office was completed, those who returned to the church testified that even after they had extinguished the lamps, the face of Girolamo shone in the darkness and seemed to light

---

[1] Paupertatem sibi placere, non sordes.

up the choir of the church." Doubtless, imagination had some part in producing these impressions ; but the candid reader will confess the existence of some extraordinary depth of devotion in the man who could so powerfully influence his contemporaries. Frà Silvestro, his most intimate friend among the brethren, declared that more than once he had seen the figure of a dove hovering over his head.

Yet the devotional and contemplative character of his life did not destroy its practical side, or lead him to dispense with the labor of study. His own native tendencies were towards philosophical speculation. We have seen that he regarded these tendencies with suspicion, fearing lest they should divert him from the true business of the religious life. Yet he did not allow himself to be driven into the opposite fanatical extreme of despising reading and study. He labored as well as prayed. With him also work was worship, even as worship was work. He often quoted the saying of Saint Francis of Assisi, that a man's knowledge was in proportion to his work, that "a man knows as much as he works." [1]

That such a man, filled with an overwhelming sense of his divine calling to speak forth the word of truth in an age which had almost forgotten God, should prove "mighty in word and deed," was a simple necessity of the case ; and so we are told his preaching was almost miraculous, "for the rapidity of his utterance, the sublimity and greatness of the things discoursed upon, and the elegance of his words and sentences were equally wonderful. His voice was clear and sonorous, his countenance animated and impassioned, and his gesture graceful and impressive."

[1] Tanto sa ciascuno quanto opera.

These testimonies, his enemies allege, are those of his friends and admirers. The objection reminds us of the well-known theory which professes to explain the spread of Mahometanism. The false prophet, it is said, propagated his religion by the sword. The retort is just: How did he get his sword? In the case of Savonarola, the power which he exercised is indisputable. To reject the testimony given to his character and work is to admit the effect and deny the only reasonable explanation of the cause.

The preaching of Savonarola was intensely biblical. We have seen how he ever, more and more, turned to the Holy Scriptures as his favorite and supreme subject of study. Nearly all his sermons started from the exposition of a passage drawn from the Bible. To us many of his explanations must seem far-fetched and fanciful; but it was the manner of his day, and he adopted it on principle. His peculiarities, as we should deem them, did not, however, consist in forcing the Bible to prove that which it did not contain, but rather in finding the recognized doctrines of the Church in texts which, to ordinary minds, seem to have nothing whatever to do with them. But whether he was a trustworthy interpreter or not, he was always a true and earnest preacher, speaking to the intelligence, the heart, the conscience. The words which he spoke were spirit and life and power. Whatever art and skill as an orator he possessed came from within, not from without. He was singularly destitute of what might be called rhetorical culture; and this explains the failure of his first efforts. The great and burning thoughts within him were laboring in vain for articulate expression. It was only as he saw more clearly the evils which he was called to denounce, and the only remedy which could be successfully applied, that the clearness of his perceptions came to be expressed in his language; and this grew to be well ordered by reason of his severely trained intellect, and again was set on fire by his deep conviction, his ardent zeal, and his fervent love for God and man. Guicciardini, no mean judge, says that, after having read and studied the sermons of Savonarola, he found them most eloquent, and of an eloquence that was natural, and not artificial. He adds that for ages there had not been seen a man so learned in the sacred writings; and that whilst no one ever succeeded in preaching at Florence more than two Lents without wearying his hearers, Savonarola was able to do so for many years, ever rising higher in the estimation of the people. Those who study his sermons most carefully will understand this criticism, and they will perceive something of the secret of his mighty power; the power itself, however, is a simple fact of history.

The popularity of Savonarola went on increasing; and he was more and more regarded, not only as the denouncer of all the frightful evils of the age, but as the steady and unflinching opponent of the enslavers of Florence, the Medici. He had predicted the death of Lorenzo, and his prediction had speedily been fulfilled; also of Innocent VIII., and he had died in the same year as the Magnificent. When Alexander VI. ascended the papal throne, if the need of renovation became more evident, the prospect grew more remote. Nothing short of some special divine intervention seemed capable of bringing about the wished-for change.

As the power of Savonarola went on increasing, and his influence was more evidently than ever lending itself to defeat the measures of the ruling family, it was natural and inevitable that he should provoke the determined enmity of the Medicean party ; and this opposition was strengthened by the accession of those who envied the Frate his success, and perhaps even more by the numerous body of ecclesiastics whose sensual and worldly mode of life he denounced with peculiar energy. Malignant men, " under the instigation of the evil one," lost no opportunity of persecuting him ; and among these, " the most bitter were the men of the most abandoned lives, and especially those prelates of the Church whose disgraceful lives were corrupting the whole world."

Brooding on these things, meditating upon the terrible evils of the age and on his own powerlessness to check them, the Frate looked ever more for divine guidance and illumination, expecting to learn from visions the will of God and the future of the Church, as he believed he had done in the past. The vision did not tarry. In the very year which had witnessed the death of the master of Florence and of the head of the Church (1492), while he was preaching the Advent sermons, he had a vision or dream which he did not hesitate to regard as a divine revelation. In the midst of heaven he beheld a hand grasping a sword, under which the words were written : *Gladius Domini super terram cito et velociter*, — " The sword of the Lord upon the earth quickly and swiftly." At the same time he heard a multitude of voices clearly and distinctly promising mercy to the good, and threatening punishment to the wicked, and proclaiming that the wrath of God was nigh. Great thunderings were heard from heaven, weapons and fire seemed to fall from the skies, and the whole earth became a prey to wars and pestilences and famines.   As the vision disappeared, Savonarola received the command to announce these chastisements, to teach men the fear of God, to bid them pray to the Lord to send good pastors to the Church, and finally to have a special care for troubled souls.   This vision became a leading subject of his preaching and teaching, — we might almost say, for a considerable time its very centre, — and was represented in numerous pictures and medals of the period.

It was not to be expected that Piero de' Medici should look upon these doings with indifference.   Indeed, as the matter would present itself to his mind, it must have seemed to be now the question whether he or Savonarola should rule Florence.   His father, when he found that he could not control the speech and action of the Frate, had left him alone.   He was wise enough in all things to remain contented with the possession of the substance of power, and to dispense with the form and appearance of it when it was inexpedient to contend for it.   It was for this reason that he had wisely preserved all the ancient forms of the government of the republic, while he was in fact supreme.   Piero was a man of a totally different spirit.   He had all the ambition and love of power which characterized Cosimo and Lorenzo; but he was entirely destitute of their policy.   Indeed, he was in most ways a striking contrast to his father, in appearance as well as in character.   He was a man of a handsome and attractive person, and his intellectual abilities were of no mean order.   Politian speaks of him as being beloved by the citizens, — " a man not less eminent for his own glory than for that of his family; combining the talents of his father, the virtues and great kindliness of his uncle, the probity of his grandfather, the prudence and piety of his great-grand-father; in short, the heart and head of all his noble ancestors."

If this description were to be taken literally, we should be forced to conclude that Piero made a miserable use of his advantages. He had, however, considerable abilities. His memory was remarkably retentive; he had a ready wit, and improvised verses with the greatest ease, and showed himself a friend and patron of litera-ture. But he knew too little of the spirit of the people of Florence, and forgot that, while they might part with the substance of liberty, they were attached to the form. Piero had all the haughtiness of the Orsini, his mother's family, and was rude and rough in his manners, — in this respect presenting a striking and unpleasing contrast to his father. Sometimes he would break into violent fits of passion at the slightest opposition, and make it too evident that in carrying out his own wishes he had little regard for those of others.

Such conduct was more offensive to the Florentines than an open violation of their laws. Lorenzo had be-sought his son to remember that, whatever his power and influence might be, he was "only a citizen of Florence." This had never been forgotten by Cosimo, *Pater Patriæ*, nor by Lorenzo himself; and the citizens were flattered by the thought that the greatest among them was still one of themselves. For such feelings Piero entertained and exhibited no respect. The ap-pearances of liberty which his father had carefully preserved, even while he was undermining the reality, the son proceeded deliberately to destroy. The widest disaffection began to spring up throughout the whole State. The leaders of the people, who had willingly followed Lorenzo, now secretly or openly fell away from his son; and a party, continually increasing in numbers and influence, was being formed against him. Savonarola, unintentionally, perhaps unconsciously to himself, was regarded, if not as the head, yet as the heart of this party; and he was looked upon by Piero as his most dangerous adversary. It was in the midst of these growing antagonisms that the crowds at the cathedral first heard the terrible announcement of the sword of the Lord coming speedily and swiftly upon Italy.

Piero could not be expected to look on with equanimity while the discontent of the people was finding expression in the first pulpit of Florence, and gathering strength from the warnings which were there proclaimed. He saw that in the Prior of San Marco lay the greatest danger for himself and his authority. But he had neither the prudence nor the self-control of Lorenzo. The Magnificent, when he could neither repress nor conciliate the preacher, would have allowed the movement which he guided to spend its force, would have temporized where he could not command. Piero was too impatient and imperious to submit to such delay. He could not silence the preacher or withdraw the people from listening to him; and therefore he used his influence with his superiors in Rome and Milan to have him removed for a season from Florence. This measure filled the brethren with grief and dismay. The prior alone was calm, resigned, hopeful. He was grateful for their affection, he told them; but, he said, "if you are too much cast down, if you begin to think that you cannot live without me, your love is yet imperfect, and therefore God has taken me from you for a season." This was in the beginning of 1493, and the same year we find him preaching the Lent sermons at Bologna.

The Bentivoglio family were still possessed of supreme authority in Bologna. He found himself hampered by the circumstances of the city, and lost much of the power and fervor which had marked his sermons at Florence. They called him a "simple man and a ladies' preacher." Still, his fame drew multitudes to hear him; and among the congregation there appeared the wife of Bentivoglio. This lady habitually came late into the church, bringing with her a large retinue of attendants, who greatly interrupted the preacher and disturbed the people. Savonarola was unwilling to take needlessly offensive measures to abate this nuisance; so, at the beginning of the interruptions, he contented himself with merely finishing his sermon, or rather, with leaving off preaching. This tacit rebuke proved insufficient. Then he would pause in his sermon, and remark on the impropriety of disturbing the faithful during their religious exercises. This indirect rebuke only inflamed the anger of the lady. She continued to come late, and every day with more noise, as if in contempt of his remonstrances. At last it became intolerable. One morning, while he was preaching with great energy and fervor, the usual interruption occurred. Then his indignation broke forth. "Behold," he exclaimed, "how the devil comes to interrupt the word of God." The proud wife of Bentivoglio in a rage gave orders to her followers to despatch the insolent preacher in the pulpit; but even they shrank from the commission of such a crime. The delay brought her no better thoughts. She ordered two of her servants to find him out in his cell, and inflict some grievous injury upon him. Savonarola encoun-

tered them with such calmness and dignity, and spoke
to them with such an air of authority, that they listened
respectfully, and departed in confusion. Happily, it was
near the end of Lent, and he had soon to depart from
Bologna. He would not have it supposed that the servant of God was driven from his place by fears for his
personal safety. His parting words from the pulpit declared his unwavering confidence in God and in his mission. "This evening," he said, "I shall take my way
to Florence with my staff and my wooden flask, and I
shall lodge at Pianoro. If any one has business with
me, let him come to me before I leave. Know, however,
that my death will not take place at Bologna."

Florence was now ever his first and deepest thought.
Even during the time of his anxious work at Bologna,
he never forgot his beloved brethren and sons of San
Marco. They were longing for his return, and he wrote
to them frequently in a spirit of the most tender affection. Sometimes in general terms he exhorted them to
keep themselves above and apart from this present
world. Sometimes he would descend to the minute
details of their daily life. Those who knew only the
preacher, "mighty in the Scriptures," knew only half
the man. It was in the words of loving wisdom which
he spoke to his brethren that all his beautiful simplicity,
all his tender love for the souls of men, all his deep
devotion to the work of God, found most attractive
expression.

On his way back to Florence many thoughts occupied
his mind respecting the state of the city, the growing
enmity against the Medici, the difficulties which beset
his future work. Villari thinks that the vision, which is
related to have occurred on his former return to Flor-

ence, took place at this time. There is one circumstance in favor of this supposition. The words which
his supernatural guide is said to have addressed to him,
when he parted from him at the gate of San Gallo, would
certainly seem better suited to this crisis in his history.
" Remember," he said, as he vanished from his sight,
" remember to do that for which thou art commissioned
of God." That he who believed himself to have peculiar intercourse with the invisible world should, at this
period of his history, have had such a vision or dream,
will seem quite reasonable. Be this as it may, it can
hardly be doubted that it was with thoughts like these,
and under the influence of the emotions which they
would excite, that he now returned to Florence. Grave
events were coming near ; and he had to prepare, as
best he could, to meet them in the strength of God.

CHAPTER VIII.

MONASTIC REFORM.

WE have already seen clearly that Savonarola hoped for a reformation of the clergy as a means towards the renovation of the Church. This was the very fountain of the evil, that the leaders of the blind were themselves blind. The bitter fountain could not give forth sweet waters. But the greatest evil, in the view of the ardent reformer, was the corruption of the monasteries. The greatest and most bitter sorrow of his heart had been aroused by discovering that the vices of the outer world had penetrated into the very heart of the "religious life" in the convent.

From the moment that he was appointed Prior of San Marco, he had entertained the purpose of effecting that thorough reform which he saw to be of absolute necessity. Removed for a season from the daily care of the society whose head he was, he had probably more leisure to meditate on its general condition, circumstances, and needs. If the monks and friars were to be reformed, if he proclaimed the necessity of this reform, how could he abstain from the endeavor to begin this reformation at home? If anything were needed to deepen his convictions and strengthen his resolves, he found it in all that he heard of the city while he was absent from it, in all that he saw when he returned.

In a sermon which he preached in the Advent of 1493 he speaks of the frightful corruption prevailing among the clergy. After giving one example of the evils which he deplores, he exclaims, —

"All the cities of Italy are full of these horrors. If you knew all that I know, — things disgusting, things horrible ! — you would shudder. When I think of all this, — of the life which is led by the priests, — I cannot restrain my tears. How do they protect their sheep? I will tell you in a word, without lacking respect for those who are good. The evil pastors have made themselves mere instruments for leading the sheep into the jaws of the wolf."

Again he exclaims, —

"O prelates ! O supports of the Church ! look upon that priest who goes tricked out with his finery and his per. fumes. Go to his house, and you will find his table loaded with plate, like the tables of the great, — the rooms adorned with carpets, with hangings, with cushions. They have so many dogs, so many mules, so many horses, so many orna- ments, so much silk, so many servants ! Can you believe that these fine gentlemen will open for you the Church of God? Their cupidity is insatiable. Look ! in the churches everything is done for money. The bells are rung from covetousness ! They resound only 'money, bread, and candles.' The priests go into the choir to get money; to vespers, to the other offices, because at these the money is distributed. See if they are at matins ! No; because there is no distribution then. They sell benefices, they sell the sacraments, they sell the marriage-mass, they do everything from covetousness ! "

There are some charges in the sermon which are too gross to be repeated here. Yet these charges were un- doubtedly true, and it was needful that they should be publicly made by one who was resolved upon the work of reform.

"The difficulty in the way of effecting a thorough reform in his own convent arose in great measure from the fact that the Tuscan congregation of the Dominican order was united with the Lombard, and was subject to the Father Provincial of Lombardy. In consequence of this state of things, it was possible for the enemies of Savonarola at any time, by means of the authorities of Lombardy or of Rome, to procure at least his temporary removal from Florence. It had not always been so. Previously to the great plague which had devastated Tuscany, the two congregations had been separate; and they had been united, in consequence of the desolation of the convents caused by that calamity, in the year 1448. Now that the numbers of the religious had greatly increased, there ought to be no difficulty in separating them again; and Savonarola set himself, with all his energies, to restore the independence of the Tuscan congregation. The Frate on this occasion showed that he was not only a great speaker, but an able doer, — as great in organization and administration as in the power of influencing men by his spoken words. By the vigor with which he took his measures he prevented opposition to his scheme being organized by his enemies.

It is indeed wonderful that Piero de' Medici should not have perceived that a most heavy blow was being aimed at his own authority, and that his great adversary was achieving an independence which was sure to be used against himself. It was only in this very year that Piero had used for his own purposes the power possessed by the Father Provincial, so as to have Savonarola removed during Lent to Bologna. It was another proof of his dissimilarity to his father that he allowed himself to be persuaded into supporting the request which Savonarola was now making. He went so far as to instruct the Florentine ambassador at Rome to give it his warmest support, and to solicit the influence of the Cardinal of Naples on the same side.[1] Savonarola was not contented with forwarding his petition and obtaining this powerful support to his cause. He immediately sent to Rome two of the members of the brotherhood of St. Mark, Frà Alessandro Rinuccini, a member of one of the principal families of Florence, and Frà Domenico da Pescia, his first disciple. This sincere and constant friend of Savonarola was the most remarkable of all his fellow-workers. Ardent and daring, he was a man of intense simplicity, of deep and living faith, and of absolute and entire devotion to his superior. Of the divinity of his master's mission he never seems to have entertained even a momentary doubt.

It was no easy matter to obtain their request. The Lombards, powerfully aided by Ludovico Sforza, made the most strenuous opposition to the separation; so that the friends of Savonarola wrote and told him that they had no hope of succeeding. "Do not doubt," was his answer; "be brave, and you will have the victory; 'the Lord . . . maketh the devices of the people to be of none effect, and casteth out the counsels of princes.'" And, in fact, the victory was obtained by what would be called a strange accident, which must have appeared

---

[1] Villari has remarked that his advocacy of the cause of the Dominicans was the more astonishing as he had always favored their rivals, the Franciscans. He suggests that he may have been influenced by his dislike to the governor of Lombardy, Ludovico "Il Moro."

nothing short of a providential interposition. It was obtained at a moment when hope was at its lowest ebb.

On the 22d of May, 1493, the Pope dismissed the Consistory, in consequence of fatigue, declaring that he would transact no more business on that day. The Cardinal of Naples alone remained with him; and believing that he had found a moment suitable for urging the claims of the Tuscans, brought forth the brief authorizing the separation, and entreated the Pope to confirm it. After some pleasantries and altercation on the subject, the Cardinal in play snatched the Pope's ring from his finger and sealed the brief. Hardly had this been accomplished when the most urgent remonstrances arrived from the Lombards, entreating the Pope to refuse his consent to the measure. But the Pope had heard enough of the matter, and refused to reopen it. " That which is done, is done," he made answer; and the Tuscan congregation was now independent of Lombardy. Even the entreaties of Piero himself, who began too late to perceive the mistake he had committed, were unavailing.

The Pope's sanction had not come a moment too soon. The Father Provincial, foreseeing the possibility of defeat, had sent an order to Savonarola and his principal adherents to quit San Marco instantly, and to disperse themselves among certain other convents, subject to his jurisdiction, which he named. It was intended that these instructions should reach St. Mark's before the papal brief arrived; and in that case, there would have been an end to all the prior's plans of reform. Again he was favored by a happy circumstance, which was also naturally attributed to the interposition of

Divine Providence. The order had been addressed to the Superior of the convent of Fiesole, to be communicated to those concerned. Through his absence from home, and the neglect of his representatives, it did not reach St. Mark's ·for more than a week afterwards. It was then of no avail, as the deed of separation had arrived. It has been suggested that even if it came in time, Savonarola may have delayed opening it, suspecting its contents. This is not impossible ; but it seems likely that it actually arrived after the papal brief.

It was now time to begin the work of reorganization and reform. Savonarola was at once elected anew as Prior of St. Mark's, and a number of convents asked to be admitted into the new congregation. First among them was the convent of San Domenico of Fiesole ; and this, after intervals shorter or longer, was followed by many others, some of them adhering spontaneously, others constrained by a little gentle pressure. To make the new congregation complete, the prior convoked a union of the various bodies, to arrange their rules and to elect a superior. At this meeting he was unanimously chosen Vicar-General; and he held this new dignity, with his accustomed gentleness and humility, to the end of his life.

From what we have read of Savonarola's own character and habits, and of the indignation with which he spoke of the luxury and self-indulgence of the clergy, we are prepared to hear that this was the first object of his attack, and the first subject of reform. The Dominicans had been a mendicant order ; but there seems to have been always some uncertainty as to the extent to which they might become possessed of property. Savonarola himself appears to have wavered on the subject; but on one point he had no doubt whatever. He was convinced that the Church ought to possess no more than was actually necessary. We have seen how he acted on this conviction, even with respect to the giving of alms. It was not fitting that the profuse bounty of Lorenzo should be distributed by the members of his society; he made it over to the *Buon' uomini* of San Martino. But there were great difficulties in giving full expression to his convictions with respect to the Vow of Poverty, especially having regard to the past history of St. Mark's.

At one time he had formed the plan of retiring to a solitary mountain with his brethren, and there living a life of solitude and poverty. He had even chosen Monte Cane, near Careggi, for that purpose; but however this scheme might have commended itself to his tastes it was at once apparent that it must defeat all his larger designs for the renovation of the Church. It is said that he gave way to the remonstrances of the younger friars, and to objections arising from the unhealthy character of the locality; but there were doubtless graver reasons for his change of purpose.

Upon the walls of St. Mark's were written the last terrible words of Saint Dominic, in which he denounced those who should introduce among his disciples the holding of property. " Have charity, preserve humility, possess voluntary poverty; may my malediction and that of God fall upon him who shall bring possessions into this order." The words still stood written upon the cloister walls; but they had been disregarded since the days of Sant' Antonino. By a new rule the convent had been declared capable of holding property; and since that time had become very wealthy. Savonarola determined to return to the original constitution. He began by selling all the property of the society, and thus cut off at once its too abundant supplies. Hence it became necessary, in other ways, to provide for their needs.

As a first measure for reducing the expenditure, he required the friars to wear less costly clothing; he made their cells simpler and less ornate; he forbade them to possess illuminated books, gold and silver crucifixes, and the like. But his reforms on the positive side were no less important. He designed that they should live by the labors of their own hands; and so introduced the study of painting and sculpture, and the art of writing and illuminating manuscripts. These occupations were assigned to the lay brethren and to those of the clerical brethren who were less advanced in the spiritual life; while the cure of souls, the hearing of confessions, and preaching, were reserved for the more advanced.

He was peculiarly anxious to raise the standard of education in his convent, and more particularly of the education that would fit the brethren for being able dispensers of the word of God. For this reason he made prominent three subjects of study, — theology, dogmatic and controversial; morals and the canons; and especially the study of Holy Scripture. To these he added a subject which at the time was even less common, — the study of Oriental languages.

The difficulty of carrying out changes and reforms so sweeping was greatly lessened by the conviction of the Superior's sincerity and earnestness, produced by his own manner of life. He imposed no restraints upon others which he had not for long willingly accepted himself; he prescribed no rules of life which he had not already more powerfully recommended by his own obedience; and for a time, at least, it seemed that the whole convent had caught his enthusiasm and become partakers of his ascetic spirit. And this enthusiasm not only gave a powerful stimulus to the studies, the labors, and the devotions of the friars, it spread beyond the walls of the convent, until men of the noblest families of Florence came forward and prayed to be admitted into the number of the brethren. A whole convent offered to change its rules for those of St. Mark, and to become incorporated into the society presided over by Frà Girolamo. The terms of the papal brief had given no such authority to Savonarola; and he declined their application, resolved to give no occasion to his enemies to bring charges against him of overstepping his own province and powers. Indeed, he had difficulties enough with the houses belonging to his own order; some of them disliking the separation from Lombardy, others probably shrinking from the more stringent discipline to which they were being subjected.

His own labors were manifold. He was constantly consulted by those who needed guidance in their perplexities. He gave himself only four hours of sleep; so much time was of necessity consumed in the work of governing, in carrying on an extensive correspondence, in prayer and meditation, in the study of the Scriptures, in the preparation of his sermons. His life was the most simple of all; and he shrank from no occupation and from the performance of no duty or service in the convent, however menial, which he imposed upon others.

Burlamacchi gives a striking account of the conventual life of this period at St. Mark's.

"After dinner," he says, "they took a moment's repose; then they gathered cheerfully around the father, who explained to them some passage of the divine Scriptures. Then they took a short walk, and reclined for a time in the shade while the father brought some passage from the sacred books before them as a subject of meditation. Then he made them sing a hymn in honor of our Lord, or took from the lives of the saints a theme for discourse. Sometimes he would invite them to dance, and accompany them with his voice. . . . In the evening they often chanted psalms and hymns with great fervor. They would attire a young novice so as to represent the child Jesus; and sitting around him, they would all give him their hearts, and ask some favor of him for themselves or others."

He was a father in the midst of a loving and trusting family, or perhaps rather an elder brother whom all reverenced and loved. He lived among them as one who expected death to come to him suddenly and by violence; but this never disturbed his serenity or cheerfulness.

It was with something of increased dignity and authority that Savonarola returned to his work of preaching. He was no longer liable to be removed from his post at the will of the Lombard Provincial. He was now himself the head of the Tuscan congregation, with a reputation for truthfulness, courage, and personal holiness which had been steadily increasing. But his theme was still the same, — the ruin of the Church, the dissolute lives of the clergy, the corruption of the rulers in Church and State, the approaching scourge of God which was to chastise the evils of the age.

It was soon after his conventual reforms, in the Advent of 1493, that he preached his sermons on the psalm *Quam bonus,* — "Truly God is loving unto Israel,"[1] — which are considered to be theologically the best of his discourses.[2] They are distinguished by a more careful diction, — probably they are better reported than some of his other courses, — by considerable argumentative force, and by the strongest assertion of the doctrine of divine grace.

"Let all Paradise come here," he exclaims, — "let the angels come, let the prophets and patriarchs come, let the martyrs come, let the doctors and all the saints come, one by one, that I may dispute with them; come all the elect of God, that I may dispute with you. Say the truth, 'Give glory to God,' confess the truth, if you have the glory, if you are happy and blessed by your own merits and by your own strength, or by divine goodness. Come here, you especially who have been immersed in sins; tell me, Peter, tell me, O Magdalene, why are you in Paradise? You certainly sinned like us. Thou, Peter, who didst confess the Son of God, who didst converse with Him, heardest Him preach, sawest His miracles, and more, who alone with two other disciples sawest Him transfigured upon Mount Tabor, and heardest the Father's voice; and nevertheless, at the words of a mere woman didst deny Him three times, and yet wast restored to grace and made head of the Church, and now possessest heavenly blessedness, — whence hast thou obtained so great good? Thou wilt say, perhaps, because thou didst return in heart, because thou didst begin to weep bitterly? Yes, O Peter, thanks to the divine good-

---

[1] Ps. lxxiii.

[2] They have been republished (Prato, 1846), together with his sermons on the First Epistle of St. John, and may still be bought.

ness which looked upon thee, as the Evangelist says:
'The Lord turned and looked upon Peter ; and Peter went
out and wept bitterly.'   Thou didst not weep until the
Lord looked upon thee ; thou didst not return in heart
until the Lord touched thy heart.   Confess then, Peter,
that it is not by thy merits, but by the goodness of God
that thou hast obtained such blessings."

Such language seems to have been understood by
some of Savonarola's biographers as indicating a tendency to Protestantism ; but this passage alone, with
its reference to St. Peter, might show that he was in
no respect at variance with the doctrines of the Church.
There was, of course, a sense in which he was a forerunner of the Reformation, inasmuch as he strenuously
opposed the tyranny and denounced the corruptions
of the Papacy ; but there is no ground for supposing
that he had any thought of protesting against the accepted teaching of his age.   Kerker's language is hardly
too strong when he says :[1] " When Meier and others
find in his expressions relative to penitence and indulgence something which anticipates the Reformation
of the sixteenth century, they prove that they are not
acquainted with the Catholic doctrine on this subject."
So the expressions on the subject of divine grace in
the passage quoted are simply the echoes of the language of Augustine, the greatest Father of the Latin
Church.[2]

[1] Wetzer and Welte's Kirchenlexicon, art. Savonarola.

[2] Hase remarks, however, with truth (Neue Propheten:
Savonarola, s. 14) : " As a prophet of the Reformation, Savonarola perceived the dawn of the ideas out of which this Reformation afterwards proceeded, —that the Holy Scripture leads us
to Christ, not to the saints nor to the Virgin ; that if Christ does
not absolve you, other absolution cannot help you ; that salva-

Savonarola's doctrine of grace did not prevent his holding firmly the freedom of man and the necessity of good works. "If any one should ask," he says, "why the will is free, we reply, because it is the will." And he adds that justification, although it be the act of God, needs the concurrence of man. "Wilt thou, my brother, receive the love of Jesus Christ? See that thou consent to the divine voice which calls thee. The Lord calls thee every day: do thou also something." Both in theory and in practice Savonarola was a worker, and held and displayed a deep faith in the power of work. His well-known motto,[1] adopted in youth, recorded by all his biographers, and repeatedly used in his sermons, indicates the spirit of his life. "A man,"

tion does not come from external works, such as the Church by its Judaizing precepts and ordinances and its refined heathenism had required, but from the surrender of the heart to the Redeemer, and from faith in the old, deep, and inward meaning of the word. But he did not think of altering anything in these ordinances, in which for nearly a thousand years the faith of Western Christianity had been established." On the relation of Savonarola to Luther, Ranke (Studien, s. 331) remarks: "If we would compare him with Luther, who regarded him as his forerunner in teaching the doctrine of justification, we shall find two points of difference. Savonarola reckoned upon supernatural signs and wonders, whilst Luther, resting simply upon the written word, not only despised them, but abhorred and opposed them. The other difference was that Savonarola held fast to the ideal of a council, and thought by this means to overthrow the Pope ... Luther's point of departure, on the contrary, was his denial of the infallibility of the council as well as of the Pope; and therefore he took his position outside of the hierarchy of the Church, whilst Savonarola held fast by this. Luther wished chiefly a reformation of doctrine; Savonarola, a reformation of life and government."

[1] See p. 121.

he says, "knows as much as he works" (*Tanto sa ciascuno quanto opera*). This theory was not in his mind at variance with his sense of entire dependence upon the grace of God, any more than it was in the mind of Saint Paul, or of Him who was Master of both.

In closest connection with the assertion of the doctrines of grace was his denunciation of the state of the clergy, — the paganism of their belief, and the unchristian character of their lives.

"They speak against pride and ambition," he said, "but they are immersed in it up to the eyes. They preach chastity, but they keep concubines. They recommend fasting, but they live luxuriously. It is the Pharisaic spirit come to life in the rulers of Christ's Church. They love greetings in the market-place, and to be called masters and rabbis; they make broad their phylacteries. They do all to be seen of men."

It was about this time that he made the often-quoted comparison between the priests and the chalices of the early and the later days of the Church. Our Church, he says, has many beautiful ceremonies and appointments, — candlesticks of gold and silver, and as many chalices as a potentate.

"You see great prelates with mitres of gold and precious stones on their heads, and a pastoral staff of silver; you see them at the altar with splendid chasubles and embroidered copes, singing those vespers and those fine masses with so many ceremonies, with so many organs and singers, that you are stupefied. . . . And people say that divine worship was never properly celebrated before, and that the early prelates were nothing when compared with these modern ones   True, they had not then so many gold mitres, nor so many chalices; and the few that they had they parted with of necessity for the relief of the poor. . . . But do you know what I have to say to you on this? In the primitive Church there were chalices of wood and prelates of gold; in these days the Church has golden chalices and wooden prelates!"

He spares the princes no more than the prelates. Naturally enough, they were still worse; and his hearers did not need to go beyond their own city for illustrations of his words. The conflict between himself and the tyranny of the age was ever thickening.

In the autumn of 1494 he resumed the exposition of the history of the flood, his sermons "On the Ark of Noah," which he had begun in 1492 and then discontinued. It is thought that the report of these sermons, which we possess in Latin, is a very incomplete and imperfect representation of those which were actually delivered. It is at least certain that these sermons produced the greatest impression upon those who heard them. They were intended to complete the series commenced in Advent, which dealt principally with the sins of Italy and the impending chastisement. In the Lent series of 1492 he proceeds to speak of the ark of safety, in which the faithful may escape from the coming deluge. He carried them on to the end of Lent; and on Easter Day he spoke of the completion of the ark, of the readiness of all things for the entrance of the people of God. The interest manifested in these discourses was prodigious. The cathedral was crowded with eager listeners. Savonarola was becoming more and more the mind, the conscience, the will of Florence.

The whole course of sermons had not completed the

exposition of this one chapter of Genesis; and Savonarola resumed the subject in the month of September, 1494, when he prepared to preach thirteen additional sermons by way of conclusion[1] The third of these sermons, on the 17th verse of the chapter which speaks of the deluge, fell on the 21st of September. It was a day and a sermon never to be forgotten by the preacher or his hearers. The cathedral was crowded, and the multitudes assembled had to wait for a long time before the preacher appeared. He ascended the pulpit laboring under the strongest emotion, which was visible to the audience. Gazing across the sea of human faces, he gave out the words of his text in a voice of awful solemnity: *Ecce ego adducam aquas super terram,* — "And behold, I, even I, do bring a flood of waters upon the earth." The words and the tone struck terror into every heart. Pico della Mirandola, who was present, relates that a shudder ran through his whole frame, and his hair seemed to stand on end; and Savonarola declares that he was himself not less moved than his hearers. The cause of this unusual emotion was not inadequate. The French had entered Italy, and the news had just arrived that their armies were descending the Alps. The event which Savonarola had expected and predicted had now come to pass; and men turned to the prophet for guidance in their perplexities. It was a great crisis in his history. The friar of Bologna, the Prior of San Marco, the preacher of Florence, was now to become the statesman.

---

[1] These sermons are, in the Venetian edition already mentioned, referred erroneously to the Advent of 1493.

CHAPTER IX.

THE FRENCH IN ITALY.

THE historian Gibbon speaks of the "expedition of Charles VIII. into Italy" as "an event which changed the face of Europe;"[1] and it certainly was an event which entailed upon Italy, immediately and remotely, the most serious consequences. The gravity of the circumstances was felt by most of the rulers and public men of Italy; but few of those who were most deeply interested in it could have dreamed of its far-reaching and enduring effects.

It has been charged against Savonarola that he showed a lack of patriotism in encouraging the invasion of Italy by a foreign army; but a judgment of this kind implies a forgetfulness both of the prevalent ideas of the period, and of the part which the great Dominican actually took in the transactions of his times. The idea of intervention was one which was perfectly familiar and natural in that age. Independent States, as we understand the word, were very few. The republics of Italy were, in theory at least, dependent upon the Empire; moreover, they hardly ever went to war without allies. In the

---

[1] Critical Researches concerning the Title of Charles VIII. to the Crown of Naples; in Miscellaneous Works, iii. 206. See also Philippe de Commines, liv. vii. c. i., who treats the claims of his master with almost undisguised contempt.

case of international disputes leading to war, there was generally a confederation of one set of States against another. There was also frequently an appeal to a power external to the contending parties.

The natural and, in theory, the rightful superior of the Italian States, to whom all their disputes ought to have been referred, was the Emperor. But the Empire had long ceased to be more than a name to Italy, and any appeal to the German Cæsar would have been valueless. Besides, France had been the old ally of Florence, and was one with the republic in its Guelfic policy. The imperial interests were represented by the Ghibelline party. To the contemporaries of Savonarola there was nothing disloyal or unnatural in the desire for an alliance with France.

It is true that Savonarola hailed with satisfaction the French invasion of Italy, and saluted Charles VIII. as the "New Cyrus;" but it was because he believed that Italy needed to be scourged before it could be regenerated, and because he saw in the French king the instrument of God for effecting this purpose. It is true, also, that King Charles referred to the prophecies of Savonarola as giving a sanction to his enterprise; but there were others besides himself who thought they saw the hand of God guiding the expedition, and it is quite certain that Savonarola's words formed a very slight proportion of the complex influences by which he was induced to lead his army into Italy.

Charles himself was a man with little capacity for such an undertaking. He must have been of a kindly disposition and of pleasant manners, otherwise he could hardly have been surnamed "The Affable," or have been so deeply regretted by his family when he died. He was, says De Commines, so good, so kindly, "that it is not possible to see a better creature." But he was most insignificant in appearance, being short of stature and very feeble in body; and his mental powers were of the most slender character, while his education had been almost entirely neglected. "But for the power and dignity of his eyes," says Guicciardini,[1] "he would have been terribly ugly." As regards attainments, it is said that he scarcely knew the letters of the alphabet. But he had, notwithstanding, inherited the ambitious sentiments of his father, the crafty and resolute Louis XI.; and having consolidated the French kingdom by the union of the great Province of Brittany through his marriage with the Duchess Anne, he began to turn his eyes eastward, and dreamed of rivalling the fame of Saint Louis by leading another crusade against the Turks. As a first step, he undertook to vindicate his supposed rights to the crown of Naples.

Those rights hardly deserve investigation at our hands. There are few questions more difficult to decide than the comparative claims of the houses of Arragon and Anjou to the kingdom of Naples; and it would be impossible to decide the questions on principles which are now generally recógnized. The law of succession was at that time very vague and uncertain. In some cases the right of a sovereign to nominate his successor, or to decide between two claimants, was acknowledged. The stain of illegitimacy was not in all cases regarded as a bar to inheritance. All these questions come up in the discussion of the subject. The French claim was

---

[1] D' aspetto (se tu lievi il vigore et la degnità degli occhi) bruttissimo, e l' altre membre proportionate in modo, che e' pareva quasi più simile al mostro, che a huomo. — *Istoria d' Italia*, lib. i.

certainly very doubtful. If the rights of the house of Arragon were not absolute, they had at least sixty years of posesssion and the consent of their subjects. On the other hand, the tyranny of Ferdinand, the ruling sovereign, and his son Alfonso had stirred up rebellion among his people, and many of them joined in urging the French king to press his claims.

The actual undertaking was brought about in a strange manner. The daughter of Ferdinand was married to Gian Galeazzo Sforza, the lawful Duke of Milan, whose inheritance had been seized by his uncle Ludovico, known, from his dark complexion, as "The Moor" (*Il Moro*). Ferdinand was incited by his daughter to assert the rights of her husband, who was kept in confinement by his uncle. Ludovico, seeing a league in process of formation against him, urged Charles of France to assert his claims to the crown of Naples, promising him assistance on his descent upon Italy. The scheme at first appeared so utterly chimerical that there was hardly a Frenchman who could be found to advise the king to undertake it. Only two of the king's councillors, both of them men of no consideration, were in favor of the enterprise, and one of these speedily changed his mind. "So that we may conclude," says De Commines, "that this whole expedition, both going and coming, was conducted purely by God; for the wisdom of the contrivers of this scheme contributed but little." [1]

The condition of Italy was at this time the most tranquil and prosperous. [2] Guicciardini, in beginning

[1] Mémoires, liv. vii. c. i.

[2] Guicciardini, lib. i. c. i.; Christophe, Papauté pendant le quinzième siècle, liv. xv.

his history, pauses before proceeding to narrate the calamities which befell his country, and looks back upon the wealth and glory which excited the admiration, and alas ! also the cupidity, of the foreigner. He speaks with enthusiasm of those great republics, then at the summit of their power, — of their numerous inhabitants, of their beauty, of the splendor of their towns, of their proud independence, of the magnificence of their princes, rivalling that of the greatest sovereigns. Italy was in truth the most civilized country in Europe, and the most advanced in all that constitutes real progress, — in liberty, in the development of industry, in literature and arts, in wealth. The Italians were not only the teachers of learning, of science, of art, they were the bankers of the kings of the earth. These potentates were frequently unable to determine whether they were in a position to go to war, until they had first ascertained whether they could obtain a loan from the bankers of Venice, of Genoa, or of Florence. If this prosperity was degenerating into luxury, if the moral condition of the country was becoming worse and worse, if faith and virtue were dying out in the hearts of the people and their teachers, these seeds of evil had not yet brought forth all their corrupt fruits. In one respect the Italians were inferior to the other nations of Europe, — they had no soldiers. The military art was almost unknown. Battles are reported to have been fought by multitudes of men, in which hardly a combatant perished.[1] The French army, on the contrary, if partly composed of inferior materials, had a large number of trained and experienced soldiers.

[1] Machiavelli says that frequently two armies were engaged for hours without a man perishing, except those who fell and were trodden to death by the horses!

Consequently, when they entered Italy, they met with no serious opposition. Moreover, if the governments of Italy regarded the invasion of their country with apprehension and aversion, the people at large were for the most part on the side of the French, and welcomed their arrival.

There was indeed no effective opposition offered to their progress. The Pope, after joining with Ludovico il Moro in inviting the invasion, had turned round and sided with the Neapolitans; but he was not prepared to take action. Piero de' Medici was the devoted friend of the house of Arragon; but the city of Florence was equally devoted to the French, and the most powerful voice among them only expressed the sentiments of the populace when it welcomed the coming of Charles. Venice was neutral, Milan was with them, Naples was almost in revolution. Ferdinand, troubled and anxious, and consumed with remorse, had died in abject misery at the beginning of this year (Jan. 25, 1494). His son Alfonso, who succeeded him, prepared as best he could to meet the approaching invaders.

Even at the last moment the French king hesitated and drew back from the perilous enterprise, when he received new encouragement from an unexpected quarter. At Lyons he was joined by the resolute Giuliano della Rovere, cardinal of San Pietro in Vincoli, well known in future history as Julius II. He was one of the few cardinals who could not be bribed to vote for the election of Rodrigo Borgia to the Papacy; and when this man ascended the throne under the name of Alexander VI., the cardinal never laid aside the bitter enmity and contempt with which he regarded the powerful but abandoned pontiff, whom he pronounced to be a "miscreant and a heretic."[1] Resolute in his determination to oppose in every possible way the man whom he regarded as a disgrace to the Church, he not only planned the assembling of a council, in order to obtain his deposition, but he made his escape into France, and used all his influence to induce the king to undertake the invasion of Italy. He told him that by his procrastination he was imperilling not only his own honor but that of his whole people. At last the king put his army in motion, Aug. 12, 1494, and crossing the Monte Ginevra, he arrived at Asti, where he was met by Ludovico.

Here the king, abandoning himself to pleasure and dissipation, brought on an illness by which he was detained at Asti for a month. When he recovered he proceeded to Pavia, where he visited his relative, the dispossessed Gian Galeazzo, kept here by his uncle, and now prostrated by disease. Isabella of Arragon, his wife, made an appeal to Charles, by which he was greatly moved ; so that he promised to use his influence to obtain their release. He was relieved from his embarrassment by the news of the young man's death, which shortly afterwards reached him. His uncle was gravely suspected of having slowly poisoned him.

While hesitating as to his future route, the king heard of the success of the French arms in other quarters. D'Aubigny, who had been sent with a small army into Romagna, had met with no opposition. The Duke of Orleans had repulsed the Neapolitan fleet at Genoa, and had taken Rapallo and put the garrison to the sword, besides slaying the whole of the inhabitants, including forty sick persons in their beds. The Italians were

---

[1] Marrano ed eretico.

unaccustomed to such ferocity in war, and the whole country was terror-stricken at the intelligence. The king was further confirmed in his resolution by the arrival of Giovanni and Lorenzo de' Medici, cousins of Piero, who came to tell him that Florence and all Tuscany was on his side. The order was now given to advance. The campaign under the king was conducted with the same savage cruelty which had distinguished the Swiss under the Duke of Orleans. The castle of Fivizzano was taken, and the inhabitants put to the sword. The invaders received their first check when they arrived before the fortress of Sarzana.

The French and the Florentines had been ancient allies ; and King Charles, before undertaking the expedition, had ordered the ambassadors whom he sent into Italy to solicit the friendship of the Medici and their city. He desired them to urge the old friendship existing between the two peoples ; to remind the Florentines that Charlemagne had· rebuilt their city, and that other French kings had afforded them assistance in their wars. The audacity of these assertions would seem more astonishing if the fable of the rebuilding of the city had not been received as history at that period, and if we were not somewhat familiar with the ludicrous notion that Charles the Great, a German king, was a Frenchman. The Florentines, however, did not need arguments, good or bad, to make them favorable to the French ; and Piero de' Medici was so infatuated with the Neapolitan alliance, and perhaps so doubtful of the reality of the enterprise, that he gave no heed to them. As he would not receive the invaders as friends, they prepared to enter Tuscany as enemies.

The feeble and irresolute Piero now began to tremble

for the result of his alliance with Naples. The rapid advance of the French seemed to paralyze what power of thought and action he possessed. If he had even now taken measures to give effect to his policy, he might have seriously embarrassed the invaders, perhaps even have finally checked their advance. While he hesitated, Florence was in confusion. The popular feeling here, as elsewhere throughout the cities of Italy, had always been on the side of the French; and the people were incensed as well as alarmed to think that they must meet as an enemy one whom they regarded as a friend. Piero at first thought of resistance, and sent reinforcements to the garrison of Sarzana; but suddenly changing his mind, he determined to try the effect of personal negotiation with the king.

Some years before, when war was being waged between Florence and Naples, his father, Lorenzo, had conceived the bold project of venturing himself alone into the hands of the king of Naples; and he had carried out his purpose with so much courage and address that he had secured honorable terms for his country. Piero determined to attempt the same experiment with the king of France. Imitations are not often successful, for the reason perhaps that they ignore the circumstances in which the original example was shown; but the imitation of a brave and capable man by one who is timid and incapable is almost certainly doomed to failure.

Accompanied by ambassadors from the republic, he set forth on his journey. On his way he found that his reinforcements had been met and defeated by the French; but they had attempted in vain to get possession of the fort of Sarzanello. In spite of this failure,

which might have been repeated, in spite of the fact
that other and still greater obstacles stood in the way of
the invaders, and probably fearing lest any attempts at
resistance on his part should not be supported by his
countrymen, he resolved to make every concession
which might be demanded of him. Without communicating with the ambassadors, he at once consented to
surrender to the king the three fortresses of Sarzana,
Sarzanello, and Pietra Santa, which were immediately
given up. He also promised to pay a subsidy, and to
yield up the fortresses of Pisa and Livorno, on condition
of their being restored after the conquest of Naples;
thus giving the French virtual possession of the whole
country. The French king might well conclude that
"God was manifestly conducting their enterprise."[1]

When the ambassadors returned to Florence and
made known the terms conceded by the unworthy Piero,
the wrath of the citizens knew no bounds. It was not
only that the conditions were ignominious beyond example, but they had been entered into without authority
from the rulers of the State and without the concurrence of the ambassadors. Even those who had hitherto
been supporters of the Medici now openly fell away
from them. It was easier, however, to quarrel with the
existing state of things than to know how to inaugurate
a better. The Florentines had lost the sense of liberty,
and the sense of power by which it is accompanied.
Accustomed to lean upon the family which had now
betrayed them, they knew not how to set to work so as

---

[1] De Commines (liv. vii. c. 9) says: "If Sarzana had been fur-
nished as it ought to have been, the king's army had certainly
been ruined in besieging it; for the country is mountainous and
barren, full of snow, and not able to supply us with provisions."

to act for themselves. There was only one man in whom general confidence was reposed. They turned to the cathedral, expecting and desiring the guidance of Savonarola.

It would be well for those who think of the Frate as a wild fanatic eager for power, burning with hatred against the Medici, and unscrupulous in his denunciation of the enslavers of Florence, to study his conduct at this crisis. One word from him, and the city would have been given up to revolt and confusion. One word from him, and the palace of the Medici and all its treasures would have perished forever. No one who considers the state of the popular mind, the readiness of the people to follow the guidance of one in whom they confided, and the influence possessed by Savonarola, will doubt the truth of this assertion.

When the time came to address the anxious and excited multitudes which thronged the Duomo, Savonarola was evidently oppressed by a painful sense of the gravity of the occasion. He felt that a fearful responsibility now devolved upon him, and that a word spoken rashly or imprudently might have terrible consequences. Instead of denouncing the authors of these calamities, he set forth the mercy and patience of God as an example to His people, and with earnest voice and gesture counselled union and brotherly love. Yet he could not avoid referring to the fulfilment of the predictions which he had so frequently uttered in their ears.

" Now," he exclaimed, " the sword has come, the prophecies are fulfilled, the scourges have begun. It is the Lord who guides these armies, O Florence ! The time of songs and dances has passed away; it is now time to bewail thy sins with rivers of tears. Thy sins, O Florence !

thy sins, O Rome! thy sins, O Italy! are the cause of these
stripes.   And now repent, give alms, offer prayers, become
united.   O people! I have been a father to thee; I have
wearied myself all the days of my life to make known to
thee the truths of the faith and of holy living, and I have
had nothing but tribulations, derision, and reproach.   May
I have at least the reward of seeing thee do good works!
My people, what else have I desired than to see thee safe,
than to see thee united?   Repent, for the kingdom of
heaven is at hand. . . ."

Again, turning his speech into prayer, he cries out:

" I turn to Thee, my Lord, who didst die for love of us
and for our sins.   Pardon, O Lórd, pardon the people of
Florence, who now desire to be Thine!"

He left the pulpit exhausted by the effort; but the
words which he had uttered were not unavailing.   His
earnest exhortations to peace and charity and unity so
moved the people that they remained quiet, their passions so kept in check by the hand which was now con-
trolling them that no excesses were committed.

The helpless condition of dependence into which
this great city, once so free, so proud, and so turbulent,
had fallen, became more than ever conspicuous when
the leading men of the State assembled to take counsel
as to their future action.   Notwithstanding the ever-
increasing hatred with which the mass of the people
regarded the Medici, they shrank from the measures
which some of the bolder began to advise.   When Luca
Corsini rose, without the usual request from the Signoria,
and declared that everything had gone wrong with them,
and steps must be taken to prevent the ruin with which
they were threatened, he was met with astonishment and

alarm, instead of applause and support. The sentiment of his hearers so reacted upon himself that he sat down in confusion, unable to proceed with his address.

He was followed by a young man named Jacopo di Tanai de' Nerli, who enforced the words that had just been spoken. Yet he too began to hesitate, as though abashed at his own audacity; and his father instantly arose and asked that the words of his son might be excused, in consideration of his youth. But there was one voice which did not fear to utter the thoughts that were laboring in many breasts, nor to point out the duty that was now incumbent upon the rulers of the republic. It was the voice of a man who bore a name illustrious in the annals of Florence, Piero di Gino Capponi.

There was something in the commanding appearance of the man, and there was in him a youthful impetuosity which his gray hairs had not tamed, which made the multitude listen with deep attention and respect to the few brief but resolute words which he uttered. He said:

" Piero de' Medici is no longer capable of guiding the State. The republic must see to itself; it is time to have done with this government of children. Let ambassadors be sent to King Charles. If they meet Piero, let them not salute him. Let them explain to the king that all the mischief has come from Piero, and that the city is friendly to the French. Let them be men of distinction, who will not fail to receive the king with all courtesy; but at the same time let them call in from the country the commanders with their soldiers, and let them conceal themselves in the convents and other secret places, together with the men-at-arms, and let them hold themselves ready in case of need. So that while we omit nothing that is right and due towards this most Christian king, nor fail to satisfy with money the avaricious nature of the French, we may be able, if he should have recourse to acts and proposals which we cannot endure, to show him our face and our arms. And above all, let us not fail to send along with the other ambassadors Father Girolamo Savonarola, who now possesses the entire affection of the people."

It wanted only such clear and decided utterances, which did but interpret the confused thoughts now struggling in the minds of the multitude, to decide their action. The ambassadors were elected on the 5th of November, and among them were Capponi himself, Nerli, and Savonarola.

It was the custom of the Frate to make his journeys on foot; so that the other ambassadors departed by themselves, and he followed, accompanied by two of the brethren of his convent. Before setting out he preached again to the people, and told them that it was God who had heard their prayers and was interposing for their safety.[1]

"He alone has come to the help of this city, when all have abandoned it. . . . Persevere then, O people of Florence! persevere in good works, persevere in peace. If thou desire that the Lord persevere in compassion, be thou compassionate towards thy brethren, towards thy friends, towards thine enemies. Otherwise there will fall upon thee the blows which are preparing for the rest of Italy. 'I will have mercy,' the Lord is calling to you. Woe to him who does not obey His commands!"

The ambassadors found the king at Lucca, preparing to depart, and they had their first interview with him in that city. Piero de' Medici remained with him; but the ambassadors, faithful to the resolutions taken at the

---

[1] This sermon, like the last, is among the Prediche sopra Aggeo (Villari).

advice of Capponi, showed him no respect, and brought him no message from the republic. Apprehensive of danger to his interests in Florence, he did his best to conciliate the king by promising him a sum of two hundred thousand ducats. Instructing Paolo Orsini, his mother's brother, to get together his soldiers and retainers and to follow him to Florence, he hastened back to the city, which he reached on the 8th of November.

The interview between King Charles and the ambassadors at Lucca was short, in consequence of the preparations he was making for his departure for Pisa. He received them very graciously, however, and seemed disposed to regard the wishes of the republic with favor. When, however, they followed him to Pisa and were permitted to have a second interview with him, they found he had been so influenced by the representations and promises made by Piero de' Medici before his departure that he listened with great coldness to the requests which they preferred on behalf of the State. He would make no promises, but simply said " he would arrange everything when he was within the great city." The ambassadors were forced to depart with the conviction that the king was anything but favorable to the city.

The arrival of Savonarola produced a greater impression upon the king and his court. Passing through the camp and the multitudes of armed men unmoved, he came into the presence of King Charles and proceeded to discharge his commission, which he believed to be derived not so much from the Signoria of Florence as from the King of kings. It was with this feeling, and in a manner and tone indicating this conviction, that he began his address.

"O most Christian king," he said, "thou art an instrument in the hand of the Lord, who sendeth thee to relieve
the evils of Italy (as I have for several years predicted),
and chargeth thee to reform the Church, which lies prostrate on the earth! But if thou wilt not be just and merciful; if thou dost not respect the city of Florence, its
women, its citizens, its liberty; if thou forgettest the work
on which the Lord sends thee, then He will choose another
to fulfil it, and He will in anger lay His heavy hand upon
thee, and will punish thee with terrible scourges. These
things I tell thee in the name of the Lord."

The king and his nobles listened to Savonarola as to
a prophet sent from God, knowing that he had predicted
their invasion of Italy; and they were evidently far
more favorably disposed towards the interests of Florence than they had been before the arrival of the Frate.

How little dependence, however, was to be placed
upon the promises of the French king, how little capable
he was even of understanding the position of affairs in
Italy and his own relation to them, was shown by his
conduct before he left Pisa. This city had for long
been subject to Florence. In some respects the very
greatness of Florence depended upon its possession of
Pisa, inasmuch as it lay between it and the sea. The
relationship had never been a kindly one. The readiness to revolt on the one side had led to oppression
and tyranny on the other. It was therefore inevitable
that Pisa should seek every opportunity of casting off
the grievous yoke under which it suffered. Here was
a chance which could not be neglected; and the citizens made the most touching appeals to King Charles
to restore their liberty. As De Commines remarks, the
king knew very little of the meaning of this appeal; but

he could not help understanding the afflictions of these people, and he replied, " he was willing it should be so; though (to speak truth)," adds his candid minister, " he had no authority to grant it, for the town was not his own, and he was received into it only in friendship, and to relieve him in his great necessities." The Pisans showed their gratitude by pulling down the lion of Florence and setting up a statue of the king in its place, with the lion under his horse's feet. " When the king of the Romans came to that town," says the same writer, " they served the statue of the king of France as they had served the lion; for it is the nature of the Italians to side always with the strongest, — rather to use the strongest, as far as they can, for their own ends. But these Pisans were, and still are, so barbarously treated that they might be excused for what they did."

Piero de' Medici, as we have heard, arrived in Florence on the 8th of November; and although he was prepared to find a change in the bearing of the authorities towards himself, he must have been surprised at the coldness of the reception which was accorded to him, — a coldness which was speedily converted into active opposition. The day after his arrival he presented himself at the palace of the Signoria with the intention of calling a parliament of the whole people, and having the government of the republic intrusted to himself alone. But the magistrates, warned of his design, received him in the most chilling manner, admitted only a small number of the multitude he had brought with him, and told him to send his people away and not create a tumult in the city. He was so confused by this reception that he could only say he would consider what he should do, and took his departure.

The next day he determined to assume a more threatening aspect; and he presented himself at the palace, accompanied by a number of armed men. But he was informed that no person could be admitted unless he was without arms; and he was forced to turn away. He had hardly done so when he was recalled by the influence of Antonio Lorini, the one member of the Signoria who still remained faithful to the Medici. Presuming on this invitation as a sign that he was still in possession of his former authority, he adopted his old tone of insolent dictation, when Nerli shut the door in his face. The people, who became aware of what was passing, needed no more to let loose their wrath and contempt. He was saluted everywhere with hoots and hisses and showers of stones. The bell of the Signoria now began to ring, and the people rushed, some armed, some unarmed, to the Piazza. Hardly had they begun to assemble in front of the palace when a fresh incident occurred which inflamed their fury. Francesco Valori, whom we have mentioned as one of the five citizens sent by Lorenzo to Savonarola with a view of inducing him to desist from his manner of preaching, had been a devoted friend of the Medici. It would appear, however, that the Prior of St. Mark's had acquired by degrees no slight influence over him, although he had still remained faithful to the ruling family. He was a man of an ardent and generous disposition, and the recent conduct of Piero had utterly alienated him; so that he now became one of the leaders of the popular party. It was this man who now appeared in the Piazza, covered with dust, having ridden all the way from Pisa, where he had left the ambassadors after their interview with the king. The excited multitude heard from him, with ever-increasing rage, that at Lucca the king had shown himself well disposed towards them, but that in consequence of the entreaties and the promises of Piero he had afterwards received them with great coldness at Pisa. It needed no more to rouse the populace to fury. Raising the cry of *Abbasso le palle*, — " Down with the balls, " — the rallying word of the Medici, they rushed forth to attack their palace.[1]

While this was going on the Medici had not been idle. Believing in the power of their name and their old-established authority, they gathered together their armed retainers and sought to arouse their supporters in the city. But the cry of *Palle* had lost its power. No one responded to it, and many threatened them from the windows of the houses. The Cardinal Giovanni, son of Lorenzo, afterwards Pope Leo X., was the foremost in defence of his family. But Piero had already consulted for his own safety. Seeing the multitude approaching, with Valori at their head, and learning that his family had been declared rebels, he set out for Bologna, where he received a very cold welcome from Bentivoglio. " I would rather have been cut to pieces," said the haughty aristocrat, " than give up my State," — a boast which was but very little verified by his own subsequent conduct. Piero continued his flight until at last he found rest at Venice, — the same city in which his great-grandfather Cosimo, but with far greater dignity, had taken refuge when he was driven away by the conspiracy of the Albizzi. He had hardly arrived at Venice when he received a message from the French king desiring his

1 The cry of the partisans of the Medici was *Palle, Palle*, from the balls in the armorial bearings of the family.

return to Florence; but he lacked courage and resolution to take a step which might have changed the whole history of his family and of Florence.

The cardinal had shown a more resolute spirit; but he too, at last, was forced to make his escape. He did not depart until he had done his best to save the most valuable parts of the splendid collection of objects of art in the family mansion. It was a remarkable proof of his own confidence in the brethren of St. Mark, and of the respect in which they were held in Florence, that he committed these treasures to their keeping.

Florence was thus expecting, in confusion and terror, the approach of the French, when Savonarola returned to announce that the king seemed again better disposed to the people, and to urge them to make preparations to receive him. His counsels were seconded by the efforts of Capponi, who had now become the foremost man in the practical direction of the State. By his advice the houses were stocked with all the munitions of war, and armed men were disposed throughout the city and kept ready in case of need. Six thousand were prepared to come forth at the first stroke of the bell.

When the advance guard of the French army entered Florence they could not conceal their astonishment at the splendor of the palaces and the general magnificence of the city. By an accident they were made aware that the conquest of the place was not so simple a matter as they had anticipated. On the 15th of November a rumor had spread abroad that Piero de' Medici was approaching. The bell sounded, the people crowded forth in multitudes, clad in armor, and filled the Piazza, the palaces were closed, the towers were armed, fortifications began to arise. The falseness of the rumor was speedily discovered, and instantly the former calm prevailed. But the impression had been made upon the French that these people would be difficult to subdue, and the Florentines had shown that they were not unprepared for the last extremity.

The palace of the Medici had been got ready for the king, and the magistrates and the leading men of Florence prepared to receive him with a respectful welcome. Charles rode at the head of his splendid army; but his magnificent attire only rendered more conspicuous the ludicrous insignificance of his person. By his side rode the Cardinal of San Pietro in Vincoli. The sight of such an army, amounting to about twelve thousand men, marching in perfect order, was as striking as it was new to the inhabitants of Florence. They passed over the Ponte Vecchio in the midst of floral decorations and to the sound of music, through the Piazza, and so on to the cathedral, where they joined with the Signoria in public prayer. The king was then lodged in the palace of the Medici. The whole city was illuminated in honor of their guests, and the next day was spent in feasts.

At last the time for the negotiations arrived. The representatives of Florence, elected by the Signoria, were Guidantonio Vespucci, Domenico Bonsi, Francesco Valori, and Piero Capponi. Of the two last names we have already heard. Vespucci was considered the most learned of the citizens in law, and Bonsi had distinguished himself as an ambassador. Capponi, who took the lead in the interview with the king, had been honored and trusted by Lorenzo de' Medici, whose senior he was by one year, and had displayed courage and ability in the discharge of the duties intrusted to him by "The Magnificent." Since the death of Lorenzo he had been the man of the State most trusted in every difficult enterprise. He had always had a repugnance to the tyranny of the Medici and a love of popular government, and since the accession of Piero he had been looked upon as one of the leaders of the party opposed to him. He knew the French people well, having been sent as ambassador to their court, and he did not hesitate to declare his opinion that "When the Italians came face to face with the French, they would cease to have so much fear of them." These convictions were not without their effect in his future dealings with the king.

Here, as elsewhere, Charles habitually acted without any fixed principles, according to the impulse of the moment and the influences which were nearest and most powerful at the time. Although Piero had fled, his mother and his wife did not fail to use every argument to induce the king to favor their side; so that he appeared inclined to espouse the cause of the Medici. He assumed an aspect of severity towards the commissioners of the republic; he put forth the most exorbitant demands as the conditions of peace; he took the attitude of one who was dealing with a conquered city. Finally, he let fall some words in favor of the exiled Piero. This was the signal for grave deliberations on the part of the magistrates, who instantly called together the leading citizens and apprised them of the threatening danger. Preparations were made for summoning the people together by the sound of the bell, and a spirit of enmity began to spring up between the invaders and the populace.

At last the king began to moderate his tone. He dropped all reference to the "conquest" of the city; he said nothing more of Piero; he was to take the title —

one which had been held by foreign sovereigns in earlier times — of protector of the liberties of the city ; he was to retain the fortresses for two years, or for a shorter time if the war should be concluded sooner. All was arranged except the sum of money he was to receive. On this point the promises of the Medici made him exacting. It was impossible for the Signoria to promise what the city could not pay, and the situation became more and more anxious and irritating. At last the king ordered his ultimatum to be read, declaring that he would not recede from it. The commissioners said they were unable to comply with his demands. The king, enraged at their resistance, exclaimed, " Then we will sound our trumpets." Capponi had with difficulty restrained himself during the negotiations ; but the brave, proud spirit of the Florentine now broke forth. Snatching the ultimatum from the hands of the secretary, he tore it in pieces, and uttered, with a gesture as impassioned as the king's own, the memorable words : " And we will ring our bells." They were words of which Florence was forever proud. Machiavelli refers to them when he says, in one of his poems, " The noise of arms and horses could not drown the voice of one capon (Cappon) in the midst of a hundred cocks (Galli)." This courageous language had more effect than many entreaties. It was agreed that the Florentines should pay the king 120,000 florins in three instalments, and that Pisa should be surrendered, with the other fortresses, in two years, or sooner if the war ended before. The conditions of the treaty were sworn to in the cathedral ; and the city, if it had lost its first warmth of feeling for the French, gave itself up to festivals and illuminations as at their first entrance.

All seemed now satisfactorily arranged ; but the king showed no disposition to depart. Trade was suspended, French soldiers filled the city, disorders of all kinds prevailed, and the king was in vain entreated to take his leave. In this emergency it was to Savonarola that the citizens again had recourse. The Frate did not hesitate to approach the king ; and he effected his purpose in spite of the opposition offered by the noblemen and officers round him, who feared lest his influence with their master should prevent their contemplated plunder of the place. Charles received him with kindness, and listened attentively to the few earnest words which he uttered : —

"Most Christian Prince," said the friar, "thy delay inflicts serious injury upon the city and upon thine enterprise. Thou art wasting time, forgetting the duty which Providence has imposed upon thee, with great hurt to thy spiritual safety and thy worldly glory. Listen, therefore, to the voice of the servant of God. Go forth upon thy way without delay. Do not cause the ruin of this city, and excite against thee the wrath of the Lord."

The part taken by Savonarola in bringing about the departure of the French has been both exaggerated and denied. It would not be correct to say that he procured the terms of agreement between the republic and the French king. The merit of that arrangement must be conceded to Capponi. But it would be equally unjust to overlook the importance of Savonarola's influence in giving effect to the treaty. Charles was too unscrupulous to care much whether he carried out the stipulations into which he had entered, either in the letter or in the spirit ; and it was undoubtedly owing to Savonarola that he now resolved to go forth out of

Florence. He left the city on the 28th of November. Few regrets could have been entertained at the departure of the French. They had behaved with insolence during the eleven days of their sojourn, and had in no wise treated the citizens as friends, but as enemies ; although the resolute enmity of that one city might have ruined their whole enterprise. The palace of the Medici, in which the king had been royally entertained, was left a mere wreck.

Savonarola had now seen a considerable portion of his predictions fulfilled, and everything was concurring to raise him higher in the public estimation. Not only were his most deadly enemies, the Medici, driven from the city, but in this very year two of the most attached friends of that family gave, in their last moments, the most convincing proof of their entire confidence in Savonarola. Angelo Poliziano died in September, at the age of forty, and requested that he might be buried in St. Mark's, in the Dominican habit; and Pico della Mirandola the elder died on November 17th — the very day on which Charles entered Florence — and made the same request. They sleep side by side in the convent church. It may have comforted them, passing away almost in their youth, to think that they would lie near the remains of him who had moved them so powerfully for good. They did not know, nor did Florence herself, what end she was preparing for her greatest man.

CHAPTER X.

REVOLUTION.

IT is one of the miserable consequences of despotism ✓ that it disqualifies a people for the exercise of liberty after they have thrown off the yoke of bondage.   It was comparatively easy for the Florentines, under the circumstances, to make an end to the tyranny of the Medici. It was a far more difficult matter to recover those habits and sentiments of independence and self-reliance which they had lost during the sixty years of subserviency to that powerful family.   When the French had taken their departure, the real difficulties of the city were first clearly apprehended.

. The ordinary method with the Florentines of effecting a change in the manner of government had been the summoning of a *parlamento*, or assembly of the whole people.   This assembly was usually called by the Signoria. At the sound of the bell the people came unarmed into the Piazza, and were addressed by the magistrates from the *Ringhiera*, — a platform in front of the Palazzo Vecchio, as it is now most commonly called.   The first step was the appointment of a *balia*,[1] or committee with authority to decide on the government of the State, or on any other weighty matter that might be intrusted to it.   Nothing

[1] The word means "power," or "authority," and was applied to the committee intrusted with authority.

could seem better adapted to elicit the true feelings of the people and to give expression to their wishes. Nothing could have been farther from the actual results of these assemblies. They were seldom called until the most careful preparations had been made to secure the ends of those by whom they were summoned. The measures to be adopted had been concocted by the party in possession of power, or desiring to become possessed of it. The names of those who were to be proposed on the dictatorship — for this was the nature of the *balia* — were all ready. It was by such means that the Medici and other dominant families had paved the way for the execution of their own ambitious designs.

The Florentines had ample experience of the unreality and mischievousness of these assemblies, but they knew of no other course to be taken in the reconstruction of their government. The bell was sounded according to ancient usage, and the people, headed by their *gonfalonieri*, proceeded to the Piazza. The magistrates proposed to them the election of commissioners, to remain in power for one year, and during that time to have authority to elect the Signoria and all the principal magistrates, and to choose a *gonfaloniere di giustizia* from their number. The proposition was accepted by the people with every demonstration of joy.

When the Medici came into power they preserved all the ancient forms of republican liberty. Finding that it was easier to reduce the authority of the old institutions to a shadow than to abolish them, both Cosimo and Lorenzo had professed to carry on the government by means of the constituted bodies, — the Signoria, the College, the Ten of War, elected every six months, the Eight, who had jurisdiction in criminal causes and were elected every four months, and the two councils, representing the two classes of the people, by whom the magistrates were elected and the laws voted. But Lorenzo, without appearing to abolish the old institutions, without summoning a *parlamento*, by means of a friendly Signoria carried through the legislative councils an important measure, which placed the whole power of the State more completely in his own hands.[1] This was the appointment of a council or senate of seventy, whom he took care to have elected from his own friends, and whom he made permanent, with power to fill up all vacancies as they occurred. To these seventy was committed the election of the other officials of the State, so that whoever had the real direction of the senate was the practical ruler of Florence.

The authority of this senate now passed to the twenty commissioners, or electors, called *accoppiatori*, who, inasmuch as they had the bi-monthly election of the supreme Signoria in their hands, became the great power in the State; for the only real check upon the power of the Signoria was the fact of its being changed every two months. Offices of different kinds might be intrusted to other hands, but the Signoria, or magistrates, had the administration in their hands, the legislation, the power of deciding cases in law, and the right of declaring war; so that the electors of this body, when they were permanent, while the Signoria was continually changing, had the most perfect control over all the affairs of State. By vesting this power of election in the twenty *accoppiatori*, chosen by the people, the Florentines believed that they were re-establishing popular power.

But they forgot that there was an energy behind the

---

[1] Cf. Von Reumont, b. v. c. i.

senate which was continually putting it in motion and guiding its action; and people, whether individuals or communities, who have been accustomed to lean on others, do not readily learn to rely upon themselves, to judge for themselves, and to act upon the judgments which they have formed. Among these electors, as among those who appointed them, there was an absence of what we might call public opinion, or what others would call party organization; and this was seen when they proceeded to the election of a *gonfaloniere*. They could not get a majority of their number to agree on any one name. Every two or three electors had their own candidate, and they became aware of their helplessness, without knowing how it could be remedied. Men who had been prompt and vigorous in action when they saw clearly the work that was to be done, were incapable of guiding the deliberations of their fellow-citizens. In this difficulty their minds turned to the constitution of Venice as offering a model which might, to some extent, become an example for themselves.

When, however, they came to discuss the subject of conforming their own constitution to the Venetian, there arose a difference of opinion among them. It was generally agreed that most of the magistrates and officials that had existed before the time of Lorenzo should be preserved or restored, — the Signoria, the Eight for the decision of criminal and political causes, the Ten as a war ministry, and the *gonfaloniere di compagnia*. But when they came to consider the constitution of the councils by which these functionaries should be elected, they could no longer agree. The two sections were led by two doctors in law, Vespucci and Soderini. According to the latter, the true method was to form a council after the model of the great council of Venice, which should consist of the popular element and have the election of the magistrates and the passing of the laws, and besides this, to have, like the Venetians, a smaller council, consisting of a higher class of men, who should decide matters that could not be properly discussed in public. Vespucci, on the other hand, represented that the great council of Venice was an aristocratic body, and that to form such a council of the people indiscriminately would be to renew and perpetuate the old excesses and disturbances which had disgraced the republic in past times.[1]

These opposing views were discussed at great length without leading to any general agreement. At last the thoughts of men turned instinctively to Savonarola. He had guided them through their difficulties with the French king, and they now looked to him for direction in their present perplexity. It is most untrue to say that Savonarola did, of his own accord, meddle with the politics of the State. He could never be indifferent to the manner in which his countrymen were governed, because he saw the most intimate connection between the government and the morals of the people. He knew that when reasonable liberty was gone, nearly all that was good and noble in men must perish with it. But he cared for politics only as the instrument of morality, and he constantly warned the citizens that the first step to true liberty and happiness was the reformation of manners.

We have seen how far he was from inflaming the passions of the populace when their wrath first broke out against Piero de' Medici. It is certain that he

---

[1] Guicciardini has preserved their arguments.

took no part in the expulsion of the Medici from Florence,[1] for he had not then returned from Pisa after his interview with King Charles. And now he began to introduce distinct political allusions into his sermons, because it was expected that he should do so, because the people needed guidance and looked to him for it, and because he believed that God had appointed him to be their teacher.

In his first sermons on the subjects of the day he exhorted the wealthy to abandon luxurious living, that they might give to the poor, who were in great distress in consequence of the cessation of business, which had not been generally resumed since the occupation of the city by the French. He said that, if necessary, he would sell the vessels of the church and the vestments of the clergy to alleviate the destitution which prevailed; but they must see at once that the shops were opened, and that work was provided for the unemployed. Undoubtedly, he told them, it was the will of God that bad government should cease, that evil customs and unequal laws should be abolished; but it was still more necessary that they should fulfil their obvious duties.

"This is a time," he said, "in which words must give way to deeds, and vain ceremonies to true sentiments. The Lord hath said: 'I was an hungered, and ye gave me no meat: I was naked, and ye clothed me not.' He never said: 'Ye built not a beautiful church or a fine convent.' He speaks only of works of charity. We must begin our work of renovation, then, with charity."

1 It has been erroneously supposed that he did so, by Perrens and others; but Villari has shown that this error arose from the wrong arrangement of his sermons, and that he had not then returned to Florence.

But this did not satisfy the expectations of the people; and at last he began, on the third Sunday in Advent, December 12th of the same year (1494), to speak more directly on the subject of politics. The opinions which he expressed in his sermons he afterwards published in his "Treatise on the Government of Florence,"[1] — a tract which he composed at the request of the Signori, and which he dedicated to them. From his sermons preached at this time, as well as from the treatise, it is evident that Savonarola was not in theory a republican. A monarchy was the form of government which he would himself have preferred; but he acknowledged that, while it was the best government when the monarch was a good and wise man, it was the worst when he was a bad man. Besides, he confessed that it was ill adapted for Italy and for Florence. There, he feared, it could only exist as a tyranny.

"The only government that can suit us," he said, "is the government of the citizens and that which is universal.[2] Woe to thee, O Florence, if thou makest to thyself a head, a chief who can oppress and domineer over the rest! From these heads arise all the evils that can ruin a city. And therefore the first law which thou shouldst make will be this: That no one must ever, for the future, be made head over thy city; otherwise thou wilt be cast down into the dust. Those men who wish to elevate themselves above all others, and who cannot endure civil equality, are the worst of all; they seek the ruin of their own souls and that of the people.

"O my people!" he exclaims, "you know that I have never wished to enter into the affairs of the State; think

[1] Trattato circa il reggimento e governo della Città di Firenze. Republished at Florence, 1847.

[2] Governo civile ed universale.

you that I should do so now if I did not see that it was
necessary for the safety of men's souls? You would not.
believe, but now you see, that my words are all proved
true; that they are not mine, but that they come from the
Lord. Give ear, then, to one who seeks only your salvation. Purify your hearts, give heed to the common good,
forget private interests; and if you reform your city in
this disposition, it will be more glorious than it has ever
been."

And then, breaking into prayer, he cries out : —

" Open, O Lord, the heart of this people, that they may
understand those things which are in my mind, and that
Thou hast revealed and commanded them."

The beginning of all reforms, he told them, must be
in the heart and life. Spiritual things are the origin
of all right principle and action, and all temporal good
ought to subserve the moral and religious good upon
which it depends. Then, referring to the well-known
saying of Cosimo de' Medici, he goes on, —

" If you have heard it declared that 'States are not
governed with Pater Nosters,' remember that this is the
theory of tyrants, of men who are the enemies of God and
of the common weal, — a theory invented to oppress and
not to elevate and free the State. On the contrary, if
you would have a good government, you must return to
God. If it were not so, I should certainly not trouble myself about the State.

" The form which is best adapted for this city," he con-
tinues, " is that of a great council, after the Venetian manner. And therefore I advise you to assemble the whole
city under the sixteen *gonfalonieri,* and let each one of
the companies choose a form ; from the sixteen thus obtained let the *gonfalonieri* select four, and take them to

the Signoria, who, after solemn prayer has been offered, shall choose the best. And that which is thus chosen, you may feel certain, will come from God. I believe myself that the form chosen will be the Venetian; but you need not be ashamed to imitate that, because they also have had it from the Lord, from whom cometh everything that is good. You see that from the time that this government has prevailed in Venice no divisions or dissensions have arisen in that city; and therefore we must believe that it is according to the will of God."

The influence of Savonarola was at this time felt to be so salutary that he was frequently requested by the Signoria to preach on these subjects in St. Mark's, and also in the palace. At last, in a sermon in the cathedral, at which only men were present, he put forth these four points as embodying the principles of true government : —

1. The fear of God and the restoration of good manners and customs.

2. The love of popular government and of the public good, setting aside all private interests.

3. A general amnesty, by which they should absolve the friends of the past government from all faults, remitting all fines, and showing indulgence towards those who were indebted to the State.

4. To constitute a form of universal government, which should comprehend all the citizens, to whom, according to the ancient ordinances of the city, the government belonged.

He concluded by suggesting the formation of a great council, after the Venetian model, but adapted to the genius of the people of Florence.

The clear statement of these principles, enforced by

the air of authority with which they were set forth, produced an irresistible effect on the people. Even those who had only a very partial sympathy with the character and action of Savonarola have expressed their admiration of his conduct on this occasion and their astonishment at the results which he produced. Men of the world living near his own time admired his talent for administration, and confessed that the government which he gave to Florence was the best that it had ever enjoyed.[1] It was reserved for scoffers of a later age to speak of him as a mixture of cunning and fanaticism. Those who study with impartiality his spoken utterances, his well-considered written testimony, his whole conduct and deportment during these times of perplexity and doubt, will see that he was speaking the truth when he said he would not have mixed in the affairs of the State but for the good of men's souls and for the glory of that Lord who had sent him to do His work.

The sermons preached by Savonarola on the Prophet Haggai in Advent, and those on the Psalms, which were delivered immediately afterwards, are not only of importance as showing the influence which he then exercised in the State, they are valuable historical documents. Every step in the reconstruction of the edifice of Florentine government was introduced by a sermon from the Frate, so that the history of the period can be traced in his successive discourses. The first step was to gain the consent of the two councils of the people to the formation of a great council; and this was done with almost entire unanimity. The council was invested with power

---

[1] Francesco Forti says: "The reform of the Frate was perhaps the only just government which Florence possessed in its republican state."

to elect all the chief magistrates and to sanction all the laws, so that it was made the supreme authority in the State.

The charge against Savonarola, that he was founding a government utterly democratic and plebeian, is entirely without foundation. Before a man could be a member of the great council he must be of the age of twenty-nine years and one of the *beneficiati* of the citizens; that is to say, either himself, his father, his grandfather, or his great-grandfather must have held one of the three highest offices in the State. This council, be it observed, was the only body which really possessed the franchise under the reformation of Savonarola; and it was so far from being merely plebeian that there were actually two classes of the citizens who had no place in it, — those called *statuati*, who were eligible to offices which would qualify them for a place in the council, and those called *aggravezzati*, who paid taxes, had the right to carry arms, and certain other civil privileges; while below these were the other inhabitants of the city, who had no part in the government or special rights of citizenship.

It was arranged that when the number of the *beneficiati* exceeded fifteen hundred, they should be divided into three parts, which should, in succession, form the great council for six months. It is said that Florence at that time contained ninety thousand inhabitants,[1] of whom only thirty-two hundred were qualified; so that the council would consist of little more than a thousand persons at a time. In order to give it a more comprehensive character, it was decided to elect sixty citizens not *beneficiati*, and twenty young men of the age of twenty-four years, as members of the council.

[1] Cf. Villari, lib. ii. c. 5.

The lesser council, which formed the senate, or upper house of government, was to consist of eighty citizens of not less than forty years of age, who were to be renewed every six months. This body was to assist the Signoria, who were required to consult it at least once a week; and these, together with the colleges of *gonfalonieri* and the other magistrates, were to nominate ambassadors and conduct other matters of importance which could not be decided in public. When it was intended to pass a new law, the *proposto* (provost or president), who was one of the Signori, and changed every day, proposed it to the Signoria; if it was passed by them and the colleges, they might then call together a committee of experienced citizens and obtain their judgment, if the matter seemed of sufficient importance, or they might carry it to the Eighty at once; and from them it went to the great council, by whose consent it became law. It should be added that these assemblies had the power of voting only, and not of discussing. Not unless their members were called upon to express their opinions could they do so, and then only in favor of the proposed law. This course, which at first may seem unreasonable, was rendered necessary by the number of persons constituting these bodies. Another provision was made at the same time, which was intended to meet the existing necessities of the State. This was the election of ten citizens who should have the power of remitting, in whole or in part, any unpaid taxes or fines imposed by the late government, and who should rearrange the public imposts and taxes, laying them principally upon real property. This last regulation, although it rendered ecclesiastical property liable to taxation, had been strongly recommended from the pulpit by

Savonarola. Villari informs us that this measure was carried out with so much prudence and justice that to this day the system introduced by the advice of Savonarola is maintained in Florence. It was provided that each citizen, without distinction, should pay to the State one tenth of the rent derived from his real property (*beni stabili*).

Savonarola had never ceased to preach peace and mercy and unity during the troubles of Florence; and a measure came now to be decided which was closely connected with the political changes which had taken place. It has been mentioned that there was a body of eight magistrates who decided upon all political and criminal offences. This body had the power, by a majority of six votes (*sei fave*,[1] " six beans," as it was called), to condemn an accused person to imprisonment, banishment, a pecuniary fine, or even to death. In consequence of the strong party feeling which often prevailed, it became necessary to have some appeal from the decision of the Eight, or from that of the Signoria, by whom the powers of the Eight were commonly appropriated.

On the general subject of appeal the voice of Savonarola was heard; but a most important divergence took place as to the body to whom the appeal should be carried. The Frate knew well that the mob was most easily made the tool of the despot, that a larger body of men were more apt to be led away by passion than a smaller and more select assembly; and he proposed that the appeal should be carried, not to the Consiglio Maggiore, but to the Council of Eighty. It was immediately

---

[1] Hence the law giving an appeal from their decision was called " La legge delle sei fave."

complained that this was to destroy the authority of the Signoria. " Surely not," said Savonarola ; " it will only strengthen their hands. If they are doing right, the council will confirm it ; if they are doing wrong, they will be glad to be set right."

It is easy now to see that Savonarola's proposal was the right one, and it is equally easy to see how it failed. The men in authority were opposed to every appeal, as taking these judicial decisions out of their hands ; the mob were jealous of such privileges being intrusted to what they regarded as a select and aristocratic chamber. Hence there was a union of forces against the scheme of the Frate which could appeal only to the reason and not to the prejudices of the people. The multitude desired that the power of revising these criminal sentences should be possessed by the greater council ; the aristocrats saw clearly that they could more easily turn the larger body to their own purposes, and they too opposed the intrusting of these powers to the Eighty. That very Vespucci who had opposed the formation of the great council, on the ground that it was intended to be democratic, and not aristocratic, as in Venice, to the astonishment of all spoke strongly in favor of these appeals being carried to the larger assembly. He wanted, he said, the equality of all the citizens, and this was the way to attain it. What he, and others like him, really wanted was a body with which they could do as they pleased ; and they used the ignorant prejudices and unreasoning passions of the multitude to gain their ends. All this was clearly perceived by Savonarola, but he was powerless to prevent the fatal decision. It may have been that his deep loyalty to the freedom of the people hindered his using the kind of argument which the other side employed. In this point, at least, his suggestion was not followed; and the most cruel part of the affair is that he has been made responsible by many writers for this mischievous law, although he did his best to prevent its being passed. Here, as in many other cases, a more minute examination of the documents of the period and of his own sermons has served to clear his memory from blame.

There was one other measure of change upon which Savonarola had set his heart, — the abolition of the *parlamento*. It has already been mentioned that the *parlamento* was an assembly of the whole people, called into the Piazza by the sound of the bell, to decide on any considerable change in the government, and to appoint a *balia* for giving effect to their resolutions. To an inexperienced mind, nothing could seem more open, straightforward, constitutional, democratic. Here were the whole people assembled to give their consent to a change which concerned every one of them. The transaction, as a rule, was as hollow as it was specious.

We who live in the nineteenth century have seen something as pretentious and as unreal in our own days. It is not long since a great nation was invited to declare its mind by a *plébiscite*. What could be fairer? Let all men say whether it is their will to have an emperor! And simple-minded English people looked on with puzzled admiration and asked: "Is not this as good as a general election, and very much the same thing?" It was, indeed, a very different thing. The people were simply asked to sanction a foregone conclusion. And if they refused, what was the alternative? It was not a change of policy or a change of ministers, it was a revolution; and that was a serious thing to face.

There was just as much unreality in the *parlamento*. Like the *plébiscite*, it was intended for the mere sanctioning and registering of a decision already arrived at, and it was the simplest and most useful instrument that despotism could employ. "I have thought," said Savonarola, in one of his sermons, "I have thought of this *parlamento* of yours, and it seems to me to be nothing else but a means of destruction, and therefore it is necessary to put it away." And again, with still greater energy: "People, when you hear the bell sounding to assemble a *parlamento*, rise up, draw your swords, and say, 'What do you want? Have we not our council, which is sufficient? What law do you want to make? Cannot the council pass it?' Therefore I want you to make a law that, when the Signoria enter upon their office, they shall take an oath not to call a *parlamento*." To these words he added language still stronger, bidding the people be ready, in case the Signoria should make such a proposal, and, the moment they set their feet on the *ringhiera*,[1] at once cut them in pieces. This language represented the Frate's deep conviction of the mischievousness of these assemblies, and not his habitual spirit and feeling towards political opponents. Already he saw signs of approaching divisions and of fresh attempts to restore the party which had been driven from power; and he may be forgiven if he used violent language in prospect of real and alarming dangers, threatening to undo the whole of the work for which he had labored with such zeal and success.

The law was passed as he had desired. On the 28th of July (1495) he preached the sermon containing the

[1] The platform in front of the palazzo, from which they addressed the populace.

words which we have quoted. On the 13th of August
it was decreed by the authority of the Signori and the
gonfaloniere of the republic, with the consent of the
councils, " that for the future it should not be possible
to make a *parlamento;* that the Signoria should take
an oath, on their entrance into office, never to convoke
one ; that whoever should plot such a thing should be
subject to the penalty of death ; and whoever should
reveal such a design should have a reward of 300
florins."

It will be remembered that one of the first subjects
which Savonarola brought before the people, when he
began to introduce the affairs of the State into his sermons, was the condition of the poor. And now, no
sooner was the constitution of the republic finally settled
than he turned his attention to the best means of reliev-
ing the wants of the needy and destitute. For this purpose he recommended the formation of a Monte di Pietà,
or " Compassionate Bank," entreating that all, and especially women who had more money than they needed,
should assist in its establishment. There was, indeed,
a great necessity for some such institution. In Florence,
as elsewhere, money-lending was chiefly in the hands of
the Jews, who charged the most exorbitant interest ; and
this again led to serious popular outbreaks against that
people. Savonarola had never joined in those persecutions, he would rather convert the Jews to the Christian faith ; but he would also take away the occasion of
their exactions. This he proposed to accomplish by the
Monte di Pietà. At first he wished that money should
be lent without any interest being charged ; but this plan
was found impracticable. He succeeded, however, in
passing a law that the bank should be established, that

the expense of its administration should not exceed 600 florins a year, and that the interest charged should not be more than six per cent.[1] It was not all that he desired, but it was a measure which brought very great relief to the class for whom he had intended it.

In the amnesty now passed, there is one case which deserves a passing notice. On the 8th of June, 1495, the magistrates decreed as follows: " Considering that Messer Dante Alighieri, great-grandson of Dante the poet, is unable to enter the city in consequence of not having been able to pay the tax imposed by the magistrates of last November and December, and judging it well to show some gratitude to the descendant of that poet who was so great an ornament to this city, they decree that the said Messer Dante shall consider himself to be, and shall be, free from every restriction or hindrance whatever." " It was," says Villari, " a tardy pardon to the memory of the great Ghibelline, an act of justice too slender to the name of the divine poet; yet it did no small honor to the republic that it should have thought of it in the first days of its new birth."

Those who would rightly estimate the intellectual capacity, the administrative ability, the moral influence of the great Dominican friar, who was now the ruling heart and mind of Florence, need only survey the work accomplished in the first year or two that had elapsed since the expulsion of the Medici. It was at this time that the statue of Judith slaying Holofernes, the work of Donatello, which had formerly been the property of

---

[1] It was in 1496 that this measure became law; but it is more convenient to give in one view the reforms which were accomplished under the influence of Savonarola.

the Medici, was set up.[1] It was intended as a monument of the triumph of the republic, and bore upon it
an inscription to the effect that the citizens had placed
it there as a memorial of the safety of the commonwealth.[2] The monument, with its inscription, has been
permitted to stand through all the changes which Florence has undergone during the space of nearly four
centuries.

One other memorial, still existing, of the changes introduced at this time should be mentioned here. It is
the Sala del Cinquecento [3] (Hall of the Five Hundred),
a chamber 170 feet in length and 75 in breadth, which
was built for the accommodation of the greater council.
There was no chamber in Florence of sufficient dimen-
sions to contain so large a body, and at the suggestion
of Savonarola a portion of the Palazzo Vecchio left un-
finished by the Duke of Athens was adapted for the
purpose. It is an interesting fact that the first Parliament of United Italy was held under King Victor Emmanuel in this chamber during the time that Florence
was the capital of the kingdom.

[1] Originally in front of the palazzo. In 1504 it was removed
to the Loggia dei Lanzi, to make room for the David of Michael
Angelo.

[2] *Exemplum sal: pub: cives posuere.* MCCCCXCV.

[3] Built under the direction of Lionardo da Vinci and Michael
Angelo, and in such an incredibly short space of time that Savonarola said, "the angels must have assisted."

CHAPTER XI.

REFORMATION OF MANNERS.

IF Savonarola was urged by the force of circumstances to take part in the political struggles of the day, he could always say with perfect truth that he had not willingly chosen this course for himself. His whole conduct proved the sincerity of his answer to those who accused him of meddling with politics, that he had done so for the safety, the well-being, the salvation of the people. In his sermons and in his public action he ever made it clear that with him politics were subordinate to religion. If he wished that Florence should be free, it was that its people might be righteous and God-fearing.

It is, indeed, one of the reproaches brought against the Frate that, in his subsequent course of action, he advocated theories and principles which were inapplicable to the actual condition of human society. If this be true, and we shall see that there is some truth in the remark, it is the best proof that he was not a mere demagogue lusting for political power. With him the claims of God were paramount. He was continually reminding the citizens that, whatever might be the form of their government, Christ was their true King. In this way he gave effect to his monarchical preferences. The rule of One was the ideal rule. But One was their master, even Christ: the only question that remained had regard to the best manner of securing obedience to His laws.

It was on the third Sunday in the Advent of 1494, in his sermons on the prophet Haggai, that Savonarola first introduced political subjects into the pulpit: It seems to have been on the following Sunday that he first broached the notion of Christ being the King of Florence.   Addressing himself to an imaginary auditory, that might prefer a monarchical government, he exclaimed, —

"Well, Florence, God is willing to satisfy thee, and to give thee a Head, a King to govern thee. This King is Christ. The Lord will govern thee Himself, if thou consent, O Florence! Suffer thyself to be guided by Him. Do not act as did the Jews when they required a king of Samuel. God said to Samuel, 'Hearken unto the voice of the people in all that they say unto thee : for they have not rejected thee, but they have rejected Me, that I should not reign over them.'[1] O Florence, do not imitate this people! Take Christ for thy Master, and remain subject to His law."

It was a thought likely to gain favor with the people at the moment; and when the Frate exclaimed, "Florence, Jesus Christ, who is King of the universe, hath willed to become thy King in particular, wilt thou have Him for thy King?" the multitude, as with one voice, acclaimed Jesus Christ as King of Florence. So eagerly was the cry taken up that Savonarola had to restrain the too-abundant expression of their zeal. It remained for long the rallying cry of his followers.

The Frate was not ignorant that his enemies would charge him with proclaiming Christ as their King, in order that he might be king himself, or at least prime minister in the new kingdom.

<hr>

[1] 1 Sam. viii. 7.

He tells them he knows what they are thinking, — that he is attempting to govern under this pretext.

" Well, then," he exclaims, " what have you given me for trying to govern you ? Where are the presents that you have sent me ? O Frate, you say, you have thousands of ducats! If any one says so, he does not speak the truth ; I have nothing, and I want nothing. It is you who want to be the first [referring to the aristocratic obstructors of the proposed constitution], and that is your reason for disliking the council. He who wants to be first seeks to overthrow the government of the whole people ; he will have no magistrates nominated without his permission ; he must be consulted about everything, even to the appointment of a clergyman to Santa Reparata. For my part, I endeavor to maintain the council. . . . Accuse me no more, then, of wanting to be minister of your city. Christ alone, I tell you, is your King ! "

We have already seen that Savonarola addressed himself to the reformation of the life and manners of the people directly after the expulsion of the Medici ; but he never forgot the supreme importance of this subject, and his sermons never became mere political addresses. The state of morality in Florence was, in truth, very degraded. Enough has been said of the moral condition of Europe and of Italy at this period ; and Florence, with its wealth and luxury, with its literary scepticism and its political subserviency and corruption, was to the full as bad as its worst neighbors. The Frate told the people that they spent their life in revelling and drunkenness and in all kinds of debauchery. " Your life," he said, " is the life of swine." And the historians of the period give no different account of their condition. They were madly addicted to gam-

bling and to the most degrading vices. They were
indecent in their attire, — a sure sign of the degeneracy of their morals, — and vices and crimes prevailed
widely which are not fit even to be named among us.
It is to be feared that these were not discouraged, — that
they were even promoted, — by the friends of the
classical Renaissance.

Savonarola was never weary of warning the citizens
— it was, indeed, the great work of his life to bear
witness — that they could have no blessing from God,
no abiding prosperity, unless they were converted from
their sins. Whatever fostered vice and ungodliness,
whatever hindered the acknowledgment of truth and
God among them, — against this he warred, through
his whole ministry, through his whole life, a continuous,
unending warfare. It has been alleged that he carried
his opposition to the borders of fanaticism when he
endeavored to suppress all gambling, when he sought
to destroy the writings[1] of the classics and of his own
countrymen, which he considered to be the fountains
of the evils which prevailed so widely in the city.

But he was not contented with urging upon the people
to abandon those habits which were ruining the city;
he entreated the magistrates to take the work in hand.

"Magistrates," he says, "it is to you that I address
myself. Put down these vices, destroy these sins, punish
this horrid passion which is against nature. And not
merely by a private fine, but in public, that all Italy may
know it. . . . Expose all the courtesans in a public place,
and send them off to the sound of trumpets. But you
say, O father! there are so many of them that this would
be to upset the whole city. Well, then, begin with one,

---

[1] We shall have to speak of this again.

then go on to the rest; and if you cannot give them chastity, you can at least teach them decency. Punish gamblers; for, be well assured, gambling still goes on. Give orders, signors, that no one shall play in the streets at great games or small. . . . Have the tongues of blasphemers pierced. Saint Louis, king of France, had the lips of a blasphemer cauterized, and said: 'I should be happy to have as much done to myself if I could at such a price have my kingdom cleared of such offenders.' Put down dancing too, for this is not a time to dance. Prohibit balls in town and country."

Then he went further, and recommended the appointment of spies to discover whether these orders were carried out. He found that the places of public entertainment were not closed at the appointed hour; that the shops were kept open on holy days; and he insisted that they should be closed, with the exception of those which were open for the sale of medicines.

If the preacher had but small success with the magistrates, it was different among the people at large, and especially with those who crowded the cathedral when he preached. These, if they became increasingly a party only of the whole inhabitants of the city, became also increasingly zealous for the objects which the Frate was endeavoring to promote. He seems at this time to have produced astonishing effects by his preaching. His hearers were influenced by the most powerful emotions as they listened to his words. The short-hand writer who reports these sermons sometimes had to cease writing. He leaves out portions of them, and explains that he was unable to go on for weeping. Men and women as they left the church tore off their ornaments and gave them as an offering to God, or took them to the magistrates for the use of the State.

Savonarola was oftentimes as powerfully moved as were his hearers. Sometimes after a sermon he was utterly prostrate, and forced to remain quiet and in seclusion. At the end of the Advent of 1494 he seemed inclined for a season to abstain from preaching; but the fire kept burning within him, as he told the people, and he was constrained to speak. In January he is again in the pulpit, preaching sermons on the Psalms, which were continued on holy days up to the beginning of Lent.

In one of these sermons, preached on the 13th of January, he gives a summary of his teaching on the reformation of the Church. It was evidently prepared with peculiar care, and was regarded as an important testimony as to the aims of the preacher; and it was printed immediately afterwards and circulated widely in Florence and elsewhere.[1] "Our intention this morning," he begins, "is to repeat all that we have said and preached at Florence these past years about the renovation of the Church; all which will soon be accomplished." This, he says, he will declare over again for the confirmation of those who have believed, and for the confusion of those who will not believe or repent.

After some remarks on the creature, on time and eternity, he says that God alone, and not even angels, can know the future; and "He communicates this

---

[1] I possess an original copy of this sermon. No reporter's name is mentioned, as is the case with another sermon published in the same manner; so that it may have been published by Savonarola himself. The title is: Predica di Frate Hieronimo da Ferrara della renovatione della chiesa facta in Sancta Maria del fiore in Firenze, adi. xiii. di Gennaio. MCCCCLXXXXIIIII. (1495, N. S.)

knowledge to whom He pleases, and to what extent and at what time He wills." Then he denounces the falseness of astrology, which pretends to have the knowledge of future events which are contingent. "Such pretensions," he says, "are equally opposed to philosophy and to faith. Prophets," he goes on, "have light from God; and He gives it to whom He will. And now you will say, 'Frate, whence have you learned the things which you have predicted for the last four years?'" At first, he says, they are not ready to receive the explanation; but at least they know he is not a madman, and that he does not excite himself without a reason. And he adds that a great part of the things which he predicted have already come to pass.

"And I tell you[1] that the rest will be verified, and not an iota of it will fail; and I am more certain of it than you are that two and two make four, more than I am certain that I touch this wood of this pulpit, because that light is more certain than the sense of touch. But I want you to know that this light does not justify men. Balaam was a prophet, and yet he was a sinner and a wicked man, although he had this light of prophecy. But I tell you, O Florence, that this light was given me for thee, and not for myself; for this light does not make a man acceptable to God. And I wish you to know that I began to see these things more than fifteen years ago, perhaps twenty. But I began to speak of them ten years ago. And first at Brescia, when I preached there, I began to say something. Then God permitted that I should come to Florence, which is the light of Italy, that you might spread the knowledge to all the other cities of Italy. But thou, Florence, hast heard with thine ears not me, but God.

1 Villari, who gives a careful analysis of this sermon, has followed the Latin translation.

The rest of Italy has heard of this only from the report of others ; and therefore thou, Florence, wilt have no excuse if thou repent not. Believe me, Florence, it is not I, it is God who says these things."

He then proceeds to repeat the reasons, such as he had often insisted upon before, " which demonstrate and prove the renovation of the Church." Some of them were probable, and might be contradicted ; some demonstrative, which could not be contradicted, because they were founded on Holy Scripture. He enumerates ten reasons, beginning with the " pollution of the prelates," saying that a good head gave promise of a good body ; but when the head was evil, the body was so also. The second was the removal of the good and righteous, by which God declared that He was bringing a scourge upon a nation. The third was the exclusion of the righteous by those in power. The fourth was the desire of the righteous. Then he mentions the obstinacy of sinners, the multitude of sinners. "See," he says, "if Rome is full of pride, of luxury and avarice and simony." Then he speaks of the insolence of the great, the want of faith, the neglect of public worship ; and finally, the universal opinion. Every one was expecting scourging and tribulations ; and every one thought it just that the punishment of so great iniquities should come. "The Abbot Joachino and many others preach and announce that a great scourge is to come in this time. These," he adds, " are the reasons for which I have preached the renovation of the Church."

After illustrating his theme by a figurative interpretation of Scripture, he proceeds to speak of the signs by which we may know of the approach of these events. There are two, he says. First, exterior signs ; and he confesses that he was mistaken in thinking the death of Pope Innocent one of these signs, — evidently meaning that the accession of Alexander VI. could hardly be the beginning of the renovation of the Church. Then there is a second class of signs, — that given to the imagination ; by which he indicates visions and the like.

"I saw by imagination," he says, "a black cross over Babylon, which is Rome, on which cross was written the wrath of God ; " and then he refers to the vision of swords and weapons of war falling to the ground, of which we have heard. And there was another cross of gold, on which was written the mercy of God. And he saw a sword hanging over Italy and descending upon it ; and this sword, he said, represented the king of France, who was now showing himself to all Italy. And then he reminds them of all the words of warning which he had spoken, and how many of them had been verified.

"Believe me, then, Florence," he exclaims ; "and thou oughtest to believe me, because of that which I have said. Thou hast not seen one iota fail until now ; and for the future thou wilt see nothing fail. I predicted, several years before, the death of Lorenzo de' Medici, the death of Pope Innocent, also that which has now happened at Florence, — the change in the State. I have not said all these things publicly ; but I have said them to those who are here at this sermon, and I have the witnesses here, O Florence ! And this light was not given to me for myself, or for my merit ; but for thee, O Florence, it has been given to me. And I have said these things to thee this morning thus openly, — this morning inspired by God that I should say them to thee, so that thou mightest know the whole, and that thou mightest have no excuse when the scourge shall come, and shouldst not be able to say, ' I did not know it.'

I could not say it more clearly to thee. Yet I know that this morning I shall be thought a madman."

In conclusion he says : —

"I warn you that already Italy is near the beginning of her tribulations. O Italy, O princes of Italy, O prelates of the Church, the wrath of God is upon you! and you have no remedy unless you repent. O Italy, O Florence, for thy sins these trials are coming upon thee! Repent while the sword is yet unsheathed, while it is not yet stained with blood. The conclusion is this : I have told thee all these things, with reasons divine and human, with moderation, restraining my language. I have besought thee. I cannot command thee, because I am not thy master, but thy father. Do thou act, O Florence! I can only pray that God may enlighten thee."

Already the enemies of the Frate were becoming alarmed at the influence of his words, and tried to have him sent to preach elsewhere. At first Pope Alexander gave an order to this effect; but afterwards recalled it, so that Savonarola prepared to preach the sermons in Lent. He chose as his subject the Book of Job. Although these sermons have come down to us in a very imperfect condition, we can see that he abstained as much as possible from allusions to politics, and devoted his attention to those matters which he had most at heart, — the reformation of the people, holy living, the union and harmony of the citizens. Even when he touches upon liberty, it is with a moral rather than a political bearing.

"The true, the only liberty," he says, "consists in willing that which is good. The good religious may seem to you not to be free, because he has subjected his will to that of another; but he has greater liberty than those who are in the world, because it is his rule to do that which others command. What liberty is there where men are ruled by the passions? And now to our point. Florence, wilt thou have liberty? Citizens, will ye be free? First love God, love your neighbor, love one another, love the common good. If you have this love and this union among yourselves, you will have true liberty."

In commending to the people the practice of piety, Savonarola made great use of the visions which he had seen, as he did when warning them of the coming scourge and predicting the renovation of the Church. We do not propose to discuss either the visions or the gift of prophecy which Savonarola appeared sometimes to claim, sometimes to disown. With regard to this apparent contradiction in his professions and claims, the solution seems easier than has generally been perceived. Savonarola evidently employed the phrase that he was "no prophet," nor "prophet's son," very much in the sense used by the prophet Amos. Probably he went farther, and meant that he had no distinct prophetic mission, — that he was not especially appointed to do the work of a prophet, like Saint John Baptist, for example. But it is quite clear that he laid claim to prophetic light. He constantly asserted that God had shown him the future; and it would be utterly absurd to question the sincerity of his pretensions. It will hardly be denied either that Savonarola did, in the most remarkable manner, forecast the future, — sometimes, it is true, by the force of his genius and by his penetrating insight into the imaginations of man's heart and into the state of the world in his own days; sometimes, also, in a manner which cannot be explained on these principles. It is useless to discuss the question whether these supposed revelations were happy guesses or strange coincidences, or whether God did actually make known to his servant some of those things which were coming upon the earth. How far men may be, in an exalted spiritual condition, made aware of the secrets of the invisible world, we cannot tell. Those who think most deeply on such questions will probably be the most backward to pronounce dogmatically on the subject. What the boundary line may be which separates a state of spiritual elevation from a state of ecstasy, which divides our ordinary experience of heavenly things from a direct intuition of the spiritual world, no wise man will attempt to determine. Of one thing we have no doubt, — that is, of the absolute sincerity of Savonarola, and, to use his own language, we know that he was not a madman. Beyond this we cannot pronounce, because we do not know.

One of the most curious instances of his dealing with the invisible was his offer to act on behalf of his hearers as an ambassador to Jesus Christ and to the Blessed Virgin. In the sermons of Lent, 1495, he relates conversations which he had with our Lord when engaged in this embassy. These communications he employs to enforce his teachings on the subject of unity. " Observe all nature," he represents our Lord as saying, "and thou wilt observe that every creature desires its own unity; every being seeks this, except the people of Florence, which wishes only for separation and division."

Speaking on the subject of good living, he again represents our Lord as saying, —

" Good is, of its own nature, diffusive; and therefore I, who am the Supreme Good, diffuse Myself in creation, and I have given being to all creatures, so that every good

which is in them is a participation of My goodness. For
this I came down among men, was made man, and died
upon the cross. This, then, will be the sign by which it
will be known who is good. When any one diffuses his
goodness among others, and makes them partakers of that
good which he has in himself, then he is truly good and
participates in My goodness. . . . Christian life," he goes
on, "does not consist in ceremonies, but in being good;
and he who is good cannot refrain from showing his goodness. . . . And in this consists the Christian religion,
which is founded in love and charity."

Those who read such reports of these sermons as
have been preserved to us will form but a slight notion
of the power which was contained in them, or the
effects which they produced. Savonarola spoke with
all the energy of his nature, soul and heart going forth
in the vehemence of his utterances, and every power
of body and mind tasked to the uttermost. He felt
that he was a witness for God in the midst of a world
which was lying in wickedness. He knew that he was
the chief guide of the deliberations of the citizens in
matters which might affect the well-being of Florence
for many years to come. He was living in times of
constant change and perplexity, when each day was
bringing forth new problems which were clamoring for
solution. He was aware that there were parties in the
State eager to seize every opportunity which might
offer itself in order to secure the success of their own
selfish designs and frustrate his benevolent efforts for
the common good. Yet none of these things moved
him. Exhausted in body and mind, he sought for
momentary repose, only to return with fresh energy
to the conflict. From the pulpit of Santa Maria del

Fiore he hurled forth his thunderbolts against every form of iniquity, secure in the consciousness of his own integrity, which he saw reflected in the convictions of his hearers. When he concluded his course of sermons on Easter Day, the reporter could not go on to the end. He was forced to add: "Such sorrow and weeping came upon me that I could go no farther." We may judge what was felt by those whose whole attention was fastened upon the preacher, his words, his tones, his gestures.

But it was not only in the momentary impression produced by his sermons that their effect was perceived. The aspect of the whole city seemed to be changed. The luxuries and indecent costumes which he had so indignantly denounced disappeared from the streets and the homes of Florence. Hymns were heard everywhere in place of the Carnival songs which had formerly been popular. Workmen devoted their leisure hours to reading the Bible and religious books. The neglect of public worship, which he had mentioned as one of the signs of the approaching scourge, no longer existed. The churches were crowded. Prayer and almsgiving seemed to be universal. Men of business were led to restore sums of money which they had unjustly acquired. Abstinence was practised to such an extent that it was thought disgraceful to sell meat on days of fasting. Schools and shops were closed during the time of preaching.

The effects of this spreading religious enthusiasm were seen in the convent of which Savonarola was the head. St. Mark's could no longer contain the candidates for admission into the fraternity. From fifty the numbers had risen to more than two hundred. It became necessary to add a neighboring building to the convent. Young men of the best families in Florence fled from the world and took refuge in St. Mark's, besides men of mature age, distinguished in literature, in science, and in the administration of public affairs. It was at this time that Savonarola was joined by a young convert named Bettuccio, afterwards known as Frà Benedetto, who was in after years to become the biographer of his superior.[1] He gives an account of his reception into the Dominican order which is interesting as illustrating Savonarola's manner of dealing with such cases. The father of Bettuccio was a goldsmith. He was himself a miniature-painter in the flower of his youth, and addicted to all the prevailing pleasures and amusements of his age and time. When he heard of the fame of the Frate, he at first refused to go with the multitude that crowded around the cathedral pulpit. On one occasion a noble lady spoke to him with enthusiasm of the preaching of Savonarola, which at first only excited his derision. At last he was induced to go to the church; but he was inclined to leave at once when he marked the astonishment caused by his unexpected presence in the congregation. When the preacher began to speak he was unable to withdraw his eyes from his countenance. The word of God spoken by the Frate took possession of him; and then, he says, he knew that he was "more dead than alive."

When the young painter left the church he went away by himself to think over what he had heard. He returned to his home a changed man. Old pleasures and habits and associates were at once forsaken. It

[1] We have heard of him as the author of the Cedrus Libani and the Volnera Diligentis.

was no easy matter for such a one to shake off his old
friends. They jested at him, treating his new feelings
as a passing frenzy which could not endure. But he
persevered. At first he did not venture into the awful
presence of the preacher who had so deeply moved
him; but he was constantly to be seen at the public
worship of St. Mark's. At last he went and cast himself at the feet of Savonarola; but even then he could
hardly utter what was filling his heart and mind. He
told him, however, that he wished to enter the convent.
Savonarola did not fail to speak to him of the danger
of a hasty decision, of the trials and difficulties of a
religious life, and advised him to think well of the matter, and to know more perfectly his real mind before
he took such a step. He counselled him also to live
first a Christian life in the world before he entered the
convent. The counsel, he tells us, was not unneeded.
He had ample experience of the conflict involved in
passing from the bondage of the world to the service
of God during that period of probation. He fell, he
repented, he showed his sincerity by his devotion, he
conquered his besetting sins; and then he returned
and asked to be received into the brotherhood. But
still Savonarola delayed to grant the boon. He was
appointed to assist the sick and to bury the dead, while
he received frequent instructions on the monastic life.
At last, on the 7th of November, 1495, he assumed
the habit, and on the 13th of November in the following year he took the vows under the name of Frà Benedetto. It was an evident proof that the numbers of the
brethren of St. Mark's had not been swelled by the
inconsiderate admission of all applicants. They were
not all destined to prove faithful to their great superior;

but it was through no fault of his that any of them entered upon a profession which they had not sufficient devotion to sustain.

It was not wonderful if Savonarola dreamed of a return to those earlier and better days for which he had so often longed, and of which he so frequently spoke. If he proposed to his disciples a standard of life which it was, humanly speaking, impossible to maintain, he had not only his own example to show, but the lives of many whom he had drawn from the service of sin. For the time at least, it seemed as though the success of the political revolution which he had guided with such ability was to be equalled by the reformation of life and manners which had been wrought by his preaching and his example.

CHAPTER XII.

DIVISIONS.

IT has been remarked that the highest order of mind has seldom been destitute of a sense of humor; and the statement has been illustrated by some of the greatest names recorded in history, ranging from Socrates to Shakespeare, and appearing in every age of the world. It is, however, equally true that the deepest thinkers and the most earnest workers have had some touch of that melancholic temperament which leads men to take desponding views of human life and to regard the most brilliant success with a feeling of distrust. When men of a less powerful build have been intoxicated with the triumph of the moment, the man of most profound and comprehensive thought has already begun to discern the signs of incompleteness and the approach of reverses and of failure.

Thus it was with Girolamo Savonarola in the midst of successes which have seldom, perhaps never, been attained in the civil reform of a State by one whose days had been spent in retirement and in preaching. While Florence was rejoicing in her newly restored liberty and in her well-ordered constitution, and lauding to the skies the man by whose exertions they had been secured, his mind, wearied by the burden it had borne, and discerning the presence of dangerous elements in the State, was oppressed by a profound sadness, mingled with the most gloomy apprehensions. "I am weary, O Florence," he exclaims at this time, "with four years of continual preaching, in which I have done nothing but labor for thee! Besides, I have been afflicted by the continual remembrance of the scourge which I have seen approaching, and the fear lest it should endanger thy safety. For this cause I have made continual prayers on thy behalf to the Lord." He had never promised that the people should continue to enjoy their new-found prosperity and happiness but on condition of their repentence; and he could not shut his eyes to the existence of evils of all kinds which abounded among the people. More particularly he must have seen, in the discussion of the "Law of the Six Beans," that there were many of the upper class who were not disposed frankly to accept the guarantees which he was endeavoring to provide for the continuance of a rational liberty, and who were ready to use the ignorance and inexperience of the multitude as a means of retaining the real power of government in their own hands.

He did not conceal from himself that his own position was one of imminent danger, nor did he hesitate to express these convictions in his public preaching. One of the most touching references to his position was given under the form of a parable. "A young man," he said, in a sermon belonging to the course which he preached on the prophet Haggai, [1] —

"A young man, leaving his home, launched forth into the sea to fish; and the master of the ship took him out into the high seas, where there was no harbor to be seen; so that the youth began loudly to bewail himself. O Flo-

[1] Advent, 1494.

rence, that youth who thus laments is in this pulpit! I
was led from my home to the harbor of the religious life,
when I entered the age of twenty-three years, solely to
obtain liberty and peace, — two things which I loved above
everything else. But there I beheld the waters of this
world, and I began to preach in the hope of winning souls;
and while there I found pleasure, the Lord brought me
down into the sea, and sent me forth into the high seas,
where I am now, and whence I no longer behold the harbor.
In all directions there are difficulties. Before my eyes I see
tribulation and tempests appearing; behind me the harbor
is lost, and the wind drives me forth into the deep. On the
right hand are the elect who are asking for aid; on the left,
evil spirits and evil men who molest and trouble us; above
I behold Eternal Virtue, and hope urges me on; beneath is
hell, which, as a man, I must fear, because without the help
of God I should certainly fall. O Lord, whither hast Thou
led me? From my desire to save souls for Thee, I am
come into a place from which I can no longer return to my
rest. Why hast Thou made me 'a man of strife and a man
of contention to the whole earth?' I was free, and now I
am the servant of all. I see in all directions war and discord coming upon me. You, at least, my friends, the chosen
of God, for whom I afflict myself day and night, do you
have pity upon me. Give me flowers, as the canticle says,
'for I am sick of love.' The flowers that I ask for are good
works; and I desire nothing else of you but that you please
God and save your souls."

Throughout the whole time of which we have spoken
in the two previous chapters, he was sensible of the
danger to which he was exposed. Speaking of the
reward of heaven and that of earth, he asks, —

"But what, O Lord, shall be the reward granted in the
other life to him who is victorious in battle? A thing which
the eye cannot see, which the ear cannot hear, — eternal

blessedness. And what the reward granted in this life?
'The servant shall not be greater than his master,' answers
the Lord. 'Thou knowest that after preaching I was cruci-
fied; so martyrdom will befall thee also.' O Lord, Lord,
grant me, I pray Thee, this martyrdom, and make me ready
to die for Thee, as Thou hast died for me! Already the
knife is sharpened for me. But the Lord tells me, 'Wait
yet for a little while, so that the things may come which
have to follow; and then thou wilt use that strength of
mind which shall be given thee.'"

It was certainly very remarkable that in these days,
in which he was the ruling mind of Florence, when
everything was being ordered in the State according to
his will, and the moral change already described was
being brought about, he should have such presentiments
with regard to his own future history. These forebod-
ings, however, can hardly be reckoned among the evidences of his possession of prophetic light. He knew
too well what was in man, — he knew too well the state
of men's minds in Florence, — to feel confidence in the
abiding loyalty of this seemingly enthusiastic and devoted
people; and he knew that the seeds of their ancient civil
discords were not dead, but only waiting for the occasion
on which they might burst forth into fresh life, and bear
their evil fruits of division, enmity, and persecution.
It will need no ordinary attention to understand the
strange combinations of the various parties in Florence,
which were brought about by the ever-changing circumstances of the republic, as each saw an opportunity of
advancing its own views or interests; but there is no
great difficulty in distinguishing the parties themselves or
the banners under which they were ranged. Foremost
among these parties were those who were called the

Arrabbiati (the madmen, the furious party), on account
of their furious antagonism to Savonarola and his policy.
The leaders of this party belonged principally to the
upper and more wealthy classes, and to the ancient
nobility of Florence. They were in favor of an aristocratic or oligarchic government such as Florence had,
at different times, possessed in its earlier days, and were
utterly opposed to every form of popular or democratic
government. From the very beginning of Savonarola's
reforms they had offered a persistent opposition to his
proposals ; and in one case, already described, they had
prevented his views from being accepted. They had
no love for the Medici, since they regarded them as
the destroyers of the aristocracy ; but common adversity
and a common opposition to what we should call constitutional principles made them frequent allies. If they
were not a numerous body in the State, their wealth
and position gave them influence ; and they had no
scruple in using for their purposes the mob whom they
abhorred and despised. Additional strength was given
to their party by the support which they received from
rulers like the Duke of Milan, who saw in the popular
revolution of Florence an event which might be used as
an example in their own States.

At the opposite extreme from the Arrabbiati stood
the *Bianchi* (the Whites, — what we should call " Red
Republicans "), or extreme democratic party, — mere
levellers, who would have governed the city by the
simple force of numbers, and therefore were opposed
to the exclusive policy on which Savonarola had proposed to form the greater council, and in accordance
with which it was finally constituted. They were not a
numerous party, and they were in a measure conciliated

by the efforts of the Frate to obtain for the republic the reality of liberty, even when he would not adopt their method. But no great reliance could be placed upon them. They gave to the moderate democracy of Savonarola a support the same in kind, but not so intelligent, as that which the republican Garibaldi gave to the constitutional monarchy of Victor Emmanuel. They were always ready to listen to proposals for sweeping changes ; and still worse, they were only too likely to be made the tools of the aristocratic party when these thought they could carry their ends by a pretence of consideration for the multitude. This actually happened in the " Law of the Six Beans."

Sometimes apart from, sometimes in union with, these two sections stood a party far more dangerous, both from its numbers and from the secrecy with which its proceedings were conducted. This was the party of the Medici, known as the *Bigi*, or Grays. When the Medici were driven from Florence, some of their friends were banished, some disappeared, and their adherents seemed to have vanished from the State. It was owing to Savonarola that the partisans of the fallen family had been included in the amnesty granted to political offenders ; and they repaid his generosity by continually plotting against the peace of the city and the influence of their benefactor. The Frate was aware of their designs. He knew that they were constantly planning the recall of Piero de' Medici, and he warned the people that there were those among them who were plotting to overthrow their liberty and to restore a despotism ; but they were so well satisfied with the changes which had been effected that they put down these warnings to an excess of zeal.

The only pronounced and open enemies of Savonarola and the *Frateschi*, by which name the adherents of the Frate were known, were the Arrabbiati. By them the followers of Savonarola were nicknamed *Piagnoni* (weepers, or mourners). It is a circumstance not without significance that, in the days in which Florence was preparing again to fall into the hands of the Medici, these two parties became united as the supporters of popular government against the pretensions of their ancient tyrants. At the time of their origin the Arrabbiati adopted a policy somewhat different. Pretending to accept the new popular government, while they were ever waiting for an opportunity of overthrowing it, they concentrated the energy of their hatred and opposition against Savonarola himself, thus hoping to gain the support of the Bigi and the Bianchi. The scheme proved only too successful, as subsequent events will show.

There were naturally subdivisions of these parties, of which we shall hear in the course of our narrative ; and there was a large class, called by Savonarola *I Tiepidi* (the lukewarm), who stood aloof, indifferent to the questions, religious or political, which were moving the republic at large.

By a kind of accident Filippo Corbizzi, a declared enemy of Savonarola and an opponent of popular government, was elected *gonfaloniere.* It was while the *Accoppiatori* were still in power, and were unable to agree upon a candidate. To put an end to the strife they decided to elect that one who should have most votes. Of the twenty electors, only three had voted for him ; but it was the largest number, and he was chosen. The new *gonfaloniere* was a mere tool in the hands of the aristocratic party, to whom he owed his elevation.

Soon after his accession to office he convoked in the Palazzo a council of theologians, consisting of abbots, priors, and canons of San Lorenzo and of the cathedral. Among those present was Marsilio Ficino, an admirer of the preaching of Savonarola, but a partisan of the Medici. As soon as they were assembled, the *gonfaloniere* explained to them that he had to complain of Savonarola for interfering in the affairs of the State, and he counted on the assistance of those who were present in his endeavor to obtain from the Frate an explanation of his conduct.

Savonarola, who had heard nothing of the meeting, at this moment entered, and was assailed by a number of those present as a disturber of the public peace. Foremost among his assailants was a certain friar[1] belonging to his own order, a member of the rival convent of Santa Maria Novella. This man had a great reputation for theological learning, and from the smallness of his stature and his subtlety in argument was surnamed *Il Garofanino* (the little Pink). He selected as a text for his remarks the words of Saint Paul, *Nemo militans Deo implicat se negotiis secularibus* (the Vulgate rendering of 2 Tim. ii. 4, "No man that warreth entangleth himself with the affairs of this life;" and that version was even more suited to his purpose than either the original Greek or our own English translation). Starting from these words, he proceeded to pour out a torrent of invectives against Savonarola for meddling with matters which did not belong to his sacred vocation.

The Frate waited patiently for the end of this ha-

[1] Named by some Frà Giovanni Carlo; in the English translation of Villari's new edition Tommaso da Rieti.

rangue, and then, standing up, he made a very calm reply to his accuser.

" In me," he said, " is fulfilled that saying of the Lord, *Filii matris meæ pugnaverunt contra me*, — ' My mother's children were angry with me;'[1] yet it grieves me to see that my fiercest opponent wears the same habit of Saint Dominic. That habit should remind him that our founder involved himself not a little in the things of this world; that from our order has gone forth a multitude of religious and of saints who have concerned themselves in the doings of the State. Will the republic of Florence remember the Cardinal Latino, Saint Peter Martyr, Saint Katharine of Siena, Saint Antonino, who all belonged to the order of Saint Dominic? It is not concerning ourselves with the doings of this world, in which God has placed us, which is to be condemned in a religious, but it is doing so without having regard to a higher end, without an eye to the good of religion."

He then challenged those present to quote a single passage which condemned the supporting of a free government in order to secure a greater triumph for religion and morality. " You will easily find," he added, "that religion should not be treated of in profane places, or theology discussed in a palace."
There was no reply ready to this defence, and they do not seem to have attempted it. By way of assailing him on a side which they thought more vulnerable, they asked him: "Well, then, tell us distinctly, do your words truly come from God, or not, that we may know whether we ought to believe you." Savonarola was contented to give back the answer of our Lord, and probably for the same reason, " *Ego palam locutus sum*

---

[1] Cant. i. 6.

mundo; . . . et in occulto locutus sum nihil, — ' I spake openly to the world ; . . . and in secret have I said nothing ; '[1] and now I have no more to add." And so the assembly broke up, little contented with the result, but unable to obtain more satisfaction. They had only added to the influence of the man whom they would willingly have crushed.

This singular gathering must have been held about the same time that Savonarola preached the remarkable sermon on the 13th January of which we have given a full account. One thing is quite clear,—that it produced little difference in his manner of preaching. In the following season of Lent, as we have seen, he restricted himself principally to religious subjects, — probably on account of the efforts made by his enemies to induce the Pope to put a stop to his preaching in Florence ; but during the interval between Advent and Lent he still recommended the people to persist . in the formation of the new government, entreating them to cultivate charity, union, and peace.

The time had not yet come for the Pope's interference. Savonarola had powerful friends at this time in Italy. The French were still at Naples ; and the Pope, although he was induced at first to send an order to the Frate to preach during Lent at Lucca, was afterwards led to withdraw his brief. He had heard of the visions and prophecies of a Dominican friar at Florence, and he knew that he was an object of dislike to a section of the population ; but Alexander also knew that his withdrawal from Florence would produce the greatest indignation in the city, and he was not prepared to excite the enmity of King Charles.

[1] St. John xviii. 20.

It was inevitable that Savonarola's sentiment of obedience should receive a shock from this conduct of the
supreme Pontiff.   It would have been a great trial to
leave Florence at such a moment, but he was prepared
to submit.   It is probable that he afterwards thought
less of papal briefs when he found how lightly they
were given and recalled by the Pope himself.   He
could not help knowing that the order was originally
issued to gratify his enemies ; and he must have guessed
that it was withdrawn from no more worthy motive.

CHAPTER XIII.

THE DEPARTURE OF THE FRENCH.

THE success which had attended the French on their first invasion of Italy accompanied them throughout their expedition. They reached Naples without having encountered any serious obstacle on the way. King Alfonso had fled, and the French rule had been established to the apparent satisfaction of the people at large. But it was not long before the Neapolitans grew weary of their new masters. They soon made it clear that they had not come to reform the government, but to plunder the inhabitants for their own benefit. At the same time, the alarm produced by the facility with which the invaders had traversed the whole country began to spread among all the princes of Italy. Those who had been the foremost to invite them, like Lodovico il Moro, now shared in these feelings of alarm; and he who had welcomed them as friends now proceeded to form a league of the Italian powers for the " expulsion of the barbarians " from the country.

The League was formed under the pretext of defending the country against the Turks; and it was signed at Venice on the 31st of March, 1495, the Pope, the Emperor, the King of Spain, and the republic of Venice entering into alliance with the Duke of Milan. Its true design, however, was immediately discerned

by the shrewdness of the French ambassador, De
Commines, who was still at Venice; and on the very
day of the signing of the treaty he wrote to his master
at Naples, informing him of the confederacy that had
been formed against him.   Burlamacchi relates that
King Charles, on receiving this intelligence, sent as
messenger to Savonarola a certain Messer Jacopo, to
ask whether there would be danger in his return to
France.   "Tell his Majesty, the most Christian king,"
replied the Frate, "that God has conferred upon him
many benefits, and has granted him to acquire so great
a kingdom without any difficulty; and although since
then he has committed many sins, God will not fail
him, and he need have no doubts as to his enemies,
for he will return with victory into his own kingdom
of France."

It has been suggested that this Messer Jacopo was
no other than Philippe de Commines, who after having
written to warn the king of the League formed against
him, had at once set out for Naples.   On his way to
join the king, he tells us that as he passed through
Florence he went to pay a visit to Frère Hieronyme,
who was reported to be a man of very holy life; and
he did so because the friar had spoken in favor of the
king, and had prevented the Florentines from rising
against the French; "for never any preacher had so
much authority in a city."

"He always affirmed that our king would come into Italy,
saying that he was sent by God to chastise the tyranny
of the princes, and that none would be able to oppose him.
He foretold likewise that he would come to Pisa and enter
it, and that the State of Florence should be dissolved on
that day.   And so it fell out, for Piero de' Medici was

driven out that very day. Many other things he presaged long before they came to pass; as, for instance, the death of Lorenzo de' Medici. And he openly declared that he knew it by revelation; as likewise he predicted that the reformation of the Church should be owing to the sword. This is not yet accomplished; but it very nearly occurred, and he still maintains that it shall come to pass.

"Many persons blamed him for pretending to receive divine revelations, but others believed him; for my part, I think him a good man. I asked him whether our king would return safe into France, considering the great preparations of the Venetians against him; of which he gave a better account than I could, though I had lately come from Venice. He told me that the king would meet with some difficulties by the way, but he could overcome them all with honor, though he had but a hundred men in his company; for God, who had conducted him thither, would guard him back again. But because he had not applied himself as he ought to the reformation of the Church, and because he had permitted his soldiers to rob and plunder the poor people (as well those who had freely opened their gates to him as the enemy which had opposed him), therefore God had pronounced judgment against him, and in a short time he would receive chastisement.

"However, he bade me tell him that, if he would have compassion upon the people, and command his army to do them no wrong, and punish them when they did, as it was his office to do, God would then mitigate, if not revoke, his sentence; but that it would not be sufficient for him to plead that he did them no wrong himself. And he said that he would meet the king when he came, and tell him so from his own mouth; and so he did, and pressed hard for 'the restitution of the Florentine towns. When he mentioned the sentence of God against him, the death of the dauphin came very fresh into my mind, for I knew nothing else that would touch the king so sensibly. This I have thought it fit to record, to make it the more manifest that this whole expedition was a mystery conducted by God Himself." [1]

This testimony is valuable, not only as furnishing us with the judgment of one who was a keen observer of his fellow-men and an experienced man of the world, but also from its entire agreement with all that we learn of Savonarola, his words and his tone, from other trustworthy sources. The man who thus addresses the ambassador of France, and who assumes no different attitude towards his master, the king himself, is the same man of whom we read in the pages of his contemporaneous biographers, and who speaks to us from the pulpit of the cathedral church of Florence.

The king did not wait for the arrival of Commines; he left Naples on the 20th of May (1495), leaving a strong garrison in the forts, and taking the rest of his army with him. On his way he visited Rome, intending to have an interview with the Pope; but Alexander had left the city and had fled to Orvieto. Continuing his march, he reached Siena on the 13th of June. The Florentines had lost all faith in King Charles and the French. They would not enter into alliance with their enemies, but they dreaded equally their friendship and their enmity. They were already discovering what Machiavelli was shortly to write of the French, that they were quite ready to make promises which they had not the power to fulfil, but that they never fulfilled those which they were able to keep. The king had promised that he would restore the fortresses which Piero de' Medici had delivered into his hands, as soon as he should get possession of Naples; but they were still

---

[1] Book viii. c. 3. Bohn's translation, vol. ii. pp. 190, 191.

garrisoned by his soldiers. The Florentines had re-monstrated with him on this breach of faith, and they had endeavored to recover Pisa by force of arms; but the Pisans received reinforcements from different parts of Italy, and even, it was said, from the French king himself. The only answer he returned to the remon-strances of the Florentines was this: "But what can I do if your Signori make all their subjects discontented with them?"

When the news reached Florence that the French had entered the territories of the republic and that Piero de' Medici was with them, the wrath and terror of the citizens knew no bounds. It was generally be-lieved that the king intended to restore the hated ty-ranny from which they had escaped. All ages and classes flew to arms, and they hastened to put the city in a state of defence. Piagnoni and Arrabbiati joined in arms, in counsel, and in prayers. The city was given up to religious exercises; and the Frate had to com-plain that some were willing to join in their prayers, but neglected to take up arms. "Offer prayer," he cried from the pulpit, "but do not neglect human precautions. We must help ourselves in every way, by every means, and then the Lord will be with us. Courage, my breth-ren, and above all things union. If you remain united and agreed in one will, even if the whole world were against us, the victory will be ours."

When the Florentines sent ambassadors to the king, asking by what route he intended to march, that they might furnish provisions, he only replied: "Provide the whole country." It was impossible that the meeting should be a friendly one when the French saw the Flo-rentines flying to arms at their approach, and the ambassadors of the State found Piero de' Medici in the camp of the king.

It was then that the citizens, as in all their most hopeless perplexities, turned to Savonarola. They knew that Charles had listened respectfully to him at Pisa when he would hardly give an audience to their ambassadors. They remembered that it was by the persuasion of the Frate that he had led his army out of Florence. By an accident a letter of his, written to King Charles, fell into the hands of his enemies, and disclosed the fact that he was carrying on a correspondence with him. But although the letter was garbled in its publication, and was actually published in order to incite the Venetian League against Savonarola, it served only to increase the esteem in which he was held by his fellow-citizens. It was couched in the same bold and imperious language which he had employed at the interviews, — the same which, as a prophet of righteousness proclaiming the will of God, he ever felt that he had a right to use.

" Most Christian Sire," he said, " the Lord wills that the Florentines should remain in alliance with your Majesty; but He also wills that, under your protection, their liberties should be confirmed, and not the authority of any particular citizen, — because the Divine Goodness has determined everywhere to put down despotism. The Lord will punish terribly those private citizens who shall wish to usurp dominion in this flourishing republic, as it has been in the past; because this new and popular government and administration has been appointed by God, and not by any man, and because He has chosen this city, and will magnify it, and replenish it with His own servants; and he who touches it, touches the apple of His eye. Wherefore, O Sire, if you will not obey, and will not maintain your promises to the Florentines, and will not restore their fortresses, many will be the adversities which will come upon you, and the people will rebel against you."

The same language which he had used in his letters he did not hesitate to employ when he again met the king face to face at Poggibonsi. Savonarola reminded him that he was now returning home, almost a fugitive; and that he had brought these misfortunes upon himself, as his monitor had predicted that he would, if he refused to accomplish the work for which God had brought him into Italy.

"Most Christian Prince," he said, "thou hast provoked the anger of the Lord by not having maintained thy faith to the Florentines; by having abandoned that reform of the Church which the Lord had so often through me announced to thee, and to which He had chosen thee by such manifest signs. For this time thou wilt escape from these dangers; but if thou resume not the work which thou hast abandoned, if thou obey not the commands repeated anew to thee by His unworthy servant, I announce to thee that still greater will be the adversities which the wrath of God will send upon thee, and another will be chosen in thy place."

The king was deeply impressed by this bold language, and by the tone in which it was uttered; and requested that Savonarola would accompany him to Pisa, whither he now conducted his army. Savonarola, however, after a second interview at Castel Fiorentino, returned home; and from the pulpit he announced, on the 21st of June, that for this time the danger was over, and took occasion again to entreat the people to be diligent in prayer and holy living, to cherish union, and to preserve the popular government.

The Pisans received the king with every demonstra-

tion of joy. After doing their best to conciliate him and
his followers by costly presents, a number of the most
beautiful women of the city came to him one day clothed
in mourning, with their hair dishevelled, their feet bare,
and ropes round their necks, representing the bondage
and misery in which they were held by Florence; and
implored him to restore their liberty. Such a request,
however reasonable in itself, it was not in the power of
the king to grant. He had contracted to restore Pisa
to the Florentines. To this engagement he had added
most solemnly his own kingly word; but we have seen
enough of his character to know how lightly he would
hold any such promises. It was a strange way that he
took of at once setting at nought the sentiments of compassion which the entreaties of the Pisan women had
awakened, and of breaking his engagements with Florence. He neither gave Pisa liberty nor restored the
fortresses to Florence, but leaving garrisons behind
him, he took his way to France. The whole expedition
was productive only of evil. The French had disgusted
their allies, they had disappointed their most moderate
hopes, and had simply left an ineradicable impression of
their own selfishness, rapacity, and faithlessness. The
king pretended that he had given orders for the surrender of the fortresses to Forence; and it is said that
in the month of September following, he sent an express
command that they should be delivered up. Whether
he at the same time sent private orders to the contrary,
or whether his generals knew that they might safely disregard the instructions they had received, the result was
the same. In January, 1496, the generals sold the
fortress of Pisa to the citizens; those of Sarzana and
Sarzanello to the Genoese; that of Pietra Santa to the

Lucchese; to the Florentines only that of Leghorn was restored. The French king had disappointed the expectations of Savonarola, and had apparently shaken off the fears engendered by his solemn warnings. When both the king and the Frate were dead, Philippe de Commines remembered these things and wrote : —

"I am sure he foretold several things which afterwards came to pass, and which all his friends in Florence could never have suggested. And as to our master, and the evils with which he threatened him, they happened exactly as you have heard, — first the death of the Dauphin, and then his own death; predictions of which I have seen in letters under his own hand to the king." [1]

Deeply as Florence had suffered from the invasion of the French, it still had reason to fear the effects of their departure. Partly from old attachment, partly from fear, partly from the state of isolation into which it had fallen, the city remained faithful to its ancient allies. The Florentines now declared Charles to be "a man without honor or shame or prudence, — an assassin, a thief, who paid no regard to his promises, and was destitute of all morality and of every trace of religion; and his ministers the basest, the most greedy, and the most perfidious men that could be imagined." But the presence of the French had at least kept their other enemies at bay; and now that the League had no longer any reason to fear the invaders, they were able to turn their enmity against the Florentines. It has already been mentioned that the principal governments of Italy had resented the expulsion of the Medici, and regarded the newly formed constitution with great aversion. The Pope and the

[1] Book viii. c. 26.

Venetians were bent upon restoring Piero; but happily for the Florentines, Ludovico of Milan not only had a personal dislike to him, but cherished some hope of forming the whole of Northern Italy into a united kingdom. His support, therefore, although it was promised to the enterprise, was of a very uncertain and untrustworthy character.

The Florentines made energetic preparations to resist this new invasion of their recovered liberties. Savonarola, who had for a time abstained from preaching, in consequence of reports from Rome that he was becoming more and more distasteful to the Pope, now returned to the pulpit; and on the 11th of October his voice was again heard exhorting them to defend their constitution, and to neglect no means of repelling those who were now endeavoring to overthrow it.

When it was in any way possible to extend pardon and amnesty, even to those whom he regarded as traitors, Savonarola's voice was ever raised in favor of clemency and mercy; but when the interests of the commonwealth were at stake, when he saw that those who had been treated with excessive forbearance were only the more bent upon overthrowing the authority which had dealt so mercifully with them, he did not hesitate to counsel the strongest and severest measures that could be taken to avert the threatened danger. Speaking of the friends of the Medici, who were now plotting to restore the fallen despotism, he declared that the punishment which was their due was death.

"You must deal with them," he says, "as the Romans did with those who wished to bring back Tarquin. . . . Do justice, I tell you. . . . This great council is the work of God, and not of men; and whoever wishes to change it, whoever wishes to set up a tyrant, whoever wishes to make a government of private citizens, will be accursed of the Lord forever."

There was to be no mercy for such; whoever they were, they were to lose their heads.

The danger soon passed away. Piero collected money and troops, and advanced against the city with the intention of forcing an entrance; but the promised reinforcements did not arrive, and he was not able to begin the attack. The government of Florence, stirred up by the words of Savonarola, declared Piero de' Medici a rebel against the State, so that he might with impunity be put to death. And they further offered a reward of four thousand gold florins to whoever should kill Piero, and two thousand for the head of Giuliano de' Medici; and officers were appointed to administer their property for the benefit of the republic.

But they did not restrict themselves to mere threats. They suspended the war against Pisa, and sent an army into the field against Piero, who was still remaining inactive, expecting the assistance which the League had promised. At last, seeing that his present enterprise had become hopeless, he fled to Rome, where he strove to embitter the Pope against Florence and its teacher, and hatched new schemes for the repair of his broken fortunes.

CHAPTER XIV.

POPE ALEXANDER VI. AND SAVONAROLA.

IT is difficult to write the simple truth respecting the man who occupied the papal throne under the name of Alexander VI. without appearing to repeat the inventions of blinded prejudice and inveterate and reckless enmity. Yet the proved facts of his personal and official life are almost as bad as any hostile fabrications could be made ; and the very fables and legends which have gathered around his history are an evidence of the impression which he produced upon his own contemporaries.

As an instance of these stories, a writer of the period [1] gravely relates that the manner of his death was uncertain, some believing that he had been carried off by a demon, others that he was poisoned by wine which he or his son had prepared for one of his cardinals. The story of the poisoning is now discredited; but it shows us in what estimation his Holiness was held.

As we have here to do with his actions in relation to the subject of this memoir, rather than with his general character or history, a very few words must suffice on these points. Rodrigo Borgia belonged to a noble Spanish family. He came to Rome during the pontificate of his uncle, Calixtus III., and was by

[1] Pico della Mirandola the younger.

him made Archbishop of Valentia and cardinal before he was twenty-five years of age. Even those who take the worst view of his character do not deny that he was a man of very great ability, and that he attained to a certain kind of political influence, and even of popularity, among his own subjects. He had at least four sons and one daughter, — all illegitimate, of course ; but that was not thought much of in those days. He obtained the papal chair by bribing a majority of cardinals to vote for him. It is said that his countryman, King Ferdinand " the Catholic," wept when he heard that he was made Pope, and predicted the evils which would follow to the Church. Crimes of the most frightful character have been laid to his charge, and his vices have probably been exaggerated. But it is agreed on all sides that there has hardly ever been a Pope who did more to disgrace the papal chair. He was impure, treacherous, and guilty of the most open and unblushing simony. A Latin couplet of the period is not too severe : —

> " Vendit Alexander claves, altaria, Christum.
>   Emerat ille prius, vendere jure potest."

> " Alexander sells keys, altars, Christ.
>   He had first bought them : he has a right to sell them.

As the most monstrous characters in history have not been without their defenders, so it has been attempted to deny nearly all the more serious charges brought against Alexander ; but it is evident that it is with a sense of the arduousness of the task that his cause has been pleaded. One of the latest of those who have sought at least to mitigate the sentence of history confesses that he would have liked to close

the history of the Popes of the fifteenth century " with
a holy and more glorious figure than his ; " and adds,
" Say, if you please, that Alexander VI. dishonored
religion and humanity, we will not contradict you ; "[1]
only his is an exceptional character among the Popes.
It will be sufficient here to deal with those of his actions which belong to our history.

When the enemies of Savonarola first reported to
Pope Alexander the bold and censorious language
which the Frate was using with reference to the rulers
of Church and State, he was inclined to regard his
words as the utterances of a fanatic who might safely
be treated with contempt; and probably the reports
of the visions and prophecies of the Frate confirmed
him in this judgment. When, moreover, he considered
that the Florentine mystic was held in honor by the
French king, he saw the inexpediency of using harsh
measures against him while so powerful a friend was
still at Naples.

Shortly after the departure of the French, the enmity
against the Frate, kept in check by the dangers of the
republic and by the necessity for union among its parties, broke out afresh. The Arrabbiati, backed up
by Ludovico il Moro, sent to Rome reports of his sermons exaggerated and distorted. He was represented
as a seditious citizen, as a disloyal priest, as the enemy
of all authority and stable government. Refugees of
the Medicean party who had taken up their residence
at Rome denounced him as the author of all their misfortunes. His old opponent, Frà Mariano da Gennazzano, did not hesitate to declare that he was a heretic.

____

[1] Abbé Christophe, La Papauté pendant le quinzième Siècle,
ii. 580.

The Pope determined at length to put an end to the work of the Florentine preacher; but he thought it best first to try the effect of flattery.

"Beloved son," wrote his Holiness, "health (*salutem*) and apostolic benediction! We have heard by the testimony of many that, of all the laborers in the vineyard of the Lord of Sabaoth, thou art the most zealous. At which we greatly rejoice and give praises to Almighty God, who has bestowed such grace on a human being. Nor do we doubt that thou hast these things from the Divine Spirit, who distributes immortal graces, and that thou canst sow the word of God in a Christian people, and bring forth fruit an hundred-fold. . . . It has recently been related to us, also, that in thy public sermons thou dost assert that those things which thou dost announce concerning the future, thou speakest not of thyself or of human wisdom, but by divine revelation. Desiring, therefore, as belongs to our pastoral office, to speak with thee on these subjects, and to hear from thy mouth, that we may by thee attain to a better knowledge and practice of that which is pleasing to God, we exhort and command thee, in virtue of holy obedience, to come to us as soon as possible. We will see thee with paternal love and charity.— Rome, 21st July, 1495."

It is useless to waste words in discussing the sincerity of this document. The influences under which it had been produced were too well known in Florence for Savonarola to stand in doubt of it for a moment. Already the attempts upon his life had begun. Already his enemies had been heard to boast that they had secured the ear of the Pope. It was therefore clear to his friends that he could not with safety accept this affectionate invitation; and yet the Frate was far from being prepared to disobey the commands of the

Supreme Pontiff, whom he regarded as the Vicar of Jesus Christ.

Happily for Savonarola, he was able to plead that he was only recovering from a severe illness, caused by the excitement of those terrible days in which all his energies were needed for the guidance of his anxious and perplexed fellow-citizens. He resolved for a season to abstain from preaching, and to put his friend Frà Domenico Buonvicini, commonly known as Domenico da Pescia, in his place. On the 28th of July, therefore, he took his leave of the people, telling them that although for the moment he regained his strength when he ascended the pulpit, he was unable at present to continue his work. He repeated to them many of the lessons which he had so often inculcated, on the necessity of moral and religious renovation, telling them of the frightful vices which still prevailed in the city. He exhorted them to a more serious life, reminding them that a time of such dangers was not a time for festivals and dances. Then he spoke of the prophetic gift. Again he besought them to retain the form of government which they had established, and said that when his health was restored, he would preach to them again, although he believed he had shortened his life by his past efforts. "And now," he concludes, "you will ask, Frate, what reward do you expect for this? I expect martyrdom. I am content to endure it. I ask it of Thee, O Lord, every day, for love of this city!"

Three days later, he sent his answer to the Pope, beginning, "Most Blessed Father, after kissing thy blessed feet," and proceeding to set forth the duty of obedience and his own desire, long entertained, to visit

Rome. In spite of this, he says, he is forced to offer excuses for not at once complying with the Pope's command; and he quotes the language of Alexander IV. as showing the lawfulness of the course he is taking. As a reason for his inability to come to Rome, he urges the state of his health, weakened by unremitting toil of body and mind in behalf of the city, in consequence of which his physicians had advised him to abstain from preaching and study, otherwise his life might be in danger. He then proceeds to inform the Pope that his presence is still needed in Florence in consequence of the change in the government and the designs of the enemies of the State, which were peculiarly dangerous while the institutions of the republic were still in their infancy. So violent indeed were those enemies that they had tried to cut him off by poison or the sword, so that it was hardly safe for him to go into the city without guards.

He then goes on to express the hope that his Holiness would not be offended by a short delay, and he would endeavor, before long, to obey his command. If his Holiness wished in the mean time to become acquainted with what he had taught concerning the future, of the scourging of Italy and the renovation of the Church, he would find a full account of it in a book which he had just caused to be printed (*Compendium Revelationum*),[1] which he had put forth that the world might know that he was a false prophet if the things which he had predicted did not take place. " I beseech your Holiness," he concludes, " to accept my most sincere and open excuses, and to believe that

[1] Published in Italian (Compendio di Revelatione, etc.) soon after, — Sept. 1, 1495. I have used both editions.

there is nothing which I more earnestly desire than to render entire obedience." The Pope gave no answer to this letter; but as Savonarola afterwards stated that he had accepted his excuse, we may infer that this assurance was in some manner conveyed to him.

To his astonishment, during the period of his retirement a new brief was issued by the Pope, and this time directed to the Franciscans of Santa Croce, the enemies of Savonarola, speaking of him as "a certain Frà Girolamo," — the same man, be it observed, who had been addressed, not two months before, as his "beloved son," — denouncing him as a disseminator of false doctrine, and commanding him at once to appear in Rome. It was evident that this was intended as an expression of undisguised anger and enmity; but it was less easy to understand the sudden change of tone. It may be that the contents of the Compendium had inflamed the Pope's mind, but it is more probable that the change had been brought about by the machinations of the Medici; for it was at this time that Piero was carrying forward his attempt to regain possession of Florence. Instead of obeying the Pope's command, Savonarola reappeared in the pulpit and delivered those sermons already mentioned, in which he besought his fellow-citizens to resist the restoration of the Medicean despotism. The Pope issued another brief, forbidding him to preach. The Frate again withdrew from the pulpit, and the Advent Sermons at the cathedral were preached by Frà Domenico.

The charges now brought against Savonarola were the more serious, as giving an authoritative expression to the accusations of his enemies at home. But he knew that the charges of heresy were only a cloak to disguise the hatred excited by his political action. If he would have refrained from denouncing the vices of those who were in high places ; if he would have allowed, without interference, Bigi or Arrabbiati to have their own way in Florence ; if he would have suffered the overthrow of that civil liberty which, next to the moral and spiritual good of the people, he most ardently loved, — he might have held and taught what opinions he pleased. Although he consented, for the time, to observe the silence imposed by the papal brief, — and at this time he was resolved not to preach until he obtained permission from Rome, — he did not for a moment waver in his convictions, nor in his determination to give effect to them in every way that might seem possible and lawful.

It was about this time that an incident occurred which has been recorded by several writers. Burlamacchi relates that a terrible sermon preached by Savonarola had inflamed the anger of a number of private persons against the preacher. These persons were chiefly " lukewarm ecclesiastics, vicious men, usurers, gamblers, drunkards," and the like, and they had made their complaints heard at Rome. Whatever the immediate cause may have been, it is said that the Pope sent some of Savonarola's writings to a bishop of the Dominican order, with instructions to examine them, in order to find grounds for condemning the author as guilty of heresy. The bishop returned the compositions, giving his judgment that the utterances of the Frate were all good and wise, inasmuch as he spoke against simony and the corruption of the priests, which were undoubtedly very great. Such a man, he said, was to be treated as a friend, and not as an enemy, and he advised the Pope to make him a cardinal.

If the story were not confirmed by a multitude of contemporaneous testimonies, it might appear too improbable to be easily believed. The evidence, however, seems too strong to be resisted; and additional confirmation is found in various indirect references to the offer in the sermons of Savonarola. The Pope was a statesman of consummate ability, and acting on the theory that every man has his price, he probably saw in this measure a more easy and ready escape from his difficulties than by the more clumsy and violent method of persecution. A Dominican was accordingly despatched from Rome, empowered to offer Savonarola the red hat, on the condition that he would alter his style of preaching.

It was to Savonarola a shocking confirmation of all his worst impressions of the state of matters at the papal court. Already murmurs had been heard of the Pope having obtained his chair by simony. The Cardinal of San Pietro in Vincoli, the same who was in the way of denouncing his Holiness as a " scoundrel and a heretic," was meditating the calling of a council to try Alexander for this crime; and in that intention he was supported by some of the princes of Europe. Savonarola was probably beginning to have his mind familiarized with the same idea. And here he had tangible proof of the manner in which the offices of the Church were conferred so as to subserve the corrupt designs of the Roman court. He was so indignant at the offer that he only returned for answer: " Come to my next sermon, and you shall hear my reply to Rome."

As the time of this offer is not quite certain, we are unable to say what sermon of his was here referred to, nor do we know whether it has been preserved. In a sermon preached in the year 1496 he makes an evident allusion to the proposal : " I do not wish for hats, nor for mitres great or small. I wish only for that which Thou hast given to Thy saints, for death. A red hat — a hat red with blood — that is what I desire." At different times he is reported as saying, " If I had wished for dignities, you know well that I should not now be wearing this ragged cloak."

By the influence of "the Ten," — formerly known as the "Ten of War," but now called the "Ten of Liberty and Peace," — the Pope had been induced to withdraw his inhibition from Savonarola and to restore to him the liberty of preaching. In spite, therefore, of the machinations of his enemies, and of the constant attempts against his life, he determined this year (1496) to preach the Lent sermons in the cathedral.

The news of his reappearance in the pulpit after his long silence (from October, 1495, to February, 1496) produced the greatest excitement in Florence, and all possible precautions were taken by the magistrates to prevent disorders arising in the city. The crowds that assembled to hear the preacher were enormous ; and a new element appeared in the audience. This was a congregation of children, for whose accommodation a special gallery had been erected. During the time of his retirement, Savonarola had turned his attention to the instruction of those who, from their tender years, were more open to the reception of religious impressions. He was specially prompted to this undertaking by the excesses in which the children had been accustomed to indulge at the time of the Carnival. His efforts had such success that he organized large numbers of

children, formed them into guilds, and instructed them
to sing hymns instead of the songs which had formerly
been heard at that season; and instead of indulging
in mischievous and dangerous amusements, they now
employed themselves in collecting alms for the relief
of the poor.[1]

When the Frate appeared outside the convent on his
way to begin his Lent sermons (February 17, 1496), he
was greeted with loud shouts of joy by the populace;
and his enemies were held in check alike by the enthusiasm of his friends and the watchfulness of the government. It was one of the significant moments in his
history. Within a period of seven months he had been
addressed by Rome as one who was little short of a saint,
and denounced as a seditious person and a disseminator
of heresy; he had been inhibited from preaching by
the Pope, and the inhibition had been removed; and
all men were wondering in what strain he would break the
long and unwonted silence to which he had submitted.

He began his sermon with a dialogue, in which he
replied to imaginary questions respecting his absence
from the pulpit. Had he been afraid of death that he
had not preached? No; for in that case he would not
be here now, seeing that he was in greater peril of death
than before. Had he, then, had scruples of conscience
on the subject? Not he. But had not his doctrines
been condemned? Let it be supposed that it were so;
he had taken himself to task, as to his life, as to his
words, whether he had spoken unadvisedly or erroneously; but he could not find that he had done so, —

"Because I have always believed, and do believe, all
that the Holy Roman Church believes. I have written to

---

[1] It was known as the Riforma dei fanciulli.

Rome that if I have preached or written anything heretical, I am content to amend and recant here in public. I am always prepared to obey the Roman Church, and I say that he who does not obey will be damned. . . . I declare and confess that the Church will never fail even to the day of judgment; and that it may be clear what I mean, as there are various opinions as to what is the Catholic Church, I refer myself to Christ and to the decision of the Roman Church."

But, he goes on, it does not therefore follow that we are bound to obey every command of our superiors, or even of the Pope. A superior could not require obedience contrary to the constitution of his order. The Pope could have no right to give a command contrary to charity or to the Gospel. "I do not believe that the Pope will ever do so; but if he did, I should say to him, ' In this case thou art not pastor, thou art not the Roman Church, thou errest.'" If a superior should require anything contrary to the commandments of God, it would be wrong to comply, because it is written : "We ought to obey God rather than man." If there were the least doubt on the subject, however, it would be a duty to obey.

He then proceeds to consider his own case, and argues that if he should be commanded to depart from Florence, he should not be bound to obey, because it was well known that not only would such a command be the result of political hatred, but obedience would be injurious to liberty and to religion ; and if he saw that his departure would be spiritual and temporal ruin to the people, he would obey no living man who should command him to depart.

He then declares that having found nothing in his own life or doctrine at variance with the requirements of the Church, and having persuaded himself that the briefs from Rome were null, because they proceeded upon false and malicious information, he had nevertheless decided to use prudence, and had therefore obeyed by observing silence. And so he would have continued but for the evils which he had seen resulting from it. He had loved peace and retirement, but he had been forced to put forth upon a tempestuous sea where the winds were all contrary.

"I should wish to go into port, but I cannot find the way; I wish to seek repose, but I find no place; I should wish to remain silent and not speak, but I cannot, — because the Word of God in my heart is like a fire which, if I do not send it forth, burns the very marrow of my bones. Now, O Lord, since Thou willest that I should sail in this deep sea, Thy will be done!"

This sermon, the first of a series on the Books of Amos and Zechariah, gave a sketch of the subjects on which he intended to speak throughout the whole season of Lent. It would appear that these were the most powerful and impressive sermons of all that he preached at Florence. Never had he spoken with more perfect self-control, judgment, and care; and yet never had he lashed the vices of the age or the corruptions of Rome with more unsparing severity. Again and again he warned his hearers that their liberties were in danger from those who had themselves no regard to the honor of God or the well-being of His people. Their enemies were in Florence, they were in Rome. Their daggers and their anathemas were being prepared for him who warned the people of their danger. But the judgments of God were coming upon the wicked. There would be such destruction of life that there would not be people enough to bury the dead. The pestilence would sweep them away in such numbers that they would have to carry them away on carts and horses, and pile them in heaps and burn them.

"Come forth," he cried, quoting the prophet Zechariah, "and flee from the land of the North, — that is, from the vices of the world, — and turn to Christ. A day of darkness is coming. It will rain fire and flames and stones, and it will be a time of trouble." The land of the North was Babylon, and the preacher could not avoid a reference to the city which he always spoke of as the existing representative of the ancient city of confusion. Taking up the passage of the prophet from which he had quoted, he proceeds again : —

"'Deliver thyself, O Zion that dwellest with the daughter of Babylon!' Deliver yourselves from it, that is, from Rome; for Babylon means confusion, and Rome has confused the whole Scripture, has confused all vices together, has confused everything. Flee, then, deliver yourselves from Rome, and turn to repentance !"

There was one element, however, which was painfully present in the sermons of this period, — the sense that he was in a manner placed upon his trial and required to defend himself from the accusations of heresy and sedition. He was not less bold, less fierce, less confident in his denunciations of evil. As has been said, he was not less powerful or less impressive in his utterances. But he was not, as in former days, the teacher, the guide, whose truth and integrity none might dare to question, although they might desire and endeavor to moderate the tone of his warnings and rebukes. His enemies not only waxed more wroth as they smarted under the lash of his terrible words, unveiling vice with a plainness which we can now hardly imagine, they were also able to arm themselves with the authority of the Church, and to proceed against their enemy as against one who was seeking to destroy the very fabric which he was professing to defend. They forced him into a position in which, by vindicating his conduct, he necessarily implied the presence of a doubt; and by excusing his action he seemed to be accusing himself.

In the last sermon of this series he returns to the subject of his dispute with the Pope, —

"Who does not know that the brief was issued to support my enemies and those of the republic who disseminated falsehoods and calumnies against me? Who does not know that my departure would not only be most dangerous to my own life, but also injurious to this people and ruinous to its liberty, that good customs would be abandoned, and religion come to the ground? It is this, indeed, that my enemies desire. I therefore believe that the Holy Father has been deceived by the false accusations of my detractors; and I obey rather that which I believe to have been his intention, and will not suppose that he desires the ruin of a whole people."

But he never lost sight of the probable end of the conflict, the end which to him, indeed, seemed ever more certain. "What will be the end of the war which thou sustainest?" he supposes his hearers to ask. "If you ask me in general, I answer that it will be victory; if you ask me in particular, I say, to die and to be cut in pieces. But that will only serve to spread this doctrine more widely, which does not come from me, but from God. I am but an instrument in His hand; wherefore I am resolved to do battle to the last."

The effects of these Lent sermons were of the most various description. The partisans of the Frate were more enthusiastic in the expression of their devotion than ever. On Palm Sunday a great procession was formed in celebration of the blessings received during Lent; and Savonarola himself arranged all its details with the greatest care, and gave direction as to its order. First came the children, then the religious and the clergy; next came the magistrates, then the men; then, a little distance apart, the women, the aged women being first. Those who were unable to join the procession were requested to keep off the streets, so as not to interrupt its progress. All who took part in it were to carry a red cross or a branch in their hands, and the children were to lead an ass in commemoration of our Lord's entrance on that day into Jerusalem.

The procession started from the church of the Annunziata and proceeded to San Marco, where each one received a small red cross; and then they took their way across the city. It is said that there were at least eight thousand children present. On the Piazza della Signoria they sang a hymn composed for the occasion; then they passed on to the cathedral of Santa Maria del Fiore, and so returned to San Marco; and there the brethren, crowned with garlands, danced and sang hymns in honor of the Most High.

Savonarola justified these things by quoting the example of King David, who danced before the ark; but it was hardly necessary, in those days and in that country, to justify practices which to us seem extraordinary and misplaced. The Piagnoni needed no justification, the Arrabbiati were little inclined to listen to it. The religious enthusiasm of the former was so great that Savo-

narola himself had to entreat them to moderate their
zeal; but the wrath of his enemies reached its height.
The Compagnacci, in particular, the younger and more
dissolute of the Arrabbiati, were driven to frenzy by
beholding the influence which the Frate was still retaining over the people.

But the fame of these sermons extended far beyond
the city in which they were preached. It is said that
the Sultan had them translated, that he might be able to
read them. From all parts of Europe there came testimonies of approval and adherence. On the other hand,
the princes of Italy began to address remonstrances to
the man who seemed to include them all in one general
sweeping condemnation. Foremost among these was
Lodovico of Milan, who represented to Savonarola his
inability to understand how one whose life was so pure
and Christian should bring such continual accusations
against himself, since he might rather find fault with
Savonarola for teaching that the Pope ought not to be
obeyed. Savonarola did not hesitate to answer this appeal with all deference, although he could entertain no
real respect for the man whom he regarded as the author
of so much mischief to Italy.

"It is not true," he replied, "that I have ever said absolutely that the Pope ought not to be obeyed, because this
would be very reprehensible, and contrary to those sacred
canons according to which I have always governed myself.
And so too it is a false accusation to say that I have
spoken against your lordship. I am affectionate to all, and
have no right to speak against any one in particular. But
if your lordship be turned to God in that mind which you
declare to be yours, then you have only to persevere; and
in this matter you can have no better judge than your own
conscience."

It was comparatively easy to deal with Il Moro; but there was a greater Italian potentate, whose anger was more to be feared than that of Sforza. The Pope, who was kept informed of the matter of Savonarola's preaching, was loud in his accusations to the Florentine ambassador, complaining not merely of the Frate, but of the Signoria who allowed him to preach. The Ten, after endeavoring in vain to soothe his anger, determined to send as ambassador extraordinary Pandolfini, the Archbishop of Pistoia. On his arrival the Pope poured out complaints against the Florentines for refusing to join the holy League which had been formed "to drive the barbarians" out of Italy; and then he complained bitterly of the support given to Savonarola in his attacks upon the Holy See. The archbishop said that the Florentines could not possibly have violated the treaties which they had made with the French; and besides, they were aware of the enmity entertained by the Venetians and the Duke of Milan against the republic. With regard to Savonarola they could hardly be to blame, seeing that his Holiness had given him leave to resume his preaching. "Well, well," broke in the Pope, "we need not speak of Frà Girolamo at present. By and by, perhaps, we shall speak better of him. As for the rest, you give me nothing but words. You want to have two strings to your bow."[1]

In order to ascertain whether there were ostensible reasons for proceeding against Savonarola, the Pope appointed a consistory of fourteen theologians of the Dominican order, to whom he gave instructions to inquire into the conduct and teaching of the Frate, as

[1] Tenere il piè in due staffe, — "To have your foot in two stirrups."

regarded the charges of heresy, schism, and rebellion against the Holy See. It is said that the majority of the consistory pronounced him guilty; but the principal reason which they alleged was his enmity to Piero de' Medici, of whose misfortunes he had been the principal cause. There could hardly have been a more convincing proof of the truth of the statement made in the sermons of Savonarola, that the true ground of the accusations made against him was political, and not religious.

It has been mentioned as a proof of the Pope's moderation, although there may have been other reasons for the course which he took, that he acted no further on the report of the theologians than to request the Signoria, through their ambassador at Rome, to take care that in future Savonarola should be more guarded in his remarks on the Holy See, the cardinals, and the prelates, and that he should imitate the manner of the best preachers, and not intermeddle with the things of this world and political affairs.

After the close of Lent Savonarola spent a short time at Prato and Pistoia, where he met his brothers. On his return to Florence he put forth a treatise on the "Simplicity of the Christian Life," — *Della Semplicità della vita Cristiana,* — which was intended as a reply to the charges brought against him at Rome, and in which he gave a popular account of the Catholic faith, stripped of theological technicalities, and rebutted the charges of heresy and schism. Along with the Latin original an Italian translation was published, with a preface in which he repeated his willingness to submit to the authority of the Roman Church, and declared that he preached and wrote with the sole intention of combating the unbelief of the times, which chilled the spirit of love and darkened the light of good works.

About this time — we are still in the year 1496 — new troubles arose in Florence. The commerce of the city had been greatly depressed by the unsettled state of Italy and of the republic; great expenses had been entailed by the exactions of the French and the preparations for war; and a grievous famine deprived the peasants round about the city of their means of subsistence. The Venetians and Lodovico were assisting the Pisans, who, instead of yielding to the assaults of the Florentines, striving to recover their most prized possession, drove back the soldiers of the republic into the hills. These misfortunes were followed by one still greater, — the death of Piero Capponi, which took place in the September of this year. He was killed by a ball while conducting the siege of the castle of Soiana. There was no citizen of whom Florence was more proud than of him who had cast back on the king of France, when he threatened to blow his trumpets, the counter-threat to ring the bells of the city. The grief was universal; and all united to do honor to the obsequies of so great a man. He was buried in the church of Santo Spirito, in the tomb which had been made for his renowned ancestor, Gino Capponi.[1]

Other misfortunes followed. The League took advantage of the difficulties of the republic to press upon its rulers to abandon the alliance with France, and to make common cause with themselves. In this case they would assist them to recover Pisa; otherwise they would

[1] The last descendant of this great family was the Marchese Gino Capponi, recently deceased, author of the History of Florence, more than once quoted in these pages.

give assistance to the revolted city. The Arrabbiati were all in favor of these proposals; but the citizens discerned in them a plot for the overthrow of their liberty, and refused to comply. Besides, the king of France had announced his intention of returning to Italy, and this expectation confirmed them in their resolution.

The League then applied to the Emperor Maximilian for assistance in opposing the threatened invasion of the French; but King Charles had his hands full at home, and abandoned the enterprise. The Emperor, however, determined to visit Italy, which was in theory, at least, still the centre of the Empire. Crossing the Alps, he avoided Milan and descended upon Genoa, when he passed on to Spezia, and made his way to Pisa. The inhabitants received him with the same joyful welcome which they had accorded to the French. He had come among them as the friend of the League, and therefore as the enemy of their tyrannical mistress, Florence.

The Florentines, seeing the preparations which were being made by the Pope, the Milanese, and the Venetians, now headed by the Emperor himself, instead of abandoning themselves to despair, proceeded to fortify Leghorn, which the French had restored to them, and which now became the key of Tuscany. As was usual in their time of difficulty, the magistrates had recourse to Savonarola, who did not hesitate to obey the call, and again appeared before the people, urging them to unity and to courage in the defence of their liberties.

The most dangerous and the most vindictive of the enemies of Florence was the Pope. He hated the city and its freedom, and resolved to restore the Medici, whom he hoped to keep in subjection to his own will.

Above all, he hated the man who was the soul of the republic and the bulwark of its liberties. If the armies of the League could not demolish the walls of Florence, he could strike at the man who alone seemed able to inspire its defenders with courage and resolution. He therefore determined to use every means to prevent him from again appearing in the pulpit. On the 8th of September[1] he despatched a new brief from Rome, addressed to the convent of St. Mark, in which he described Savonarola in the same terms as those which he used in his letter to the friars of Santa Croce the year before. Again he was described as " a certain Frà Girolamo, a friend of novelty and a disseminator of false doctrine." He told them that this friar had advanced to such a pitch of madness that he had made the people believe that he was sent by God and had converse with him; and this without any miraculous proof or any special testimony of the Holy Scriptures, such as the canon law required. He then spoke of the patience which he had exercised towards Savonarola, in the hope that he would repent, and desist from continuing that scandalous separation from the congregation of Lombardy which he had been deceived into sanctioning. He then required that the brethren of St. Mark and their vicar should recognize the authority of Frà Sebastiano de Madiis, Vicar-General of Lombardy; commanding Savonarola to prepare to go where he should be ordered, and in the mean time to desist from all preaching whatever, either public or private. The convent of St. Mark was to be at once reunited to the congregation of Lombardy, and Frà Domenico, Frà Salvestro, and Frà

---

[1] See, in Vilari, the reasons for assigning this date to the brief here described, lib. iii. c. 5.

Tommaso Bussino were to present themselves in nine days at Bologna. And all this under pain of excommunication.

It was quite clear to Savonarola that these orders could not be obeyed; but he determined to try what could be done by submission. He addressed a respectful letter to the Pope, dated the 29th of September, about the time that Capponi was being laid in the tomb of his ancestor. He reiterated his willingness to submit to the Church, saying that his enemies had deceived his Holiness. He denied that he had claimed to be a prophet, as he had denied it nearly two years before, as he was to deny it again in some yet more solemn hours of his life. Even if he had put forth this claim, he said, it would not be heresy; but he had only predicted certain events, some of which had taken place, and others would in the future. He then reminded the Pope that the bull of separation had been solicited by all the brothers, and had been granted after a lengthened discussion. To refer their cause to the Vicar of Lombardy was to make their adversary their judge. Besides, since the separation, their rules had been made more strict and severe, and therefore to reunite them would be to increase the enmity already existing, and to give rise to great dissensions and scandals. There was no reason for this reunion, since he was not guilty of the offences alleged as rendering it necessary, seeing that he preached the doctrine of the Church and of the holy doctors; and he repeated anew what he had always said, that he submitted himself and all his doctrines to the correction of the Holy Roman Church.

The Holy Father saw that by going too far he might fail in the main object of his brief, which was to prevent Savonarola from preaching. He therefore appeared to lay aside his resentment, and on the 16th of October he despatched another brief addressed to Savonarola. The Frate was again his "beloved son." He begins by referring to the mischief caused by his preaching and his pretensions to prophecy. Still, he was greatly rejoiced to learn from brethren who were cardinals of the Church, and from his own letters and messengers, that he was prepared to submit himself to the judgment of the Holy Roman Church. "We have begun to persuade ourselves that thou hast not preached these things from an evil mind, but rather from a kind of simplicity and a zeal for laboring in the vineyard of the Lord, although experience may seem to teach the contrary." But for all this, he adds, he must not be so negligent as to dismiss the matter entirely, and therefore he commands him, "in virtue of holy obedience, further to abstain entirely from all preaching, both in public and in secret."

Savonarola was not in the least deceived by this fatherly forbearance, knowing very well that the Pope was, by a different path, trying to reach the same end, and prevent his preaching at a time when his voice was most needed by the citizens. Besides, he learned from the ambassador that the Pope was more enraged than ever against him; and he knew that he was acting in concert with the Emperor and Il Moro. He was convinced that an attempt would be made, as soon as there appeared any hope of success, to effect the restoration of Piero de' Medici. Yet the tone of the Pope's brief had placed him in a difficulty. To defy a command addressed in a spirit so benignant might bring worse evils upon himself and the city; and therefore he determined for a season, at least, to refrain from preaching.

In the mean time fresh clouds seemed to be gathering around the fortunes of the republic. Leghorn was besieged by the imperial troops; the Venetian ships blockaded the port, so the provisions could not be brought into the city; and famine and pestilence were making terrible ravages among the inhabitants. The Florentines made the most heroic efforts to relieve the suffering city, but the pestilence began to ravage their own homes. The misery of the city was extreme. The Arrabbiati were triumphant; now they were clear that the Frate had deceived them. This was the happiness he had promised to Florence! Surely it was time to change a government which had succeeded so badly.

The magistrates in this extremity had recourse to the divine offices. They ordered that a miraculous image of the Madonna, to which they had frequent recourse in times of danger, should be carried in solemn procession through the city. Again they turned to the only man who had been able to help them in former times of perplexity, and entreated Savonarola to speak to the multitude. It needs not to be told how his compassionate heart had bled for the miseries of the people whom, with all their faults, he so dearly loved. Whatever might be his fate, he could not resist the appeal which was now addressed to him.

On the 28th of October he was again in the pulpit. Friends and foes were gathered around him. He knew what was passing in many minds, and he at once addressed himself to the unuttered thought.

" I ought not to have spoken? But I come in obedience to the Signoria, and to call you once more to repentance. *You are clear?* And I tell you that I am clear, and that everything I have said to you will be verified to the smallest iota. . . . Be ye then clear that, unless you change your life, you will have woes. Vices still prevail among you, O Florence, — gambling, bestiality, — and in this way you draw down the scourge upon you. Yet if you return to the Lord, I am confident that some great grace will be bestowed upon us, and we shall have need to fear no one."

He then rebuked them for putting their trust in man, and told them that, first of all, they must return to God; then they must put away all thoughts of human help; all the money they could spare they must lend to the city, and without interest; they must be united and have no dissensions. If they would do this, "listen," he said, " to the words that I say to you : I am willing to lose my head, if we do not drive away our enemies. I say that, if you do this, I will be the first to go forth against them, crucifix in hand, and we will make our enemies flee as far as Pisa, and further." Two days later, the miraculous image was carried into Florence in solemn procession. An enormous multitude followed, showing every evidence of the deepest devotion. Sadness was on every countenance. Money was freely given as the Frate had required. The procession had reached Por Santa Maria, when a messenger arrived on horseback with an olive-branch in his hand, on his way to the Palazzo. Caught by the bridle, he was required by the multitude to deliver his message. His news were almost incredible. The promised succor had arrived from Marseilles, and had been wafted by a favorable wind into the harbor of Leghorn, before the Venetian ships were able to come up. Joy sat on every countenance, which but now had been clouded with sorrow. The intelligence flew from mouth to mouth. The bells rang out peals of gladness; the churches, which had but recently been filled with multitudes humbling themselves in penitence, were now crowded with the same multitudes pouring forth their joy and gratitude. Even the most embittered enemies of Savonarola were silenced. They were almost ready to confess that, for once at least, his predictions had been verified.

Two days later, on the festival of All Saints, Savonarola preached again, exhorting the people to gratitude. Surely the mercy of God must lead them to repentance and amendment. Surely they would now put their trust in God alone. At the same time he warned them against the transports of joy to which they were abandoning themselves. They ought not, he said, to be so easily overcome by joy and by sorrow. The next day, All Souls' Day ("the day of the dead"), he preached on the way to die well, and produced a deep impression on his hearers. He then desisted again from preaching. He had obeyed the call of duty; but he would not further give his enemies occasion to censure him for disobedience.

The Pope did not delay for a moment to take further action against the man who was resolved ever to cross his designs. On the 7th of November a new brief was issued, addressed to all the Dominicans of Tuscany. Instead of reuniting them to the congregation of Lombardy, the Pope now proposed to form a new Tusco-Roman congregation, with a vicar of its own who should be elected every two years by the various priors of the new congregation, without, however, derogating from the authority of the Vicar-

General at Rome. For the first two years the Pope would himself nominate the Cardinal of Naples, who had always been friendly to St. Mark's and its prior. The Pope had outdone himself in the astuteness of his policy. He had heard Savonarola's remonstrances; he would not unite the hostile congregations. He would give them a vicar who was a known friend of their own. But there was something beyond all this. Such a scheme would annihilate the independence of St. Mark's, and render Savonarola dependent upon the new vicar, who might after two years be the creature of his adversaries.

In this emergency Savonarola again put forth a protest, not this time addressed to the Pope, but to the public at large. In this pamphlet, entitled " An Apology for the Congregation of St. Mark," he declared that the proposed union was "impossible, unreasonable, injurious." The brothers of St. Mark should not be obliged to accept it. The order had been obtained by false accusations, and therefore it became a duty to resist a command which was contrary to charity. " When the conscience rejects a command received from one's superiors, it is necessary first to resist and humbly to correct the error; but if that does not suffice, it is then necessary to do as Saint Paul did, who 'withstood Peter to the face before them all.'" There could be no uncertainty as to the meaning of those words. The immediate dangers which had threatened Leghorn now passed away. The Emperor abandoned his undertaking against Florence and returned to Germany, complaining bitterly of the untrustworthiness of his allies. Savonarola, apparently abandoning all hope of a reconciliation with the Pope, again ascended the pulpit on the 26th of November, reminding his hearers of the dangers through which they had passed, and of the debt of gratitude which they owed to their Divine deliverer ; showing also the blessings of the government which they enjoyed.

He now commenced his sermons on the prophet Ezekiel, eight of which were preached in this Advent, the remainder in the following Lent of 1497. In a prayer uttered in the course of his first sermon, he declared his purpose in preaching. "O Lord," he said, "I ask of Thee a life of adversities. I begin again to preach this morning, only to repeat that which I have already said, and to confirm it anew; and I am willing here to lay down my life." Turning to the people, he said, "If I depart from this, say that this brother contradicts God and lies in his throat, and stone me and cast me out of this pulpit."

In this strain he continued throughout the season of Advent, repeating the lessons of religion and politics which he had so often inculcated before. The year ended with increased power and popularity to the Frate, but also with multiplied dangers. Henceforth the struggle with the Pope was to be looked upon as unending. Did the Frate hope that the wished-for council might meet, and Alexander be deposed, and a better take his place, and the Church be renovated? It may be so. But it is equally certain that he saw clearly enough the other alternative; and the prospect of a violent death was now seldom absent from his mind.

CHAPTER XV.

THE BURNING OF THE "VANITIES."

IN his recent conflict with the Pope, Savonarola had received his chief support from the Ten, although it is apparent that the Signoria had not been hostile to him, and had not failed to use his influence with the people when the necessities of the republic seemed to require it. It was an evidence of the position which he now held among the citizens, obtained by his labors and the effect produced by the marvellous relief of Leghorn, that in the beginning of the year 1497 a Signoria devoted to his interest was elected, and Francesco Valori was appointed *gonfaloniere.*

This is that Francesco Valori of whom we have heard as at first a supporter of the Medici, and one of the five citizens sent by Lorenzo to restrain the Frate in his style of preaching, — the same who afterwards became one of the foremost opponents of the dominant family when they were driven from Florence, and one of the most faithful and attached friends of Savonarola. He was a man of undoubted courage ; and if his discretion had equalled his bravery, he might have used this opportunity to repress the dissensions which were rending the city.

Savonarola suggested that the constitution of the greater council should be so modified as to exclude those who plotted against the republic. Valori thought the best manner of guarding against such danger was to secure a larger representation of the people ; and for this purpose he reduced the age at which those otherwise qualified for election might be admitted into the council, from thirty to twenty-four. His object was, of course, to counteract the influence of the aristocratic party, who were the most dangerous enemies of the constitution ; but the actual effect of the measure was to introduce the younger members of the Arrabbiati, who have already been mentioned as the most violently opposed to the teaching and the policy of Savonarola.

There can be little doubt, in these days, that the great mistake which was made by Savonarola was the attempt to repress every kind of immorality, and those amusements which he regarded as productive of immorality, by physical force and by the arm of the law. It would be utterly false to describe him as of a persecuting or intolerant spirit ; but the horror inspired in his mind, from his earliest years, by the frightful immorality which he saw prevailing everywhere, led him to imagine that only the strongest measures could be effective and successful.

In his opinions on these subjects he was neither better nor worse than his best contemporaries. At that time, and for long afterwards, it was thought right and expedient to repress by law whatever was regarded as hurtful to the community. On this ground heresy was punished, and customs which seemed in any way dangerous to the social, the moral, or the religious interests of a country. Those who suffered from what they regarded as persecution were themselves ready to persecute when their turn arrived to wield the power of the sword.

In the English Puritan revolution these principles were the source of the unity and strength of the party which then came into power. They were resolved to set up the kingdom of God upon earth, and they carried out their resolution with the Word in their mouths and a two-edged sword in their hands. Their enemies can hardly deny that this was their original intention, however they may accuse them of a growing lust of power, of unreality and hypocrisy. In a world like this, and with creatures like ourselves, such efforts must fail. We have now discovered that it must be so. We have learned that to paralyse personal liberty, beyond what is required for the protection of others, is to induce evils far greater than any which we are able to repress. To put a stop to all amusements is to drive those who will have them to deception, and is very likely to engender vices as base, because more morbid, than those which are exterminated. We have learned that, to a great extent, we must leave it to the individual conscience to decide whether an amusement is innocent or hurtful. That Savonarola did not grasp these principles was nothing wonderful or discreditable; they did not belong to his time. Holding that vice should not be tolerated, and holding this conviction in a most vicious age, he went to war with the overwhelming majority of his countrymen. It was clear to himself that they must be converted, or he must perish. He would not, he could not, abandon his design; and he saw with ever-increasing clearness, with ever-deepening sorrow, what the end must be.

The prohibition of balls and festivals enraged the younger members of the Arrabbiati beyond all power of self-control. To them life without pleasure was insupportable, and the Frate was resolved that they should not have their pleasures in their own evil way. In order to carry on the contest with greater unity and vigor, they formed themselves into companies, and placed at their head one of their own number named Dolfo or Doffo Spini. These companies went about armed, and committed assaults on the Piagnoni as they had opportunity. From their organization they were called *Compagnacci.* Many of these young men, who had had only an indirect influence on the government, now became members of the greater council, and consequently more dangerous than ever.

About the beginning of this year Savonarola was anxiously occupied in preparing for publication that which was perhaps his most famous composition, "The Triumph of the Cross." In this way he was withdrawn from his more active labors among those who were under his spiritual guidance. His deputy at such times, whether in the pulpit or as an administrator of the affairs of the convent, was ordinarily Frà Domenico. This brother had preached in his place when the strife with Rome had first begun. It is said that he was but a feeble echo of his great master; but he was a true echo, and a faithful and devoted friend. He had the most unswerving faith in his superior. He knew him for a man of God, a man who lived above this world, its cares and its interests. He saw how deeply he was himself penetrated by those convictions to which he gave such eloquent and powerful utterance. He went beyond his master in thinking that he was endowed with miraculous powers, as well as with prophetic gifts. If he was too credulous, this fault may easily be forgiven when his sublime devotion is remembered, — a devotion which became touching and heroic at the end.

As the time of the Carnival drew near, it became clear that the Compagnacci were determined that it should be celebrated as in the days of the Medici. The songs of Lorenzo should be sung, the indecent dances should be danced, the games should be resumed, and everything, down to the most irrational of their old practices,[1] should be as it had been before the Piagnoni had interrupted their pleasures. To Frà Domenico had been given the training of the children who had played a part so important in the previous Carnival. When he knew of the preparations of the Compagnacci, he determined to meet them with preparations of his own. Day after day he drilled his youthful bands, preached sermons to them, and wrote them letters. By means of new laws, passed by the friendly Signoria, he carried out the reforms which Savonarola had commenced in the preceding year.

It was determined to make an onslaught more thorough and sweeping on the luxurious and lascivious manners and customs of the people, and especially of the women. The children scoured the town, and knocking at the doors of the rich, asked to have given up to them the things which they had been taught to designate as vanities (*vanità*) or anathema. Everything which ministered to luxury, everything which tended to immorality, was to be given up, — masks, dresses with immodest figures upon them, musical instruments, books containing indecent or immoral tales. It was determined, by a solemn and public *auto-da-fè*, to declare before the world that Christ was

---

[1] Such as the throwing of stones by the children of the city, —one of those absurd and dangerous practices which Savonarola had stopped when he organized his bands of children.

King of Florence, and these things should not be allowed to defile His kingdom.

To whatever extent the will of Savonarola may have have been resisted during the Carnival, all were prepared, when its last day arrived, February 7th, to think of nothing but the religious festival which was being prepared. Burlamacchi gives a detailed account of the proceedings of the day. In the morning multitudes of men and women received the communion from the hand of Savonarola. At two o'clock they came together and formed a solemn procession, which was to traverse the streets, finishing at the Piazza della Signoria, where the great event of the day was to take place. Here is Burlamacchi's description of the scene : —

"In the procession the boys carried a *bambino* [he says it was *devotissimo*], full of splendor, which gave the benediction with the right hand, and with the left held out the crown of thorns, the nails, and the cross; it was of stupendous beauty, being the work of that most rare sculptor Donatello. This was supported by four most beautiful angels upon a portable altar, very rich and wonderfully adorned, and over it a most beautiful baldacchino was supported by twelve children. Around these were other children, who sang psalms and hymns with sweetest melody. Before went the other children, walking two and two in order. Behind came the guardians with their officials, men who bore silver vessels to receive alms for the poor of St. Martin, who received more in that day than they ordinarily did in a whole year. Behind these came the men with small red crosses in their hands. Last of all came the girls and all the other women."

They took their way first to the Duomo, where they sang "the most beautiful lauds," and all the people made an offering of Florence to the Queen of Heaven. They then proceeded to the Piazza, where complete preparations had been made for the work they had in hand. A huge bonfire had been erected in the centre of the square, in the shape of an eight-sided pyramid, which rose to the height of thirty braccia, or sixty feet, and measured at its base one hundred and twenty braccia, or two hundred and forty feet. Each side had fifteen steps, upon which were deposited all the *vanità* collected during the Carnival; and a huge image surmounted the pyramid, which was filled with inflammable materials. Each of the eight sides had objects arranged with some attempt at classification. On the first were dresses with immodest figures; on the second, pictures of the beauties of Florence; on another, chess-boards and cards; on another, music, harps, lutes, guitars; on another, the *vanità* worn by women, — false hair, phials, looking-glasses, perfumes; on another, lascivious books written by Latin and Italian poets, among them Boccaccio and others; on another, masks, beards, and other orna-ments used in the Carnival; finally, pictures and sculptures in ivory and alabaster.

The Piazza was crowded with people, and the children were arranged on the *Ringhiera* and under the *Loggia dei Lanzi*, where they kept singing re-ligious songs and denouncing the Carnival. At a signal given, the four guardians set fire to four corners of the pyramid, the smoke and flames leapt up into the air, the trumpeters of the Signoria blew a blast, the bells of the Palazzo rang out, and the multitude raised a shout of rejoicing.

We can imagine that these transactions were regarded

with very different emotions by the onlookers. Doubtless there were many who heartily participated in the religious enthusiasm which had been evoked by Savonarola, — many who now, as in the former Carnival, freely gave up useless ornaments to be disposed of for the benefit of the poor ; many, too, who burned " with sacred rage " those things which, in their past life, had ministered to their lusts. But there were others who regarded the scene with very different feelings, — some who had parted with their vanities from fear of those terrible children who went in bands to execute the will of the Frate ; some, probably, who had utterly refused to give them up. To very many these young tyrants must have appeared in the light of a simple nuisance. Burlamacchi relates, with a gravity bordering upon the ludicrous, that "notwithstanding, these good children endured a most cruel persecution from ill-disposed and lukewarm men, which they bore with great serenity of mind, and with so much joy that they filled every one with astonishment, and seemed nothing less than angels of Paradise."

It is impossible to form a judgment on an event which happened in times so different from our own and in a season of such intense religious excitement. Those who consider all the circumstances and the customs of the people among whom it took place will probably experience no great astonishment. If we could enter more fully into the feelings of that day we might be led to understand that it was a spectacle in no small degree calculated to produce a wholesome effect upon those by whom it was witnessed. The greatest danger was, perhaps, that it might be drawn into a precedent ; and we shall see that a similar " burning " took place at the next

Carnival. It is a remarkable fact, however, that none of the contemporaries of Savonarola should have brought this forward among the offences charged against him.

The demonstration has not fared so well at the hands of more recent writers. Savonarola has been denounced as a Vandal, a barbarian who had destroyed antiquities and curiosities of priceless value; he has been represented as an ignorant and blinded fanatic, who looked upon literature and art with contempt and detestation.

It is very possible — it is indeed probable — that Burlamacchi, who looks back upon these days with all the delight of an ascetic, with all the satisfaction of a religious who knew that his own order had made a holocaust of the vanities of the age, was guilty of unconscious exaggeration. For instance, he represents the number of children present as being nearly equal to the whole population of Florence. He speaks of a Venetian merchant as offering an incredible sum of money for the *vanità* which were consumed in the fire. But there is no doubt that there was a considerable destruction of costly dresses, ornaments, and books; and in judging Savonarola we must have regard to his motives and to the state of the society to which he belonged.

If the *auto-da-fé* had been meant as a condemnation of all poetry, the Frate might plead that he had at least the favorite author of the new literary school on his side; for Plato could find no place for poets in his ideal republic. But there is no foundation for such a charge. From his youth he had himself written hymns and poems, and had procured hymns to be composed for the Carnival, to be sung in place of the old lascivious songs.

If it be charged against him that he caused to be

burned the works of Boccaccio, one of the most elegant
of Italian prose writers, we need not urge the somewhat
unfavorable literary judgment pronounced on Boccaccio
by the late Gino Capponi.   It is certain that Savonarola,
in this case, thought little of the literary merits or de-
merits of the books which he prepared for the flames.
It may be more to the point to ask whether his accusers
would like to have Boccaccio as the favorite author in
the libraries of their daughters, or whether they would
tolerate the reading of the Decamerone in their families.
It is said that it was one of the favorite books of the
nuns at this period; and it is not to be believed that
it tended to improve the moral purity of the convents.
Savonarola was often wellnigh maddened by the thought
of the foul and bestial streams of sensuality which were
flowing through this fair city, almost under his eyes ; and
the burning of every indecent volume in the world would
have seemed to him a small price to pay for the salvation of one human soul, for the rescuing of some of those
little ones whom he was striving to protect from the evil
that was in the world, from the moral contamination
which was prevailing everywhere, and which it seemed
almost impossible to escape.   Was Savonarola the only
reformer who ever burned indecent books?   History
tells us of some who burned heretical men.   To ourselves it may seem unwise and impolitic to make this
display of our condemnation ; but there are others, and
those men not destitute of learning and piety, who think
such an exhibition may be edifying.   Little more than
a generation has elapsed since a book directed against
divine revelation was burned in the hall of a college in
one of our great universities, and this in the middle of
the nineteenth century ; but what danger has existed in

the Oxford of these days which could for a moment be compared with the condition of Florence at the end of the fifteenth century?

An interesting proof was given this very year that Savonarola was not to be classed with the fanatic who burned the Alexandrian library, on the principle that it could be of no value because all that was good in it must be contained in the Koran, and that which was contrary to the Mahometan Bible must be mischievous. In consequence of the financial straits of the republic, it became necessary to dispose of the library of the Medici, which had become the property of the State when the family had been declared rebels and their goods confiscated. There was great danger that this magnificent collection of books would now be dispersed. Such a loss would have been irreparable ; there was no library in Europe which at that time contained so complete a collection of Greek and Latin classics. It happened that the convent of St. Mark's could then command a considerable sum of money, in consequence of the sale of all unnecessary property which Savonarola had recommended. They agreed to pay two thousand florins at once, and to be responsible for an additional sum of one thousand ; and thus they secured to Florence that *Biblioteca Laurenziana* which is to this day one of its principal glories. And this was the work of a man who has been represented to be an ignorant fanatic, the enemy of literature and art ; and the transaction took place in the very year which witnessed the *bruciamento delle vanità !*

The defence of Savonarola from the charge of despising the arts of painting and sculpture is no less easy. If he set his face against the prostitution of these arts, it is equally certain that he desired to see them consecrated to the service of morality and religion. To speak of Savonarola as a mere ignorant iconoclast is to ignore the clearest evidence to the contrary. The walls of St. Mark at this very day are adorned with the same sacred pictures upon which the eyes of its greatest prior must have rested. Instead of being the enemy of art, he was the friend, the patron, the guide of artists. One of his dearest friends was the great painter known as Frà Bartolommeo, a member of his own convent. Lorenzo di Credi, according to Vasari, was a "partisan of the sect of Frà Girolamo." Michael Angelo, who long afterwards took part in the same struggle for freedom in which Savonarola was so prominent, was one of his hearers in his youth, and in his old age took pleasure in reading his sermons and other writings. Vasari, who was not a contemporary, and who is not always to be depended upon when he relates the events of his own age, records that Frà Bartolommeo, or Baccio della Porta, as he was commonly called, burned some of his own pictures among the *vanità*. If this were so, we may be assured that he acted on grounds which satisfied his own conscience. One proof of his lasting attachment to his master is the well-known fact that for four years after his death he entirely abstained from painting.

So far was Savonarola from making an indiscriminate attack on literature and art that he actually taught and wrote on the subject of poetry and of painting. But while he defended poetry and demonstrated its utility, he declared that there was in his own time "a false kind of pretended poets, who did nothing but follow in the footsteps of the Greeks and Romans, using the same forms, the same metre, and invoking the same gods, — nay, more, finding it impossible to use any other names or words than those which were sanctioned by the ancients. But he did not, for this or any other reason, include all the poets of Greece and Rome under one sweeping condemnation. He says that some of them condemned base actions and exalted those which were generous and brave. " These," he says, " have made a good use of poetry, and I neither can nor ought to condemn them."

So far was he from depreciating the beautiful in nature and art that he took pains to explain its true character, and declared that it was a kind of reflection of the beauty of the Maker of all. A holy soul, he said, actually participated in the beauty of God, and diffused His celestial beauty throughout the body. But he had little toleration for the delight in mere material beauty, and in the endeavor to increase it without regard to that higher spiritual beauty which was the true glory of man and of woman. He told them that women who gloried in their ornaments, their hair, and their hands, were simply void of reason (*brutte*). If they would see true beauty, they must look upon a face that was purified by devotion and prayer. That would be a reflection of the beauty of God Himself, — a countenance that would be almost angelic.

From these principles he took occasion to condemn many painters who made sacred subjects a mere vehicle for the display of dresses and ornaments, and, still worse, took for their models those who were distinguished for mere physical beauty, and in some cases those who were notorious for their evil life, instead of trying to represent countenances of elevated

and spiritual loveliness, such as might raise the thoughts
of the beholders to better things.   " Painters," he
exclaimed, "in this you do wrong; and if you knew,
as I do, the scandal that results from it, you certainly
would not do it."   Such things were a public injury.
"You bring all the 'vanities' into the churches," he
exclaims.   "Do you think that the Virgin Mary should
be depicted in the manner in which you paint her?   I
tell you that she went attired like a poor, humble
woman."

In the Lent which followed the Carnival of 1497
and the *auto-da-fé* on the Piazza, Savonarola completed the course of sermons on Ezekiel which he
had begun in the previous Advent.   In these sermons his favorite topics were prominent, — the need
of love and unity and holiness, the evils of luxury
and self-indulgence.   But throughout the whole course
there was evidence of the expectation of a new struggle
with Rome.   It came at first in a form for which he
was not quite prepared, except that he was always
expecting to hear of the plots of the Medici; and when
this danger passed away, he found himself confronted
by another, — the deadly enmity of the Supreme Pontiff,
which led to one last conflict; a conflict that was to
end only when the man who was its object had passed
beyond the bounds of earthly strife.

CHAPTER XVI.

TREASON.

AFTER the failure of his attempt upon Florence in the autumn of 1496, Piero de' Medici had returned to Rome, determined to wait his time and to watch for such changes in the affairs of the republic as might seem favorable to his hopes. His life at Rome was of the most scandalous description, — too scandalous, in fact, to be described. Rioting, drunkenness, gambling, sins of the flesh which cannot be named, consumed his nights; and half of the day was spent in sleeping off last night's debauch. His wastefulness and extravagance plunged him in debt, from which the generosity of his brother the cardinal was insufficient to preserve him. There was hardly a vice with which he was not familiar. He was destitute even of the virtue of tyrants, — gratitude to the agents of their tyranny. Men who devoted themselves to his interests were used, and cast away when they seemed likely to be troublesome. Some of them were despatched with poison or the dagger. But amid all his recklessness and self-indulgence, he deeply cherished the design of returning to Florence, and nursed a most bitter enmity to its inhabitants. One of his happiest meditations was the thought of the vengeance he should wreak on the men whom he considered the authors of his misfortunes. The work of reprisals executed by his ancestors upon their enemies in former days should be outdone by himself. The exiles and confiscations which followed the restoration of Cosimo after his expulsion by the Albizzi, the deaths which were inflicted after the conspiracy of the Pazzi, were to be a mere trifle to what he would do when his turn came. He would take effectual means to prevent another expulsion from Florence. He did not even pretend to have the slightest regard for the interests of the city. When he was told that he could govern very well with a council of twenty or thirty citizens, he replied that he wanted no council at all; he would prefer to rule badly by his own counsel than well by that of others. Trusting to the support which would be afforded to him by the princes of Italy, to the large party still attached to his family in Florence, and to the chance of dissensions and divisions among the citizens, he was resolved, when the fit time should arrive, to force his entrance by the power of arms.

Circumstances arose sooner than he could have expected to give reality to his hopes. The two months during which the Signoria, elected in January, 1497, held office were coming to an end. Francesco Valori and his fellow-magistrates had attempted too much, and had chilled the ardor of some of their supporters. The quarrels and contests between the Arrabbiati and the Piagnoni had given the *Bigi*, the Medicean party, an opportunity of carrying on their secret plottings and maturing their plans. Some of the Arrabbiati, despairing of being able to carry out their own designs, began to make common cause with the Bigi as the only means of destroying the influence of the Piagnoni. Frà Mariano da Gennazzano, the ancient enemy of Savonarola, again appears on the scene. While at Rome he lost no opportunity of keeping alive the exasperated feelings of the Pope; and now he suddenly presented himself in Florence.

At the beginning of March a new Signoria was elected, by whom Bernardo del Nero, a citizen of reputation and eminence, but a devoted adherent of the Medici, was chosen *gonfaloniere.* The Bigi had for some time acted as a party in the great council, standing aloof from the Piagnoni, with whom they had professed to co-operate. By degrees they became more bold and outspoken in their opposition to the existing state of things; but their joy knew no bounds when they had secured the election of one of their party to the post of chief magistrate of the State. Still they forbore to reveal their designs, and secretly despatched a messenger to Rome to bring word to Piero of the happy turn which affairs had taken at Florence. He knew that he could depend upon the Pope and the other members of the Italian League, and he now received the assurance that a large number of the citizens would declare themselves on his side if he could force his way into the city.

Thus assured, Piero began to collect men and money. Some of his more cautious friends at Florence counselled delay, as they were by no means sure that the state of the popular mind was favorable to his attempt. But Piero could bear no longer suspense, and set out for Siena, the place appointed for meeting his fellow-conspirators. There he found the magistrates on his side, and he at once determined to make his way to Florence, with thirteen hundred men who had gathered to his standard. To prevent the disclosure of his plan, he endeavored to stop all the travellers who were on the

same road ; but a fall of rain arrested his progress, and
gave time for some of the peasants to reach Florence by
a circuitous route, when they instantly gave the alarm to
the government.

It became at once apparent that the city was not
prepared to welcome back its old masters. The citizens
flew to arms, and the members of the Signoria who were
favorable to the attempt were forced to conceal their
sentiments. The gates were closed, the walls were
armed, and all preparations were made to meet the
enemy. In this moment of suspense one of the Signoria,
named Filippo Arrigucci, a friend of Savonarola, sent off
Girolamo Benivieni, the poet who had written the hymns
for the Carnival, to consult the Frate respecting the
fortunes of the city. The story is told, not only by the
contemporaneous historian Nardi, but in a letter afterwards written by Benivieni himself to Pope Clement VII.,
so that there can be no reasonable doubt as to the facts.
He relates that, even before he had been able to deliver
his message, Savonarola turned to him with the words of
Christ to Saint Peter, "*Modicæ fidei, quare dubitasti?* —
'O thou of little faith, wherefore didst thou doubt?'
Tell the Signoria that Piero de' Medici will come to the
gates, and will turn back again without obtaining any
result." The attempt failed utterly and ridiculously.
Piero, finding the gates shut against him, and the whole
city prepared as one man to resist his entrance, retired
without drawing a sword. It was the end of May; and
to give the last blow to his hopes, on the very day that
he appeared before the gates of Florence, a new Signoria
was elected, pledged to resist the attempts of the Medici
and to punish the conspirators within the city.

Although their attempt had failed, the conspirators did

not abandon their design, as we shall see hereafter ; and the hatred of the enemies of Savonarola waxed still more fierce. The government now fell chiefly into the hands of the Arrabbiati, who as a party were opposed to the Bigi, but were still more hostile to the Piagnoni. The Compagnacci under their leader, Dolfo Spini, began to consider how they could best give effect to their enmity against St. Mark's. Frà Mariano was about this time making one of his accustomed attacks on his rival in a sermon which he preached before the Pope. "Cut off," he cried out, "cut off, most blessed Father, this monster from the Church of God." To attacks like these Savonarola always replied with the greatest gentleness and self-control. His wrath, his denunciations, were reserved for the enemies of God and of the liberties of Florence. For his personal enemies he had always forbearance and charity. This generosity only drove his adversaries to greater rage and violence.

Savonarola, who had for some time abstained from preaching in public, had determined to speak to the people from the pulpit of the Duomo on the following Ascension Day (May 4, 1497). The new Signori, whether in sincerity yielding to the known wishes of the people, or hoping that things might fall out unfavorably for the Frate, gave the assurance that the sermon might safely be delivered. The Compagnacci, who had been for some time seeking an opportunity of attacking him, first of all thought of making an attempt upon his life on this Ascension Day. Among other schemes suggested, there was a proposal to blow up the pulpit while he was preaching ; but they feared to bring down the public indignation upon themselves. Desisting from this scheme, they next considered in what way they might best expose their adversary to ridicule and contempt. First, they collected all kinds of filth and placed it in the pulpit; then they drove nails into the wood at the places where the Frate was accustomed to strike his hands on the pulpit when preaching; finally, they set up in his place the skin of an ass. Their method was as childish as it was brutal; but they hoped that in the confusion which would certainly ensue, they might find an opportunity of carrying out their design against the preacher's life.

These projects could not be kept secret; the whole city was full of confusion, and on the vigil of the Ascension the Signori gave out a decree that no one should interrupt the preaching on the following day. The friends of Savonarola were far from being reassured by these precautions. They came and entreated him to abstain from preaching; but he received the advice with indignation. " I cannot," he said, "from fear of man, leave the people without a sermon on that day on which the Lord commanded His disciples to go into all the world and preach the Gospel."

On the morning of Ascension Day the Piagnoni went to the cathedral and removed all the filth which had been heaped up in the pulpit. Just before twelve o'clock Savonarola came out of the convent, accompanied by his friends. All the biographers tell of the remarkable appearance presented by the congregation assembled in the cathedral, — the Compagnacci, richly attired and perfumed, with a smile of scorn and derision on their faces, contrasting strikingly with the modest and devout appearance of the Piagnoni. The preacher began by speaking of the power of faith.

" Faith," he said, "is omnipotent, and despises the life of earth, because it is assured of the life of heaven. The times predicted are now drawing near, — the hour of danger, when it will be seen who is truly on the Lord's side. The wicked thought to hinder me from preaching to-day; but they must know that I have never shrunk from my duty through fear of men. No man on earth, be he great or small, can boast of having hindered me in my office. O Lord, deliver me from these adversaries who call me a seducer; deliver my soul, for I have no fear for my body. I call as witnesses the Lord, the Virgin, the angels, and the saints, that the things revealed by me come from God, and that I have received them by divine inspiration in the vigils which I have passed for the good of this people which now plots against me."

He then warns the righteous of the trials which are coming upon them, — wars and excommunications, the sword and martyrdom.

"It is the will of God," he goes on, "that I should be the first to endure them. I have already told you that I shall meet with great ingratitude, and the lukewarm [*i Tepidi*, who are often heard of during these two years] will treat me as did the brothers of Joseph, who sold him to the Egyptian merchants. These say that I am no prophet; but they are only bringing about the fulfilment of my predictions. I repeat to you that Italy will be devastated by barbarous nations; and when they shall say peace and safety, then sudden and repeated destruction shall come upon this perverse Italy. But, ye righteous, make your prayers unto the Lord, and ye shall have His help.

"And as for the wicked [here a great murmuring arose throughout the church], Lord, be not angry with them; convert them, forgive them, for they know not what they do. Ye believe, O sinful men, that ye are fighting against the Frate, and ye are making war on the Lord; because I do not fight against you from hatred of you, but from love of the Lord. You say that I sow discord; but Christ came not to bring peace on the earth, but a sword. Why do you not turn to virtue, for then you would have peace ? But you say I have no right to preach, for the Signoria has prohibited me ? That is not true, nor ought I to abstain from preaching from fear or at the command of men. I shall be silent only when my preaching may do harm, when I shall fear to cause scandal."

The enemies of the Frate seemed determined to take him at his word, for at this moment a great crash resounded through the church ; and instantly noise, confusion, and disorder were everywhere, and many rushed out of the building. The cause of the uproar was a certain Francesco Cei, one of the Compagnacci, who had laid hold of the alms-box of the church and dashed it to the ground, while another beat upon a drum, some knocked upon the benches, and others slammed the doors. Savonarola's friends rose up to defend him, some gathering round the pulpit, others rushing off to procure arms, which they had placed ready in a neighboring street. These, to the number of sixty, speedily returned fully armed, and took their place around the pulpit. This movement only increased the alarm of the multitude, who took the armed men for Compagnacci. In the midst of the confusion, which now became greater than ever, two of the Arrabbiati, who were also members of " the Eight," thinking that their dignity would protect them, endeavored to make their way to the pulpit, with the intention of putting Savonarola to death. But they found his adherents ready to do battle in his defence ; and one of them, named Giugni, received a heavy blow on the ear, — an insult, it is said, never previously inflicted on one of " the Eight."

It was a terrible moment for the preacher. " Wait,"

he cried aloud; " have patience." Then, raising the crucifix aloft, he exclaimed: " Hope in this, and fear nothing." But he soon saw that it was impossible to gain a hearing, and therefore, kneeling down in the pulpit, he prayed for a few minutes in silence; and when the tumult had a little subsided, he came down and placed himself in the midst of his defenders, who received him with loud shouts of joy. Some held up their swords and spears, others their crosses; and all accompanied him to the convent, with loud cries of *Viva Cristo*, their favorite watchword. In the garden of the convent he concluded the sermon which had been so rudely interrupted. He told his hearers that they need not fear, — the wicked would fall into the pit which they had digged for others. "Then," he adds, "I will sing praises to the Lord, and peacefully depart from this life." In spite of the tumult the sermon was reported by Girolamo Cinozzi, who published it, with an account of all that he had seen in the Duomo during its delivery.

Savonarola was as good as his word. He would not continue his preaching when it could be only injurious and cause scandals. But he could not refrain from publishing his testimony to the world in another manner; and therefore he addressed a letter " to all the elect of God and faithful Christians," saying that, in imitation of the Lord, who often gives place to wrath, he would for a season abstain from preaching; but in order that the Word of God might not cease to go through the world, he would say by letter that which he could not utter with his voice. They were not to be troubled, but to rejoice at tribulations. His prophesies would still be verified. His enemies had been trying to procure his excommunication, and because they had failed, they were making attempts on his life. They must prepare for still more grievous persecutions, but their faith would be strengthened to endure them ; and they must pray to God that He would deign anew to open the mouths of His preachers, because when He commands there is no power which can resist Him.

The failure of their last effort had not damped the ardor of his persecutors. The real authors of the disturbance were not punished, and many innocent persons of the popular party suffered death in their place. This was the work of the Eight, whose office it was to carry the law into effect, but who, as we have seen, were themselves implicated in its violation. The Signoria now ordered that no friar of any order should preach, — they went so far as to consider whether they might not pronounce a sentence of banishment against Savonarola ; but the fear of the people deterred them from this outrage. At the same time, every effort was made by the Arrabbiati to induce the Pope to issue the threatened excommunication, — a step which his Holiness was the more inclined to take, as he judged, from the disturbance of Ascension Day, that the party of the Frate was less powerful than he had imagined.

Savonarola resolved to make another attempt to propitiate the man who so unworthily occupied the apostolic chair. He complained respectfully that he had never been heard by the Holy Father, who, on the contrary, had given a too ready ear to the false accusations of his enemies, and had not read his sermons, which were printed, and from which he might learn what he had actually preached. He denied the truth of the assertions made by Frà Mariano, and protested his readiness to submit to the judgment of the Church as to whether he had not preached the doctrine of the holy Fathers. " But if," he concludes, " all human help shall fail me, I will put my trust in God, and will make clear to the whole world the iniquity of those who will perhaps be led to repent of the work which they have begun."

Savonarola wrote this appeal on the 22d of May, and did not know that the Pope had issued the brief of excommunication ten days before (May 13). The brief — which was addressed, not, according to the ordinary form, to all believers throughout the world, but to the brethren of Santa Annunziata — had been intrusted to a theologian named Giovanni da Camerino; but when the bearer reached Siena, he stopped there a few days, and fearing that the Frateschi would tear him to pieces when they knew his errand, he went back again, leaving its delivery to other hands, so that it did not reach Florence until near the end of the month. When it did arrive, many of the clergy refused to publish it, on account of the irregular manner of its presentation; but it was at last posted on the doors of the principal churches of the town.

It was a remarkable production. Savonarola was again a " certain Frà Girolamo," who was, according to his own representation, vicar of St. Mark's in Florence, who had sown pernicious doctrine, to the great scandal and unsettlement and ruin of simple souls who were redeemed by the blood of Christ. Then it was set forth that the Supreme Pontiff had commanded him that he should entirely cease from preaching, hoping that he would become convinced of his errors and retrace his dangerous way; but to this prohibition he had given no heed.   Further, he had been commanded, on pain of excommunication, to unite the convent of St. Mark to the new Tusco-Roman congregation, founded by a papal brief; but he had still remained firm in his pertinacity, and therefore the Supreme Pontiff commanded the brethren of the Annunziata, publicly before the people, to declare him, Frà Girolamo, excommunicated because " he has not obeyed our apostolic admonitions and commands."

Although the Pope showed the weakness of his cause in accusing Savonarola of heresy — for there was absolutely nothing in the brief to support such a charge — he still exhibited his subtlety and ability as a statesman by fastening upon the undeniable and undoubted fact that the accused man had not obeyed his commands. It was, of course, perfectly true that those orders had been issued, not with the intention of crushing a heretic, but with the design of shutting the mouth of a political opponent. Still, the charge of flagrant disobedience was a serious one, and Savonarola could not deny that he had evaded the command to proceed to Rome, and that he had taken no steps to unite his convent to the new congregation. As he could not deny these acts of disobedience, he proceeded to justify or excuse them. On the 19th of June, the day after the publication of the papal excommunication in Florence, he wrote an " Epistle against the Surreptitious Excommunication, to all Christians and beloved of God." In this letter he repeated the assertion of the soundness of his doctrine, and declared that the excommunication was invalid, because it had been procured through the false accusations of his enemies. In a second letter, " Against the Sentence of Excommunication," he proved, by quotations from Gerson, that there was no reason for fearing an unjust condemnation, and that to yield obedience to such a sentence were to show "the patience of an ass and the silly timidity of a hare."[1] Following the same authority, he discussed the lawfulness of an appeal from the Pope to a council, although he expressed some uncertainty on this point; but he declared further that to resist the Pope, when he used his authority for the destruction of the Church, was not only a right, but a duty.

The excommunication was publicly pronounced on the 18th of June.[2] This was done with all possible solemnity, in the presence of the clergy and the brethren of the various monastic orders settled in Florence. The sentence was read in the cathedral to the sound of bells; and after the reading was concluded, four lighted tapers were suddenly extinguished, leaving the place in gloom and in silence.

It would have been difficult, by any other means, to show how powerful for good had been the influence of Savonarola in Florence. The brief had commanded that no intercourse should be held with the excommunicated man, and the Augustinian and Franciscan friars refused to take any part in celebrating the approaching Feast of St. John if the brethren of St. Mark were allowed to do so. There was now no check put upon the vicious mob, which had been so long kept in subjection by the terrible voice which was now silent. It was as though the days of the Magnificent had come again. The Signoria, composed

---

[1] Est asinina patientia, timor leporinus et fatuus.

[2] Burlamacchi fixes a date a few days later, but this seems to be the best attested.

principally of Arrabbiati, encouraged the multitude in their excesses. The indecent attire which the Frate had shamed men and women into destroying or concealing, reappeared in the streets; the obscene Carnival songs again resounded throughout the city. Shameless vice and indecency were everywhere. Any other pontiff but the detestable Borgia would have blushed to hear what work his anathema had wrought in the fair city of Florence.

If the stern Puritanism of Francesco Valori had produced a reaction in favor of a party opposed to the Frateschi, it could hardly fail but that these excesses should open men's eyes to the true interests of their city. Within a week of St. John's Day a new Signoria was chosen, and this was found favorable to Savonarola. No sooner were they elected than they began to use their influence with the Pope to obtain the recall of the excommunication; and the Pope expressed his willingness to submit the consideration of his doctrines to the judgment of six cardinals. While this negotiation was proceeding, Savonarola received an intimation, through the Cardinal of Siena, — afterwards the successor of Alexander in the Papacy, under the name of Pius III., — that if he would pay the sum of five thousand scudi, the excommunication would be withdrawn. If this offer showed the Frate that the wrath of the Holy Father was not unappeasable, it filled him with indignation as a fresh proof of the venality which prevailed at Rome.

But the Pope had at this time trials of his own which must have made his war with the rebellious vicar of St. Mark's a very insignificant matter. The history of the Borgias is involved in great difficulties; and it is now affirmed with confidence that the re-nowned Lucrezia was not the vicious creature that she has been represented. Whether she was in any way the occasion of the tragedy which was now enacted, there is no doubt that her brother, the eldest son of the Pope, who was Duke of Candia, was at this time most foully murdered; and there is little doubt that the instigator and author of the crime was no other than his own brother, the infamous Cæsar Borgia.

It was a strange thing to see an excommunicated man writing to the Pope who had pronounced the anathema, and exhorting him to penitence; but Savonarola probably judged that now, if ever, the Pontiff was open to better and more sacred impressions. And, in fact, there was probably no moment in the life of Alexander VI. in which he did more seriously reflect on the error of his ways. Savonarola wrote to the "most blessed Father," and reminded him that it was the faith of Christ, proved by miracles and con-firmed by the blood of martyrs, which could alone give peace and consolation to the heart of man. It was this which could support men in adversities and make them joyful in tribulation. "Respond, then," he goes on, "to the blessed call, so that soon your sadness may be turned into joy. Blessed Father," he concludes, "I write under the guidance of love, and in the hope that you may be truly consoled by God. Already 'His wrath is kindled' a little; and 'blessed are all they that put their trust in Him.' May the Lord of all mercy console your Holiness in your tribulations!"

Whether the Pope was really touched by this appeal coming to him in the hour of his bitter sorrow, or whether it was that his mind was too much pre-occupied with his own sorrowful thoughts to give heed to it, it would at least appear that he showed no resentment at the time against the writer. But the season of mourning and of transient penitence soon passed away, and then he remembered that the insolent Frate had dared to intrude upon his sorrow.

Petitions and counter-petitions now went up to the Holy Father from Florence on the subject of the excommunication. The Arrabbiati entreated him to confirm his sentence. The whole of the brethren of St. Mark, to the number of two hundred and fifty, sent up a petition for its removal, representing the purity of the doctrine preached by their vicar, and the holiness of his life. Another petition, on the same side, was circulated in the city, and had in a short time received three hundred and sixty-three signatures, when the outbreak of the plague put a stop to the proceedings of both parties.

Savonarola has been blamed because he did not go forth from his convent and minister to the sufferers who were stricken by the pestilence; but it has been overlooked that he was at this time under the sentence of excommunication, so that his ministrations would not have been allowed or accepted. It would be absurd to accuse such a man of cowardice; for apart from the proofs which he had already given of his fearless spirit, when the people were now rushing in crowds from the plague-stricken city he remained steadfast at his post, ministering to the sick brethren of his convent; for the pestilence did not spare

St. Mark's. He resisted the entreaties of his friends that he would provide for his own safety, and remained reading to the sick such passages of Scripture as were calculated to afford them strength and consolation, and even writing counsels for the guidance of those whom the scourge might smite.

The pestilence soon passed away; but it was followed by a discovery which filled the minds of the people with alarm. The conspiracy of the Bigi in the spring of this year had ended in ridiculous failure; but during the supremacy of the Arrabbiati no success had attended the efforts to discover its promoters in Florence. Soon after the appointment of the new Signoria a letter was discovered on the person of a certain Lamberto dell' Antella, a partisan of the Medici, by means of which the names of the principal conspirators were discovered.

The inquiry was committed to the Eight, who speedily found that some of the chief men of the State had been concerned in the plot, and especially the majority of the late Bigi government, together with their *gonfaloniere*, Bernardo del Nero. These disclosures were so embarrassing that the Eight hardly knew how to deal with them, and they applied to the Signoria for advice. By these a number of additional judges were appointed to assist them in their examination of the facts. Lamberto dell' Antella, who had indeed little reason for attachment to a vicious and ungrateful master, on being promised a free pardon disclosed the names of the friends of Piero in Florence. He further disclosed the intention of the conspirators to make a new attempt to bring the Medici back in this very month of August.

It was an anxious moment for the Eight and the other twelve who had been appointed to assist them; but they determined not to flinch from their duty, and they took an oath that they would do justice without respect of persons. They then ordered that the Piazza should be held by armed men, and that care should be taken that no one was allowed to leave the city. In the name of the Signoria they required the presence of the men who were most compromised by the revelations of Lamberto dell' Antella. Some of them instantly sought safety in flight; others presented themselves before the magistrates, when it was found that five of these had been implicated in the conspiracy. Of these five, two were relatives of Piero de' Medici, — Niccolò Ridolfi and Lorenzo Tornabuoni. It will be remembered that the wife of the elder Piero, the mother of Lorenzo, was one of the Tornabuoni family. Besides these were Giovanni Cambi and Gianozzo Pucci; the latter, like Tornabuoni, belonging to one of the most distinguished of the old Florentine houses. Finally, there was the aged Nero, who had been the *gonfaloniere* of the Bigi government. He was a man of high character and reputation, and was now seventy-five years of age. It will be remembered that although a partisan of the Medici, he had not committed himself to any overt acts in their favor; and it was now urged on his behalf that his only offence was that he had known of the conspiracy and had not disclosed it. But such an offence in the chief magistrate of a State was one of no ordinary magnitude.

The twelve citizens who assisted the Eight had acted as a kind of jury, and they now left those whose duty it was to pronounce the sentence. But these experienced the same difficulty which had embarrassed them when they were first made acquainted with the names of the accused. It was their simple duty now to pronounce the sentence of death against the five men who had been proved guilty of treason against the republic; but they were afraid to incur the enmity of the powerful families to which the guilty men belonged. They turned again to the Signoria, who again reminded them that it was their own duty, and not the duty of the supreme magistracy, to take the responsibility of the sentence. At last, however, Domenico Bartoli, the *gonfaloniere,* proposed that they should bring the matter before the Consiglio Maggiore, to whom, according to the recent law, the final appeal might be carried. This was objected to by the friends of the accused. Seeing the indecision of the magistrates, and knowing that the time was approaching when a new Signoria had to be chosen, they hoped that by a short delay they might see their party in power, and so put a stop to the proceedings. But the accusers were equally resolved to bring the trial to an end.

The Signoria gathered together an assembly consisting of the various magistracies and representatives of Florence, the Ten, the Eight, the *gonfalonieri* of the companies, the senate, or lesser council, besides themselves. There were one hundred and thirty-six persons in all, and the rule was suspended which forbade those present to express an opinion contrary to that of the Signoria. It was not long before the decision was given. The five men were found guilty and condemned to death, and their goods were confiscated. It was found, however, that there were four votes among the Signoria favorable to the accused; and their friends, hoping to take advantage of this circumstance, required that the votes should be given individually. This device was frustrated by Valori, who immediately presented himself at the table and gave his vote that these citizens were worthy of death, and that their goods should be confiscated, — an example which was followed by all. The Eight were now compelled to give their sentence, which they did by a majority of six over two.

This decision was the signal for new discussions. The defenders of the condemned men now declared for an appeal to the greater council, according to the "Law of the Six Beans." Their prosecutors well knew that this appeal was made only for the purpose of gaining time; and they replied that it could not be granted, because the accused had already refused to be judged in this way, and because they had not been condemned by the tribunal from which this appeal was allowed. The public excitement and indignation against the traitors was greatly increased by letters which arrived at this time, showing that the old enemies of the republic, the Pope and the Duke of Milan, were preparing to act against their liberties.

The popular feeling was expressed by some of the leading citizens. While the people were threatening to attack the houses of those who were seeking to delay the execution of the sentence, Francesco degli Albizzi stood up in the meeting at which the appeal was being discussed, and called out in a voice of thunder, "Let justice be done!" while the Bigi party were doing their best by noise and disturbance to confuse the proceedings and prevent a decision being arrived at.

The people were almost unanimous in favor of refusing the appeal; but the final decision of the question remained for the Signoria, and they still hesitated to commit themselves to either course. The sitting was protracted and tumultuous. They had passed the night in debate and noise, when Valori, who now became the leading actor in the government, rose up in great wrath, and seizing the ballot-box, advanced to the table, demanding that the votes should be taken and justice done. Luca Martini, who was the Proposto, was constrained to put the question to the vote. The four who had stood by the accused at the beginning were still firm, and voted for the appeal. But Valori was not to be baffled. What was the use, he asked, of calling all these citizens together, if their decision was thus to be disregarded? Was it not clear that these men had been condemned for conspiring against the liberties of the republic? Had not the citizens declared that they would defend those liberties, and that the traitors must die? It would be well if we could believe that Valori was influenced solely by the love of liberty. There can be little doubt that he was also moved by hatred of Nero, who had succeeded him in the office of *gonfaloniere*. His impetuosity, however, carried the day, backed as it was by the indignation of the people. Again the Proposto put the question to the Signoria: Was it their will that the sentence of condemnation should be carried out; that instructions should be given to the Eight this very night to carry out the sentence of death against these five citizens? The four dissentients, seeing no hope of escape, and probably fearing the violence of the people, voted for instant execution; and the order was given.

A last attempt was made to excite compassion, by bringing the five men, chained and barefooted, into the meeting. It was in vain; the sight of them only inflamed the wrath of their judges. The condemned bore their punishment with firmness and dignity. At seven o'clock in the evening their heads fell in the court of the Palazzo del Capitano; and the same night the Signoria wrote to Rome, giving an account of the execution, concluding with these words:—

"The city has been quite united against these perfidious and parricidal citizens; even their own relations have desired that justice should be done. And now it is to be hoped that the State may be in safety; for the whole body is resolved to root out every evil plant. May God have mercy upon the souls which, by betraying their country, have need of such punishment!"

It has been brought as a charge against Savonarola that he did not interpose to save the lives of the five men, and especially that of the aged Bernardo del Nero. Such an accusation will be supported only by those who wish to blacken his memory without regard to truth or justice. There is no doubt that he tried to save the young Tornabuoni, although he had played a double part and deceived him. He afterwards declared himself that he was opposed to the death of Nero; but it was impossible for him to interpose openly, and Valori had made up his mind that the guilty men should die. This accusation is of the same kind with the charge brought against him that he was concerned in the expulsion of the Medici at a time when he was not even present in the city. Let it be remembered, too, that Savonarola, while he strove with all his might to obtain the best possible government for the republic, never interfered in the administration of its affairs.

Savonarola, still under excommunication, was at this time retired from public life and preparing for publication his great work, the " Trionfo della Croce." Our limits do not allow us to give a complete account of this work,[1] which is perhaps the best adapted to convey to the mind of the present day an accurate impression of the power and comprehensiveness of its writer's intellect. Its primary object was to show the entire accord between the teachings of the Gospel and the reason of man.[2] In its form, at least, the argument was new to the age in which it was produced. The writer first discourses on the existence and attributes of God. In the second book he discusses the truth and excellence of the Christian religion, showing that while it is above reason, it is not contrary to it. In the third, he treats of particular Christian doctrines, — the Incarnation; Original Sin, the Passion of Christ, the Morality of the Church, the Sacraments. In the fourth and last, he shows that the Christian is the only true religion.

In this work,[3] the author was careful to give to the Pope his true place [4] according to the theory of the age. After pointing out that Jesus Christ had established Peter

[1] It was written in Latin and Italian. There is a good English translation by Mr. O'Dell T. Hill (Hodder & Stoughton, 1868).

[2] Villari remarks that in this work Savonarola was "the glorious initiator of that noble school which was afterwards honored by the names of Bossuet and Leibnitz."

[3] Lib. iv. cap. 6.

[4] It is a pity that the English translator has thought good to omit this passage.

as His vicar upon earth, and promised that His Church should continue forever, he goes on, —

" But it cannot be said that this power was given to Peter alone, and that he had no others to succeed him, Christ having promised that His Church should remain to the end of the world. . . . Whence it follows that in the vicariate of Peter He is succeeded by those whom He has called into His place, so that there shall always be one head in the Church, who holds the place of Christ, and who has the same power which Peter had. Whence, that the Roman bishops are the successors of Peter, is a thing manifest, and that the Roman Church is the guide and mistress of all others, and that all faithful Christians should be united to the Roman Pontiffs."

When we remember that these are the words of a man then suffering under a papal excommunication, we may easily perceive how far he was removed from that which we mean by the name of Protestant.

CHAPTER XVII.

RENEWED CONFLICT WITH ROME.

IF the death of his son had for a moment drawn the attention of the Pope away from the man towards whom he entertained a mingled feeling of hatred and contempt, it was evident that he had never really laid aside his animosity and resentment. Equally clear was it that it was from no doubt, much less from any conviction, of the unsoundness of his faith, that he had determined to paralyse the influence of Savonarola in Florence. As the Frate frequently declared, he was hated, not as a heretic, but as an advocate of the political liberties of the people; and this aversion had become strengthened by the boldness of the preacher in denouncing the evils of the Church and the immorality of the priests.

It is not, therefore, wonderful that the publication of the "Triumph of the Cross" produced no change in the feelings or in the intentions of Pope Alexander. Still, the Frate waited in silence, hoping that time would work a change in the policy of Rome. Since the disturbance on Ascension Day his voice had not been heard in the Duomo; and Florence, deprived of her conscience and left to her own evil heart, had gone from bad to worse. What was the Frate to do? He had vindicated his soundness in the faith. He was no heretic, he was no schismatic; for he had plainly declared that the chair of Peter was the centre of the Catholic Church. His only offence was his refusal to obey the command which summoned him to Rome; and he knew Rome too well to hope for justice there. To venture into the den of the lion was to court sudden death or endless imprisonment.

It only remained for him, therefore, to treat the excommunication as null; and on Christmas Day he proceeded to celebrate the three masses appointed for that festival, and to communicate the brethren and the multitudes who came together to receive the Sacrament at his hands. That his new course of action might be clear to the world, he and the members of the convent, at the close of these services, went in solemn procession around the Piazza of San Marco.

And now preparations were made by his supporters for his resuming his place in the cathedral. The galleries were erected, the seats put in order, and the consent of the Signoria obtained to his preaching. This step was not to be allowed without opposition from the ecclesiastical authorities. Lionardo de' Medici, vicar-general to the Archbishop of Florence, Rinaldo Orsini, not unwilling to enforce the papal commands, which in any case he could hardly have overlooked, forbid him the pulpit of the Duomo, and strictly prohibited the clergy of the diocese from taking any part or being present at the service; and threatened any who might be among his hearers that they would be refused absolution, and that they would not be admitted to the Communion or receive Christian burial. To these threats the Signoria replied by announcing to the vicar that if within two hours he did not quit his office, he should be declared a rebel. This is certainly a fact which may well be considered by those who profess to look back to those happier days in which ecclesiastical authority was supreme, and mourn over the interference of the civil power in the evil days upon which we have fallen. All obstacles being now removed, on Septuagesima Sunday, February 11th, 1498, he stood in the cathedral pulpit surrounded by an immense congregation.

It was impossible for Savonarola, after so long a silence, and appearing as he did in defiance of the papal censure, to avoid the subject of the excommunication. He accordingly declared, as he had done before, the lawfulness and necessity of disobedience under certain circumstances. At the close of the sermon he referred to the expectation of miracles in support of his teaching, and, unfortunately for himself, he seemed in a measure to sanction this expectation.

"In his own time," he said, "the Lord will stretch out His hand. But already you have seen so many signs that there is no more need of miracles. What miracle greater than the increase of this doctrine in the midst of so many contradictions? Citizens, women, it may be needful to lay down our life for this doctrine. I turn to Thee, O Lord, Thou didst die for the truth. I pray Thee that Thou mayest require me alone to die in its defence, for the salvation of Thine elect and of this people."

Four days later, in St. Mark's, he returned to his favorite theme, the corruption of the clergy : —

" When I think of the lives of the priests, I must weep. O brethren, O my children ! weep for these evils of the Church, that the Lord may call the priests to penitence ; for it is clear that there is a great scourge upon them. It

is the clergy who support every wickedness. Begin with
Rome. They make sport of Christ and of the saints; they
are worse than Turks, worse than Huns. Not only are they
unwilling to suffer for God, they go so far as to sell the
Sacraments. . . . Can you believe that Jesus Christ will
longer endure it? Woe, woe, to Italy and to Rome! Come,
come, ye priests; come, my brethren, let us see if we can
awaken a little the love of God. O Father, you reply, we
shall be put in prison; we shall be persecuted and killed.
Be it so. Let them kill as much as they will, so long as
they cannot take Christ from my heart. I am willing to die
for my God.

"You have been at Rome and know the life of these
priests. Tell me what you think of these supporters of the
Church, of these temporal lords? They have courtesans
and squires, and horses and dogs; their houses are full of
carpets, of silk, of perfumes, of servants. Does this look
like the Church of God? Their pride fills the world, and
their avarice is no less. They do everything for money;
their bells ring only to gratify their avarice, and call only
for bread and money and candles. They are present in the
choir at vespers, because then they are paid. You will not
find them at matins, when no money is distributed. They
sell benefices, they sell the Sacraments, they sell marriage
masses, they sell everything. And yet they are afraid of an
excommunication! . . . Lord, send now Thy sword."

On Sexagesima Sunday he again spoke of the papal
authority and of the excommunication. "But why do
they set themselves against me at Rome? Perhaps
you think it is for religion? Not at all. They want
to change the government; they want to introduce a
despotism; and they do not care for the holy living of
the people, which rises with our teaching and falls with
it." And again on Quinquagesima Sunday (February 25)
he returns to the same subject: "But, O Father, what

will you do, if all the world come against you? I shall stand firm, because my doctrine is the teaching of good living, and therefore it comes from God." The Carnival was drawing to an end, and he announced to the people that he would give a solemn benediction on Shrove Tuesday, in the piazza of the convent; and he added:

"When I shall have the Sacrament in my hand, I beseech every one of you to make fervent prayer to the Lord that, if this work does not come from Him, He may send a fire which shall draw me down to hell. Make such a prayer throughout these days. Write it and proclaim it to all."

On the last day of the Carnival, after giving the Sacrament to a great number of the people, there was a procession; and then the Frate ascended a temporary pulpit which had been placed near the principal door of the church. There he knelt in prayer, while the brethren sang psalms; and then, standing up, he requested the people to offer the prayer he had taught them. Then, holding the Sacrament in his hand and blessing the kneeling multitude, he prayed, " O Lord, if I do not act with sincerity of mind, if my words come not from Thee, strike me with Thy thunder this moment." The people saw written on his face, while he spoke, the expression of a confident faith in his words.

And then came, for a second time, as on last Shrove Tuesday, the "burning of the vanities." On the Piazza stood a pyramid larger than that of the former year, and on the top of it a representation of Lucifer surrounded by the seven deadly sins. Again the torches were applied amid the triumphant singing of the Te Deum and the exulting shouts of the beholders. For the moment Savonarola had resumed his full sway over the people of Florence.

The Pope was more furious than ever.   Nothing was talked of at Rome but the audacity of this presumptuous friar, who treated with utter contempt the excommunication of the Pope, and held up the lives of the clergy to the detestation of mankind.   His enemies gave Alexander no peace ; and Frà Mariano was foremost among those who called for vengeance.   In the church of the Augustinians he upheld the authority of the Supreme Pontiff, " who spoke by the Holy Ghost."   " This is the true light, and not he of Ferrara, who preaches in the light of the devil, and dares to say that the Pope is a broken weapon (*ferro*)."   And here he could not contain his rage, but broke out : " The great drunkard, the scoundrel, the thief, the robber, who has treasures hidden away in secret !   O Pope, O cardinals, how can you endure this monster, this hydra?   Has the authority of the Church come to such a pass that a drunkard like this can thus ignominiously cast it under his feet?"

The Pope was desirous of using his last weapon ; he prepared to smite Florence with an interdict : but first he addressed a brief to the Signoria (issued the very day before the new *auto-da-fe*), in which he recounted the offences of the Frate against the Holy See, and urged them " at least to separate this corrupt member from the rest of the people, and keep him in custody, that he might not sow new scandals ; " but if they would not consent to this, he " must have recourse to an interdict, and to other remedies still more efficacious."   At the same time he gave strict orders to the canons of the cathedral to prevent him from preaching in their church.

It was now the time for a change of Signoria.   Those elected in January had cared no more for the papal briefs than Savonarola himself; but the March election gave a decided majority to the Arrabbiati; and one of these, named Piero Popoleschi, and known as a most determined adversary of Savonarola, was chosen *gonfaloniere* of justice. He was a cousin of Piero de' Medici, and had formerly borne that name, but had chosen that of Popoleschi after the expulsion of his relatives, and had joined the aristocratic party.

It was a terrible change which had taken place in one short week, and Savonarola knew that the papal commands would now obtain a different reception at the hand of the authorities. On the day on which the new Signoria was installed, he preached in the cathedral on the briefs that had just arrived from Rome.

"They call me," he says, "the son of perdition. Let this be sent back for answer: ' The man whom you thus designate has neither harlots nor concubines, but gives himself up to preaching the faith of Christ. His spiritual children, those who listen to his doctrine, do not pass their time in the commission of crimes ; they go to confession, to communion; they live virtuously. This friar labors to exalt the Church of Christ, and you to destroy it.' "

He would not lower his tone even in that moment of danger ; but he judged it best to retire from the cathedral and continue his sermons during Lent at St. Mark's.

The Signoria were in a difficulty. Some of them would gladly have carried out the Pope's instructions, but they feared the people. The minority, who stood by the Frate, urged the mischief that his removal would cause to the State. The Signoria yielded to these considerations, and wrote to the Pope to say that Savonarola had retired to his convent, that they could not further interfere with a man whose doctrine was so pure, whose life was so holy. "It would be unworthy of the republic; it would be unjust to a man who had deserved so well of his country; it would be a cause of popular discord and of great danger to many."

And so the Frate was permitted to go on with his sermons at St. Mark's. The congregations were so large that they were forced to exclude women from the sermons. These had to go to San Lorenzo, where Frà Domenico was preaching; afterwards, when that was shut against him, to San Niccolò. But they would not be satisfied until Savonarola consented to preach to them alone, on Saturdays, at St. Mark's.

In the sermons preached during this Lent, Savonarola discussed the fallibility of the Pope, and declared that a man who said the Pope could not err because he was the Pope, might as well say that a Christian could not err because he was a Christian.

When the Pope received the answer of the Signoria to his demands, he sent for the ambassadors of the republic in great wrath, and declared that he would place the city under an interdict unless Savonarola were delivered into his hands, or at least prevented altogether from preaching. In addition to this verbal communication, he wrote to the Signoria, rebuking their audacity in defending this rebel against his authority.

"Your conduct," said his Holiness, "has gravely displeased us. . . . Take mature counsel on your affairs. . . . In any case, answer us no more with letters, but only with acts, because we are most firmly decided no longer to tolerate your disobedience; and we will place an interdict upon your whole city, which shall remain so long as you continue to show favor to this your monstrous idol."

It is, however, remarkable that the Pope, in these communications, withdraws the charge of false doctrine. When the government of Florence urged the holy life and good teaching of Savonarola, the Pope allowed that there was no question of these things, but only of his disobedience to the papal commands and prohibitions, adding that, if he would come to Rome and make his submission, he should receive absolution. There can be little doubt as to his fate, if he had gone to Rome.

On the 17th of March, 1498, a meeting of the Signoria was held. By the influence of the *proposto* of the day, Giovanni Berlinghieri, and the *gonfaloniere*, both of them determined enemies of Savonarola, it was decided that he should be inhibited from preaching. It was no more than was to be expected. It is honorable to the Signoria that some of its members should still have protested against the sentence. Savonarola was not surprised. On the following day, the third Sunday in Lent, he announced to the congregation his resolution to obey, and bade them farewell. It was his last sermon.

He told the people how often he had resolved to abstain from preaching on the things which had been revealed to him; but he said he had been unable to contain himself. " The word of the Lord has been within me as a consuming fire, shut up within my bones and my heart, and I have not been able to restrain it, because I have felt myself all on fire with the Spirit of the Lord." He then told them of the order he had received, the day before, from the Signoria. He did not regret it for himself. He could return to his studies, which were his delight; but he was not equally satisfied that his retirement was right. " But," he said, " we will do with prayers what we cannot do by preaching. Lord, I commend to Thee the good; Thou wilt forgive their shortcomings, for human frailty is great. *Benefac, Domine, bonis et rectis corde,* — 'Do well, O Lord, unto those that are good and true of heart.' O Lord, I pray Thee, delay no longer to fulfil Thy promises!" And then, reciting the Lord's Prayer, he added, " O Lord, deliver us from all evil. I commend unto Thee the souls of our adversaries; enlighten them, O Lord, that they go not down into hell! I commend to Thee this whole people. Give them, O Lord, Thy benediction."

The grief of his supporters was profound and intense; the joy of his enemies was unbounded. The Pope was at last satisfied that his faithful children at Florence had done their duty.

There was only one resource left for the persecuted man. He would still make an effort to give effect to the thought which had long dwelt in his mind; he would see whether a council might not be convoked for the reformation of the Church. In this desire he had been encouraged by the Cardinal of San Pietro in Vincoli, and he knew that it was favored by the King of France. He determined to appeal to him and to the other princes of Europe. The life of this man who disgraced the chair of Peter should be condemned by the Church; if possible, his election should be declared simoniacal and void. He now penned his famous "Letter to the Princes of Europe," telling them that the Church was full of abominations, and they made no attempt to remedy them, so that the Lord was grievously displeased, and had left the Church without a pastor; for, he says,

"I testify now to you, *in verbo Domini,* that this Alexander is not Pope, nor can he be retained as such; for leaving alone his most wicked sin of simony, by which he obtained the papal chair, and the fact that every day he sells the ecclesiastical benefices to whosoever will buy them, and apart from his other manifest vices, I affirm that he is not a Christian, and that he does not believe there is a God."

Before sending forth this letter to the Emperor, the King of Spain, and the other princes, Savonarola thought it advisable to address himself to Charles VIII. of France, in whom he placed his chief reliance for the assembling of the council. His letter was intrusted to a courier, who fell into the hands of the soldiers of the Duke of Milan. Lodovico, rejoiced at this opportunity of wreaking his vengeance upon an old adversary, immediately sent on the letter to the Pope. Before his Holiness could give expression to his indignation, fresh events occurred which hastened on the approaching crisis; but this crowning audacity of the Dominican vicar was not forgotten when the time of vengeance arrived.

CHAPTER XVIII.

THE ORDEAL BY FIRE.

IT has been asked how it was that Socrates, after thirty years of " public, notorious, and efficacious discoursing,"[1] lost his hold at last upon the people of Athens; and the reason has been found in the character and circumstances of the Athenians. In the case of Savonarola the change was far greater and more remarkable, and the causes perhaps more various. He exercised a power and a sway over the mind and history of Florence which was never possessed by Socrates in Athens; and the people turned against him with a completeness and bitterness of revulsion which exceeded the madness of the people of Athens.

We have already referred to the severe and uncompromising Puritanism of Savonarola as having within itself the sure prophecy of failure; but the causes at work were too multifarious and diverse to be easily identified and distinguished. It was a serious thing for a man to set himself as an accuser before the vices of a vicious age. It was a still more serious thing to proclaim war upon those vices incarnate, as they were, in the rulers of Church and State. Those who have position, power, and wealth, however feeble in themselves, however incapable of accomplishing

---

[1] Grote's History of Greece, viii. 634; Stanley's Jewish Church, iii. 211.

any great object even for their own advantage, are often terrible enemies, because they become a focus for discontent, and can sustain a warfare which they could not originate or conduct. It must be added that the position and pretensions of Savonarola were peculiarly difficult and dangerous. That he was sincere and honest we cannot doubt. He believed with all his heart in the claims which he advanced. But there was a point at which he became uncertain of himself. His biographers have collected accounts of miracles supposed to have been wrought by him. We cannot find that he ever laid claim to such powers himself; but he certainly did not discourage the supposition that such evidence might be granted in confirmation of his doctrine.

It is, in truth, one of the most convincing proofs of his entire sincerity. An impostor might have known that, as his revelations were inventions, so he could have no pretensions to work miracles except as the mere deceptions of jugglery. Savonarola believed that the fire which burned in his heart was kindled by God, and therefore he might well ask himself why the same Spirit should not appear by signs and wonders, and confirm the words which He had taught His servant to speak. "God could stretch forth the hand in His own time," he said. He did not promise that it should be so; but he did not feel that he had a right to repress the expectation.

The changing humors of the upper and middle classes of the people had been faithfully reflected in the changes of the government. At the beginning of Lent (1498) the public opinion of these classes was decidedly hostile to Savonarola; yet they were not prepared to proceed to extremities. Many of them sincerely respected him; and they knew that the masses of the people still believed in him, and were prepared to defend him. If they went beyond what the absolute necessities of their circumstances might require, if they proceeded to lay hands upon the excommunicated Frate, they might provoke a war, in which the popular element would be their adversary and destroyer.

While these conflicting forces were pausing for some change which should set them in motion, an event occurred which was destined to have the most powerful influence upon the course of this history In the previous year Frà Domenico Buonvicini had been preaching at Prato, when a Franciscan, named Frà Francesco di Puglia, who was preaching in the same town, made a violent attack upon the teaching of Savonarola. He went so far as to say that he was ready to enter the fire with Frà Domenico, that it might thus be made manifest which of them was a witness for the truth. This offer was eagerly accepted by Frà Domenico, and a day was fixed; but before that time Frà Francesco pleaded that he was ordered by his superiors to depart elsewhere on important business. It has been thought that this course was taken because there was no prospect of striking at Savonarola himself by means of such a trial.

Be this as it may, in the Lent of 1498 the same Francesco was preaching at the Franciscan church of Santa Croce, when he again attacked Savonarola in the most violent manner as a heretic, a schismatic, and a false prophet, and challenged him to enter the fire with him, to prove whether his doctrine was true.

When Frà Domenico heard of this new attack, he claimed to take the brunt of the battle upon himself, because it had arisen out of the quarrel of the previous year at Prato. He declared himself ready to defend the doctrines of his master, who was at this time prohibited from preaching, and willing to submit to any ordeal in defence of their truth. Savonarola discouraged this rashness in every possible way. He had already proved the truth of his doctrine, and none had ventured to point out the slightest heresy in his teaching. He could not undertake such a mode of defending himself without a clear divine sanction.

Frà Domenico was not to be restrained. He published a set of propositions which he was prepared to maintain, in defence of which he was ready to enter the fire: 1. The Church of God needs renovation. 2. It will be scourged. 3. It will be renovated. 4. Florence, too, after the scourge, will be renovated and prosper. 5. The infidels will be converted to Christ. 6. All these things will take place in our times. 7. The excommunication lately issued against our father, Brother Hieronymus, is null. 8. Those who do not observe it do not sin.

To this Frà Francesco replied that he had no quarrel with Frà Domenico da Pescia, but with Frà Girolamo, whose doctrines he called in question; and it was he whom he challenged to the ordeal. The matter might have died out as a passing folly which deserved no serious notice; but the enemies of Savonarola saw their opportunity, and determined that it should not be lost. If Frà Francesco could only be made to persevere with his challenge, they might now forever ruin the man whom they hated. If Savonarola should venture to enter the fire, he would be burned. If he refused, his credit with the populace would be gone for ever.

There can be little doubt that the Compagnacci were at the bottom of the movement. Dolfo Spini and his friends induced the Signoria, who were only too ready, to take the same view of the position. Privately they assured Frà Francesco that there would be no real necessity for him to enter the fire; and the assurance emboldened him to persist. He had no pretensions, he said, to compare with Frà Girolamo, but it was with him that the trial must be made: he had nothing to do with Frà Domenico; and he added that his challenge was made "at the instance and request of the magnificent Signori."

The Signoria were not entirely of one accord in this matter; but the thing had gone too far, and it only remained to see it carried out. Burlamacchi asserts that Savonarola, although he never approved of the ordeal, offered to submit to it on condition that the ambassadors of all the Christian princes and the Pope's legate were present. This requirement was probably advanced, not only from the just suspicion that unfairness might be used in conducting the trial, but also to remove all doubt as to its lawfulness. His adversaries replied that these excuses were vain, and that they were advanced only for the purpose of wasting time.

It was at last agreed that the ordeal should take place. Savonarola was forced to withdraw his opposition. It is said that he was encouraged by a vision of Frà Salvestro, who declared that he had seen the angels of Frà Girolamo and Frà Domenico, who had assured him that these brethren would come out of the fire unhurt. This Frà Salvestro, or Salvestro Maruffi, was a man who had an influence over Savonarola out of all proportion to his real power. He was one of those weak, nervous, emotional people who are unable to distinguish between facts and fancies, between reality and imagination; and his power of converting his wishes and the impressions made upon him by the teaching and preaching of Savonarola into visions and revelations was a gift most dangerous to himself and others. But in this matter the whole brotherhood were of one mind. They came forward in a body to offer themselves for the *Sperimento*. For every Franciscan that would enter the fire, there was a Dominican ready to go along with him. After several had announced their willingness to undergo the ordeal, on the second of April, Frà Malatesta Sacramoro da Rimini and Frà Roberto di Bernardo Salviati da Firenze subscribed the challenge. The "Ten" sent an account of the proceedings to Rome, together with the reasons assigned by the brethren of St. Mark for accepting the trial. It was finally agreed that Frà Domenico alone, on the side of St. Mark's, should undergo the ordeal, and that the Franciscans should be represented by Giuliano Rondinelli, Francesco professing his readiness to go into the fire, provided Savonarola would do the same.

The sixth of April was originally fixed as the day by the Signoria; but they put off the trial to the seventh. It is believed that they had some hope that a brief might arrive from Rome forbidding the " experiment " to take place. In this, however, they were disappointed. The place appointed for the ordeal was a platform, about eighty feet in length, ten in breadth, and three in height, which extended from the 'Tetto de' Pisani, on the western side of the Piazza, to the Marzocco, the marble lion, which stands in front of the Palazzo Vecchio. The platform was covered with earth and bricks, and was piled up with wood and other more combustible materials, leaving a passage in the middle, four feet in width, for the two men to walk in. It was arranged that it should be lighted at one end, that they should enter at the other, and then that the pile should be lighted behind them.

On the morning of April 7th, the monks of St. Mark's, who had spent several days in constant prayer, assembled for the celebration of a solemn mass, "their hearts full of such joy," says Burla-macchi, "that it showed itself on their countenances, through the certainty of victory" Still it was an awful moment, and Savonarola addressed them with unusual solemnity and diffidence. He had no faith in the intentions of his adversaries; he probably knew that the Signoria were embarrassed as to the lawful-ness of the trial which they had sanctioned, and he showed in his words the hesitation inspired by these considerations.

"I cannot be certain," he said, "that the ordeal will take place, because this matter does not depend upon us ; but I am able to tell you that, if we come to the event, the victory will certainly be ours. O Lord, we have no need of these miraculous proofs in order to believe in the truth; but we have been challenged, and we could not refuse to defend Thine honor! We are sure that the devil will not be able to turn this thing to the injury of Thine honor, or against Thy will; so that we go to do battle for Thee. But these adversaries of ours adore another god, for their works are different from ours. O Lord, this people wishes only to serve Thee ! "

Then, turning to the people, he asked, " My people, are you willing to serve God?" Every voice answered, " Yes ; " and then he bade the men offer up prayer while he was preparing the brethren to go forth, and the women to continue in prayer until they returned. By the time the preparations were finished, a message arrived from the Signoria to signify that all was now in readiness for the trial.

A strong guard of soldiers had been placed on the Piazza by the Signoria to prevent outrage and disturbances ; but each party had taken the precaution to arm their own adherents and station them near the scene. The Arrabbiati had five hundred men under Dolfo Spini, and the Frateschi three hundred under Marcuccio Salviati.

The adherents of the Frate formed their line of procession in the piazza of San Marco. First came the acolytes, and after them the friars ; last of these Frà Domenico, attired in a red vestment,[1] with a crucifix in his hand, a deacon and a sub-deacon walking on either side of him. Last of all came Savonarola, in a white cope, bearing in his hand a silver reliquary which contained the blessed Sacrament ; on one side of him Frà Francesco Salviati, on the other Frà Malatesta Sacramoro, also wearing copes. The face of Frà Domenico was calm and joyous, as of one going to certain victory. Behind them came a great multitude of men and women, carrying lighted tapers in their hands. The singers led

---

[1] Burlamacchi seems to say a chasuble, others a cope. I follow Burlamacchi chiefly in this account.

off, in a loud voice, the 68th Psalm : *Exurgat Deus, et dissipentur inimici Eju.,* — "Let God arise, and let His enemies be scattered." As they entered the Piazza the people took up the psalm, and the earth seemed to tremble under the tramp of multitudinous feet.

The Loggia de' Lanzi had been set apart for the two bodies of friars, the Dominicans occupying the western division, and the Franciscans the eastern. The latter were already stationed in the place allotted to them, and standing silent, when the Frateschi marched into the square to the thunder of their psalm, and took their places. But now it was found that Frà Giuliano Rondinelli, the champion of the adversaries, was not there.

Up to this time Savonarola appears to have been tortured with doubt as to the rightness of the trial which he had been forced to sanction. But now all misgivings seemed to vanish. He felt assured that his cause was the cause of righteousness and of God, that he had not chosen this mode of vindicating himself, and that God would be with him. He saw depicted on the face of Frà Domenico a joyful eagerness to undergo the trial ; and he was anxious that it should begin at once. But the challengers did not appear. They were still in the Palazzo, in consultation with the Signoria. The *ringhiera*, from which the Signoria were to watch the process, was empty. Instead of coming forth and bringing the Franciscans to the appointed spot, they sent a message to Savonarola, asking why he did not begin.

The accounts of this scene are tolerably consistent, and they show that the party opposed to Savonarola had no real intention of undergoing the ordeal. All their efforts were directed to inducing him to enter the fire alone, or take the responsibility of retreating from the trial. In either case they were victorious. Nay, more, they knew that if anything should happen to prevent the ordeal being gone through, the popular fury would turn against Savonarola, because he was the man whose claims and whose doctrines were in question.

Hence they began to invent every possible pretext for delay. First of all they declared that the red vestment worn by Frà Domenico had been enchanted by Savonarola, and insisted on his taking it off before he entered the fire. To this the Dominicans consented, although at the same time they declared that the demand was absurd, as they did not believe in incantations. The Franciscans next said that his habit might also be enchanted, and he consented to retire and exchange dresses with another of the brethren of St. Mark. But still they feared to let him stand beside Frà Girolamo, lest he should enchant this habit as well; and so he consented to be placed between two Franciscans. And now he insisted that the trial should begin; he had complied with their wishes, and there could be no reason for further delay.

But still his opponent did not appear. People were going to and fro among the Franciscans, showing their sympathy with that side, and sneering at the Dominicans because they would not ascend the platform alone. Savonarola became impatient, and demanded that the Franciscans should appear; but it was becoming more and more apparent that they had no intention of doing so. The people now began to give signs of restlessness and indignation. They had come there to see the Frati enter the fire, and no one would gratify them. The enemies of Savonarola took advantage of their impatience, and stimulated them to cry for the beginning of the

Sperimento. It had been the hope of the Arrabbiati that, in case of a tumult arising, they might be able to lay hold on the Frate and despatch him without further trouble. They now believed they saw their opportunity. Stationed under the Tetto de' Pisani, they occupied the side of the Piazza nearest to the Dominicans. They began to advance towards the place where Savonarola was standing ; but their attempt was observed by Salviati, who, keeping his men in their place in front of the Loggia, made a line on the ground with his sword, and shouted, " Whoever passes this line shall know the strength of the arms of Marcuccio Salviati," which stopped the movement.

The Signoria were perplexed, and knew not how to act, when suddenly a thunderstorm broke over the city, and heavy rain began to descend. But the people would not be driven from their purpose, and remained standing in the Piazza until the rain ceased. Still the Franciscan did not appear ; and his party began to invent new reasons for delay, and to make new complaints of the conduct of their opponents. Frà Domenico had walked forth from St. Mark's bearing the crucifix in his hands, and now they demanded that this should be given up. Savonarola advised him to do so, and bid him enter the fire with the Sacrament in his hand. Burlamacchi says that Frà Salvestro had seen a vision, in which it was revealed that Domenico should not undergo the ordeal without bearing the Sacrament with him. The Franciscans then objected that such a course involved a fearful sacrilege, as the host would be burned. It was of no avail that it was answered that the accidents only could perish, — a proposition which was supported by the authority of many doctors of the Church. For the first time the party of Savonarola resisted the demands of their adversaries. They now had the pretext they had been seeking for refusing to go on with the trial. Both sides stood firm; and in the midst of the dispute the Signoria sent their command that the ordeal should not take place.

The spectators were furious. They had waited for hours to see the doctrines of the Frate put to the proof, and now they were to be baulked. They forgot that it was the Franciscans who had refused the test, and thought only of the fact that it had not been undergone by the man who, they were made to believe, had occasioned the challenge. Even the Piagnoni began to exclaim that the Frate ought himself to have entered the fire, and thus finally have vindicated the truth of his doctrine. His enemies went about among the people declaring that now the falsehood of his pretensions was demonstrated. The Franciscans began to depart in triumph, having accomplished their purpose. They had disgraced their enemy and turned the fury of the populace upon him. Returning to Santa Croce, they sang a solemn Te Deum in celebration of their victory.

Savonarola, seeing the danger to which his brethren were exposed from the rage of the mob, requested a guard from the Signoria to protect them on their way back to San Marco. Upon this, Marcuccio Salviati brought forward a band of his most trusted and courageous soldiers, and forming them into a crescent (*luna*), said, " Father, follow me, for I will defend you as long as my life shall last; " and so receiving Savonarola and the brethren into the midst of his men, conducted them back to the convent.

Savonarola, returning to the church, found the women

still kneeling in prayer, and gave them an account of all that had happened.   He then returned, weary and sad, to his cell.   The howls of the disappointed mob that filled the piazza of San Marco came into his ears as he knelt in sorrowful prayer, and told him with no doubtful meaning of the days that were approaching.

CHAPTER XIX.

MARTYRDOM.

THE ordeal by fire was the beginning of the end. Savonarola had lost his hold on the people of Florence, and he was not destined to recover it. Whether there was still a possibility of his regaining his former sway if different measures had been taken, is open to discussion; but those measures were not taken. To many of the Frateschi it became at once apparent that active preparations must be made to defend themselves, perhaps even to assume the offensive. This was the view of Luca degli Albizzi and others; but Valori, strong in the righteousness of their cause, would not hear of it. Albizzi and many others declared that this inaction was throwing away their lives, and instantly left Florence, to provide for their own safety.

A speedy collision seemed inevitable; and the Piagnoni were certainly imprudent, in so far as they neither prepared for it nor avoided it. They appeared to catch the spirit of the sorrowful words which their leader addressed to them on the morning of Palm Sunday, the day after the ordeal. He seemed to be aware that he was speaking to them for the last time, and he expressed himself ready for the sacrifice, prepared to give his life for his flock. After vespers at St. Mark's the Piagnoni proceeded to the cathedral to hear the sermon, which during Savonarola's retirement had been preached in Lent by Mariano degli Ughi, one of the brethren who had offered to undergo the ordeal on behalf of Frà Girolamo. The Arrabbiati were determined to prevent the sermon. The Piagnoni were assaulted on their way to the Duomo. In the church itself noisy discussions took place. The Signoria were that day deciding that Savonarola should be banished from Florence, and the brothers inhibited from preaching. Whatever opposition to extreme measures had previously existed seemed to have been removed by the events of the previous day. The Compagnacci had probably become aware of this decision. From words they proceeded to blows; and at last the cry was raised: "To San Marco!" and "With fire!"

The signal once given, they lost no time in carrying out their purpose. Rushing furiously along the streets, they killed on their way two known adherents of the Frate. A number of the congregation had remained at St. Mark's after vespers, and were engaged in prayer in the church. A shower of stones was poured into the building by the assailants. The women and the principal part of the worshippers hastily dispersed in terror. The doors were closed and locked, and only a few of the citizens remained to defend the convent. It is said there were about thirty of them, some of the most loyal and devoted of Savonarola's adherents.

Although they had not been able to agree as to concerted measures for self-defence, yet some of the brethren, foremost among them Frà Benedetto,[1] had

---

[1] Frà Benedetto was one of the most loyal and devoted of the adherents of Savonarola. After his master's death he was first exiled, and then long imprisoned for his attachment to him. He was at this time about twenty-four years of age. Cf Padre Marchese in the Archivio Istorico.

collected a quantity of arms and ammunition, without the knowledge of Savonarola, for use in case violence should be attempted against them. When the assault commenced, they prepared for the defence. Frà Benedetto, with a helmet on his head and a breastplate over his Dominican habit, was rallying his forces ; and shouts of *Viva Cristo !* were heard mingling with the noise of armor, disturbing the quiet of those cloisters so long the abode of silence, prayer, and meditation.

Savonarola and Frà Domenico endeavored in vain to appease the tumult, and entreated the brethren to lay aside their armor. When words could avail nothing, Savonarola, attiring himself in a cope, and taking a crucifix in his hand, proposed to go forth and offer himself a sacrifice to the mob, " as it was on his account that the storm had arisen." Held back by the lamentations of his friends, he then took the Sacra-ment in his hands, and calling upon the brethren to follow him, he went in procession around the cloisters, and afterwards proceeding to the choir, told them that prayer was their only lawful weapon. Nearly the whole of the community joined him in prayer, singing before the sacrament : *Salvum fac populum Tuum, Domine,* — " Save Thy people, O Lord ! "

It was probably about this time that a messenger arrived from the Signoria, bearing the news that Savonarola had been sentenced to exile, and ordering him to leave the territory of the State within twelve hours. The tumult without was waxing louder, the assailants probably being emboldened by the absence of re-sistance from within. Savonarola seems to have re-mained in the choir in prayer, there awaiting the issue of events. Francesco Valori, at last convinced of the

wisdom of the advice which he had rejected, got over
the walls at the back of the convent, hoping to raise
the Piagnoni in defence of their master. If Marcuccio
Salviati could have been there at once with his Iron-
sides, all might have been different; but it was not so
ordered. Valori hastened home to make his preparations, but was instantly summoned to appear before
the Signoria. Confident in the righteousness of his
cause, he at once obeyed. But the days of his
supremacy had not been forgotten, nor the death of
the Medicean conspirators, which had been in great
measure his work. Members of the Tornabuoni and
Ridolfi families set upon him and killed him under the
eyes of his wife, who, hearing the tumult as he left the
house, had rushed to the window. They perished
together; she was shot from the street as she looked
upon the murder of her husband, and their house was
immediately sacked and burned.

The assault on the convent waxed fiercer, and fire
was now applied to burn down the doors. The
brethren flew again to arms. The enemy had penetrated into the cloisters and into the church. , Frà
Benedetto, again marshalling his forces, poured down
upon them a shower of stones and missiles of every
description. The friars met their assailants with determined courage, striking with whatever weapons they
could lay hold of. Those who had nothing better
used their crucifixes; some, it is said, had attached
pikes and knives to the burning tapers they had been
carrying, and struck home with such vigor that they
seemed to their adversaries under supernatural guidance. The grotesque and the pathetic were curiously
mingled in this strange conflict. Burlamacchi tells us

of a certain German Frate, named Herico (Heinrich, no doubt), who, in defending the choir, "got up into the pulpit with an arquebuse, and shot a good many of the enemy in the church, exclaiming as he fired, *Salvum fac populum Tuum, Domine, et benedic hæreditati Tuæ,*" taking up the refrain of the psalm which Savonarola had made them sing before the Sacrament. The vicar and some of the brethren were still before the altar in prayer; sometimes ministering to the wounded and dying. While Herico is discharging his arquebuse from the pulpit, and stones and sticks are flying in all directions, there is a youth wounded to death borne into the choir, who receives the Sacrament at the hands of Frà Domenico, murmuring, as he dies, happy in dying near his beloved teacher: *Ecce quam bonum et quam jucundum habitare fratres in unum,* — "Behold how good and pleasant it is for brethren to dwell together."

It has been the opinion of many that the brethren were quite holding their own against the mob, and might, with the assistance of their friends, have driven them off; but the Signoria now began to take more active part in the quarrel. There is no doubt that they had become the declared enemies of Savonarola. To keep up appearances they seem to have issued simultaneously a decree declaring the assailants of St. Mark's rebels, and another giving the same name to all those of the brethren who did not leave St. Mark's within an hour; demanding at the same time the surrender of Frà Girolamo, Frà Domenico, and Frà Salvestro.

By these means assistance was rendered to the besiegers, who pushed forward and burned down the door of the choir, forcing an entrance there. The defenders retreated behind the high altar, our German and another brother, also armed with an arquebuse, pouring their shots from both sides of the great crucifix. How far Savonarola had taken part in this conflict is doubtful. He had successfully interposed at the beginning of the assault, and had induced the brethren to lay down their arms. A fresh attack had been begun, and hostilities had been resumed, while he was at prayer in the choir. Some of the assailants having broken into the convent, they and the besieged had got mingled together, so that any effort to put an end to the conflict was hopeless, and his friends would not allow Savonarola to expose his own person. When the choir was broken into, he took again the Sacrament in his hands, and beseeching the brethren to follow him, he proceeded to the Libreria Greca (the Convent Library), and there prepared himself for the end. Gathering around him such of the members of the fraternity as could be collected, he addressed to them the last words he was to speak within those walls.

"My children," he said, "before God, before the consecrated Host, with the enemy already in the convent, I confirm to you my doctrine. That which I have spoken I have received from God, and He is my witness in heaven that I do not lie. I did not know that the whole city was to turn against me; but the will of the Lord be done. My last counsel is this: let faith, patience, and prayers be your arms. I leave you with anguish and grief, to put myself into the hands of my enemies. I know not whether they will take away my life; but I am certain that if I must die, I shall be able to aid you in heaven more than I have been able to do on earth. Be comforted, embrace the cross, and with that you will find the harbor of safety."

The commander of the guard of the palace now appeared with a written order from the Signoria, requiring that the three friars should be immediately given up, and enforcing the demand with a threat to destroy the convent by artillery.[1] Several of the brethren entreated their prior to save himself by flight; and for a moment he seemed to hesitate. His course was finally decided by the counsel of Frà Malatesta Sacramoro. This man had been an ardent believer in the teachings of his master; he had gone so far as to offer himself for the ordeal. The failure of that project and the subsequent conduct of the people had changed the faithful disciple into a Judas. It is the name given to him by Savonarola's friends, especially by Frà Benedetto, who was a witness of all that took place. He now turned against the Frate, through fear or some revulsion of feeling. While others were urging Savonarola to flee, he interposed with the plausible question, "Ought not the shepherd to lay down his life for the sheep?" Savonarola was deeply touched by these words. Turning to the brethren, he gave them, and first among them Malatesta himself, a last embrace. Salvestro had hidden himself.[2] With the faithful and ever resolute Domenico by his side, he went forth and gave himself into the hands of his enemies. He would not leave the convent without speaking one last word of comfort to the afflicted brethren. "My dear brothers

---

[1] Villari says that this had been suggested by Frà Malatesta Sacramoro; I cannot find the authority for this statement. Burlamacchi says it had been required by Savonarola himself.

[2] Vasari says that Frà Bartolommeo also concealed himself. It is possible, and not discreditable; but there is no contemporary evidence, and Vasari is a very untrustworthy authority.

(*Fratelli miei*)," he said, "remember you have no need to doubt. The work of the Lord will ever go forwards, and my death will only hasten it."

If the change of fortune had made friends to fall away, it had strengthened the attachment of others. An impressive scene took place shortly before he left the library. A young man named Girolamo Gini had been long desirous of taking the habit at St. Mark's, and was in the church when the siege of the convent began. He had laid down his arms at the command of the Frate, but he had resolved to show his devotion to his cause. When the enemy broke into the cloisters he had run into the midst of them, armed only with his crucifix, as if to seek death. Seriously wounded, he hastened back to the library, and kneeling down before the Frate, he requested now to be received into the brotherhood. It was Savonarola's last act of authority to grant his request.[1]

If the enemies of Savonarola had resolved and planned that his persecutions, his sufferings, and the circumstances of his death should resemble those of his Divine Master as nearly as possible, they could hardly have acted differently towards him from this moment to the hour of his death. No sooner was he in the hands of the soldiers than the mob crowded round him and heaped upon him every imaginable insult. They raised cries of joy, of execration, of blasphemous reproach. It was now about eight o'clock, and many bore torches and lanterns. Turning these upon his face, they cried out, "There goes the true light." They rushed against

---

[1] Other proofs of devotion were given. Frà Benedetto cast himself into the crowd, and asked that he should be taken along with his master.

him and struck him, exclaiming, "Prophesy, who is it that smote thee?" They kicked him behind, and howled in derision, "It is there he has the gift of prophecy." It was with difficulty the officers were able to conduct him to the Palazzo. He was at once brought before the *gonfaloniere*, who asked him if he persisted in his assertion that he had spoken by divine revelation. When he and Frà Domenico answered in the affirmative, they were immediately committed to custody. The cell in which he was confined is still shown; it was the same in which Cosimo de' Medici had been imprisoned by the Albizzi. The Signoria had promised when he gave himself up that he should be set at liberty after he had been interrogated. This promise was not kept. The next day Frà Salvestro, coming out of his hiding-place, was in his turn betrayed by the Judas of the convent. The three Fratri were now kept for their more formal trial.

The joy of Savonarola's enemies knew no bounds when they heard of the success of the trick played by the Compagnacci and the Franciscans, of the failure of the ordeal, of the consequent revulsion in the popular mind, and the arrest of the three Dominicans. Briefs arrived from Rome telling the brethren of Santa Croce, and Frà Francesco in particular, how deeply the Holy Father had felt, and how earnestly he would hold in eternal remembrance their "holy zeal and evangelical charity." As regarded the Signoria, they were declared to be true sons of Holy Church, and every blessing and absolution was pronounced upon them. But a greater joy awaited the Pope and his firm ally, the Duke of Milan. Savonarola had still one friend, somewhat of a broken reed, it is true, yet dangerous to his enemies, if

not entirely to be trusted by his friends.   It was to the
king of France that the Frate had turned as a means
of assembling a council ; he could not help thinking of
him as a protector in his hour of adversity.   Alas, this
hope too must now fail him !   On the very day of the
ordeal Charles VIII. had died at Amboise.

The enemies of Savonarola had determined that however his trial might be conducted, his condemnation
should be obtained.   The Compagnacci exhibited in
public the arms which had been collected for the defence of the convent, and told the people that these
were the proofs of the miraculous powers of the Frate,
and of the love which he bore to Florence.   The
Signoria, knowing that the Ten and the Eight were still
favorable to Savonarola, determined to bring him before
a special and hostile tribunal.   For this purpose they appointed a commission consisting of seventeen examiners,
with two canons.   They took care to place on the commission some of his bitterest enemies ; among them Piero
degli Alberti — one of the chief promoters of the ordeal,
and the first who had objected to the vestment worn by
Frà Domenico as being enchanted — and Dolfo Spini,
the leader of the Compagnacci.   The constitution of the
tribunal was so manifestly unjust that one of the commissioners left it in indignation, declaring that he "would
have no share in this homicide."[1]

When Savonarola was brought before the commission
he gave the same answer as he had already given to the
Signoria, — his doctrine was of God.   To those who
demanded a different reply he said, "Ye tempt the
Lord."   We have here the whole substance of his

[1] Burlamacchi gives the name as that of Francesco degli
Albizzi.   Villari shows that it was Bartolo dei Zati.

defence.   Throughout the entire period which intervened between his arrest on Palm Sunday to the day of his death, on the eve of the Ascension, he never wavered, except under torture, in the profession of his faith.   It is now impossible to recover the true answers which he returned to the particular questions of his judges.   At first he was allowed to write his replies ; but these were found so unsatisfactory for the purpose of his condemnation that they were destroyed, and his oral answers were so garbled that it is impossible to place any reliance upon the reports.

The first examination took place on the Monday in Holy Week, before the commission was made up.   On the Tuesday he was taken to the upper hall of the Bargello,[1] interrogated afresh, and when he refused to give the desired replies, put to the torture.

Pico della Mirandola gives a minute account[2] of this horrible punishment as applied to Savonarola.   His hands were bound behind his back with the strongest chains.   They were then tied to a rope attached to the roof of the building, by which he was first drawn up to a great height, and then let fall with great violence, so that his feet did not quite touch the ground ; and his body, remaining suspended in the air, sprang upwards again, so that his shoulders were put out of joint and his muscles strained and torn.   Instruments of torture were set before his eyes.   Insults were heaped upon him, he was struck and spit upon, his torturers demanding all the time that he should recant his prophecies and disavow his pretensions to be a messenger of God.

[1] Opposite to the church of the Badia, formerly the Palazzo del Podestà, now a museum.

[2] Cap. xvii.

Burning coals were then applied to his feet, so that the flesh and nerves were half burned, in order that he might be induced to retract. He refused to do so. Again and again they repeated the torture, and he repeated his innocence, crying out with the prophet Elijah : *Tolle, tolle, Domine, animam meam,* — "O Lord, take away my life !" When the torture was over and he was led back to his cell, he immediately knelt down and prayed, in the words of Christ, " Father, forgive them, for they know not what they do."

It is difficult to say how often the torture was applied to him during his two examinations before the commissioners, each of which lasted several days; but it is certain that the pain which he endured was extreme, and almost maddening. He was of a most delicate and sensitive organization, and while ready and willing to die, he was unable to endure the agony which was thus inflicted upon him. In the delirium produced by his torments it is said that he gave utterance to many equivocal expressions, and even that he confessed to being influenced by the desire of glory and power. His biographers relate that he used the same method before his judges that Christ employed before Pilate.

However this may have been, his enemies found it impossible to convict him out of his own mouth. Their questions had reference to three points, — his religious teaching, his political conduct, and his prophecies. They could obtain nothing from him on the first point which they could torture into a charge of heresy. On the second he is said to have been equally clear and distinct. On the third his utterances were more uncertain and wavering.

When they found that even the torture could extract

from him nothing that was sufficient for their purpose, they employed a notary named Francesco Ceccone, who promised that he would so misrepresent his words as to make him confess himself guilty. This man had been concerned in the conspiracy of the Bigi, and is said to have been saved by the interposition of Savonarola, whom he thus repaid. Preserving some of his words, he distorted their meaning by omissions and additions which changed the whole impression they were calculated to produce. For instance, says Burlamacchi, he was asked why he had done such great things for Florence; and when he replied, "I have done everything for glory," — meaning for the true glory of the State, — Ceccone wrote down "for human glory."

It is almost certain that something of this kind took place, and Signor Villari, in printing the false reports which were published by the Signoria, has indicated passages which are evident interpolations; but it is impossible to arrive at the truth. The stories told by his own biographers represent rather the view taken by Savonarola's own friends than any ascertained facts. Burlamacchi relates that Ceccone had bargained with the Signoria for four hundred *scudi* for the work which he had to do; but the magistrates were so little satisfied with the result that they paid him no more than thirty. Complaining of this injustice to one of the citizens who happened to be an adherent of the Frate, he thus revealed the treachery of which he had been guilty.

Pico relates a very probable example of this falsification, which is said to have taken place on the 19th of April. The Frate, he says, had the examination read over to him, and was asked by Ceccone, in the presence of eight witnesses, of whom six were friars of St. Mark's, whether that which was read was true or false.

" To which the man of God replied, ' What I have written is true.' ' Altogether ? ' he asked. ' Altogether,' he replied. ' To the letter (*ad verbumne*) ? ' he was asked again. ' To the letter,' he answered. And then, turning to his friends who were present, he told them that no one was ignorant of his doctrine and manner of life, and asked to be commended to the novices, and sent them an exhortation to live in the fear of God, as they had been taught; and entreated that they would offer earnest prayers to God on his behalf, because the Spirit had almost left him."

In reference to this, Pico says his enemies declared that he had said, not " What I have written is true," but " What is written," — meaning the report of Ceccone.[1]

If Ceccone failed to satisfy the Signoria, the remembrance of his treachery is said to have been a heavy burden on his own conscience, which became insupportable as the hour of death drew near. He was taken ill at his villa, and had only one maid-servant with him at the time. Two Dominicans came to the door, asking alms, while he lay dying, and the maid entreated them to come and try to bring her master to confession. But all was vain; " he said his sins were unpardonable,

---

[1] Among the brethren of St. Mark's who were thus present was the Judas, Fra Malatesta, who, apparently desirous of knowing the truth, now asked Savonarola, " But are the things you have subscribed " (meaning the report of Ceccone) " true or false ? " To this question Savonarola gave no reply, but turned away from the traitor in indignation. Sacramoro then said, " Out of thy mouth I believed thee; and now out of thine own mouth I disbelieve thee."

crying out that Judas had betrayed only one, but he had betrayed three ; and so he died without confession and absolution."

The words which Savonarola had spoken to his friends on the loss of the spirit of prophecy represented with truth his habitual feelings during this period of his imprisonment ; and these feelings are probably represented in many of the expressions contained in the falsified report. That he said he was no prophet is very probable : he had said the same in the days of his prosperity and power ; and such a profession was in no way incompatible with the declaration that he had received from God the message which he had delivered to Florence, to Italy, and to the Church at large. But these simple statements were not sufficient for his cruel judges. They plied him with questions so artfully contrived that he could hardly answer them without giving the appearance of equivocation and evasion. Whether his revelations were from God or were the imaginations of his own heart, it would be impossible to answer questions respecting them that would satisfy men blinded by passion and hatred. Many of his answers, therefore, were probably ambiguous ; but we may safely put down a great deal of the report of the examination as an entire fabrication. For instance, when he is represented as saying, " This was my hypocrisy, it was my pride," and the like, we see in these words, not the utterances even of the tortured and delirious victim, but the invention or the distortions of the notary ; and it is certain that, when he was before the commissioners, he repeatedly asserted the truth of his visions, at the same time that he protested against these being made a ground of accusation against him, inasmuch as they did not concern the State and were not matters which they could either examine or condemn. If it should be believed, as some have believed, that Savonarola did, under the torture, employ language which bore one meaning in his own mind and another to his hearers, this will not seem surprising if it is remembered how the last few days had been passed before his trial. On the Saturday he had stood for hours in the Piazza della Signoria, tormented by the tricks of the Franciscans, insulted and reviled by the people; the next day was the terrible Palm Sunday, on the evening of which he surrendered to the magistrates. On the Monday he had been questioned, with every expression of insolent hatred and amid the tumult of the populace, in the Palazzo della Signoria, and on Tuesday he was put to the torture in the Bargello, — a process which seems to have been repeated day after day during his examination.

When the report of this trial was published — and this was not done until it had been altered again and again — it proved so unsatisfactory that the Signoria withdrew all the copies and destroyed as many as they could lay hold of, and published another version; but even then it was found to contain nothing which could be regarded as constituting a capital offence. Having thus failed, the Signoria determined to have a second trial, which was conducted in the same manner as the first, and with very nearly the same results. To crown the injustice of the proceedings, instead of reading the conclusion of the trial before the people and in the presence of the accused, in accordance with the law, it was read simply by one of the Eight, who announced that Savonarola had declined to be present, for fear of being stoned by the people, — a statement which no one believed.

The examination of the two companions of Savonarola was conducted in a manner equally illegal, and if possible, more cruel and deceitful. They were tortured, of course ; but they were put to the still more cruel torture of being compelled to hear the falsehood that the master whom they loved had confessed himself a deceiver. But one at least stood firm. They could extract no word from Frà Domenico which could by any device be perverted into a recantation or a disowning of the truth which he believed he had received. Finding that they could not entrap him in his words, they permitted him to write his defence. To this they made great additions. Happily the two versions are preserved, so that we can ascertain the kind of changes which the falsifier of these documents introduced.[1]

In this document Frà Domenico, after declaring that he spoke the truth, proceeds to state that he and Frà Hieronimo had been opposed to resistance by arms. He says that he went to the ordeal by fire willingly, and did not take the Sacrament with him to prevent its taking place. When he was told that Savonarola had recanted, he said that he had always believed, and until he was shown better always should believe, in the prophecies of his master; and after enumerating them, he said they could be no injury to himself or to the city; "and in these things every one is free to believe what he will." He said that Savonarola had never told him what to preach, but had let him be led by divine inspiration. When he was pressed to say more, he

---

[1] Villari prints copies of both among the Documenti at the end of the second volume of the Italian edition of his work.

declared that he knew no more, and that he had simply occupied himself with holy living and with Jesus Christ, King of Florence. If they tortured him again, they could make him say nothing different. When, after being again tortured, he was asked to write what he had further to say, he declared that he had always believed in the goodness and sincerity of the Frate, and had rendered him obedience as his superior with all simplicity and care. "I have said," he goes on — and these are his last statements — "in the pulpit, to the brethren and also to laymen, that if I had known in Frà Ieronimo the least error or deception, I should have discovered and published it. To himself, too, I have testified several times that I should have done it; and I should do it now, if I knew of any duplicity in him."

It was very different with Frà Salvestro. His character has been already described, and we have heard how he showed his timidity on the evening of Palm Sunday. When he was examined he had only one thought, — how to avoid the torture. Even his answers, however, Villari thinks, have undergone alteration at the hands of Ser Ceccone; but a careful perusal of his whole testimony leaves upon the mind the impression that no real accusation could be brought against Savonarola.

When the brethren of San Marco were told of the recantation of their vicar their faith failed them. They were perplexed and dismayed by the rapid succession of changes and misfortunes which had fallen upon them. Even Frà Benedetto wavered for a season, only, however, to return in penitence and increased conviction to his former faith. On the 21st of April the fraternity made their abject submission to Borgia, and his Holiness gladly gave them absolution, especially as they disowned and abandoned "the head of the whole error, Frà Girolamo Savonarola!"

But the time was coming near for the election of a new Signoria; and in spite of the reverses which the fortunes of the Frate had experienced, his enemies had some dread of his party returning to power. If this happened, their cruel injustice would instantly be discovered. They took effectual precautions to prevent such an event. On the day of the assembling of the great council for the election of the Signoria they took care to exclude a large number, some say as many as two hundred, of its members who belonged to the popular party. By this means a new Signoria, of the same kind as their predecessors, were elected, headed by a *gonfaloniere* named Vieri de' Medici, "who was worthy of the name which he bore."

The Pope had for some time been insisting that Savonarola should be sent to Rome to be tried for his offences. The old Signoria had temporized, evaded the request, put off giving a final answer, until they had secured the election of their successors; and then the Pope was informed that they were unable to grant his request. Amidst the masses of falsehood it is impossible to discern their whole reason for this refusal. Certain pretexts were addressed to the Pope himself; other more private reasons were assigned in a letter to their own ambassadors. It may have been that they were unwilling to part with their authority. They may have wished that the death of the Frate should take place at Florence, to strike terror into the hearts of his adherents; so at least they said. Burlamacchi suggests that they were afraid of the falsifications committed at their request by Ceccone being found out. They requested his Holiness to send two commissioners to try the accused in his name. The Pope at last agreed, and the commissioners arrived at Florence on the 19th of May. They were Giovacchino Turriano, General of the Dominicans, and Francesco Romolino, *Auditore* of the Governor of Rome, a Spanish doctor. They were commissioned by Alexander "to examine the errors and crimes of those three sons of perdition," — a strange description of men who were to be tried and examined !

Nearly a month had elapsed from the last examination of the three prisoners, and Savonarola had employed this interval in writing short commentaries on the 31st and the 51st Psalms. In this work he seems to have recovered all his old energy, and writes as he preached. Still he dwells upon his favorite thought of the renovation of the Church, and finds consolation in the conviction of its accomplishment. He is a penitent sinner, but an undoubting believer. " I will hope, then, in the Lord," he writes in his commentary on the Miserere,[1] " and soon I shall be delivered from all tribulation. And by whose merits? Not by my own, but through Thine, O Lord ! I do not offer my own righteousness, but I seek Thy mercy. The Pharisees gloried in their righteousness, so that they have not that of God, which is by grace alone ; and no one will ever be righteous before God by having done the works of the law alone." One other work he composed in prison : it was his " Rule for a Good Christian Life," written at the request of his jailer, who had been so deeply impressed by the sanctity of his deportment that he asked him to provide him with such a rule.

[1] This commentary soon ran into thirteen editions. It was republished by Luther in 1524.

When the papal commissioners entered Florence, they were greeted on all sides with shouts of "Death, death to the Frate!" There was no doubt of that from the beginning. Romolino told some of the Signori that he had brought a sketch of the sentence with him. The trial was a mere farce. It had been determined by the Pope, as by the Signoria, to perpetrate a judicial murder. There was no attempt made to discover the truth, but only to get hold of something which might criminate the accused. As threats and abuse had no effect upon him, he was put to the torture. When this was being applied, he turned to the magistrates and said aloud, "Now hear me, magistrates of Florence, and be my witnesses. I have denied my light through fear of torture. If I have to suffer, I am willing to suffer for the truth. That which I have spoken I have received from God." These words were remembered and placed on record. Under the torture he became delirious, and seems again to have had recourse, consciously or unconsciously, to his former ambiguity of language. This was when speaking of his prophecies. There was no ambiguity in his utterances concerning the faith or the Church. The next day (May 21st) they put him to the torture again; but still his answers were inconclusive. Seeing that no more could be extracted from him, Romolino told him he must return to-morrow to hear his sentence. "I am a prisoner," he replied; "I shall come if they bring me." The result of this examination was so unsatisfactory that it was not even published. Ceccone seems again to have done his best, but even his garbled report could only demonstrate the innocence of the accused.

On the 22d of May they met to decide the question of the guilt of Savonarola and his companions. By way

of making a show of fairness, Romolino suggested that
the life of Frà Domenico should be spared ; but he was
told that in that case the whole doctrine of Savonarola
would remain alive. To which Romolino instantly made
answer : "A wretched friar (*frataccio*) more or less
makes little difference ; put him to death, then ! "
When the Signoria met there was still one man who
refused to consent to the condemnation. His name,
which deserves to be remembered, was Agnolo Pandolfini.[1] To him "it seemed a very serious fault to put to
death a man of qualities so excellent that such an one
was hardly to be seen in a century. Such a man," he
said, "would not only bring back faith to the world, but
also the sciences, with which he was most highly endowed.
I therefore counsel you to keep him in prison, if you so
wish, but preserve his life and allow him to write, that
the world may not lose the fruits of his genius." The
answer was worthy of the whole transaction. "No one,"
it was said, "could trust the new Signoria that might be
elected within two months. The Frate would certainly
be set at liberty, and would again bring confusion and
destruction upon the city. A dead enemy makes no
more war." It was decided that they should be first
hanged, and then burned.

The sentence of death was communicated the same
night to the three condemned men. Savonarola received
the announcement with perfect calm. He was engaged
in prayer when the messenger arrived. He returned no
answer, but only continued more earnest and fervent in
his prayers. A member of a society which attended
on the condemned in their last hours, named Jacopo

[1] Thus Villari in his first edition. In his second he gives the
surname as Niccolini.

Niccolini, came to pass the night with him. "I do not come," he said to Savonarola, "to recommend resignation to one who has brought back a whole people to the paths of virtue." "Do your duty," was the only reply. He refused to sup, lest it should interrupt his meditations. After confessing to a Benedictine monk, he asked Niccolini to let him lay his head upon his knees. In this attitude he fell asleep; and as he slept he talked and smiled. It was a presage of the coming peace and joy.

Frà Domenico received his sentence with the same composure which he had shown throughout. He rejoiced to suffer with his master and for his cause. To the friars of Fiesole, of which convent he was prior, he wrote a letter bidding them farewell and giving them his last instructions. After asking for their prayers, and bidding them salute the brethren of St. Mark's, and especially those of Fiesole, he gave a touching evidence of his faithfulness unto death. "Collect from my cell," he writes, "all the works of our Father Girolamo; have them bound, and place one copy in the library, and another in the refectory to be read at table." Frà Salvestro was completely overwhelmed by the intelligence of the sentence.

Before they went to rest for the night Savonarola had prayed Niccolini to obtain for him the last favor of an interview with his two brethren. After some hesitation on the part of the Signoria the request was granted. They met in the hall of the great council, — the very chamber which had been erected by the patriotic efforts of Savonarola himself. It was the first time that they had seen each other since the night when they left St. Mark's for the last time. It was to be a short interview, and Savonarola turned at once to Domenico and said he knew that he wished to be burned alive; "but," he said, "it is not given to you to choose the manner of your death. Receive with cheerfulness that which God has prepared for you. Who knows if you will be able to bear that which He has appointed? — since that depends, not upon your own virtue, but on the grace of God. It is not, therefore, expedient to tempt God." Domenico received this counsel in silence.

Turning then to Frà Salvestro, he said, "I know that you wish to declare your innocence before the people. I require you to abandon such a thought, and rather to follow the example of our Lord Jesus Christ, Who not even upon the cross would speak of His innocence." Without answering a word they both knelt down before their superior, and received his benediction in silence. They were then reconducted to their cells to snatch a brief repose, and then to prepare themselves for death.

The place of execution was the same as that appointed for the ordeal; and on the same ground which had been occupied by the scaffold on that occasion was now raised another, about the height of a man, on which were piled all kinds of inflammable materials, and at the western end a gallows with two arms, in the form of a cross. The resemblance, indeed, was so striking that they cut off pieces from the ends of the cross-beam. From the arms of the cross hung three nooses and chains, the chains intended to support the bodies in the fire after they were strangled. The crowds on the Piazza were enormous, as on the day of the ordeal; but a feeling of deeper solemnity seemed to pervade them. On that occasion they had been swayed by doubt, suspense, eager curiosity; now they knew what Florence, what Rome had decided to do with the man who had built up for them their new system of government. Many there were who looked on with savage exultation, knowing that the voice which had rebuked and condemned them could now no longer disturb them in their evil courses. Others — and among them some of his political adversaries — were agitated and terrified at the success which had attended their endeavors. The horror of the scene was increased by the presence of a number of criminals let loose from prison by the Signoria. These wretches had come, as was evident from their words and gestures, to enjoy a festival; and by the insults which they heaped upon the condemned men they showed that they understood the reason of their liberation.

The platform was united to the *ringhiera* by a kind of wooden bridge, over which the condemned men were to proceed to the place of execution. On the *ringhiera* itself were erected three tribunals. The first, which was nearest to the gate of the palace, was for the Bishop of Vasona. He had been appointed with a refinement of cruelty to superintend the degradation of the Frate as a Dominican who had himself received the habit at the hands of Savonarola, although he had afterwards become a member of the congregation of Santa Maria Novella. The second was for the apostolic commissaries; the third, nearest to the Marzocco, was for the *gonfaloniere* and the Eight.

In the morning the three Frati met again to receive the Holy Communion. Savonarola, before communicating himself, took the host in his hand and offered an earnest prayer, " with wonderful joyfulness of mind," says Pico.

" I know, O Lord," — thus he prayed — " that Thou art the Supreme God, who didst make heaven and earth and the whole universe. I know also that Thou art perfect and indivisible Trinity, comprehending three distinct Persons, the Father, the Son, and the Holy Ghost. I acknowledge the Son as the Word of the Eternal Father, who came down from heaven to earth into the womb of the Virgin Mary. Thou, O Lord, didst ascend to the wood of the cross, and didst shed Thy most precious blood to deliver us wretched men from sin. I pray and beseech Thee that Thy blood may not have been shed in vain, but for the remission of my sins. For all of these which I may have committed, from the day in which I was washed in the sacred waves to this hour, I pray that I may obtain pardon of Thee, as well as for every offence and injury which I may have done to this city, and for every error of which I may be ignorant." [1]

He then took the Communion, and gave it to his two companions. Shortly afterwards they were told that they must proceed to the Piazza.

As they descended the stairs of the palace they were met by a Dominican of Santa Maria Novella, who had orders to despoil them of their habits, so that they came before their judges wearing only their woollen tunics, with their feet bare and their hands bound behind them. Savonarola received this unexpected insult with calmness, but with deep grief. " O sacred habit," he said, as it was removed, " how much I desired thee! By the grace of God thou wast granted to me ; and I have

---

[1] Before he left his cell he had told Niccolini of the calamities which were to come upon Florence, and that they would happen under a pope named Clement, — all of which took place. Cf. Villari, lib. iv. cap. 10

preserved thee unstained to this moment. Now I do not abandon thee, but thou art taken from me."

He then took his place before the first tribunal, that which was presided over by his old disciple, the Bishop of Vasona. It was no agreeable task that was assigned to him, to degrade an innocent man, and one whom he had formerly venerated as his master. He could hardly look up, and seemed more like the condemned criminal than the judge. The three friars were placed before him, vested again in the religious habit. The confusion of the bishop showed itself in his words. It was his office to separate the prisoners from the Church on earth ; but as he stammered forth the words, " *Separo te ab Ecclesia militante* (I separate thee from the Church militant)," he added in his confusion, " *atque trium-phante* (and triumphant)." " *Militante,* yes," replied Savonarola at once ; " but *triumphante,* no ! for this does not belong to you."[1] They were words which were heard by many, and could never be forgotten.

They were then led in their tunicles before the two papal commissioners. They had just been excommunicated, and now they were to be restored ! Romolino declared that he was empowered to grant them plenary indulgence. " His Holiness, our Lord Alexander VI., is pleased to deliver you from the pains of purgatory, giving you plenary indulgence of your sins, and restoring you to your first innocence. Do you accept it ? " They assented by inclining their heads.

They were then taken before the tribunal of the Eight, who as a matter of custom went through the

---

[1] Pico : Militante, non triumphante ; hoc enim tuum non est. Burlamacchi : Della militante si, ma della trionfante no, questo a voi non appartiene.

form of voting, and declared that they were unanimous in their condemnation. They expressed their decision in these words : —

" The *gonfaloniere* and the Eight, having well considered the trials of the three friars, and the enormous crimes which they reveal, and especially having considered the sentence of the Pope, which consigns them to the secular tribunal for punishment, decree that each one of the three friars shall be hanged on the gallows, and then burned, in order that their souls may be entirely separated from their bodies."

They were then led to the place of execution. The platform had been so roughly constructed that gaps were left between the planks. Through these some of the mob thrust sharp stakes, to wound the naked feet of the condemned as they passed along. Then Frà Salvestro, who up to that time had shown the greatest timidity and terror at the near prospect of death, seemed to become inspired, and his face shone as he told Savonarola that they must now endure death with a ready and courageous mind. Savonarola exhorted him and Domenico to remain steadfast, to dismiss all fear and anxiety, saying that they should thus the sooner come to heaven, where they would sing that psalm of David, *Ecce quam bonum,* — " Behold, how good and how pleasant it is for brethren to dwell together in unity ! "

Amid the insults which were poured upon them as they passed, there were not wanting expressions of grief and sympathy. Some exhorted them to die with a willing mind; some are said to have offered them food. "Why," asked Savonarola, "should you offer such things to me, who am about to leave this life?" and again, " In the last hour only God is needed to comfort mortals." A priest named Nerotto asked him, "With what mind do you endure this martyrdom?" He simply replied, "Should I not die willingly for Him who suffered as much for me?" and raising up his eyes to his crucifix, he kissed it.

Frà Domenico was worthy of himself to the last. He was so serene and cheerful that he seemed like "one going to a dance, and not to death." He wished to sing the Te Deum aloud as he went along; but at the request of Savonarola he desisted, saying, "Accompany me then in an undertone;" and so they recited it throughout; after which he added to those nearest, "Remember that the prophecies of Frà Girolamo must all be fulfilled, and that we all die in innocence."

Frà Salvestro was the first to die. He mounted to his place with a firm step, in silence, but "with some tears in his eyes;" and murmuring, "Lord, into Thy hands I commend my spirit," he gave his neck to the executioner, and speedily was dead. He was followed immediately by Frà Domenico, whose face shone with joyful hope, as though he were already in the antechamber of heaven.

Last of all came Savonarola, softly reciting the Apostles' Creed. He was so absorbed in devotion that he seemed scarcely aware of what was passing around him; but ás he took his place under the cross he cast one look of sorrowful reproach upon the multitudes whom he had so often taught, guided, and comforted. How different were those upturned looks from the faces which had hung upon his words a few short months before! An awful silence fell upon the people as they stood to witness the death of their prophet. It was broken by a harsh voice which shouted in deri-

sion, " Now, prophet, is the moment to work a miracle."
Others he saw with torches in their hands, ready to set
fire to the pile which was to consume the bodies. It is
said that his last words were : "O Florence ! what hast
thou done to-day?" "He died," says Guicciardini,
"convinced of his innocence and penetrated by the
most lively feelings of charity. Sustained by hope, he
suffered no loss of firmness and composure. No word
escaped from him either of confession or protestation."
It was the 23d of May, the vigil of the Ascension, 1498,
about ten o'clock in the forenoon; and he was now
forty-five years of age.

The executioner, thinking to please the mob, began
to act the buffoon over the dead body as it swung from
the beam, and in doing so very nearly fell off the
scaffold. Exclamations of horror broke from the by-
standers, and the magistrates sent him a severe reproof.
Some tried to kindle the pile so that the flames might
reach the body before life was extinct; but he had
died. One man shouted as he applied his torch, "I am
at last able to burn the man who would have liked to
burn me." As the flames arose, the wind blew them
aside ; and the excited people, ready for any prodigy,
exclaimed, " A miracle ! a miracle ! " and many fled
across the Piazza. But the wind fell, and the flames soon
consumed the cords which bound his arms. His right
hand and arm, raised by the action of the fire, seemed
to the eyes of his adherents as though lifted up to bless
the people that had murdered him. Some of them
knelt down on the ground, regardless of the place and
the beholders. His enemies took no less part in the
scene. Showers of stones were thrown at the burning
bodies, and pieces were struck off and scattered over

the Piazza. A child picked up one of Savonarola's fingers and carried it home to its mother. The bodies were conveyed in carts and cast into the Arno; but fragments which fell out by the way were gathered up and preserved as relics. Pico della Mirandola tells us that he secured a portion of the heart of the Frate, which had been recovered from the river. It was believed that miracles were wrought by means of these relics.

History tells us of the miseries which were in store for Florence in the future. The bitterest enemies of the Frate knew their error too late, when they were forced to make common cause with the Piagnoni against the tyrants who sought to bring them under their former bondage. The excellence of Savonarola's policy has been acknowledged, not by mere partisans, but by historians who had little sympathy with his prophecies or with his religious reform. The ruin of Florence was the result of the restoration of the Medici, and from that time it has never recovered its ancient position in Italy and in Europe. Some of the causes which led to the failure of the work of Savonarola we have endeavored to indicate. Of the man himself, of his intellectual and moral greatness, of his simplicity and godly sincerity, of the nobility of his aims and the sanctity of his life, none will doubt who carefully and candidly consider the testimony of his words and deeds. If there are any who will still bring against him the mere vulgar charges of fanaticism, or even of imposture, we can only say, "Wisdom is justified of her own children."

"From his early youth to the day in which he was led forth to die on the gallows," says the Padre Marchese, "he was always equal to himself in the innocence of his life, in the love of truth, in his charity towards the human race. It must be confessed that if perchance he erred in the selection of the means which he adopted in order to attain his ends, he had not for his object, as some assert, an ambition for worldly power, or any less noble end, but only the elevation of that most degraded generation of the fourteenth[1] century to the sublime perfection of Christianity."[2]

[1] As we should say, fifteenth.
[2] Avvertimento to the Lettere Inedite of Savonarolain Archivio Istorico.

THE END.